DEADLY
SECRETS

Other books by Keith Hoar

<u>NOVELS</u>:

Edge of Madness

RAGE

<u>NONFICTION:</u>

DECEIVED The Assault of Revisionist History

DEADLY SECRETS

Keith Hoar

First Edition

Zhetosoft Publications

Published by: Zhetosoft Publications

Cover design by Keith Hoar

Library of Congress Cataloging-in-Publication Data

Hoar, Keith.
DEADLY SECRETS/Keith Hoar.
Library of Congress Control Number:2019919913

1. Christian Mystery & Suspense 2. Romantic Suspense
3. Christian Suspense 4. Suspense Thrillers
5. Terrorism Thrillers

ISBN(13): 978-0-9994590-8-9 (paperback)

[AUTHOR'S NOTE]

The events that occur in **DEADLY SECRETS** follow immediately after those that take place in the novel **RAGE**. To fully enjoy the Zach Templeton thriller series as intended, I highly recommend you read ***Edge of Madness*** first, followed by **RAGE**.

Edge of Madness, the first book in the Zach Templeton thriller series, introduces the key characters, their backgrounds, and their motivations. The challenges and dangers they face in the first two books lead directly to the events that will take place in this book.

This novel is set in various locales in the United States and in other countries. Seemingly incorrect grammar that is contained within quotes may reflect broken English that is used by some foreign characters. For example: "I not see you long time." would be typical speech for someone who has a poor command of the English language.

<u>Special Note:</u> Research for this book began in August of 2019 with the outline being completed in very early 2020 before anyone had heard of the current pandemic. The emergence of the Chinese Coronavirus was entirely coincidental to the premise of this book.

Prologue

Port of London – Borough of Tilbury,
London, England

Sha'ban Rabi Bahar, known also by his Arabic nom de guerre as al-Ta'abin—The Snake—dressed in black trousers, black overcoat, and a black skullcap, crept cautiously down the dark and gloomy street. He stopped before reaching the edge of the last building on the block. Edging forward, being careful not to move beyond the shadows, he squinted into the darkness, trying to read the street sign at the corner. Obscured by a dense fog, he could not make out the street sign in the feeble light provided by one lone street lamp. Inching forward as far as he dared, he squinted into the foggy gloom again. Confirming he had arrived at the intersection of Lansdown Road and Calcutta Road, his intended destination, he drew back into the shadows and waited.

Only a few blocks from the Port of London, spread out for miles along the Thames River, the haunting, forlorn sound of a foghorn rumbled through the fog. The sound of footsteps. Sha'ban stiffened, his hand, inside his overcoat, instinctively closing around the gilded hilt of his jambiya—the curved dagger worn by all males from his country of birth.

"al-Ta'abin, is that you?" a voice called out from the darkness. "It is me, Mislav."

"Quiet, you fool," Sha'ban whispered, withdrawing his hand from the jambiya. "Over here."

Mislav Berislav followed the sound of Sha'ban's voice and stepped into the shadows.

"Your mother's name?" Sha'ban asked.

"Hermina," Mislav answered.

"Follow me," Sha'ban ordered, hearing the agreed upon response. He grabbed the man's arm and directed him into an alleyway between two buildings. "Do you have the items I requested?"

"Yes. Nebojša prepared all items you asked for," Mislav replied. "The passport and the documents in envelope."

Sha'ban took the envelope and tucked it under his coat.

"What of the man I asked about? Were you able to locate him?"

"Yes," Mislav answered, holding out a folded piece of paper. "I write name on paper. He in United States. Place called Ok-la-hom-a."

Sha'ban took the paper and stuffed it in his pocket. "Is he absolutely certain he located the right man?"

"Yes, he swear," Mislav gulped, deathly afraid of the man standing in front of him.

"You must swear to never speak of this. Agreed?" Sha'ban warned, pulling the double-edged jambiya out of its sheath. Mislav shrank back against the wall upon seeing the menacing dagger. "You must promise," Sha'ban warned again.

"Yes, promise. I say nothing," Mislav whimpered, turning to leave the alleyway.

Sha'ban, The Snake, stepped quickly behind Mislav. With one hand he pulled Mislav's head back by the hair and with his other hand he drew the curved blade quickly across the man's throat. The razor-sharp blade sliced through Mislav's flesh like warm butter, severing his jugular vein and vocal cords. Sha'ban released Mislav's hair and shoved the man forward with his foot. Unable to make a sound except for the gurgling of blood in his throat, Mislav fell face first onto the alleyway. Mislav twitched for a few seconds then lay still, his blood quickly spreading out across the cold asphalt.

al-Ta'abin, Sha'ban's Arabic nickname, was earned and well deserved. The Arabic word "al-Ta'abin", translated as "*The Snake*", referred roughly to a snake called the Black Mamba, one of the most feared creatures in the world. Those that fear its extremely poisonous bite called it "death incarnate." The deadly Black Mamba, the source of many myths and legends, was widely known for being highly aggressive, very fast, and attacking without provocation. That description fit Sha'ban perfectly. He needed no provocation whatsoever. Having no conscience, he killed simply for gain and because it gave him a sense of power and control, *and* he enjoyed it.

Sha'ban, The Snake, stared at the jambiya in his hand, stained red with blood, not only from the man laying before him, but also from the man named Nebojša and the two dim-witted fools that worked for him. Sha'ban poked at Mislav's lifeless body with the toe of his shoe. He bent over and wiped the jambiya's blade across Mislav's jacket, then shoved it back into its sheath.

"Stinking infidel," Sha'ban snarled, kicking the lifeless body again. "You came with greed in your heart but you found death." He stepped over the lifeless body, turned right on Cal-cutta Road, and headed for the Tilbury Town rail station. On his way to the rail station, he stripped off and discarded his overcoat and skull cap, wadding them up and dropping them in a trash barrel. He retrieved a briefcase he had hidden nearby. After entering the rail station, he paid the eighteen euro fare to the Russell Square tube station in central London with cash and selected a seat close to the door where the next train would arrive.

He slipped the piece of paper Mislav had handed him out of his pocket and unfolded it. Staring at the name—Zachariah Templeton—written on the paper, he envisioned the joy he would feel when he slit the throat of the man that had ruined his first plan to bring in the New World Order. He would shout praises to Allah as he watched the infidel's blood pour out upon the ground.

Sha'ban fingered the hilt of his jambiya, savoring the im-ages of his latest "kills". Years earlier, before emigrating to England, he had paid dearly for the jambiya now hidden inside his jacket. He paid more than the highest-paid workers in his home country of Yemen earned in an entire year. Although now illegal, the hilt made of rhinoceros horn, had turned a greenish-yellow color, attesting to its great age. Also confirm-ing its great age were two silver Venetian ducats affixed to the top and bottom of the hilt. In Yemen, no man was complete without his jambiya, but in his fabricated identity as Bailey Gibbons, corporate financial officer, it could never be worn openly and had to remain well hidden.

Sha'ban smiled as he thought forward to the day he would destroy America, the Great Satan he hated with every fiber of his being. He would use their arrogance and softness against them. *"The Americans are weak-willed and impotent,"* he thought, fighting hard not to laugh. *"They think only of their cars, their houses, their money, and their vile music. They are spineless cowards and care only about themselves. I will watch them snivel and beg for mercy. Then I will laugh as I watch them die like the pitiful cowards they are."*

The lights from an approaching train lit up the outdoor platform. Sha'ban got up off the hard, wooden bench, exited the station, and boarded the closest car. Selecting a seat at the far end of the car, he settled in for the hour-long ride to the Russell Square station, scheduled to arrive at approximately seven a.m. He would spend a short day finalizing some financial reports and then he would hurry home to prepare for a flight to Sardinia, Italy.

A secret initiation ceremony to induct two new members into the Holy Order of the Illumined Elite had been called. Sha'ban, presiding as Worshipful Master, would convene and lead the conclave. Therefore, he must not be late. Even the highest and most elect supreme council members of the Holy Order had no concept of the *Deadly Secrets* hidden in the mind of al-Ta'abin—The Snake.

An ancient and sinister evil was resurfacing upon the earth, but *nobody* was watching.....

Chapter One

May River Road
East of Bluffton, South Carolina

The night was pitch black, a steady drizzle falling from a heavily overcast sky. A dark blue Chevrolet sedan drove down Palmetto Bluff Road, slowing as it approached the intersection with May River Road. Well past ten o'clock, no other traffic approached from either direction. The driver, Warren Pearson, former FBI Field Agent, stopped briefly at the stop sign and turned right onto May River Road. As the Chevrolet drove eastward, the drizzle turned to a steady light rain. The only sound inside the car was the rhythmic whump-whump of the wipers as they slid back and forth across the rain-streaked windshield.

Continuing eastward, staying just under the posted speed limit, the driver glanced in the rearview mirror every few seconds. He continued driving eastward on May River Road, skirting the south side of Bluffton, South Carolina. Nearing the intersection with Heyward Street, the driver spotted a car approaching the intersection from the North. He drove past his intended street and turned left onto Promenade Street. After driving around the block, he returned to May River Road, and turned back west.

Seeing no traffic in any direction as he approached the intersection, he turned left onto Wharf Street, shut off the headlights, and drove slowly to the end of the street. At the end of the street he drove around the Dead End sign, stopped, and killed the engine. Sitting in the dark with his hand on the ignition, he waited a full ten minutes to be certain no one had noticed. Satisfied he had not aroused anyone's suspicions, he carefully pushed the door open and slipped out. The open-door sensor had been taped over to prevent the interior lights from coming on.

He reached inside the car, righted the body that was slumped against the passenger door, and slid it over into the driver's seat. After positioning the seatbelt across the body and clicking it into place, he started the engine. Another quick check down the dark street revealed no activity. Leaning inside the car, he pulled the gear lever into Drive and pushed the door closed. Slowly the car rolled forward toward the river, picking up speed as it rolled down a slight incline. The car hit the water with enough momentum to cause it to float twenty feet out into the river. Standing with his back against the Dead End sign, the man watched as the Chevrolet sank and disappeared from sight.

Stepping around from behind the sign, the man pulled a cigarette lighter out of his pocket and flicked it. He allowed the flame to remain lit for five seconds, returned it to his pocket, and started walking down the street. A black Jeep Cherokee with darkened windows started, backed out of a driveway, and met him at the intersection. He jumped into the passenger seat, stripped off his rubber gloves, and stuffed them in his pocket as the Jeep drove off down the street. The driver, careful to obey all traffic laws, maintained his speed just below the posted limit. Being pulled over by law enforcement would be disastrous as neither man carried any identification.

The driver of the Jeep Cherokee, Alfred Grant, Senior FBI Field Agent, drove through town and turned onto a major highway, relaxing as they passed into the country and the relative safety of darkness.

"Are you certain the authorities will not suspect foul play?" the driver asked.

"I think it is highly unlikely," the passenger answered. "I inserted an extremely fine needle between the woman's toes to deliver a lethal overdose of potassium chloride. The overdose of potassium immediately induced a severe heart arrhythmia, leading to a heart attack. If the body remains in the water even one day, the bloating will mask any evidence of the small needle prick. The mildly elevated level of residual potassium in the body's blood, even if detected, will simply indicate heart muscle damage. The medical examiner will almost certainly rule the cause of death as sudden cardiac arrest. No one will suspect a thing."

"Great work," the driver said.

"Thank you, Sir," the passenger replied. "But, what of the old man? He was very upset. Can we trust him to stay silent?"

"I believe he will remain silent," the driver answered. "He has pledged his unending loyalty to the Holy Order as did we *and* he knows we do not make idle threats."

"I hope you are right."

"Not to worry. Assign someone to watch him closely. If it appears he may be thinking about revealing our secrets, kill him. And be sure to make it very painful. Then kill his family as well. It will serve as a warning to any other members that may be thinking about talking. We must be certain there are no leaks."

"I need you to track someone down in Oklahoma," the driver said as he handed the other man a piece of paper with a name written on it. "Use someone you can trust."

"Yes, Sir. I have just the man. He's a former Tulsa Policeman. What do we do after we locate him?"

"Keep your eyes on him, then report back to me."

"Understood, Sir. I will see to it."

Villa Dieci Stelle
Oristano, Sardinia

On the far side of the world, a small group of very rich and extremely powerful men met secretly to set off an evil conspiracy, one man's plan, intended to plunge the world into unthinkable chaos. Those assembled, cold-blooded psychopaths, called upon evil secrets concealed for centuries from all except the Elect. Using false explanations and shadowy misinterpretations of the secret order's ancient rites and symbols, one man deliberately misled the other council members, using them to advance his plan. To usher in and fulfill the ancient prophecy, the Worshipful Master of the Supreme Council of the Illumined Elite would need the assistance of several highly placed individuals. The Sovereign Grand Inquisitor, Worshipful Master and highest ranking member of the Supreme Council, had carefully chosen two initiates, blinded by ego and completely oblivious to anything but their own ambition, to do his bidding. The initiates had been summoned to stand before the Supreme Council and be initiated into the revered rank of Grand Elect Knight of the secret order.

The Sovereign Grand Inquisitor of the Supreme Council, excused the other four Supreme Council members and sent them off to prepare for the initiation ceremony that would begin soon. He smiled as the four men exited the room and pulled the door shut. *"It is laughable how easily the other council members are fooled,"* he thought. Only one other council member, Timothé Alex Durand, the Grand Prince of the Royal Secret, knew the Worshipful Master's American name, Bailey Gibbons. Neither Durand nor the three other council members had the slightest idea that Bailey Gibbons was not American.

Bailey Gibbons was, in fact, Arabic. He had been born Sha'ban Rabi Bahar in the remote and sparsely populated province of Shabwah, Yemen. Sha'ban was fair skinned and possessed American features, inherited from his American mother. Growing up listening to the vehement rantings of the mullahs, he grew to hate his mother because of her American ethnicity. Not only did he not weep when she was murdered in the marketplace, he laughed because it brought him great joy that another infidel had died.

For as long as he could remember, Sha'ban hungered to know the joy and feel the glorious satisfaction the mullahs promised would come from annihilating thousands of infidels. At night, lying on his pallet, he dreamed of one day bringing the Hadhramaut to America.

Sha'ban did not know the exact origin of the word "Hadhramaut". The mullahs had declared it described a region where much death had come. They often recounted an ancient legend, claiming it was the nickname of "Amar ibn Qahtan", a brutal invader whose battles always left many dead. One of their legends claimed the word Hadhramaut identified with a Biblical character named Hazarmawet, the son of Joktan, who also identified with Qahtan and to whom Arabic writers traced their purest and most ancient genealogies. Whatever origin was true did not really matter. To Sha'ban it meant the "Place Where Death Comes". His purpose in life was to bring much death to the infidels in America.

To fulfill that purpose, Sha'ban knew he must have a position of significant power. He worked very hard, excelling in every subject in school. After much study and hundreds of hours of practice alone in his room with a recording device, his Arabic accent disappeared. His English became flawless. With his education and language preparation complete, he moved to Europe and assumed a false American name. Relying on his American features and shrewdness, he rose quickly within the business world. He manipulated and used anyone and everyone to gain power and stature. Those that could not be manipulated were often found dead in some dark alley.

Not long after arriving in Europe, a business associate saw much promise in Sha'ban and recruited him into the Order of the Illumined Elite. Sha'ban could hardly believe his good fortune. Most assuredly Allah had smiled on him. The secret Order was exactly what he needed: secret handshakes, deals made in secret, threats of death for violating oaths, and power in the hands of a tiny few. Power. Enormous power. To Sha'ban it was always about power. He excelled, rising quickly within the Order. Sha'ban was patient, seizing every opportunity. In a few short years, he was elevated to the Supreme Council. Another few years and two bodies that would never be found later, he attained the revered position of Sovereign Grand Inquisitor and became the Worshipful Master of the Order's Supreme Council.

The first attempt to destroy America, his hated enemy, had failed. Overconfidence had led to a flawed plan that relied too much on men who lacked the boldness to accomplish their assigned goals. Sha'ban vowed he would not fail again. Allah had provided everything he needed: the position, the power, and the resources. The time *The Snake* to strike had come. Soon, Allah would guide him to victory and his lifelong dream would be realized. He would turn America into a "Place Where Death Comes".

Cagliari Elmas Airport
Cagliari, Sardinia, Italy

John Lewin, recently arrived from Atlanta, Georgia, paced back and forth in front of the seating area adjacent to baggage claim number three in the lower level of Cagliari Elmas Airport. Waiting for nearly an hour after retrieving his bag from the carousel, he had grown impatient and had begun to pace. Thinking perhaps he might have missed the other initiate summoned to the secret ceremony, he walked down the concourse toward the main terminal, stopping at a display listing arriving flights. He consulted his daytimer to check the flight number he had been given for the fellow-initiate he was supposed to meet.

Flipping the pages of the daytimer, he located the page for the current day. His fellow-initiate had been booked on Alitalia flight 1591. He scanned the display looking for a matching flight number. Shaking his head, a deep sigh escaped his lips when he saw the flashing "Delayed" symbol next to the flight number. The new arrival time for flight 1591 was still forty-five minutes away. Rather than return to the waiting area, he located a small snack bar and purchased a cup of coffee. Sitting next to a dirt-streaked window, he slowly sipped his coffee and watched disinterestedly as airport workers scurried between the aircraft loading and unloading baggage.

Tipping the paper cup up, he poured the last swallow of the bitter coffee into his mouth. He frowned as he tossed the empty cup into a trash receptacle sitting nearby. A hundred times he had asked himself why he continued to purchase the bitter slop airports concessions called coffee. Forty minutes had passed. He grabbed his bag and headed for the baggage claim area, stopping by the inbound flight display. Baggage from Alitalia flight 1591 would be arriving at baggage claim number one. Continuing down the concourse to baggage claim number one, he selected a seat, and sat down to wait.

Mr. Lewin, in his early-forties, sported a mop of dark brown, unruly curls and gray-green eyes. Fashionably dressed in gray slacks, a navy blazer, a white silk shirt, and an expensive-looking silk tie in muted shades of gray that matched his slacks, he looked as if he was headed to a company board meeting. He crossed his legs and watched as a throng of passengers gathered around the adjacent baggage claim, impatient and jockeying for a position next to the conveyor belt, each one wanting to be first. Gradually the crowd dispersed as they located bags, yanked them off the belt, and rushed off to find rental car or hotel buses.

Not long after the last passenger located his bag and departed, another throng of passengers began to gather around baggage claim number one. Mr. Lewin scanned the crowd looking for a man matching the vague description he had been given. Noticing someone that loosely matched the description, he watched the man grab a bag and exit the baggage area. Turning back toward the baggage carousel, he spotted a man walking toward him.

"The weatherman said it was going to rain," the man said as he walked up to Mr. Lewin and stopped.

"You can't trust the weatherman," Mr. Lewin responded, barely able to conceal his shock. *"This is the man that is to join me at the ceremony?"* he wondered as he stood there staring at the shabbily dressed man standing in front of him. The man asked the proper identifying question so it had to be the man he had waited for.

Mr. Adam Conley, from Reston, Virginia, somewhere beyond fifty with coal-black, slicked-down hair, and dark, close-set eyes, exhibited the exact opposite appearance of Mr. Lewin. Rumpled and untidy, Mr. Conley's face was colored by dark stubble of more than a day's growth. Carelessly dressed in stained khaki trousers, a wrinkled, blue denim shirt, and heavily scuffed shoes, he looked as if he was headed to work at a construction site. What Mr. Lewin did not know was that Mr. Adam Conley wielded unimaginable power, his shoddy attire a deliberate ruse to conceal his true identity. No one would have guessed he was Deputy Assistant to the President of the United States.

"Let's go," Mr. Lewin said as turned and headed for the airport's VIP pickup area.

The two men arrived at the VIP pickup area and located a driver holding up a sign with the name Alfred Whitmore, Mr. Lewin's traveling identity, written in block letters. Necessitated by their prominent positions, both men carried flawless, but fake, identification papers created by one of the world's best forgers. The limousine driver directed them to the VIP parking area and opened the trunk of a black Lincoln Towncar. The driver loaded the bags into the trunk while the two men climbed into the backseat.

The black limousine exited the airport located on the far northeastern edge of Cagliari and headed east on superstrada 391. A short two kilometers east the driver turned north on superstrada 131. The two men settled in for the long one hundred twenty-five kilometer ride as the limousine began its journey toward their destination of Villa Dieci Stelle (Villa of Ten Stars), high in the mountains near Sorgono. With nothing else to occupy their minds, the two men stared out the windows as they passed the ancient, megalithic stone towers, called nuraghi, that speckled the Sardinian countryside.

Mr. Lewin attempted to persuade the driver to stop and let them explore one of the sacred wells he had read about in the airline's *InFlight* magazine. The article Mr. Lewin had read stated that archaeologists believed the Nuragic people gathered around the sacred well temples during times of special celebrations to worship the *Mother Goddess*, performing the so called *Cult of Water*. The limousine driver adamantly refused, knowing that if he was late delivering his passengers to the villa, the

Worshipful Master would be furious, a fate he had been warned never to experience.

The limousine driver drove much too fast as the limousine rose up into the mountains and encountered the winding switchback road. The two men clutched their armrests tightly. Fearing for their lives, they scarcely noticed the brightly colored maquis filling the air with its aromatic scent. The maquis, a scrubland vegetation common in the Mediterranean region, was composed primarily of leathery, broad-leaved evergreen shrubs or small trees. Sardinia's hills and mountains were covered with mastic trees, laurel, Arbutus, Smilax, and Cistus. Mixed in among the scrubby maquis were oleander bushes covered with vibrant red blossoms. Despite the limo's windows being rolled up, the interior was filled with the spicy scent of lavender, thyme, myrtle, and rosemary also growing on the fertile hills.

After the last harrowing forty-five minutes of the ride up the mountains, the limousine reached its destination and pulled onto a narrow parking pad that had been hewn out of the stony ground and stopped. Adjacent to the parking pad stood an ornate iron gate. A pressure sensor under the parking slab set off a security alarm in the guard shack. In response to the alarm, a tall, slender man dressed in a security guard uniform exited the small shack-like structure and walked up to the driver's side window.

"Identification and password," the guard ordered.

The limousine driver climbed out of the car and pushed the door shut. "Mah-hah-bone," he replied as he held out a plastic ID card in his left hand and made a hailing sign with his right hand.

Satisfied the man standing before him was the individual he had been told to expect, the guard said, "Have the men step out of the car, then get any luggage they might have brought with them and set it over there by the gate."

The driver pulled the rear door open. "Out of the car please and present yourself to the guard." While the two men scrambled out of the car, the driver opened the trunk, retrieved two small, carry-on suitcases, and set them by the gate as instructed.

The guard glanced at two photographs affixed to the clipboard in his hand to verify the identity of the two men. "You may go now," he said to the limousine driver. The driver climbed back into the limousine, backed up, turned around, and sped off in the direction from which he had just arrived.

The grounds of the Villa of Ten Stars, purposely selected for its location high in the hills above Oristano, Sardinia, were remote and far away from prying eyes. Surrounded on three sides by steep, craggy slopes, access to the villa, other than by the western, gated wall, was virtually impossible.

Completely encircled by a ten foot high wall, the villa was guarded twenty-fours a day whether occupied or not. By standing order, only members of the Illumined Elite Order and their pre-approved guests were allowed to enter. The security guards were tasked with safeguarding the villa, but they were never allowed to set foot within its walls.

Naiveté and blind acceptance of carefully controlled accounts of history, shrouded in secrecy and darkness, had blinded all but a hand-picked few individuals to the frightening network of hidden powers that conducted its secret business within the villa walls. The cryptic words, deeds, gestures, and veiled language of the world's ultra-powerful men pointed to an ancient, prophetic, and terrifying secret. The enormous, yet unseen, power wielded by the hand-picked men drove global affairs and accelerated the world toward a horrifying upheaval.

A malignant force, foreboding and evil, had reawakened upon the earth, but no one was watching. What had been hidden in plain sight for hundreds of years prepared to reveal itself to humanity. An evil power so organized, so scheming, and so insidious that the few political and influential leaders that knew of its existence were afraid to even speak of it.

Inside the walls of the Villa of Ten Stars, five ultra-wealthy and powerful men gathered to prepare the way for a New World Order. Calling themselves the Illumined Elite, they were about to set the clock ticking toward an event that would change the world forever. In a very short time the clock would begin edging ever closer to the beginning of an unspeakable nightmare. The occult desire of the ages, more evil than the world could comprehend, was about to be unleashed.

John Lewin and Adam Conley had each been summoned by a hand-delivered, encrypted message. After years of advancing through higher and higher degrees within the order, they had been selected to advance to the pinnacle of the order. Each man had spent hours studying the ceremony and memorizing the oaths that would be required. The two men now stood before the iron gate waiting to be admitted to the villa for the initiation ceremony.

"Here, put these on," the security guard ordered, handing each man a black hood with two small eyeholes cut out. "When you enter the inner temple, you are to keep your eyes downcast at all times unless otherwise instructed. Unenlightened initiates, do not forget your old degree and identity ceases the instant you step through this gate. The penalty, if you forget, will be swift and severe," the guard cautioned as he released the latch and pushed the iron gate open.

By order of the Supreme Council of the Illumined Elite, inside the villa walls, personal names were absolutely forbidden and only sacred order degrees or titles could be used. As John Lewin and Adam Conley passed through the gate and into the villa's courtyard, their old degrees and titles ceased. No longer holding degree or title and personal names forbidden, John Lewin became *Initiate One* and Adam Conley became *Initiate Two*. Later, upon conclusion of the initiation ceremony, each man would be advanced to his new sacred order degree and title.

Gooseflesh rose on the two new initiates' arms as they walked across the courtyard in anticipation of what was to come. The Temple of the Supreme Council, seen only by a tiny handful of carefully chosen individuals, stood at the easternmost edge of the property. A large expanse of granite pavement covered the ground in front of the temple building, leading to white marble steps that narrowed as they rose upward toward the temple's entrance. Flanking the temple entrance, stood two Sphinx-like granite lions with women's heads, the neck of one entwined by a cobra and decorated with the "*ankh*", the Egyptian symbol of life and deity.

Adorning the neck of the other was a symbol of fertility and procreation. Carved into a marble slab, just in front of the tall, bronze temple doors, were two Egyptian swords with curved, serpentine blades. Inscribed between the two swords in gleaming brass letters, "The Sacred Temple of the Ancient and Revered Supreme Council of the Illumined Elite."

High above the temple entrance, partially concealed by immense, white marble columns, an elaborate image of the Egyptian sun god, backed by a radiating sun and flanked by six large, golden snakes, stared down at them.

The Knight of the Sun, the last Supreme Council member to arrive, was quickly admitted through the large iron gate. He strode hurriedly across the courtyard and entered the temple through a rear door.

Standing in the temple's vestibule, the two initiates stood in awe as they took in the exquisite elegance displayed on every surface. The floors were white marble, polished to a mirror-like sheen. The decorations were fashioned from rare exotic woods and gleaming gold. Statuary depicting honored former members of the Supreme Council stood on marble pedestals lining the outer walls.

Small twinkling lights set into the dark blue ceiling gave the appearance of stars. Large serpents, decorating the walls, created a strange jumble of sensations, creating the atmosphere of being in a temple but at the same time exuding a tomb-like feeling. Something sacred, yet threatening at the same time.

Drawing their eyes away from the elaborate decorations, the two initiates hurried across the dimly lit vestibule and entered a small dressing room. Each initiate removed his shoes and socks and all clothing, dressed in simple cotton trousers, draped himself in a long, black robe, and looped a rope noose around his neck. Properly attired as instructed, the two men walked over and stood in front of the double doors leading to the temple's inner chamber. They stood quietly, hoodwinked, the original hood having been replaced with one containing no eye holes, devoid of all metal, a cable tow draped around their neck, with eyes downcast.

A shrill squeal pierced the eerie silence as the double doors slowly swung open. Gloved hands flashed out from the darkness within the chamber and jerked the men inside. The doors closed quickly with a dull thud.

At eye level around the walls inside the inner chamber, a black marble frieze circled the entire chamber, inscribed in bright, bronze letters:

FROM THE OUTER DARKNESS OF IGNORANCE
THROUGH THE SHADOWS OF YOUR EARTH LIFE,
WINDS THE BEAUTIFUL PATH OF INITIATION
UNTO THE DIVINE LIGHT OF THE HOLY ALTAR

The Sovereign Grand Inquisitor and ranking Supreme Council leader struck his gavel, calling the conclave to order. As the initiation ritual began, each initiate was led around a raised platform by a *Conductor*, holding a gleaming sword in his left hand. As they circled the platform, oblations and signs were given at each point of a five-pointed star inscribed on the floor. At the end of the circuit, each initiate's *Conductor* yanked off the hoodwink, signifying the initiate had been ushered into the Glorious Light of Knowledge. Arranged upon the altar before the two initiates lay four *holy books*: the Bible, the Koran, the Book of the Law, and the Hindu Scriptures. The Sovereign Grand Inquisitor turned toward each initiate, in turn, and commanded, "Kiss the book of your religion."

The Sovereign Grand Inquisitor rose from his throne and directed the initiates to repeat the first required obligation.

In unison, the two men repeated the sacred Oath of Obligation, "We swear true allegiance to the Supreme Council of the Illumined Elite above all other allegiances, and swear never to recognize any brother as being a member of the Supreme Council unless he also vows eternal loyalty to the Absolute and Unending Authority of this Supreme Council."

One of the two men assigned as *Conductors* that had led the initiates around the stage stepped down off the platform and handed each initiate the top half of a human skull, turned open side up, half filled with wine and commanded them to drink.

Upon finishing the wine, each initiate repeated his second and irrevocable oath, "May this wine I now drink become a deadly poison to me, such as the Hemlock juice drunk by Socrates, should I ever knowingly or willfully violate my allegiance or my oath to this Revered Supreme Council."

At the instant the second initiate completed his second oath, the Grand Elect Knight, and the Grand Prince of the Royal Secret, convincingly dressed like skeletons, leaped out from the shadows and threw their arms around the initiates. The two initiates concluded the final sealing of their obligation with yet another chilling oath, "And may these cold, dead arms forever encircle me should I ever knowingly or willfully violate my oath or my allegiance."

The Sovereign Grand Inquisitor stepped to the very edge of the platform and placed the point of his sword against the neck of *Initiate One*. The initiate flinched as a narrow ribbon of blood trickled down his neck. "Initiate, you shall henceforth and forevermore be called Knight of Vengeance," The Sovereign Grand Inquisitor announced. Placing the tip of his sword against the neck of *Initiate Two*, once again producing a slight trickle of blood, he announced, "Initiate, you shall henceforth and forevermore be called Prince of the Golden Serpent."

The Sovereign Grand Inquisitor raised the gleaming sword above his head and gave the initiates their final charge, "Worthy Initiates, you have now been accepted into the revered and all-wise Supreme Council, having been guided from outer darkness into the Divine Light. Your former essence has been extinguished and you have pledged your full and faithful service to our dreaded Overlord. It is an ominous and solemn pledge you make here this day. You are now bound for eternity to perpetual silence, unshaken loyalty, and unconditional submission to the Holy Order. Speak of this day and this temple to no one. The tiniest violation of the oaths you vowed here today shall result in a death so hideous and so painful as to defy human comprehension."

The Sovereign Grand Inquisitor turned and solemnly approached the Altar of Knowledge, bowed at the waist three times, and closed the meeting of the Supreme Council by means of the *Mystic Number*, striking the altar with his sword seven times.

The newly accepted initiates bowed three times and quickly withdrew, backing out of the temple with eyes downcast. The Sovereign Grand Inquisitor raised his hand and gave the grand hailing sign to the other Supreme Council members. The initiation ceremony now concluded, he and the remaining four Supreme Council members withdrew to an anteroom to discuss a matter of the most extreme urgency.

West Elgin Street
Tulsa Oklahoma

Some days are bleak and excruciating. For Zachariah James Templeton, known as Zach to family and friends, today was one of *those* days. You know the days; when the entire world seems to conspire against you. When the universe seems dark and scheming. When you just want to run back to your bedroom and hide under the covers. Drowning in an ocean of grief, Zach teetered back and forth between anger and depression. No longer able to deny the excruciating loss of his beloved wife, he wandered through his empty house night after night, agonizing over the pain of her absence. No matter how desperately he wanted to turn around, wake up from a ghastly nightmare, and see her standing there, he could no longer refuse to acknowledge the undeniable truth. She was dead, lost forever. He wanted to scream and pound his fists against the wall. Never again would he see her bright smile. Never again would he feel her tender touch.

Six months earlier President Paul Cantwell had personally presented Zach the Presidential Medal of Freedom with Distinction, the highest civilian honor awarded by the United States. The rarely given designation "with Distinction" recognized those people who had made "an especially meritorious contribution to the security or national interests of the United States". Zach had responded to a plea for help from his country, risking everything, including his life. Noble though it was, his sacrifice had exacted an enormous personal cost.

What should have been a mountain-top experience, however, only reminded him of the enormous price he had paid. As the President read the citation describing Zach's heroism, Zach's mind flashed back to the final encounter with the evil men he had pursued. The horror of that scene indelibly and forever stamped in his memory. The vision replayed itself over and over in Zach's mind as if it was on an endless loop. Over and over and over it played in his mind. It would not stop.

After the ceremony, Zach had smiled and greeted dozens of high-ranking military officers, government officials, and even some foreign dignitaries. Inside he had wanted to run away and hide. The dinner and social gathering after the ceremony had been agonizing for Zach, but he had graciously accepted the congratulations and pats on the back from dozens of people he did not know. Finally, three tortuous hours later, the event had finally ended. Zach had said his farewell to the President and his old friend, Rear Admiral Charles Hadley, had placed the medal in its velvet-lined presentation case, and had retreated to the privacy of his hotel room.

After his return to Tulsa, Zach had perfunctorily gone about his daily tasks, living off of a meager savings account and whatever short-term, temp jobs he could find. Out of desperation after three months of fruitless job hunting, he had accepted a low-level position with a California-based company that had acquired a local communications service company. With no other opportunities in sight and money running low, he had accepted the fact that he was left with no other choice. He had accepted the position despite being greatly overqualified.

Zach had endured much to reach this point in his life. Over the past several years, Zach's life had been marked more by tragedy and pain than anything resembling normalcy. His best friend and former SEAL teammate had been murdered. His company, a lifelong dream, had failed. Angie, his beloved wife, had been murdered. Zach, being a former Navy SEAL, stoically attempted to accept the tragic events as his lot in life.

Zach stood five feet nine inches tall and tipped the scale at one hundred ninety pounds; hardly any of it fat. Only family and a few close friends would have guessed he was forty-eight years old. Holding to a rigorous exercise program as much as was possible, he still maintained the chiseled physique developed from years of serving as part of the US Navy's SEAL Team Four.

All but one of the external scars he carried, received while participating in fierce battles in faraway places, remained hidden beneath his clothing. His one visible scar, the result of burning-hot shrapnel, had been received during a night mission behind enemy lines. The jagged scar started just below his left earlobe and extended down below the collar of his shirt.

In the darkness along a leech-infested jungle stream, SEAL Team Four, Delta Platoon had been ambushed. A screaming mortar shell landed twenty feet to Zach's left, right beside Lieutenant Vincent Mitchell. The quiet jungle erupted into a deafening fire fight. For twenty long minutes the battle raged, lighting up the jungle as grenades exploded and tracer rounds streaked through the darkness. Despite their valiant efforts, outnumbered three to one, Delta Platoon was completely overwhelmed. Zach and one teammate, Fred Hargrove, were the only two platoon members that survived. Using the jungle stream to mask the noise of their escape, Hargrove dragged Zach, seriously wounded and semi-conscious, several miles down the muddy stream. Applying a field dressing from his combat first aid kit, Hargrove managed to keep Zach alive until they were rescued by a CSAR (Combat Search and Rescue) Team.

On that tragic night, as on every other, SEAL Team Four, Delta Platoon had two objectives: complete the mission and come home alive. Above everything else, completing their mission took precedence. On that night, not only did they fail to complete the mission, fourteen brave SEALs perished in the jungle.

The physical wounds represented by the scars had healed and over time the physical scars had faded, becoming far less noticeable. However, the emotional scars Zach carried, though hidden, had not faded. The deepest emotional scar Zach carried was the loss of fourteen brave comrades. After retiring from military service and returning to civilian life, he struggled with nightmares. Sudden noises or movement would often cause him to react with cat-like reflexes, ready to pummel some poor unsuspecting soul. Even years later, in the darkness when all was still and quiet, the sense of failure and loss returned.

The one person that could defuse such episodes was his beloved wife, Angie. A tender touch, a word, or her worried look, would pull him back from the darkness that threatened to engulf him. But now, she too was gone. The demons clawed at him with renewed force. Who would pull him back from the darkness now that Angie was gone?

Settling into a permanent job, albeit a job he disliked and one that gave him no satisfaction whatsoever, he put on a brave front and did his best to live a normal, routine existence.

He went to work.

He paid his bills.

He mowed his lawn.

He ate.

He went to bed.

Then he got up and did it all over again.

Every day he told himself, *"If I can just get through one more day…"*

Day after day, the horrible emptiness dragged on. Grief nagged at him during every waking hour and routinely invaded his sleep. The dreary days and long empty nights merged into a dull, monotonous blur.

The past month had been particularly unkind to Zach. He had lost fifteen pounds, the result of having no appetite. Food seemed as dull and unsatisfying as the long, empty days he endured. Physically, he was doing mostly okay, but mentally he was losing the battle. On one of the rare good days, he would feel somewhat like his old self, but on the far more frequent bad days, he felt his world spinning out of control. He was beginning to doubt if he would ever be okay.

Each day it seemed a little harder to get up and do it all over again. Zach became more moody, distant, and forgetful. One day he arrived home from work, walked into his house, and could not remember how he had gotten there. Knowing it was a huge mistake, he often gave in to the deep emptiness in his soul and wandered around the house looking at mementos and photographs. On one quiet and lonely evening, he stopped in front of the fireplace and stared at one photograph in particular sitting on the mantle. It was his favorite photograph of Angie. She was leaning against a palm tree on a picturesque sandy beach on the island of Roatan. He never got tired of looking at that picture. She was so beautiful. *"What am I going to do without her?"* he asked himself.

If he had not told her where he was going.
If he had not let her get involved in the confrontation.
If only he had made her wait in the lobby.
If he had been a little faster in Henry Tang's penthouse.
If, if, if, if…..
But he had not….
He had failed her…
And now she was dead.

Tears welled up in his eyes as he turned away from the photograph. Gut-wrenching guilt washed over him. His beloved Angie was dead and it was his fault. He felt miserable, empty, and alone. With no appetite or desire for dinner, he sat and stared out the window until long past dark. He forced himself out of the chair, walked into the bedroom, crawled into bed, and pulled the covers up around his neck.

In the quiet darkness, Zach's eyes flew open, awakened by the same recurring, ghastly nightmare. Drenched in sweat and gasping for breath, his heart hammered inside his chest as if he had just run a marathon. In the terrible nightmare, his archenemy sucker-punched him in the gut. Then, unable to escape, he had fallen into the clutches of his archenemy. As it often did, the nightmare felt so real it left him startled and uneasy.

Still shaking, he pushed the covers aside, slipped out of bed, and stumbled into the bathroom. He bent over the sink and splashed cold water on his face. Straightening up, he stood there dripping water on the floor, gazing into the mirror. The face staring back at him looked haggard and dull. Despite knowing further sleep would be unlikely, he forced himself back to bed. Lying there staring up into the quiet darkness, he tried to convince himself the upcoming day would be better.

He could not have been more wrong.

Tomorrow would be another very, very bad day.

"Twenty minutes left," Zach groaned as he glanced at the digital alarm clock sitting on the dresser, as he had done many times during the long night. Refusing to lie there any longer, he threw the covers back and swung his legs over the side of the bed. "*Would today really be a better day?*" he wondered. He certainly hoped so because he could not take much more.

Groggy from lack of sleep, he stood up and grabbed the corner of the rumpled sheet, intending to make the bed. "What's the point?" he sputtered, letting go of the sheet. He turned off the alarm clock and headed for the bathroom, hoping a hot shower would revive him.

After the shower, he got dressed for work and walked out into the living room. Taken aback by the mess, he stopped and shook his head. Several day's worth of newspapers lay scattered on the sofa and strewn across the floor. He bent over, gathered up a handful of newspapers, and straightened up. "Arghhhh!" he growled, hurling the newspapers across the room. The newspapers swirled in the air and settled back onto the floor in more disarray than before. "What difference does it make? What difference does anything make?" he shouted as he turned and continued on into the kitchen.

He wasn't hungry, but having skipped dinner the previous evening, he knew he had to eat something. He dumped a generous mound of fresh coffee grounds in the coffeemaker and punched the On button. While the coffee brewed, he rummaged through the cabinets looking for something that might spark his interest. Finding nothing that appealed to him, he dropped a slice of bread in the toaster and pushed the lever down, settling, as he did most mornings, for just toast and coffee.

The toaster popped up so forcefully it threw the slice of toast out onto the counter. Zach grabbed the slice of toast, slathered on a liberal amount of butter, and laid it on a small plate. He poured a cup of coffee and set the coffee and toast on the dining table. Scrounging through the scattered papers, he located the front section of the previous day's edition. With the newspaper in hand, he sat at the table and munched on the hard toast as he scanned the front section of the newspaper.

Zach managed to stay focused enough to read several articles. Working on his second cup of coffee, his mind had wandered, as it often did, and he ended up staring blankly into space. He sat there staring long enough that his coffee had gone cold. Zach bent over and dropped his head into his hands, trying desperately to chase away the image of Angie dying on the floor of the New Jersey penthouse. His rate of breathing increased and his face flushed as the images in his daydream aroused his anger and frustration. Suddenly, his hand lashed out and launched the half-full cup of coffee against a cabinet door, smashing it into pieces.

"Good grief," Zach exclaimed as he scrambled out of the chair and grabbed for the roll of paper towels. He gathered up the larger pieces and dumped them into the trashcan. He pulled off several sections of paper towel and mopped up the coffee, repeating the process several times.

He sat back down at the table, annoyed and disappointed over his loss of self control. "Why can't I get past this?" he moaned. The *bong-bong-bong*… from the wall clock in the living room reminded him that he needed to head for work immediately or he would be late, again.

As he opened the garage door, a bright, early morning sun reflected off the light snow that had fallen. Late fall weather in

Tulsa could be quite deceptive, sometimes changing drastically overnight. Zach squinted against the dazzling sunlight reflecting off the snow. The day had barely started and already it was getting worse. Now he would be late for certain.

He backed his car out of the garage, shoved the gear lever into Park, and stepped out to close the garage door. Running late and in a hurry, he neglected to be careful of the snow-covered driveway. He took one step, his foot slid out from under him, and he went down hard. Using the car door as leverage, he pulled himself up and dusted the snow off his trousers and jacket. He slammed the garage door down so hard it bounced up a foot and slammed down again. Storming back to the car, he got in and yanked the door shut.

In the car, giving in to the rising frustration yet again, he slammed his fists on the steering wheel repeatedly. A lengthy sigh escaped his lips as he let his hands drop to his lap. He sat there for a long time, struggling to get his emotions under control.

"If this is the way the rest of the day is going to go, I'm in deep trouble," he thought as he slipped the car into gear and backed out onto the street.

"Will the pain and turmoil ever end?" Zach asked himself as he sped off down the street.

Zach did not know it, but the day was about to get worse. Much, much worse. Another crushing event, looming on the horizon, would propel Zach beyond the prison of anger, guilt, and depression in which he was trapped. If he had known what lay ahead, he would have gone back into the house, leaped into bed, and pulled the covers up over his head.

Chapter Two

Villa Dieci Stelle
Oristano, Sardinia

The Sovereign Grand Inquisitor and the four other Supreme Council members had removed their regal garb and were seated around an ornate oak table in a dimly lit anteroom next to the temple's inner chamber.

"Sovereign Grand Prince, can you explain to me what happened to our carefully conceived plan?" the Sovereign Grand Inquisitor asked as he turned and looked at the man seated on his right.

"*Meister, es lief wie geplant,*" the Sovereign Grand Prince answered, swallowing hard.

"Sovereign Grand Prince, English please," the Sovereign Grand Inquisitor admonished.

"Sorry, Master. It was going as planned. Even though the idiot we recruited made a serious mistake, we could still have been successful. Somehow, the people we had in place were discovered."

"Is there a link back to the council?"

"No, absolutely not. Absolutely no one had any knowledge of the council. We used the fools' unrestrained greed and blind obsession to their ideology to recruit them. We controlled them as if they were puppets on a string."

"So then, what happened?" the Sovereign Grand Inquisitor asked, a threatening look clouding his face.

"Someone got sloppy and careless, for which he would have spent the rest of his miserable life in prison, but it seems he had an unfortunate accident," the Sovereign Grand Prince chuckled.

"Will this happen again?"

"No, Master. This time we are using only carefully selected devotees who have sworn the holy oath. I can assure you they will willingly die rather than fail."

"Good. How soon will it begin?"

"As we speak, the process is already underway. I have been told the prototype vector is ready to be tested."

"Sovereign Grand Prince, we *must* not fail. If the New World Order is to come to light, we must *make* it happen. I will expect you to personally take charge and direct the final delivery. There will be no failure allowed. Listen to me," the Sovereign Grand Inquisitor warned, drawing close. "No cost is to be considered too great. Do you understand me?"

"Yes, Worshipful Master. I understand fully. I have pledged my life for the will of the Supreme Council and for the Holy Order."

"What of the initiates?" the Sovereign Grand Inquisitor asked, looking across the table.

"They are being driven to a private airport using the vehicle hidden in the maintenance building," the Grand Prince of the Royal Secret answered. "From there, they will be flown to the mainland and then they will board commercial flights."

"There is another matter of the utmost urgency we must address," the Sovereign Grand Inquisitor announced as he stood and faced the other four council members. "You know that someone may attempt to disclose the Secret Key and thereby reveal the *Eneffable Name*."

"Yes, we are aware of that...," the Grand Elect Knight began, interrupted by Worshipful Master's raised hand.

"We *must not* allow that to happen," the Sovereign Grand Inquisitor declared, turning to look directly at the Grand Elect Knight. "What can you tell me, Worthy Knight?"

"We believe we have identified the woman that inadvertently discovered the Secret Key and the vellum on which the hidden location of the golden triangle was written. That person will tell no one, I assure you."

"How can you be certain?"

"I spoke with the Grand Knight of Haman, just before arriving for the ceremony. He informed me that she has paid the ultimate price for her heinous deed."

"That is good, but what of the missing vellum?"

"An extensive search has, so far, been unsuccessful," he answered sheepishly. "But American members of the Order are still searching."

"Did this woman have help?"

"We do not believe so. It appears the materials may have been left unguarded and exposed through an act of negligence."

"Negligence," the Sovereign Grand Inquisitor bellowed. "Everyone knows their extreme importance. What do you intend to do?"

"The only possible source is the Knight of the East. He is being watched twenty-four hours a day. It matters not if it was simple negligence. Once we determine how the exposure occurred and we extract the information we need from him, he will pay the price for his carelessness. His flesh will be stripped and his bones will sink to the bottom of the ocean."

All Supreme Council members rose to their feet, raised their right arms into the air with their index and middle fingers extended, and shouted the *Eneffable Name*, a name so revered and so powerful it can only be uttered inside the walls of the temple and only by members of the Supreme Council.

"Fellow members of the Revered Holy Order," the Sovereign Grand Inquisitor announced. "Another group has falsely claimed to have the authority to return the world to its proper order. For centuries they have lied. Only our Holy Order can be traced back to the beginning of man. It is built upon mountains of bones and the suffering of many noble knights and princes. Only we have the authority and charge to set the world aright and bring enlightenment to the blind and ignorant."

"*NOVUS ORDO SECLORUM. NOVUS ORDO SECLORUM. NOVUS ORDO SECLORUM...*," the other members chanted.

The Sovereign Grand Inquisitor held up his hand to silence the members and continued, "The day has come my fellow Supreme Council members that we must swear and reaffirm that our sacred duty is the eradication of all ordered governments, private property, patriotism, family, and all religion but our own. We pledge our allegiance to the New World Order. We swear to use any and all means at our disposal: deception, mind control, financial enslavement, blackmail, murder, and even far more grave means such as wars, famine, and depopulation. We will unleash a genocide like no other before it."

Once again the other members chanted, "*NOVUS ORDO SECLORUM. NOVUS ORDO SECLORUM. NOVUS ORDO SECLORUM…*,"

The Sovereign Grand Inquisitor smiled and allowed the chanting to continue for several minutes before silencing the other members and advising them they all had important obligations to perform.

The five men stood, donned their regal robes once again, returned to the inner chamber, and gathered inside the great circle inscribed on the floor. On the east side of the inner chamber stood a grayish-bronze sculpture formed in the likeness of a man's body. The legs were crossed at the ankles and instead of feet; the legs had hooves. Attached to the neck was the head of a goat. A pair of folded wings sprouted from behind the shoulders. The figure's right arm was extended making a right angle at the elbow with the index and middle fingers pointing upward in the grand hailing sign.

Behind the goat-man stood a gleaming black obelisk with a pentagram inscribed inside a circle emblazoned at the top. A young girl and a young boy stood on either side of the goat-man's legs, gazing up admiringly at the creature. In the center of the chamber, each council member stood on one point of a five-pointed star inscribed inside the large circle, exactly matching the symbol on the obelisk behind the goat-man.

The five men reached their left arms toward the center of the circle, bowed their heads, and repeated the Luciferian Oath known only to the five Supreme Council members and to absolutely no one else, "Our unrivaled religion should be, by all of us initiates here of the righteous and noble degrees, maintained in the purity of our Luciferian doctrine. We have now well-learned the mystery of our Sacred Order. The seething energies of Lucifer flow through and from our hands. Before we may step onward and upward, we must worthily and forever accept his ability to guide and apply our energy."

As the men raised their heads and stepped backward outside the circle, the Sovereign Grand Inquisitor handed the Sovereign Grand Prince a small, silver box containing a single white tablet.

The Sovereign Grand Prince looked directly into the Sovereign Grand Inquisitor eyes and proclaimed, "I swear, O Worshipful Master, I shall myself strangle the words in my throat before uttering or revealing a single word of what has transpired here."

The men turned and bowed to each other, removed their robes, and then hurried from the Temple building, heading to their respective parts of the world to put their portion of the Supreme Council's devilish plan into effect.

Interstate Highway
Tulsa, Oklahoma

While driving along the interstate highway toward downtown Tulsa, Zach's mind, as usual, had drifted to the unpleasant events of the past. Suddenly, the sound of blaring horns and screeching tires wrenched him back to reality. He slammed on the brakes and steered his car off onto the shoulder, missing the line of traffic stopped in front of him by mere inches. His knuckles stood out white as he tightly gripped the steering wheel. He shook his head, breathing hard from the sudden surge of adrenaline coursing through his body.

The driver of the car that had been following Zach pulled up beside Zach's stopped car, made an obscene gesture, and gunned his engine as he passed. Zach had no excuse and simply shrugged his shoulders.

Zach waited for the effects of the adrenaline to wear off. Seeing an opening in traffic, he stomped on the accelerator, and steered his car back into the driving lane. For the rest of the trip to work, he drove like his ninety-year-old grandmother, being extremely careful, much to the distress of the impatient drivers behind him. Turning off the expressway onto the Forty-First Street exit, he headed for the building he worked in. He turned into the building's parking lot and drove down the ramp into the underground parking area. Pulling in next to the elevator, he parked in his assigned spot.

Zach didn't much care for his current job as a low-level communications analyst. The work was okay. He did not dislike the work, but he found it rather boring and tedious. Just over a year earlier, he had owned his own company in the same building. As the owner and Chief Design Engineer of his company, he was directly responsible for a number of contracts supporting sophisticated microwave communications systems. The responsibility had been very demanding, but it was satisfying, until it spiraled out of control.

As the company prospered and grew, it caused a deep rift between him and his wife, Angie. The demands of running the company required an ever-increasing portion of his time. He spent as much time with Angie as he could, then worked into the early morning hours trying to keep the company operating. The stress and long hours exacted a heavy physical toll on Zach.

Unexpectedly, conditions at the company began to go sideways. System issues that Zach and his technicians could not solve caused the premier client to threaten to cancel their contract. By the time Zach identified the source of the problem, it was too late to satisfy the client and Zach's company lost its most important and lucrative contract. Without the cash flow from the premier client, Zach's lifelong dream of owning his own company imploded.

As Zach stood in front of the elevator, he remembered the last day his company existed as if it were yesterday. With great sadness he had watched as a building maintenance worker scraped the last remnants of the company's logo and name off the door. Inside the office, movers wrapped the remaining furniture, hauled it out on wheeled dollies, and loaded it onto a large truck. Zach had donated the furniture to an organization that helped new startups get established.

The one bright spot in the disheartening demise of his company was that Angie had finally understood what the company had meant to Zach. With the company's demands no longer consuming his attention, Zach had lots of time to spend with Angie. They had moved back in together and they were on the road to being truly happy again. And now she was gone, just like the company.

Zach sighed deeply. Yes, he remembered very well. On the last day of his company's existence, he had stood in that exact same spot. His company's offices had been in this same building, two floors below where he was now headed. If it had not been so painful, Zach might have laughed at the way fate seemed to be playing kickball with his life.

A smirk crossed his face as he reached out and pushed the Up button. He stepped into the elevator and leaned against the back wall as the elevator made its quick trip up to the eighth floor. The elevator door slid open and he entered the offices of Matrix Data Services.

He walked through the reception area, greeted the receptionist, and walked into the outer office. Penny Wilson, who served as a shared administrative assistant, looked up as he entered. As a highly skilled and capable assistant, she often anticipated Zach's needs and kept him on schedule as much as she could, considering she also served as assistant to two other analysts.

"Good morning, Zach," she said. "You're limping. What happened?"

"When I got out of the car to close the garage door, my foot slipped on the snow and I fell on the driveway, hard," Zach responded.

"I'm sorry to hear that," Ms. Wilson offered. "Mister Hanson has already been here looking for you. He didn't seem too happy."

"Yeah, I know. I'm late again," Zach answered. "On the way in, I was distracted and nearly ran into a line of stopped cars on the expressway. I slid clear off onto the shoulder. It really rattled me. Did Mister Hanson say what he wanted?"

"No. Not a word. He just turned and walked out. He seemed rather annoyed."

"Guess I'd better get to work," Zach said, turning and limping into his office, or, rather, a closet as he described it. He hung his jacket on a hook on the back of the door and set his briefcase beside the desk. After retrieving his non-spill coffee cup from the bottom, right-hand drawer of his desk, he trudged to the break room and filled the cup with coffee. Back in his office, he set the cup on the desk and dropped into his chair. The day had only just begun and already he felt exhausted, as if he had been sitting at his desk all day.

He pawed through the hanging files in the bottom, left-hand drawer of his desk and pulled out a thick file folder labeled, East Side Tower Project.

He opened the file folder and spread the various topographic maps, site layout drawings, FCC filings, and lists of installation materials across the top of the desk. Zach yawned as he bent over the papers, forcing himself to concentrate on the top priority project. The project encompassed all the necessary FCC fillings and land acquisition forms for relocating a five hundred fifty foot tall guyed steel radio tower. Complicating the large relocation project was the fact that fourteen separate radio systems would be located at various heights on the tower. Each one of the radio systems required a separate propagation study and also a frequency harmonics analysis. The FCC filings for the approval to construct the enormous radio tower were due by the end of the week and he was determined to complete the project on time.

An hour later, working on the landowner agreements for the four guy wires that would be required to support the tower, he looked up when Penny entered his office and stood beside the desk.

"Mister Hanson called. He wants to see you in his office immediately," Penny announced.

"Do you know what he wants?" Zach asked.

"No, but I saw Daniel Butler walk into his office about ten minutes ago."

"Great. Just great," Zach complained as he pushed himself back from his desk and stood up. Besides being a contemptible and extremely unlikable man, Mr. Daniel Butler had a well-known and well-deserved title as the *Corporate Hatchet Man*.

Zach gulped down a large swallow of lukewarm coffee and braced himself for what he knew would likely be a very unpleasant meeting.

"This should be loads of fun," Zach added as he hurried out of the office.

Zach had formed an immense dislike of Mr. Butler from the instant he first met him. Butler's arrogance and insulting mannerisms were well known and a frequent topic of discussion throughout the entire communications industry. If there had been even the slightest hint of a job opportunity elsewhere, Zach would have walked out of the interview after less than five minutes. Zach stopped in front of Mr. Hanson's office door, took a deep breath, and knocked on the door.

"Enter," Mr. Hanson hollered through the closed door.

Zach pushed the door open and entered the office. The first face he saw was that of Mr. Daniel Butler. As usual, he was sloppily dressed, wearing faded blue jeans and a ratty yellow polo shirt. A scraggly goatee sprouted from his chin. Even though Butler appeared to be in his early thirties, he possessed the stooped shoulders of someone much older, reducing his six-foot frame by more than an inch. A pair of scuffed loafers sat beside a chair on the right side of the desk. Another one of Butler's infuriating mannerisms was to walk around the office without shoes. In stocking feet, Mr. Butler stood beside Mr.

Hanson's desk, an ominous grimace spread across his swarthy face.

Mr. Hanson's office was impressively furnished. Side chairs covered in vibrant, cobalt blue velvet adorned with shiny silver accents sat on either side of a large mahogany desk. Behind the desk stood a large bookcase crafted from rich brown wood. Two walls of the office displayed large, and expensive, original oil paintings.

Mr. Hanson, Zach's boss, was seated behind the impressive desk wearing a starched, white long-sleeved shirt with the sleeves unbuttoned and rolled up to his elbows. An expensive gold wristwatch hung loosely around his left wrist. A muted, brick-red tie hung slightly askew below the unbuttoned collar of his shirt.

Mr. Hanson rose from his chair and informed Zach Mr. Butler wanted to talk with him. Mr. Butler slipped into Mr. Hanson's seat as Mr. Hanson hurried out of the office and pulled the door shut. Mr. Butler pointed toward a chair in front of the desk. A chill ran down Zach's spine as he sat down and faced Mr. Butler. An uneasy feeling grew in the pit of Zach's stomach.

"Templeton, we have decided to make some organizational changes that will affect the project you're working on." Mr. Butler said.

"But…," Zach started.

Mr. Butler held up his hand, interrupting Zach. "The decision has been made and will take effect immediately. We're sorry about what happened to you, but we have a company to run. Now that the acquisition is complete and the major issues have been resolved, your position is being eliminated."

Zach opened his mouth to respond but stopped. He knew arguing with Butler would be a waste of breath and he knew he would likely lose his temper, which would only make a bad situation worse.

"Nothing to say, Templeton?" Mr. Butler questioned.

Zach shook his head and remained quiet.

Mr. Butler glanced at his wristwatch and continued, "It's now ten-thirty. We will give you till noon to clean out your desk and turn in any keys or other company property in your possession. Oh, by the way, someone in the corporate office is reworking the project you've been working on. Your work papers will no longer be needed."

Without another word, Mr. Butler got up, walked over to the door, pulled it open, and waited. Zach stood up and started for the door. "What about the company car? How will I get home?" Zach asked.

"That's your problem," Butler sneered.

Zach shuffled through the open door without saying another word, dazed by the suddenness of his position being eliminated.

Chapter Three

Shady Oaks Cemetery
Bluffton, South Carolina

One thousand miles from Tulsa, Oklahoma, in Shady Oaks Cemetery, located just outside the small town of Bluffton, South Carolina, a large white hearse and two white Lincoln Towncars sat parked next to a three-sided, blue tent. The open side of the tent faced a newly opened grave. Many other cars of various makes and models lined the nearby gravel pathways of Shady Oaks Cemetery. The immediate family and close friends of Marguerite Watts sat quietly on metal folding chairs under the blue tent. A large imitation grass-like tarp covered the large mound of dirt piled beside the open grave.

In an older section of the cemetery, the Watts family plots had been in the family for many years. Leaning at precarious angles, many of the moss-covered gravestones in the older section, had settled unevenly into the ground over the long years. The family names had weathered away to the point of no longer being legible. Those gravestones stood mute, no longer able to identify the long-dead souls that lay interred below.

Just beyond the weather-beaten fence that marked the southern boundary of the cemetery, immense live oak trees draped in large clumps of Spanish moss stood with their huge limbs spread out. The dense canopy of leaves and stringy moss allowed only narrow shafts of filtered light to seep through. The air, scented with the earthy odor of damp, rotting foliage, hung heavy in the cemetery. An early morning mist floated just above the ground, swirling eerily around the bases of the silent tombstones.

On any other day the Spanish moss-draped live oak trees might have evoked a sense of awe and wonder, but given the sad and gloomy mood of the gathering, the silver-gray strands, hanging like natural Halloween decorations, produced a somewhat spooky appearance. The stringy clumps of Spanish moss decorating the gigantic oak trees summoned up images of old plantations, mysterious bayous, and dark, forbidding swamps like those seen in movies.

When the Native Americans first saw the tangled clumps of moss swaying in the wind, they called it 'tree hair'. The early French explorers dubbed it 'Spanish Beard' as an insult to the Spaniards, so the Spanish quickly changed the name and called the moss 'French Hair'. Surprisingly, the plant is not moss at all, but, rather, it is a distant member of the pineapple family, growing longer and longer until it appears as if it were dripping from the large trees.

On the other side of the cemetery, a grassy meadow rose gently until it reached a thick line of trees one hundred yards to the north. The line of trees angled off toward the Northeast. At the very northeastern edge of the meadow, a sparkling, crystal-clear stream meandered its way down from the top of one of the nearby hills.

Clumps of Bitter Switchgrass mixed with Indiangrass and Turkey Grass dotted the meadow outside the perimeter fence surrounding the cemetery. Droplets of water from a heavy dew glistened and sparkled on the blades of the grasses as the sun peaked through breaks in the cloudy sky.

Sadly, on this sorrowful day, the beauty of the lush meadow and the glistening stream was lost, overshadowed by the unexpected death of a dear loved one.

A large number of mourners had gathered to pay respects to their dear friend Marguerite Watts. Those that could not fit under the tent milled around nervously, speaking in hushed voices as they waited for the pastor to begin the graveside service. Several late arriving mourners hurried between the moss-covered gravestones to join the assemblage.

Despite a temperature in the mid-seventies, the foggy mist persisted, hugging the ground and obscuring the bottom of the tree line at the far edge of the meadow.

Holding above ninety percent, the humidity created an oppressive and uncomfortable dampness, further adding to the unpleasant mood of the day. Many of the mourners were already fanning themselves with the funeral bulletins they had received at the funeral home.

Satisfied everyone was listening, Pastor Norman Stone rose from his chair and began. "We gather here today to lay to rest the body of your servant and our dear friend Marguerite Watts. She lived a full life and was deeply loved by all those that knew her. Here today, we commit to the earth only that which is of the earth. The Scriptures teach us that our bodies are made of the dust of the ground and to the dust of the ground we will return. Almighty God, into your hands, we commend your servant Marguerite Watts in the sure and certain hope of the resurrection unto eternal life through Jesus Christ our Lord," Pastor Stone proclaimed in a forceful yet solemn tone.

Pastor Stone, slightly over six feet tall with snow-white hair and a rich, baritone voice, turned slightly toward the family and continued, "It is especially hard when a loved one is taken from us so suddenly and without explanation. I have known this dear woman for twenty-plus years and I cannot remember a single time when she was not the first one to volunteer to run an errand or care for someone that was sick. She loved everyone she met. Our community will certainly miss her infectious laugh and gentle, loving spirit. We grieve deeply that we will no longer hear that laugh or see her smiling face or experience her tender compassion. Our lives will seem a little more empty and a little less bright without the presence of this dear woman. But do not grieve for Marguerite, for she is in the loving arms of her Lord and Savior."

Pastor Stone stopped for a moment, pulled a handkerchief from his pocket, took a deep breath, and wiped away the solitary tear that had rolled down his cheek. He smiled and continued, "Over the years, I have had many enjoyable conversations with Marguerite. Some time ago she slipped me a note and made me promise to share it when the time came for me to conduct her funeral. I am deeply saddened that it had to be so soon. I will now fulfill my promise to her."

Pastor Stone pulled a small sheet of notepaper from his inside jacket pocket. He unfolded it and began reading, "Dear friends that are gathered here to say a last farewell, do not grieve for me. Please try not to be sad. I am now in a place where the light never fades. You need not fear death. Scripture tells us that whosoever shall call upon the name of the Lord shall be saved. My dear friends, it really is that simple. Death is but a release into eternity. I wish I could be there to hug each one of you and say a proper goodbye. Please know that I loved you all so very much and my deepest desire is for you to have a faith greater than mine. Marguerite"

Many of those assembled were reaching for handkerchiefs or tissues, greatly moved by the simple, yet moving, words written on the notepaper. Great tears rolled down the face of her beloved daughter, Anna Mae. Marguerite's husband, Edwin, dressed in his only suit, the elbows of the jacket frayed and nearly worn through, sat staring at the casket. He gripped the folding chair so tightly his knuckles stood out white. At sixty-two years of age, Edwin was a thin wispy man with gray thinning hair. Time and a hard farm life had aged Edwin well beyond his years. Slightly stoop shouldered, his skin tanned dark, looking like leather, the result of long hours in the blazing sun sitting atop some piece of farm machinery as he tended their one hundred sixty-acre farm.

Edwin had attended a fair number of funerals during his sixty-two years. Funerals were especially difficult for Edwin, having lost both his parents when he was a child of only ten. His parents had been killed in a tragic farming accident. One sweltering summer day he had come running up to the wheat field from playing in the creek and had witnessed the grisly scene. The vision of that scene dancing before his eyes and the pain he had felt on the day of the funeral ripping at his heart was still as vivid as the day it took place fifty-two years earlier. Mightily he fought against the flood of emotions screaming to be released. His face was taut and his lips were drawn pencil-line tight as he struggled to maintain control. Edwin, a very private, reserved man, refused to surrender to those emotions in front of his family and friends. He would cry later, in private.

Anna Mae noticed that her father was struggling. She reached over, placed her hand over her father's hand, and whispered in his ear, "Daddy, it's okay to cry. Nobody would think less of you. We'll get through this together."

Edwin released his grip on the chair and took Anna Mae's hand in his, but his gaze remained fixed on the casket. Despite his valiant effort to maintain control, he failed and the tears rolled down his cheeks, dripping onto his old, worn jacket.

Pastor Stone refolded the notepaper and slipped it into his jacket pocket. Taking a step closer to the casket, he placed his hand on the casket and began his summation, "These mortal remains we now commit to the ground. Earth to earth, ashes to ashes, dust to dust. Blessed are the dead who die in the Lord. Lord, we thank you for those we have loved so dearly but can see no more in this life. We rest assured that one day we will be reunited. Receive into your loving arms your servant Marguerite Watts. Amen and Amen."

Anna Mae and her father rose from their chairs and shook Pastor Stone's hand. "I know she would want you to have this," Pastor Stone said as he removed the folded note from his jacket pocket and slipped it into Anna Mae's hand.

"Thank you, Pastor Stone," Anna Mae said, her voice quavering. "It was a beautiful service. I know Mother would be pleased."

The crowd of mourners outside the tent stood back and waited as the family and close friends filed out of the tent. As the last person filed out, the other mourners walked away from the gravesite and headed for their cars. Anna Mae and her father walked over next to the casket and stood there in silence. Two cemetery workers watched them from a distance, patiently waiting for everyone to leave so they could finish their task. After several minutes, Edwin put his arm around Anna Mae and squeezed her tight. He let go and said, "Honey, we need to go."

"I know, Daddy. I just can't believe she's gone. It doesn't feel real." she sniffled.

"Yeah, I know. I feel that way too."

Edwin took several steps, stopped, and squatted in front of the simple white stone that marked his dear grandmother's gravesite. He bowed his head, reached out, and placed his hand on the rough stone that had been placed there only three months earlier. Anna Mae struggled as she looked down on her father, seeing his shoulders shake. Her father was a deeply private man and only once before had she seen him cry openly; the day they had buried Ada Mae Watts, her great-grandmother. *"Life seems so unfair sometimes,"* she thought as she waited for her father.

Edwin stood up and wiped his cheeks with the back of his hand. He reached out and grabbed his daughter's hand, and together they started toward the funeral home's limo. Part way to the limo, Anna Mae stopped and turned back toward the gravesite. She watched as one of the cemetery workers tripped the suspension release and the casket slowly lowered and disappeared from sight.

"Oh, Daddy," she wailed as she fell against her father's chest, clutching him tightly.

"I know. I know," her father choked. There were simply no words that could ease their grief. The pain was too fresh and too raw. Edwin put his hands on Anna Mae's shoulders and pushed her back. "Anna Mae, we need to go. They're waiting for us."

"Sorry, Daddy," Anna Mae sputtered, dabbing at her eyes with the handkerchief clutched in her hand.

As they walked arm-in-arm toward the white Lincoln Towncar parked directly behind the hearse, Anna Mae again dabbed at her swollen, red eyes. She stole one last look toward the gravesite and saw the cemetery workers disassembling the lowering device upon which the casket had sat. She shivered involuntarily despite the warm temperature.

She reached out and tapped her father on the arm. "Dad, I just don't understand," she exclaimed, using her more grown-up term for her father. "Mom just suddenly vanished. And then two weeks later they found her car submerged in the May River up by Bluffton. She was an excellent driver. The weather had been good. She wouldn't have just driven into the river. It just doesn't make sense."

Her dad just looked at her with a pained expression, tears once again forming in his eyes. He shrugged, not knowing what to say.

"The medical examiner's report said because of the length of time she was in the water, the lab tests were mostly inconclusive. The ME said the only test outside normal range was a slightly elevated level of potassium. He said he was not convinced but had no choice but to rule the cause of death as *sudden cardiac arrest*," Anna Mae confided. "Dad, something's missing. Mother hadn't been sick. How could she just have a heart attack? This is just not right!"

Nearly overcome with grief and teetering on the edge of breaking down, her dad shrugged again as he climbed into the limo for the ride back to the funeral home. Sensing that her father was in no condition for further conversation, Anna Mae fell silent and climbed in beside him.

Anna Mae was thirty-seven and had never married. She had remained single because in her early teens she had made a promise to herself that she would only marry a good, Christian man. Immediately after high school graduation, she went off to college and put all her efforts toward her education, graduating with honors and a degree in accounting. After college, she had returned to Bluffton and had gone to work for a small manufacturing firm. Five years later, when the company's only other accountant retired, she was offered his position and became the head accountant.

Anna Mae was very attractive with sparkling blue eyes and beautiful, long auburn hair. Her beauty combined with her kind and gentle spirit drew the attention of a fair number of Bluffton's young men. Even though a number of those young men had expressed an interest in Anna Mae, she had turned them all down flat. Having lived in Bluffton all her life, she either knew them or had heard about them. From their reputations, it was obvious they were anything but Christian. All of Anna Mae's friends and high school classmates had long-since married. Many of them now had children, some already entering middle school. Anna Mae could not help but notice the quick glances as she walked down the streets of Bluffton. She also had noticed her friends whispering, but she did not care in the least. She had made a promise and she always kept her promises.

Anna Mae often dreamed about what it would be like to have a husband to share life with. Someone to share the good times and the hard times. This was one of those dismal days when she longed for a strong, loving man to hold her in his arms and tell her everything would be okay. Often she had watched her parents as they went about their daily responsibilities. Despite their having lived a difficult, hardscrabble life, they were genuinely happy. For her parents, life was not about *possessions*. Their life centered around little things: sharing a cup of coffee on the porch, walks by the creek on a cool evening, or scratching the ears of their old Redbone Coonhound, Tripp. The clumsy and adorable puppy had received his name from the fact that he often tripped over his own feet. Her parents found joy in the simple things of life that could not be purchased with money.

"Would she ever find someone to share her life with?" she silently asked herself, sighing heavily. Would God bring a good man into her life? Whether or not that happened, she convinced herself she had much to be happy about. After all, being happy was not an accident driven by circumstance. It was a choice.

As Anna Mae sat silently staring out of the limo's window, her mind churned with the baffling mystery surrounding her mother's sudden and mysterious death. She adamantly refused to believe her mother had had a heart attack and had driven off the road and into the river, but what other explanation was there? Everyone, her father included, told her to just let it go, but she could not accept that. Something deep inside her refused to be silenced. Something unsettling and troubling demanded to know exactly what had happened to her mother.

Anna Mae had sensed a definite nervousness in Beaufort County Sheriff, Lonnie Overton's expression the day he had notified her of the grim discovery. Sheriff Overton had been uneasy and he had lied. She was certain of it, but she could not fathom why.

Why had her mother driven to Bluffton?

Why had she been near the river?

Why would Sheriff Overton lie?

What did he have to gain?

What could he be hiding?

She continued to stare at the lush landscape, asking herself the same questions over and over as the limo headed for the funeral home. "*Am I wrong?*" she asked herself silently.

"*No, she was not wrong!*" she answered almost immediately.

The facts simply did not add up and she was determined she was going to find out what had happened?

Darlington Avenue
Tulsa, Oklahoma

Zach walked down the hallway mumbling angrily to himself, fuming that his boss had not even had the decency to stay for the meeting. He rounded the corner and met his boss heading back to his office. The two men stood there facing each other for several seconds, Zach looking down on Mr. Hanson as he stood only five foot three inches tall. With an embarrassed look on his face, Mr. Hanson started to say something.

Zach held up his hand and stopped him. "Don't say a word. Not one word!" Zach snapped through clenched teeth as he stepped sideways around Mr. Hanson and continued down the hallway.

As Zach walked back into his office, Penny could not help by notice the distressed look in Zach's eyes.

"Mister Templeton, is something wrong?" she asked. "You look stressed."

"My position has been eliminated. No warning. I have till noon to clean out my desk," Zach grumbled as he walked past her and into his office. He stopped beside his desk and just stood there. After a long pause, Zach bent over, picked up his briefcase, and placed it on the corner of his desk. He sat down and began stuffing his few personal items into the briefcase: one of his favorite photos of Angie, his nameplate, an architectural ruler, two drafting pencils, and a small assortment of plastic design templates.

"Hey, Penny, can you come in here please," he called out.

Penny stuck her head into Zach's office and said, "What do you need, Mister Templeton?"

Zach picked up his half-full coffee cup and held it out. "Can you rinse this out for me while I go through my desk, I mean the company's desk?" Zach remarked. "I want to get out of here as quickly as possible."

"Absolutely, I'd be happy to," she said, grabbing the cup and heading for the break room.

Zach opened each desk drawer and searched through its contents, finding nothing else that belonged to him.

"Not much to show for six months work," he thought as he closed the briefcase and set it on the floor. As he stood up, he looked at the project papers he had been working on still scattered across the desk. He pushed the trashcan close to the side of the desk and pushed all the papers off into it. He lifted the plastic bag out of the trashcan and tied the corners together in a tight knot.

"There. All done. Six months of my life gone. Wasted. Kaput. El-Finito," he grumbled, brushing his hands together as if shaking off unwanted dust.

Grabbing his coat from the hook on the door, he laid it over his arm, snatched the bag of trash, picked up his briefcase, and exited his office without so much as a glance backward. He stopped at Penny's desk just as she returned from the break room. She held out the coffee cup. Zach took the cup from her and added it to the other personal items in his brief-case.

"Thank you, Penny, you've been a wonderful assistant. A friendly piece of advice: if I were you, I would look for a different job," he said, holding out his hand.

Penny took Zach's hand and grasped it firmly. "I'm so sorry, Zach. I hope things work out for you. You've been a great boss," Penny responded. "I think I will take your advice about the job. I don't like it here much either."

Zach pointed at the plastic bag. "Butler said someone from the corporate office is already reworking the project. So, all that is trash."

Zach walked out of his office, not intending to say a word to anyone else. Halfway to the elevator, he stopped, returned to his office, and grabbed the set of car keys he had left lying on the desk. He winked at Penny as he exited his office for the last time and headed for Mr. Hanson's office.

Still reeling from the morning's events, he decided he did not care if he burned this bridge as he had no intention of ever working for them again. Without knocking, Zach pushed the door open and walked into Mr. Hanson's office, interrupting the meeting that was underway. Zach walked over beside the desk and glared at Mr. Butler as he dropped the keys to the company car on the desk.

"I wouldn't want to inconvenience anyone. I'll just call a taxi." Zach turned and walked out of the office without another word.

Chapter Four

Miami International Airport
Miami, Florida

Panting and out of breath, Klaus Herrmann stopped, leaned against a billboard advertising acne cream, and mopped his face with a handkerchief. He had just made a grueling twenty minute trek, dragging his suitcase from Terminal E to the Customs and Immigration entry point at the far end of Terminal D at Miami International Airport. Afraid to loiter any longer, Klaus grabbed the handle of his suitcase and entered the large, international arrivals hall.

Stopping to get his bearings, he looked up at the overhead signs to determine which line he should join. The signage indicated the international arrivals hall was split into three separate lines: Visitors, Residents, and Citizens. He walked over and stopped under the sign for Visitors. Looking back in the direction he had just come from, he noticed the long line of travelers extended nearly out the door of the arrivals hall. He hurried back to the end of the line and joined the long line of people.

As he shuffled along with the mass of visitors, he pulled out his passport, his visa, and the ETSA form (Electronic System for Travel Authorization) the flight attendants had passed out on the plane. For the third time, he verified that he had filled in all the required spaces and then he dug in his wallet for the required fee. Klaus had been warned that entering the United States would require an enormous amount of patience because US immigration laws were some of the strictest in the world. Even though Klaus possessed a pre-arranged visa, he knew that fact alone did not guarantee him entry into the United States.

The final permission to enter would be determined solely by a Customs and Border Protection Officer. Ever since 9/11, US immigration officials had become extremely suspicious of everyone, which meant they would question each visitor for as long as they deemed necessary. Acting nervous, arguing, or lying to the customs officials would almost assuredly get you singled out for *special* questioning which could take hours or, worse, could cause your entry to be denied.

In his native country, Klaus was president of a mid-sized bank and quite wealthy. To minimize potential suspicion, he had purchased a new casual wardrobe of pleated, gray linen trousers, a collared, green polo shirt, and simple black loafers. All chosen to make him look like any other tourist. Klaus was a large man with an angular face, square chin, dark penetrating eyes, and light brown wavy hair. He deliberately stooped to lessen his height.

His trip had begun over twelve hours earlier in Frankfort, Germany, with a three-hour layover and plane change in Amsterdam. Adding the time to pack and drive to the airport, in all he had been travelling for well over fifteen hours. Dark stubble colored his face, giving him a shadowy appearance.

Klaus shifted his weight, leaned to his left, and sighed deeply as he looked down the long line slowly creeping its way toward the front of the hall. He shrugged his shoulders and settled in for what would likely prove to be a long, grueling wait.

Two minutes shy of one and one-half hours later, Klaus stopped at the red line and waited for the next CBP officer to wave him forward.

"Next," CBP Officer Thomas Mosley called out, motioning Klaus to come forward.

Klaus stepped up to the counter and handed Officer Mosley the paperwork he had been clutching in his right hand for nearly two hours. Officer Mosley eyed Klaus suspiciously as he did everyone while comparing the passport photo to Klaus's face. Officer Mosley had worked for Customs and Immigration for over three years and had become quite adept at identifying travelers that were hiding something. Satisfied that Klaus matched the passport photo, Officer Mosley slid the passport through an OCR Slot Reader.

"What is the purpose of your visit, Mister Herrmann?"

"A vacation to see an old friend," Klaus lied.

"How long and where will you be staying, Mister Herrmann?"

"Just a week. I'll be staying with my friend in Delray Beach, Florida," Klaus lied again.

Neither Klaus's face nor his mannerisms gave any indication whatsoever that he was lying. Being a skilled liar, no change in expression showed on Klaus's face because he had no conscience. His purpose in life and everything he did was to serve the Supreme Council. In his mind, the council's plan was pure and righteous. Therefore, he concluded, he was not really lying as it served a higher purpose. Neither did he worry about using his true identity because when the purpose for his visit was complete, he would have no need of a passport.

Officer Mosley instructed Klaus to open his suitcase. After poking around in its contents for several minutes, Officer Mosley pulled out a gold-colored box. "What is this?" he asked.

"You may open it if you like," Klaus answered. "It is a gift for my friend in Delray Beach. It is expensive cologne you cannot buy here."

Officer Mosley eased the top flap open, tipped the box down, and slid a gold accented bottle out into his hand. He held the bottle up to his nose and sniffed. "Very nice scent," Officer Mosley remarked. He slid the bottle back into the box, closed the flap, and laid the bottle back in the suitcase. "You may close it up," he said.

Cleverly hidden inside the bottom of the bottle of cologne was a small silver box containing one white table. While Klaus straightened the contents of his suitcase and closed the lid, Officer Mosley opened the passport to a blank page, stamped it with an "Admitted" stamp, and scribbled Mr. Hermann's entry class and expected exit date in the appropriate blanks.

"Have a pleasant stay, Mister Herrmann," Officer Mosley said as he waved up the next visitor in line.

Klaus grabbed the handle to his suitcase and hurried off toward the baggage area to meet his associate. He smiled and hummed his favorite tune, knowing the grand and glorious day that was his sole focus would arrive soon.

Chapter Five

Darlington Avenue
Tulsa, Oklahoma

Zach stepped off the elevator on the ground floor and walked across the lobby. About to push the main door open, he turned, walked over to the south side of the lobby, and dropped into a chair to calm down and gather his thoughts. He knew his outburst in Mr. Hanson's office had been childish and accomplished nothing. The anger and frustration that had been building in him for weeks had reached the tipping point and he had lost control.

"Well, maybe the outburst had accomplished something," he thought. He had desperately wanted to tell Mr. Butler what he thought of him from the very first day he met him. The release of some of the pent-up emotions had been therapeutic. Although he was now unemployed, he actually felt relieved that he would no longer have to endure the horrible job. A job he hated.

"Now what am I going to do and how am I going to get home?" he asked himself as he sat there deciding what to do next. Without a job, he really did not want to spend the money on a taxi. Left with no other choice, he swallowed his pride and called his dad.

"Hey, Zach. How's your day going?" James Templeton, Zach's dad asked.

"Not so good, actually," Zach answered. "I'm at work, but I need a ride home. If you aren't busy, could you come by the office and pick me up?"

"What's going on? Are you sick?"

"No. I'm not sick. I'd rather tell you in person. If you're busy, I can call a taxi."

"Absolutely not. I'm not busy and I'd be glad to come get you. All I have to do is put on some shoes and grab my car keys. Where exactly should I meet you?"

"I'll be waiting in the lobby."

"I'll be there in…. say twenty minutes or so," James Templeton said after glancing at his watch.

"Thanks, Dad. I really appreciate this."

"No problem. Glad to help. See you in a few minutes."

Zach ended the call and dropped the cell phone back in the holster clipped on his belt. He sat there staring out the window wondering how he was going to pay his bills. After agreeing to help Admiral Charles Hadley chase down the perpetrators of the bombing in Sacramento and the expense of having Angie's body shipped home from New Jersey and then the funeral, he had been struggling to meet his expenses. Having only worked at the job he just lost for a few months, he would not qualify for unemployment benefits. A quickly developed plan would be critical as he only had enough money in his bank account to last for a few weeks.

Twenty-five minutes later James Templeton, Zach's dad, drove into the parking lot and stopped in front of the lobby door. Zach pushed himself up from the chair, exited the building, and climbed into the passenger's seat.

"Thanks Dad. I really appreciate the lift."

"You're welcome. Sorry it took me a little longer than I said. I had trouble locating my car keys. I think your mother hides them," Zach's dad said with a smile on his face.

"Mom wouldn't do that. You're just getting old," Zach quipped.

"Yeah, happens to all of us. Where to?"

"Home."

Zach's dad put the car in gear and drove out of the parking lot, heading for the freeway. The overnight snow had already melted except for a few small patches in shaded areas. Zach's dad grabbed a pair of sunglasses lying on the dashboard and slipped them on to shield his eyes from the bright mid-day sun. Zach sat in silence, staring out the window as his dad drove down the street.

Every few seconds Zach's dad glanced over at his son with deep concern. He could tell from his son's countenance that something serious was troubling him. Zach was leaving work in the middle of the day and he had full use of a company car. So, why did he need a ride? Something was definitely out of the ordinary. James had avoided pushing his son to talk, well aware of the enormous strain he was under. Angie's death had been a horrible blow to everyone, but Zach seemed to be near the breaking point. *"Maybe I've been too careful,"* James thought as he glanced over at his son again.

"Zach, I'm deeply concerned. I can tell something is troubling you. If I can help, all you have to do is ask."

Zach did not answer, continuing to stare out the window with a vacant expression on his face. Zach's dad drove down the street for eight more blocks, then turned right onto the entrance ramp for the freeway. He merged into the south-bound traffic and seeing a break in the line of cars behind him; he moved over into the center lane. He tried once more to get his son to open up.

"Zach, I think you need to talk about what's eating at you. I know something's going on. Maybe your mother or I could help."

Zach turned toward his dad. "I just got fired. Hit the bricks, pal. Scram. Sayonara. Don't let the door hit you on the way out. Not even any severance pay," Zach burst out, anger and frustration evident in his voice. "Said they didn't like the quality of my work. My coward of a boss didn't even have the decency to stay in the room. He let the sniveling, corporate hatchet-man Butler do it."

"Zach, I'm sorry," Zach's dad groaned. "What are you go-ing to do?"

"I don't have a clue," Zach answered. "It took weeks to find that job. And it was a lousy job, I might add. It was the only genuine lead I had after two months of looking."

"Your mother and I will help in any way we can. You know that, right?" Zach's dad offered.

"Yes, I know that and I really do appreciate that, but something has to change. I can't keep going on like this."

"What do you mean *change*?" Zach's dad questioned.

"Dad, I feel like I'm dying inside. A major part of me is missing. Every day I miss Angie a little more. I just can't seem to focus on anything for more than a brief time."

"I understand that. Your mother and I miss her too, but Zach, life has to go on. What kind of change are you looking for?"

"Everywhere I go I see something that reminds me of Angie," Zach blurted out. "And not just in the house. On the drive to work I see our favorite restaurant. I see the park where she went jogging. I see the fabric store where she bought material. Even in the grocery store, I see her hand reaching up to pick something off a shelf. In our house… I mean my house, she's everywhere. Dad, I just can't take it anymore!" Zach's hands were balled into fists. He wanted to lash out at something. Anything. He felt overwhelmed and helpless. Having been a Navy SEAL, he had battled enemies that stood in front of you. Enemies you could see and touch. Now he was battling an unseen enemy. An enemy just as destructive as a physical enemy.

"But how are you going to change any of that?" Zach's dad questioned.

"I'm going to put the house up for sale and then I'm going to look for a job somewhere else. I need a place where I don't see Angie's face everywhere I look." Zach responded.

"I understand why you would want to do that, but are you certain that's the best thing to do?"

"I have to, Dad. I'm going crazy. I need a complete change."

"Okay, Zach. If you're absolutely certain, your mother and I will support you. You know your mother is going to be more than a little disappointed."

Yeah, I've thought about that, but this is what I have to do. Do you want me to tell her?"

"No. I think it would be better if I told her."

The two men rode in silence the rest of the way to Zach's house. James pulled his car into the driveway of Zach's house, slipped the gearshift into park, and turned the engine off.

"Earlier you said you were going to look for a job somewhere else. Exactly what does that mean?"

"Somewhere warm. In the Southeast, I think. Georgia sounds good to me."

"How on Earth are you going to find a job in Georgia?"

"I'm going to call in a favor," Zach answered. "Remember, after the award ceremony in Washington, I told you President Cantwell said if I ever needed anything, to call him."

"Yes, I seem to remember something like that."

"Surely the President will know someone in Georgia that could use my skillset."

"How soon is all this going to happen?"

"As soon as I can make it happen. I'm going to call a real estate agent tomorrow. I'll discuss setting a sale price that will make the house sell quickly. Then, I'm going to call the President and see if he knows of a company that is hiring in the Southeast, and Georgia specifically. Part of me hates to use his influence, but I have never needed a favor more in my life."

"You seem pretty certain about this. I suspect I couldn't change your mind."

"I'm certain, Dad. I have to do this. Tell Mom I'm sorry."

"After I explain it to her, I think she will understand. I know she wants to see you happy again. If that has to happen in Georgia, we're behind you."

"That means a lot to me, Dad. To know you support me will make leaving a little less difficult."

"Do you need me to come in and talk for a while?"

"No. I'm okay. Believe it or not, I actually feel much better now that I've made a decision. I just hope it's the right one."

"Me too, Zach. Your mother and I love you very much. Keep us informed."

"I love you guys too. I'll call you tomorrow and let you know what the realtor and the President have to say," Zach answered as he slipped out of the car and closed the door.

James started the engine, slipped the car into gear, and backed out of the driveway. Zach waved at his dad as he drove away. He continued to watch as the car travelled down the street, turned the corner, and disappeared from sight.

Zach dug a ring of keys out of his pocket and headed for the front door. He slid the key into the deadbolt lock and unlocked it. Then Zach unlocked the doorknob, pushed the front door open, and walked into the house. He dropped the briefcase just inside the front door and headed for the kitchen with a smile on his face. He was hungry for the first time in weeks.

Some of the weight lifted from his shoulders and he stood a little taller. Having made a decision, he now had a goal to work toward. Despite the fact that it might be a rather short-term goal, at least it was a start.

He hoped the President would be able to fulfill the promise that he had made six months earlier.

Underground Laboratory, Unknown Location

Klaus Hermann, the Sovereign Grand Prince, climbed down the ladder and stepped off into the secret underground facility. He walked across the rubberized floor, the sound of his footsteps barely registering above a whisper. At the far side of the small room, he pressed a button next to the heavy access door that led into the laboratory's Class Eight anteroom. After thirty seconds with no response, he reached out and jabbed the button again.

A distorted face peered at him through a thick glass view port. Klaus heard a soft clunk as the door's locking mechanism released. He heard a whoosh and felt air rushing inward as the door was pushed open. A hand reached out, grabbed him, and pulled him inside as the door was quickly resealed. The man that had pulled him inside the anteroom stepped sideways and checked the air pressure indicator to assure himself negative pressure had been reestablished. It was critical to always maintain air flow from clean areas to contaminated areas to prevent the escape of airborne particles or infectious microorganisms.

A rumpled looking, sixtyish man, rail-thin, wearing khakis, rubber-soled shoes, and a stained white lab coat turned from reading the air flow gauges. The man smoothed his wild hair down, pushed a pair of bent wire-rimmed spectacles back up on his nose, bowed slightly, and introduced himself, "Sovereign Grand Prince, I'm Doctor Mark Bristol, senior virologist. We have been expecting you. Welcome to our facility."

"Doctor Bristol," Klaus acknowledged. "As I suspect you must already know, I am sent by the Worshipful Master of the Supreme Council."

Dr. Bristol noticed the Sovereign Grand Prince glance across the room at the man seated in front of the binocular viewer of a large scanning electron microscope. "That is Doctor Randall Weaver. He is a biotechnologist with a sub-specialty in genetics. May I show you what he is working on?" Klaus nodded agreement. Dr. Bristol led Klaus across the workspace. The hum of the florescent lights, the steady whirring from multiple power supply fans, and the rush of air blowing out of the ventilation system masked their quiet footsteps as the two men walked up behind Dr. Weaver.

Intensely absorbed in his task, Dr. Weaver was oblivious to the two men that had walked up behind him. Dr Bristol tapped him on the shoulder. Dr. Weaver, hunched over the microscope's viewer, lurched and pulled his head away, and reached for his right eye.

"Hey, what the.....?" he blurted out, startled by the unexpected touch on his shoulder. "Someone should have warned me we were going to have visitors. Slater is in charge of security," Dr. Weaver complained, still holding his eye. "Where is he anyway?"

"I'm right here," Harvey Slater announced as he sauntered out to the control room. "I saw our friend here as soon as he entered the clearing. He matches the photo they sent me, so I let him enter and watched him on the monitor as he climbed down the ladder."

Dr. Weaver glared at Slater, having a great dislike for the man because of his overbearing mannerisms. Dressed in black slacks and a black turtleneck, Slater stood one inch over six feet tall. Even though he was wearing a light jacket, his muscular build, the product of lifting weights, was quite obvious. His hair, trimmed short into a flattop, hinted of a military background. His weathered face seemed permanently fixed in a grimace. An ominous lump, barely concealed beneath his jacket, provided the men ample reason to be wary of Mr. Slater.

"We did not expect anyone until next week," Dr. Weaver said, still holding his eye.

"I am the Sovereign Grand Prince from the Supreme Council." Klaus repeated for the two men. "The Worshipful Master is more than a little concerned. He feels this will be our last chance. He instructed me to come and personally oversee the prototype assessment and the final preparations."

"Our work is progressing just fine. We do not need babysitting," Dr. Weaver sneered, as he turned away from the equipment and stood directly in front of Klaus. "And what qualifications do you have to interfere with our work?"

"Doctor Weaver," Klaus responded, taking a step forward until he was not more than six inches from Dr. Weaver's face. "I have been warned about you and your arrogance. You would be wise to hold your tongue, Doctor. We have many biotechnologists available to us. Perhaps you would like to be found floating in the river?"

"Humph," Dr. Weaver grunted as he backed away and turned back toward the equipment.

"I will assume that means no," Klaus remarked. "Now, Doctor Bristol, please continue. Has the prototype assessment begun?"

"Yes, Sovereign Prince," Dr. Bristol answered. "We have released two tests and we are very optimistic, but it will take some time before we can fully assess the pathogen's efficacy."

"How can you be certain of the target once you release the vector?" Klaus asked.

"The vector is exceptionally aggressive. It seeks a host immediately upon release," Dr. Bristol replied.

"If the vector is so aggressive, how can you control the spread of the test?"

"We have engineered the delivery vector to have a very short life. A few hours to no more than two days. I will explain how we do that later."

"What is the pathogen's incubation period?"

"That depends somewhat on the host's immune system. Anywhere from twelve to twenty-four hours."

"Very well," Klaus replied. "Can you explain how you can edit the specific, targeted gene?"

"The process is quite complex, Sovereign Prince, but I will do my best to explain the basic concept," Dr. Bristol said. "We can edit a genome using the CRISPR-Cas9 process."

"Huh, what's that?" Klaus asked, a puzzled look spreading across his face.

Dr. Bristol pushed Dr. Weaver out of the way and directed Klaus to take a seat in front of the microscope. Klaus leaned forward and looked into the binocular viewer as Dr. Bristol began his explanation.

"What you are looking at in the viewer is the result of our latest effort. The process we are using was adapted from a naturally occurring genome editing system used by bacteria. The acronym CRISPR stands for clustered regularly inter-spaced short palindromic repeats. The Cas9 suffix refers to an enzyme that bacteria use to cut a virus's DNA molecule apart, thereby disabling the virus. Sovereign Prince, Do you understand the difference between RNA and DNA?"

"I'm not certain. Enlighten me, Doctor."

"RNA is a single-stranded molecule whereas DNA is a molecule composed of two molecule chains that coil around each other, forming a double helix. A DNA molecule carries all the genetic instructions required for the development, functioning, growth, and reproduction of all known organisms and specifically, in our case, viruses. Is that clear?"

"Yes, go on, Doctor."

"During early research, scientists identified repeating DNA sequences in many species. Later in their research, they discovered that bacteria capture the repeating snippets of DNA from invading viruses and use them to create new DNA segments known as CRISPR arrays. The CRISPR arrays allow the bacteria to *remember* a specific virus or one that is closely related. If the virus attacks again, the bacteria produces RNA segments from the CRISPR arrays to target the virus's DNA and destroy it. We have adapted this molecular process and can identify and change any chosen position in a virus's DNA code. Once the Cas9 enzyme cuts the DNA at the position we have selected, the cell attempts to repair the break using whatever available DNA it can find. So, at that point we inject the new genetic sequence we want the cell to insert."

"But, as I understand it, a cell has billions of pieces. How does the new gene find the right place to embed itself?" Klaus asked.

"Yes, a cell has three billion pieces of information, give or take," Dr. Bristol answered. "We don't need to see the DNA we are editing through the microscope. It's much too small. We also don't need to position the DNA sequence either. The cell uses a random diffusion process called Brownian motion. The cell itself guides the new *donor* DNA along until it finds a place in the DNA strand where it fits, and then it is permanently stitched into the DNA strand via the cell's natural DNA repair mechanisms. Pretty amazing when you think about it."

"I'm afraid I must take your word for it, Doctor."

"The viruses we start with are Yellow Fever and Dengue Hemorrhagic Fever, both are from the virus family *Flavivirus*. We stitch them together using the CRISPR process and then we edit a specific section to make it particularly virulent."

"How virulent, Doctor?"

"Extremely," Dr. Bristol answered. "We have further modified the virus using genetic DNA material from the HIV virus because it is an envelope type virus. The new virus attaches itself by fusing its viral envelope to receptor proteins on a host cell's membrane. The virus punctures the cell membrane and then empties its virus material into the host cell. Once inside the cell, viral replication begins within seconds. The infection rate is staggering."

Klaus turned away from the microscope and looked at Dr. Bristol, "Continue, Doctor."

"Our tests on lab animals have produced a mortality rate over ninety-seven percent. Because the virus has been altered, any organism that it infects cannot recognize it and sees it is as an unknown virus which leaves the organism completely defenseless. There is simply no cure."

"How will you spread this unknown virus?"

"For the initial dissemination, we have genetically modified a particularly nasty mosquito named *Aedes aegypti*. We have made it even more aggressive than it normally is. Our tests indicate that it will seek a victim within mere seconds after being released."

"How then do you control these mosquitoes once they are released?"

"As I said earlier, they live for only a short time. The mosquitoes will be genetically modified to include a safeguard, using a self-limiting gene that reduces its lifespan to no more than a day or two. That will allow us to have complete control over the area of initial infection."

Klaus shivered involuntarily, knowing what would happen when the genetically altered mosquitoes were released in large quantities. "Is the final run complete?" he asked.

"The final steps are being completed as we speak. You can watch from over here," Dr. Bristol answered as he ushered Klaus over to the large viewing window of the containment room. "As you can see, Doctor Weaver is just now completing the primary containment of the final run."

The two men watched as Dr. Weaver moved about the biolab's class four containment room in his positive pressure personnel suit. Dr. Weaver moved about the room effortlessly, carefully avoiding the coiled air supply line that followed him. Many hours of work in the containment room had acquainted him with where the supply line would reach and where it would not.

The suit had been double-sealed and pressurized to protect him from the most dangerous and lethal pathogens known to man. In Dr. Weaver's case, the suit was critically important as the mutated virus he was working with had been altered to be exceptionally potent. Exposure to an amount as small as a nanogram, one billionth of a gram, would be fatal. The original virus had been altered enough so that to an infected host, it would present as an entirely new and unknown organism, leaving the host totally defenseless. Death would follow exposure in twenty-four to thirty-six hours, sometimes less, depending on the host's immune system. Nothing medical personnel tried would lengthen that length of time or minimize the patient's suffering.

Dr. Bristol tapped Klaus on the shoulder and pointed toward a polished metal container. "Next, Doctor Weaver will move the primary storage biocontainers to an adjacent holding chamber. The chamber will be pumped down to a vacuum and then flooded with ethylene oxide, a powerful sterilizing gas. Only then can the biocontainers be placed in the secondary containment canister. Doctor Weaver must be exceptionally careful as there is no vaccine and, as I said earlier, if exposed, there is no treatment. For practical purposes, it can be considered absolutely one hundred percent lethal."

"But the final biocontainer looks rather small," Klaus observed.

"Do not be fooled, Sovereign Prince. There is enough pathogen in that biocontainer to kill every living sole a hundred times over," Dr. Bristol remarked.

Klaus watched intently as they completed the sterilization and final containment. The secondary containment canister was sealed, the holding chamber was flooded with ethylene oxide gas, and then the secondary containment canister was pushed through a double airlock into the receiving area.

"While I await the confirmation to release the material, perhaps you should begin working on a backup batch," Klaus instructed.

"That would be unnecessary," Dr. Bristol replied.

"Doctor, I did not ask you if you thought it necessary. I expect you to do as I say," Klaus snapped, taking a step closer to Dr. Bristol.

"As you wish, Sovereign Prince," Dr. Bristol replied. "We will begin immediately."

"Dr. Bristol, have the canister moved to the agreed location for pickup."

"It will be done immediately, Sovereign Prince," Dr. Bristol responded, bowing at the waist.

Chapter Six

Old Miller Road
Bluffton, South Carolina

Early on a Sunday evening, Victoria Jean Pickett, Anna Mae Watts' cousin on her mother's side, flitted around the tiny kitchen of the modest house she and her husband, Joshua, shared. Sporting a headful of fiery red hair and a face liberally dotted with freckles, she busied herself preparing supper for her husband and their two-year-old daughter, Mazie.

Born just two days shy of her paternal grandmother Margaret Pickett's birthday, Mazie was the absolute joy of Victoria's and Joshua's life. The instant the nurse placed the newborn in Joshua's arms, he looked over at Victoria and mouthed the name Margaret. Even though she was exhausted from the delivery, she smiled and nodded her head in agreement. Joshua was instantly smitten with their new bundle of joy. He gently rocked the baby and cooed, "My little Mazie." And so, little Margaret's nickname became Mazie from that day forward.

Mazie inherited her mother's red hair and, it seemed, her freckles as well. When she turned two, the freckles darkened somewhat and became more prominent. She was a happy little child, giggling at the slightest provocation. Her infectious smile, framed on either side by huge dimples, completely disarmed her father. Had it not been for Victoria's protestations, the house would have been full up to the ceiling with toys.

Victoria would often lose track of little Mazie and would have to go hunting for her. Most often she would find her in her room quietly playing with a favorite toy. Occasionally, Mazie would jump out from behind the bed and shout, "Peeboo." Victoria would run after her, wiggling her fingers, pretending to be the tickle monster. Mazie would turn and run away, shrieking with delight.

While stirring a pot of macaroni, Mazie's favorite food, Victoria glanced over to check on Mazie, finding her happily playing on the floor of the kitchen with her pink, plastic horse. Victoria placed her hand against her forehead. She felt unusually warm. Her throat had felt raw and sore when she crawled out of bed that morning. As the day passed, her condition steadily worsened. By the time evening rolled around, she had a ferocious headache. She reached out and put her hand on the stove to steady herself, fighting off a wave of nausea. *"Probably picked up a bug of some kind,"* she thought as her attention returned to preparing supper.

She sniffled and wiped her nose with the back of her hand. Alarm set in when she glanced at her hand and saw a large bloody smear covering the entire back of her hand. What started out as a slight trickle of blood quickly grew and became a steady drip. She ran for the sink, leaving a trail of bright red droplets on the floor, and grabbed the dish rag draped over the edge of the countertop. She pulled a chair away from the dining table, sat down, and pushed the rag against her nose.

Victoria had suffered occasional nosebleeds in the past as do many people, but this was different. She became concerned when she felt blood running down the back of throat. "Joshua, come here please," she mumbled with the rag held tight against her face. She waited, but there was no response from the living room where her husband was watching television. Full-blown panic set in. Pulling the rag away from her face, she screamed, "Joshua, come quickly. I need help!" In the short time the rag was away from her face, blood had streamed down her chin, creating a large red stain on her dress.

"What do you need, Hon?" Joshua called out as he rounded the corner of the wall separating the living room from the kitchen. Shocked by the sight of Victoria's blood-stained dress, he rushed over to where she was sitting. "What happened?" he asked as he knelt down beside her.

"I don't know. It just started bleeding. I didn't do anything."

"Here, let me have a look," Joshua urged, tugging at the blood-soaked rag.

"I'm scared," Victoria sputtered as she allowed Joshua to pull the rag away. Immediately, blood ran from her nose, staining her dress even more.

Joshua pushed the rag back against her nose. "Hold this tight while I get another rag." He ran to the cabinet beside the sink, yanked out the drawer, grabbed a handful of dish rags, and raced back to where Victoria was sitting. "Use this clean rag while I get some ice." He dropped the blood-soaked rag in the sink and ran to the freezer to get some ice. Armed with a dish rag wrapped around several ice cubes, he ran back to Victoria and gently pressed the ice-filled rag against the side of her nose.

"Let's see if the ice is helping," he said five minutes later. Cautiously Victoria pulled the rag away. The same as last time, blood ran freely from Victoria's nose. She jammed the rag back against her nose.

"It won't stop! Joshua, what are we going to do?" Victoria cried out, fear evident in her eyes.

"I'll grab some towels. Then we'll get you in on the couch so you can lean your head back. Maybe that will help."

Joshua ran off to the hall linen closet and grabbed an armload of towels. In the living room, he draped several towels over the couch then returned to the kitchen. "You hold the rag tight," Joshua ordered. "Give me your other hand and I'll help you up. Don't strain. Just hang on to my hand and let me pull you up."

Joshua spread his feet and pulled Victoria to an upright position. Once she was on her feet, he guided her into the living room and eased her down onto the couch. "Lean your head back against the couch and let me hold the ice against your nose. We'll wait fifteen minutes and see if it's getting any better."

After only ten minutes, Victoria pushed Joshua's hand away and mumbled, "I can't stand the cold any longer. I don't think it's getting any better."

"Let's see," Joshua said as he eased Victoria's hand away from her nose slightly.

Worse than before, blood streamed down Victoria's chin, dripping onto her dress. Joshua became as panicked as Victoria. He pushed the rag back against Victoria's nose. "You sit here and hold that tight and I'll get Mazie buckled in the car seat," Joshua shouted as he turned and headed for the kitchen. "Then I'll come back and get you. I'm taking you to Emergency Care."

Three minutes later, Joshua raced back into the living room. He pulled a kitchen towel off the oven handle, folded it twice, and handed it to Victoria. He took the second blood-soaked rag and threw it in the sink. "Let's go," he barked, grabbing her free hand and pulling Victoria to her feet.

"But Joshua, my dress. I can't...."

"Don't' worry about the dress. We can't take the time for you to change. We've got to go."

Victoria stood on shaky legs. "Honey, the stove."

Joshua rushed into the kitchen and turned off all the burners and ran back into the living room. He pushed Victoria toward the front door and out onto the porch. Without bothering to turn off any lights or even lock the front door, he got Victoria into the front seat of their car. He started the engine, slammed the car into gear, and roared down the driveway, kicking up a plume of dust and gravel.

Fortunately, there was little traffic on the roads. Had there been, Joshua would have missed the medical facility's driveway in his state of panic. When he pulled into the parking lot of St. Joseph's Immediate Care six and one-half miles later, he had no idea how fast he had been driving. His only thought had been to get his precious wife to a medical facility.

As Joshua helped Victoria into the immediate care facility, the on-duty staff sprang into action when they saw the blood-stained dress. "Nosebleed. Won't stop," Joshua shouted, out of breath. "Two-year-old in the car. Be right back." Once Joshua was satisfied the on-duty medical personnel were attending to Victoria, he ran back out to the car, grabbed Mazie, and ran back into the care facility.

"Where? What room?" Joshua asked the receptionist at the check-in desk.

"You can't go in right now. The doctor is examining her," the young lady behind the desk answered. "Besides, it wouldn't be a suitable place for the child to be. I need some information."

Joshua spent the next ten minutes answering questions and providing insurance and ID cards. With the paperwork completed, he paced back and forth across the patient waiting area while keeping his eyes fixed on the doorway leading to the exam rooms. He spied a box of toys on the far side of the room. His arms were getting tired from holding Mazie, so he took a seat beside the toys. He let Mazie down. She stood beside the box, looking at the various toys. She settled on a bag of blocks, sat down on the floor, dumped them out, and stacked them together.

Joshua kept a watchful eye on Mazie, glancing at the doorway to the exam rooms every few seconds. Joshua waited what seemed like hours but in actuality was only slightly over twenty minutes. A youngish, early thirties looking doctor wearing blue scrubs emerged from the exam room door and walked over to where Joshua was sitting.

"I'm Doctor Bryan Depue," he announced. "Are you Victoria's husband?"

"Yes, I'm Joshua Pickett," Joshua answered, extending his hand. "Is she okay?"

"She's pretty weak from the loss of blood, but she is doing okay. We don't think a blood transfusion is necessary at this time. Has Victoria suffered nosebleeds in the past?"

"No. Well, maybe an occasional one, but nothing serious. Certainly nothing like this."

"That was a rather nasty bleed she had. It was a good thing you brought her in when you did. I cauterized a blood vessel in her nose. The bleeding appears to have stopped, at least for now. I will let you take her home, but she must go straight to bed when you get home. She may sit up in a chair occasionally, but only for short periods. No more than ten minutes at a time. Understood?"

"Yes, Doctor. No more than ten minutes."

"Okay, I'll sign the release paperwork. You go get your car and drive up to the side door over there," Doctor Depue said, pointing to a door on the south side of the waiting area.

Joshua helped Mazie gather the blocks and put them back in the bag. He picked her up, exited the building, and walked over to his car. Once Mazie was buckled into her car seat, he drove over to the side door Dr. Dupue had indicated. Just inside the door, a nurse was waiting with Victoria seated in a wheelchair. Joshua scrambled out of the car and held the door open while the nurse pushed Victoria over next to the car.

Joshua helped Victoria stand up. On shaky legs, Victoria eased herself into the passenger seat and buckled her seatbelt.

"Mommy, Mommy" Mazie cried out.

"It's okay, Sweetie," Victoria stammered, weak from her ordeal. She reached over the seat and took the little girl's hand. "We'll be home soon and you can have some macaroni. Then it's off to bed for you."

Joshua climbed into the car, eased the car into gear, and drove out of the emergency care center's parking lot. Joshua drove slowly, avoiding potholes as best as he could, fearing too much jostling might restart Victoria's nose bleed. The trip home was uneventful. Joshua got Victoria settled into bed then dished up a plate full of macaroni for Mazie. While Mazie worked on her supper, Joshua tiptoed into the bedroom to check on Victoria, finding her already asleep. He sighed heavily, finally able to relax.

Back in the kitchen, Mazie had devoured the plate of macaroni and was begging for more. He grabbed the plate, scooped on two more spoonfuls of macaroni, and set it before Mazie. As he watched the little girl finish her supper, exhaustion set in. He had been more frightened than he could remember. Once Mazie gobbled up the last morsel of macaroni, he picked up the plate, put it in the sink, and wiped her face. "It's off to bed, young lady," he said, tossing the rag toward the sink.

Joshua carried Mazie to her bedroom and laid her in her crib. He picked up her favorite stuffed toy from the floor and tucked both of them under the covers. Leaning over the crib, he stroked the little girl's hair until she fell asleep. Tears filled his eyes as he stood there staring down at his precious little Mazie. He whispered a brief prayer, thankful that the two most important people in his life were okay. Satisfied the little girl was asleep, he turned and headed for his bedroom.

Careful to make as little noise as possible, he slipped into the bedroom and walked over to Victoria's side of the bed. He stood there a long time listening to her soft breathing. Leaning over, he checked the pillow. Relieved to find not even a trace of blood, he walked around to his side of the bed, turned off the table lamp, and slipped under the covers as carefully as he could.

Lying there in the darkness waiting for sleep to come, suddenly he jerked and slapped at his arm. As tired and exhausted as he was, he awakened every hour. He would lift his head off the pillow, listen for Victoria's breathing, then settle his head back on the pillow. Each time as he drifted off to sleep, he reached down and scratched the itchy spot on his arm.

Early the next morning, Joshua stopped by his boss's desk on the way to his cubicle and explained the reason for his being a little late that morning. His boss was understanding and advised Joshua to check on his wife throughout the day and go home if needed. His only request was for Joshua to let him know if he had to leave. Joshua thanked him profusely, then hurried off to his cubicle to get some work done.

He had been reluctant to head off to work, but Victoria convinced him she would be fine. The nosebleed had not returned, but Joshua was concerned that Victoria had a temperature of slightly over one hundred one. He walked into his cubicle, turned on his computer, and headed for the break room to put his lunch in the refrigerator. He poured himself a cup of coffee and returned to his cube.

Thirty minutes later, sleeves rolled up to the elbows, Joshua was hunched over the keyboard staring at the computer monitor. Becoming more and more annoyed, he was mystified that he could not get the subtotals on the spreadsheet he was working on to add up to the grand total. He had been over the formulas twice and had found nothing wrong. Scratching at the raised, red bump on his left arm, he leaned in even closer to the screen, ready to go through the formulas for a third time. Deep in concentration, he jumped when the phone rang.

"Joshua Pickett, may I help you?" he announced into the phone.

"Joshua, I'm scared! I have a horrible headache and the bleeding is worse than last night," Victoria stammered, her voice filled with terror.

"When did it start?" Joshua asked.

"Ten or fifteen minutes ago. I leaned my head back and I tried ice, but nothing is helping. Joshua, what should I do?"

"Stay as calm as you can," Joshua advised. "Go sit on the couch and lean your head back. I'm going to call an ambulance."

"Joshua, hurry! I'm scared."

"I'll be there as quick as I can," Joshua barked into the phone. He depressed the hook switch to disconnect the call and then dialed 9-1-1. As quickly as he could, he explained the situation to the emergency operator. He gave the operator their home address and said he would leave immediately and, hopefully, meet the ambulance at the house.

Joshua hung up the phone and took off at a dead run for the exit. He stopped by his boss' office and poked his head in the doorway, "My wife's nosebleed is back and it's worse. I called an ambulance. I've gotta go." His boss hollered out his hope that his wife would be okay, but Joshua never heard it.

He had already burst through the exit door and was running across the parking lot toward his car. Roaring out of the parking lot, he drove as fast as he dared down Red Cedar Street, turning onto State Highway Forty-Six. State Highway Forty-Six, also called May River Road, a major route through Bluffton, allowed him to increase his speed. Nearing the intersection with Old Miller Road, he caught a glimpse of the ambulance just as it turned north onto Old Miller Road.

Two minutes later, Joshua turned down the lane that led to their house. He flew down the lane and slid to a stop beside the ambulance as the EMT's were dragging the stretcher out of the back. Following on their heels, he explained to one of the EMT's the quick run to the emergency care center the previous evening. Leaping onto the porch ahead of the EMT's, he pushed the front door open and held the screen door out of the way.

Surprised by the sight of Victoria leaning back on the couch covered in blood, the EMT's stepped up their response. The senior EMT began his assessment of Victoria's condition while the other EMT got the stretcher ready.

The senior EMT yelled at his partner, "I need packing, quick." The junior EMT dug around in the drug box and pulled out a package of nasal packing, a balloon covered by a bio-compatible self-lubricating fabric. He tore open the package and handed the packing device to the senior EMT. He held it out while the junior EMT dribbled a small amount of normal saline on the tip, then inserted the deflated packing device into Victoria's nostril. Using a standard syringe, he pushed in enough air to inflate the device. The device exerted sufficient pressure to close off the blood vessels within Victoria's nose. With the bleeding temporarily under control, the senior EMT began taking a set of vital signs.

Victoria's pupils were sluggish and slow to respond to light as the EMT swung a small, pocket flashlight back and forth across her eyes. A slow or delayed pupillary response can be caused by a number of underlying conditions, all of them serious. When the EMT saw the digital thermometer register one hundred three point four, he stopped and looked over at the other EMT, "This is more than a nosebleed. We need to get her loaded up and get out of here quickly. I can wait to take the rest of the vitals once we're on the road," the senior EMT shouted.

Together they lifted Victoria off the couch, laid her on the stretcher, covered her with a blanket, and tightened up the strap to hold her securely on the stretcher. "Mister Pickett, can you grab the drug box while we get your wife loaded into the ambulance?" the senior EMT asked.

"Sure thing," Joshua responded as he closed the drug box and picked it up. "Where are you taking her?" he asked, pushing the screen door open with his free hand.

"Beaufort Memorial Hospital," the junior EMT responded.

"No," Matt Blumenthal, the senior EMT corrected. "Memorial University Medical Center in Savannah would be a better choice. They'll just end up transferring her at Beaufort. Besides, I think Memorial might even be a few miles closer."

The EMT's hurried out the door and across the yard. With Victoria securely loaded in the ambulance, the senior EMT instructed the junior EMT to drive so he could attend to their patient during the thirty-plus mile trip. About to close the rear door of the ambulance, the senior EMT motioned Joshua over. Joshua handed him the drug box.

"Mister Pickett, you can follow us, but if we get separated, the ER department is on the south side of Memorial. Turn off East Sixty-sixth Street onto Ranger Street. You'll see the ER sign straight ahead."

The senior EMT slammed the rear door shut and the ambulance sped down the lane and turned left onto May River Road. Zach ran back into the house and snatched up Mazie. Heading out the door, he reached over and flipped off the lights. He twisted the door lock, slammed it closed, and raced over to the car. By the time he got Mazie buckled into her car seat, started the car, and turned out onto May River Road, he had lost sight of the ambulance.

The fifty-minute drive to Memorial University Medical Center in Savannah, Georgia, was the most agonizing fifty minutes of Joshua's life. When he wasn't talking to Mazie, he was praying for his wife. Never more scared in his entire life, he battled against the urge to mash the accelerator pedal to the floor and drive as fast as their old car would go.

West Elgin Street, Tulsa, Oklahoma

After entering the house, Zach made a beeline straight for the kitchen, starving for the first time in weeks. He pulled the refrigerator door open and took stock of his choices. There was not much to choose from, but he did not want to go out and hunt for a restaurant. Settling on a breakfast, he pulled a package of bacon out of the meat drawer and sniffed it. "Phew," he exclaimed. "I'm certainly not eating that!"

He stuffed the package of bacon in the trash and dug a package of hashbrown potatoes out of the freezer. After starting a pot of coffee, he turned his attention back to preparing breakfast. The frozen hashbrowns had been in freezer for weeks and had accumulated a lot of frost. If he tossed the potatoes also, he would be left with nothing but eggs and toast, so he decided to use them anyway.

He dumped the hashbrowns in the skillet. He sorted through the day's mail while waiting for the hashbrowns to need turning. Finished with the mail, he turned the hashbrowns and shoved two pieces of bread into the toaster. He cracked three eggs in the skillet beside the hashbrowns. The toast popped up. He quickly buttered it then slid the eggs out onto a plate along with the hashbrowns.

He set the plate loaded with eggs and potatoes on the kitchen table and poured a cup of coffee. After quickly devouring the breakfast, he put the empty plate on the counter and poured another cup of coffee. Sitting at the table, enjoying the second cup of coffee, he mentally went over a list of things that needed to be done before he could sell the house. "*What should I do first?*" he wondered. He recalled hearing a realtor say the most important thing in selling a house was to depersonalize it. With that objective set firmly in his mind, he headed to the garage to bring in some empty boxes. Back in the living room, he propped his armload of boxes against the wall. He selected a medium-sized box, grabbed the tape dispenser, folded over the bottom flaps, and ran three strips of tape across the bottom of the box.

Armed with the empty box, he decided the living room would be a good place to start. Stopping in front of the mantle, he picked up a photo of Angie. He sat on the floor and stared at the photo for ten long minutes, remembering the good times they had shared. There was sadness in his heart, but not the deep depression that had overwhelmed him before. Not just mentally but emotionally, he had finally accepted what had happened and do the best he could to salvage the rest of his life.

Arising with renewed resolve, he went around the house packing photos, mementoes, and personal objects into boxes. Two hours later, with the depersonalizing task complete, he returned to the living room and gathered up the scattered newspapers and stuffed them into the recycle bin.

He dusted all the furniture, then dragged out the vacuum and vacuumed every room in the house. "*Enough work for one day,*" he thought, deciding the bathrooms could wait.

Rummaging through the top drawer of his desk, he located the card President Cantwell had given him at the awards ceremony. He grabbed his cellphone, poured another cup of coffee, and sat down at the kitchen table. Before he officially listed his house for sale, he would call the President and see if he could help him in finding a job. He lifted his cellphone out of its holster and was about to punch in the number when he glanced at his watch. Being an hour later in Washington, D.C., it was too late to call the President.

Too keyed up to just sit around the house, Zach took a shower, changed clothes, and drove over to his parent's house. Explaining his decision to sell the house and move would not be easy, but it had to be done. His intention was to treat them to dinner and explain why he felt a complete change was so crucial.

During the twenty-minute drive to his parent's house, he rehearsed what he was going to say over and over. Fearing his mother's reaction, his pulse rate was already increasing as he pulled into the driveway of their house.

"Wow! What is that delightful aroma?" Zach called out as he pushed the front door open. He sniffed the air again as he headed for the kitchen. "Wait, I know that smell."

"Yep, meatloaf and cheesy potatoes," his dad announced, rising from the chair he was sitting on. He met Zach halfway into the kitchen, gave him a bear hug, and clapped him on the back. "I was about to call you and invite you over. Thought you could use some cheering up."

"My thought was to take you and Mom out to dinner," Zach countered. "But no way I'm missing out on Mom's meatloaf."

"Zach, let's just enjoy each other's company. Don't talk about the move until after dinner. I mentioned it when I got home and I could tell it hit your mother hard."

"Absolutely," Zach agreed. "I concur."

Zach and his parents chit chatted about trivial stuff until dinner was ready. Zach helped his dad get the plates and silverware on the table while his mother dished up the meal and brought it to the table. Zach's dad asked the blessing for the food and they dug in.

Two platefuls of delicious meatloaf later, Zach pushed himself away from the table stuffed to the gills. "That was absolutely great, Mom," Zach exclaimed.

"How about let's have coffee in the living room where it's more comfortable," James Templeton suggested. "Zach, you take the cups into the living room and I'll grab the pot of coffee."

"Good idea," Zach answered as he placed three cups and saucers on a small serving tray and headed for the living room.

Zach set a cup and saucer on a side table at each end of the couch and one on the table beside his dad's easy chair. James filled the coffee cups and sat in his chair. Silence gripped the living room as the three quietly sipped their coffee, no one wanting to broach the uncomfortable subject.

Zach decided it was his decision to move that was causing the tension. He took a deep breath and began, "Mom, I know Dad told you about the decision I shared with him while he was driving me home. I feel like I don't have any choice. I just have to…."

"Son, you don't need to explain," Martha Templeton interrupted. "You may find this hard to believe, but I agree with you. I know how hard these last few months have been for you. I feel it too. Everywhere I go, I see Angie. I cannot begin to imagine how hard it is for you to walk into that empty house every night."

"I can't tell you how much it helps to know you understand," Zach said feeling as if he grew an inch as the weight of disappointing his mother was lifted. "Part of me doesn't want to go, but I know I have to."

"We will certainly miss you, but we want what's best for you," his dad added.

For nearly an hour, the three of them discussed what Zach might do and where he thought he might end up. Only able to give them generalities, Zach promised he would call and keep them up to date.

On the drive home, the relief that came from deciding to move and the fact that his parents understood and supported him, gave Zach a peace he had not felt in a long, long time. Suddenly, he felt very tired. Not a tiredness that came from being beat down and overwhelmed, but a tiredness that came from having a full belly and the knowledge that the people that love you stood behind you and supported you.

Zach turned into his driveway, pulled into the garage, and switched off the ignition. He entered the house, went straight to the bedroom, and climbed into bed. Sound asleep in less than two minutes, he began snoring softly.

How long would Zach's new found feeling of peace last? Was there another catastrophe waiting just around the next corner? Sleep soundly Zachariah Templeton while you can.

Chapter Seven

Memorial University Medical Center
Savannah, Georgia

Driving as fast as traffic would allow, Joshua Pickett merged onto Harry S Truman Parkway from US Highway 17 and headed south toward Memorial University Medical Center. A short four miles later, he exited the parkway onto the Hospital Access Road exit. Following the EMT's instructions, he continued on the access road until it turned into Metts Drive and turned east, traversing the south side of the medical center. At the intersection with Ranger Street, Joshua spotted the sign pointing toward the hospital's emergency room entrance.

He parked in the first empty spot he could find, collected Mazie from the back seat, and ran toward the emergency entrance. Inside the hospital, he scanned the various signs, looking for an information desk. Not finding what he wanted, he stopped the first hospital employee he saw and asked, "Excuse me. An ambulance just brought my wife in. Where can I find her?"

"See that desk over there," the employee said, pointing to a desk on the west side of the entrance. "The ER admin nurse will be able to direct you."

"Thanks. I appreciate your help," Joshua panted as he turned and dashed off toward the desk.

Standing in front of the desk, puffing and out of breath, he shifted his weight back and forth from one foot to the other. The nurse either did not see Joshua or ignored him.

"Sorry, I need to know where my wife is," Joshua blurted out. "An ambulance just bought her in."

"Name?" the nurse asked, looking up from the notebook she had been writing in.

"Victoria Pickett. She has a severe nosebleed."

The nurse tapped a few keys on a computer keyboard. After scanning the information on the screen, she shook her head and said, "I don't see that name listed. The ER department may not have had time to enter her information yet."

"She's here somewhere," Joshua complained "I need to know where she is."

One of the EMT's that had brought Victoria in walked up to the information desk and tapped Joshua on the shoulder. "Mister Pickett, I was about to leave the ER and I saw you standing here. Come on. Follow me. Nurse, I can take him back."

"Fine. Thanks," the nurse answered, nodding her head as she went back to the notebook she had been working on.

With Joshua in tow, the EMT pushed open the double doors leading into the emergency department. "Your wife is over here in exam room three," the EMT advised, pointing ahead and to his left. The EMT pushed the exam room door open and Joshua panicked when he saw that the room was empty.

Alissa Reed, the ER Charge Nurse, carrying an armload of supplies, noticed the panicked look on Joshua's face. She dumped the supplies on a metal cart sitting next to the wall and approached Joshua. "Are you family of Victoria Picket?" she asked.

"Yes. I'm Joshua, her husband," Joshua answered. "The EMT said she was in room three, but nobody's there. What's going on? Where is she?"

An ER nurse for over twelve years, Nurse Reed had experienced all manner of angry, frustrated, confused, and desperately frightened family members. Her calm demeanor and natural ability to deal with distraught patients and family members made her a highly valued employee at the hospital. Knowing the first step in calming someone was to redirect their attention, she held out her hand to the little girl in Joshua's arms.

"Who is this pretty young lady?" she inquired.

"This is Mazie, our daughter," Joshua answered. "Actually, her name is Margaret, but we call her Mazie."

"Mazie. I just love that name," Nurse Reed smiled as she shook the hand Mazie had offered. "She is the prettiest little lady I have seen in a long time." Nurse Reed could see that Mr. Pickett was relaxing slightly, his face less drawn and pale. She touched his arm and pushed him out of the way of another patient being wheeled in from the ambulance bay.

"Mister Pickett, your wife arrived about fifteen minutes ago. Doctor James Volker, the ER Attending Physician, was concerned that your wife's nosebleed was not just a simple nosebleed. He sent her off for an emergency CT scan to see what might be causing it. CTs don't take too long so we should know something soon."

Nurse Reed and Matt Blumenthal, the EMT that had escorted Joshua, were long-time friends, their paths often crossing in the ER department. She looked at him and asked, "Matt, can you show Mister Picket and Mazie where they can wait?"

"Be glad to, Alissa," he replied. "Mister Picket, follow me. The emergency department's waiting area is back through the double doors and to your left."

"Oh, Mister Pickett, I'll come find you and let you know what the results of your wife's test are," Nurse Reed called out as Joshua and the EMT passed through the double doors.

"I've got to go. I sure hope your wife is okay," the EMT said as he turned and rushed off toward the ambulance bay.

Joshua started to say something, but the EMT was already halfway across the waiting area. His arms were getting tired from holding Mazie and she was getting squirmy. Spying a small children's table in the corner of the waiting area, he sat Mazie in one of the chairs and selected a picture book from a rack beside the table. With Mazie occupied, Joshua paced back and forth, fear gripping his mind.

For twenty minutes, Joshua paced back and forth while keeping an eye on Mazie and glancing at the ER department doors every few seconds. Growing increasingly concerned, he picked up Mazie and was about to head to the information desk to find out what was taking so long. He stopped when he saw the double doors swing open and a man dressed in scrubs covered by a long white coat emerge. The man walked over to the waiting area.

"Are you Joshua Pickett?" the man asked with a thick accent.

"Yes, I'm Joshua Pickett."

"I am Doctor Radha Choudhary," the man said, holding out his hand. "Follow me, please."

Joshua shook the doctor's hand and followed him to a small patient conference room located next to the information desk. Inside the room, Dr. Choudhary pointed to a chair and asked Joshua to sit.

"Would you mind if one of the nurses entertained your little girl for a few minutes so we can talk?"

"Ahh, ahh… okay," Joshua stammered, becoming more apprehensive with each passing second. Dr. Choudhary stepped out of the room and returned a few seconds later with a nurse. After introductions and a little coaxing, the nurse took Mazie and returned to the children's area in the waiting room. Dr. Choudhary pushed the conference room door shut and sat down opposite Joshua.

"I am the head of the Hematology Department here at Memorial University Hospital. The ER attending physician was quite concerned with your wife's condition during his initial exam. He ordered an emergency CT scan and called me for a consult. Before I explain the results of the CT scan, we packed your wife's nose. The critical concern was to get the bleeding under control."

"How is she doing, Doctor?"

"Her condition is guarded for the moment," Dr. Choudhary answered. "Her blood loss was significant. The ER attending is starting a unit of blood right now. As soon as that is in place, she will be moved to the critical care unit where she can be monitored more closely."

Joshua sank in his chair as the color drained from his face. He started to say something, but the words stuck in his throat.

"I know this is frightening, Mister Pickett," Dr. Choudhary consoled. "We have one of the best hematology departments in the country. Your wife is getting the best care possible."

Joshua pushed himself up in the chair. "You said you were going to explain the CT scan results."

"Yes. The CT scan revealed Victoria has a bleed in her brain in addition to the nosebleed. I consulted with a colleague and our initial assessment is that it may be a hereditary hemorrhagic telangiectasia or HHT for short. When she is stable enough, we will perform a more definitive test to confirm." Dr. Choudhary noticed the bewildered look on Joshua's face. "Let me explain. An HHT is an extremely rare genetic disorder characterized by a small group of blood vessels that failed to develop properly. Those blood vessels then form into an abnormal tangle known as an arteriovenous malformation, or AVM. What puzzles us is that ruptured AVMs are even more rare in people with HHT, and it also would not explain Victoria's nosebleed or her high temperature."

"What can be done to treat that?" Joshua asked.

"The first thing we….," Dr. Choudhary stopped speaking when the door suddenly opened.

A nurse from the ER department rushed into the room and blurted, "Doctor, we need you. NOW!"

Dr. Choudhary leaped up from his chair and ran out of the room, leaving Joshua sitting there dumbfounded and more than a little alarmed. Having no idea when the doctor would be back, he exited the conference room and walked over to the children's area. Mazie saw him coming and ran over to meet him, jabbering excitedly about a toy she and the nurse had been playing with.

"Thank you for watching Mazie," Joshua said to the nurse.

"How is your wife doing?" the nurse asked.

"I'm not certain. A nurse rushed into the room and told the doctor they needed him. He got up and ran out of the room without a word."

"You stay here with Mazie. I'll go see if I can find out what happened."

Joshua sat down on one of the small children's chairs and watched Mazie as she continued to play with the toy. A few minutes later he saw the double doors open and the nurse walked out looking tense and on edge, heading his way. Joshua stood up and waited for the nurse to arrive.

"I found out they had already transferred your wife to the CCU. Shortly after arriving in CCU, she went into crisis."

"What kind of crisis?" Joshua blurted.

"I'm sorry, Mister Pickett. I don't know," the nurse answered. "CCU is on the third floor. When you get off the elevator, turn right. You'll see the CCU waiting area on the right."

"Thanks for taking care of Mazie."

"You're welcome. It was fun," the nurse replied to Joshua's disappearing back as he ran off in search of the elevator.

Upon arriving in the CCU waiting area, Joshua selected a large comfortable chair toward the back of the waiting area near a window. With Mazie snuggled in his arms asleep, Joshua dozed off, letting his head fall back against the chair. Barely asleep, Joshua awoke with a start when another person came into the waiting area and slumped down in the chair next to him, pushing it several inches until it bumped up against the wall. Like a thousand fingernails on a blackboard, the chair's feet screeched unbearably as they scraped across the floor.

Mazie squirmed and whimpered. Joshua whispered in her ear and patted her on the back and she soon went back to sleep. Not really in the mood for conversation, Joshua did his best to ignore the middle-aged woman who had occupied the chair beside him. She seemed acutely distraught. He decided it was likely she needed someone to talk to. Joshua shifted Mazie to the right side, leaned to the left side of the chair, and introduced himself to the woman. "Hello. My name is Joshua Pickett. My wife is in CCU. I'm waiting here to find out how she's doing."

Joshua learned the woman's name was Elizabeth Harman and that her husband, Paul, had been involved in a serious auto accident. He had been air-lifted to the medical center with life-threatening injuries and she had not been told anything other than he was in a coma and was responding poorly to treatment.

"I'm sorry I'm blubbering so, Mister Pickett," she sobbed. "I have five children at home, two under the age of six. I don't know what I'm going to do if Paul doesn't make it."

"Do you have family that can help you out?" Joshua asked.

"No. Paul was an only child and his parents are dead. My family all live on the West Coast," she answered, dabbing at her eyes with a soggy scrap of tissue.

Joshua grabbed a box of tissues from a side table and held it out to her. She plucked one out of the box and held it to her cheek, overcome by another round of weeping. Joshua started to say something, but he saw a nurse headed their way. The nurse stopped in front of Mrs. Harman and shook her head.

"Come with me," the nurse urged. "The doctor would like to speak with you."

Joshua shuddered inside as he watched the nurse help the sobbing woman up, put her arm around the woman, and lead her toward the information desk. The woman's shoulders shook as she shuffled across the waiting area. Joshua's mind rebelled, filled with images of someone coming to give him the same dreadful news.

All the commotion had finally awakened Mazie. "Daddy, where Mommy?" the little girl questioned.

Not exactly certain what he should tell her, he decided the simplest explanation was the best. "Mommy doesn't feel well. The doctors are trying to make her better."

"Dow pease," Mazie insisted, squirming her way out of Joshua's arms. Once her feet hit the floor, she made a beeline for the other side of the room and another children's area filled with books and toys. Joshua stayed seated and watched as Mazie looked over the various books and toys, selecting, as she usually did, a box of blocks. Mazie had stacked and restacked the pile of blocks three times when Joshua caught sight of Dr. Choudhary as he pushed the sliding door open and stepped out of the critical care unit.

Dr. Choudhary was just past forty and quite short, standing only five feet six inches in his stocking feet. He stopped and glanced at Joshua. Standing there, he looked even shorter, exhaustion showing in his face. No longer wearing his white coat, his scrubs were soaked with sweat. Instantly alarmed, dread filled Joshua's mind when he saw the grim look on the doctor's face. Dr. Choudhary strode across the waiting area and took the seat recently vacated by Mrs. Harman.

"I wish I had better news, Mister Pickett," Dr. Choudhary sighed. "Remember when I described the arteriovenous malformation earlier?" Joshua nodded his head. Dr. Choudhary continued, "We are having much difficulty getting Victoria's bleeding under control. We no longer think the HHT is the underlying cause. Have you or your wife been out of the country in the past two to three months?"

"No. We've never been out of the country."

"Any family members been out of the country?"

"No. Nobody we know has been out of the country."

"Well then, does Victoria have any history of serious bleeding disorders?"

"No. Absolutely not. She may have had an occasional nosebleed, but nothing beyond that. She has always been very healthy. Hardly ever sick. Not even the flu."

Dr. Choudhary pulled a handkerchief out of his pocket and wiped his face. He leaned forward with his elbows on his knees and shook his head. Born in Chennai, India, capital of the far southeastern Indian state of Tamil Nadu, Radha Choudhary grew up poor. Radha never really knew his father who had abandoned the family when Rahda was barely four years old. His mother, Sarala, worked whatever menial jobs she could find to support the family. It was a difficult life for Radha and his two brothers, but they survived by scrounging for food while their mother worked.

Life for the Choudhary family improved when Sarala was fortunate to land a job as a housekeeper for a major hotel. She worked long hours and came home exhausted, but finally; the family had money enough to buy decent food. Life took a dreadful turn for the Choudhary family not long after Radha turned twelve. One day his mother came home from the hotel coughing and sneezing. Eight days later she was dead. Over the following two weeks, both his brothers developed the same symptoms and died. The local hospital, such as it was, told Radha it was likely his mother had contracted one of the hemorrhagic fever viruses from a guest at the hotel. The doctors had no idea why Radha had not been affected by the deadly disease.

Radha lived on the streets until the Greater Chennai Police apprehended him and handed over to a local orphanage. The director of the orphanage noticed something different in Radha. He was very intelligent and chattered non-stop about how he wanted to be a doctor someday and cure diseases like the one that had ravaged his family. The director spent his own money to purchase books for the young man. On a Tuesday afternoon nearly two years later, a middle-aged couple met with Radha upon the director's insistence. They also were greatly impressed by Radha. A few weeks later, with all the adoption papers in order, Radha left the orphanage and India, headed for Philadelphia in the United States.

The disease that was eating away at Victoria Pickett reminded Dr. Choudhary of the ravaging disease that had destroyed his family. In his mind it seemed like only yesterday, but it had actually been twenty-nine long years ago. Dr. Choudhary returned from his reverie, straightened up, and faced Joshua.

"I hate to alarm you, but we may be losing the battle. Victoria has already had four units of blood and is starting on a fifth. We just can't seem to get the bleeding under control. Whatever is causing this is beginning to affect multiple organs. It is damaging her blood vessels, affecting the body's ability to regulate itself. There is now involvement in her lungs and we believe in her liver as well. I ordered a full body scan to determine the extent of the involvement."

"Don't you have some idea what is wrong?"

"We thought it might be one of the viral hemorrhagic fevers. Her symptoms mimic the effects of Ebola, Marburg, or maybe even Yellow Fever, but the progression of the symptoms in your wife's case is much more rapid and you said neither of you have been out of the country."

"What are you going to do, Doctor?" Joshua pressed.

"We will continue to give her blood. Hopefully, the full body scan will tell us something. We will….," Dr. Choudhary stopped when he noticed a nurse come rushing out of the CCU area.

The nurse hollered from halfway across the waiting area, "Doctor Choudhary, come quick. Misses Pickett is in severe hematological crisis!"

Dr. Choudhary scrambled out of the chair and followed the nurse. Joshua watched in horror as they disappeared into the critical care unit.

West Elgin Street
Tulsa, Oklahoma

Zach had finished a quick lunch and had placed the dirty dishes in the dishwasher. After wiping down the countertop and stuffing an empty potato chip bag in the trash, he glanced at his watch. Earlier that morning, he had called the office of the realtor he and Angie had used to purchase the house and learned that Jeffery Kimbal was out and would not return for an hour. Rather than waste an hour, he called President Cantwell.

Zach walked into the spare bedroom he used as a home office and sat down in front of his desk. He picked up the President's card he had propped against the monitor stand the previous evening, tapped in the phone number, and pressed the call button.

After hearing six rings with no answer, he was about to hang up when he heard a voice. "White House. President Cantwell's assistant. Who's calling, please?"

"This is Zach Templeton. I was there six months ago for an awards ceremony. The President said to call if I ever needed help. Well, I could very much use his help."

"Mister Templeton, I remember you. He awarded you the Presidential Medal of Freedom. We don't give many of those out. The President just finished a meeting. Hang on while I check and see if he can talk with you."

Zach listened to soft music coming from the receiver. From memory, he could visualize the assistant slipping in the side door of the Oval Office and walking over to the President's desk. Zach waited, doodling on the ever-present scratch pad that lay on his desk.

"Zach Templeton, how are you?" President Cantwell asked.

"Mister President, I wasn't certain you would remember me?"

"Are you kidding? How could I forget?" the President exclaimed. "After what you did for our country and for me, there is no way I could ever forget you. Now, tell me how you're doing."

"I'm surviving," Zach responded, halfheartedly.

"That certainly doesn't sound very convincing."

"Well, you know, Sir. Good days and bad days, but mostly bad days to be honest."

"I'm sorry to hear that," the President remarked. "Given the loss you suffered, I can't say I'm surprised. Is there anything I can do to help?"

"Yes, Sir, there is," Zach declared. "I can't take it here in Tulsa. I see Angie everywhere I go. Two days ago I lost my job. So, I've decided to sell the house and move. I could really use some help finding a job."

"If I can help in any way, I will. You will get my highest recommendation. Do you have an idea where you would like to end up?"

"I was thinking something different. Somewhere warm, preferably. I was thinking Georgia, or maybe South Carolina."

"You know, I already have an idea. Let me make a call and I'll get back to you."

"That would be fantastic, Mister President. I can't tell you how much I appreciate this."

"I'm glad I can offer my assistance, Zach. It's an insignificant price to pay considering your sacrifice."

"Thank you, Sir."

"You bet," President Cantwell said as he ended the call.

Zach ended the call on his cellphone and sat there staring at it. He had just talked with the President of the United States and he had offered to help him and not only help him, but he would personally vouch for him. "*Maybe, just maybe, this whole mess was going to turn out okay,*" he thought.

Excited that the President already had an idea for a potential lead, Zach picked up his cellphone and called Jeffery Kimbal again. Fortunately, Mr. Kimbal was not out of the office on a showing this time. He picked up the phone almost immediately. Zach explained briefly to Mr. Kimbal his current situation, emphasizing his desire to turn the house quickly.

"We're in luck, Zach," Mr. Kimbal said, after tapping a few keys on the keyboard sitting in front of him. "I have the old file for your house up on the monitor. I can transfer most of the information to the new listing contract."

"That's great," Zach responded. "I want you to list the house for two thousand less than current market value."

"I can certainly do that. But if you do that, you are going to lose money," Mr. Kimbal cautioned.

"I understand that, but a quick turn is more important than losing a little money."

"Very well. I will get started on it right away. Can you stop by the office tomorrow afternoon and sign the contract?"

"Yes, I can do that. I'll see you tomorrow afternoon," Zach answered. He ended the call and laid the cellphone on the desk. "Things are looking up," he said with a smile as he pushed his chair back from the desk.

Armed with a new resolve, he headed for the garage to grab more packing boxes. "Great," he groused, kicking at the pile of boxes lying in the garage, finding nothing but small book boxes. He lifted his old stepladder off the wall hooks where it was hanging, unfolded it, and pushed it under the trapdoor in the ceiling that provided access to the attic. Standing on the first step, the old stepladder creaked and wobbled. Zach made certain the hinges were pushed all the way down and continued up the ladder. Stopping on the next-to-last step, he pushed the access panel up and out of the way.

Zach grabbed the string hanging down from the light fixture and gave it a yank. Surveying the contents of the attic, he realized he and Angie had accumulated little in the brief time they had owned the house. Fortunately, that meant there was little that would need to be sorted through. He located the pile of old packing boxes at the far end of the attic. Placing his hands on either side of the access opening, he pushed upward with his legs. The wobbly old ladder creaked and fell over, leaving Zach dangling half in and half out of the attic.

Zach leaned forward and grabbed onto one of the roof trusses with his right hand. He struggled and dragged the rest of his body up through the opening. On his knees, he looked down through the opening at the ladder lying on its side. "Well, that went about as expected," he grumbled.

Uncertain what sizes or how many boxes he would need, he grabbed the entire pile. Three or four at a time, he dropped the boxes through the access hole. With all the boxes scattered on the garage floor, he sat down on the edge of the opening, grabbed the edge, slipped through the opening, and dropped onto the scattered boxes.

He piled the boxes in stacks according to size on the side of the garage where Angie had always parked her car. Shortly after the funeral, Zach had sold her car because he could not stand to see it sitting there every time he entered the garage. He stood the ladder upright, making certain the legs were stable. Back up the ladder, he muscled down the box full of packing paper. Back up the ladder again, he slid the access panel back into place and hung the ladder back on the wall hooks.

He grabbed several boxes of each size and stacked them in the hallway near the spare bedrooms. Finished with the bedroom that had been used as storage, he was half finished packing up the spare bedroom when his cellphone rang. Zach looked at the display, surprised the see the President's number.

"Mister President, I didn't expect your call so soon."

"Rather than take a chance I would get sidetracked, I made a call as soon as I hung up. The gentleman I called was in a meeting, but he called me back as soon as it ended. The company is Silverline Communications in Savannah, Georgia. That's right on the border with South Carolina. Right where you said you wanted to be."

"That's incredible, Mister President," Zach exclaimed.

"The man you want to talk to is Grant Hollins, the owner of the company. He's waiting for your call."

"He's waiting for my call?" Zach choked, hardly able to believe the good news. Zach scribbled Mr. Hollins's phone number as the President read it off.

"Yes, now," the President affirmed. "I've got to run to a meeting, Zach. I'm thrilled that I could help."

"I can't believe....," Zach stopped and looked at his phone. The President had already hung up.

"Amazing. Absolutely amazing," Zach beamed, feeling like he needed to pinch himself to prove this wasn't all just a dream and he was about to wake up. Zach took a deep breath, dialed the number, and waited.

"Hello, Grant Hollins, Silverline Communications. May I help you?" a booming voice tinged with a deep southern accent answered.

"This is Zach Templeton. President Cantwell gave me your number. He said he had just spoken with you."

"Yes he did," Mr. Hollins answered. "You might want to know the President spoke very highly of you. He is a very close friend of mine. We had a brief conversation a week ago and I mentioned that my company landed a very nice contract and I was looking for someone with communications and data analysis experience. He seemed to think you were just the man I need. Said you were tenacious and never give up."

"I'm flattered to say the least. I hope I can live up to the nice things he said about me." Zach learned Mr. Hollins had also served in the Navy and had similar communications experience. Mr. Hollins's outgoing demeanor quickly put Zach at ease. The two men made an instant connection and they talked like they were old friends. They spent thirty minutes discussing Zach's experience and data analysis skillset.

Mr. Hollins, satisfied the President had been correct in his assessment of Zach, made Zach an offer without ever meeting him face-to-face. "The President told me I'd be a fool if I didn't hire you. I believe he was correct. Zach, the job is yours if you want it. One thing I hadn't mentioned yet is that the job is a telecommute job except for two days a month here in the office in Savannah for meetings. The company will pay the monthly fee for a high-speed data line wherever you would choose to live. Oh, we will also furnish any specialized equipment you might need. Whatever you were making at your previous job, I will double and I will cover all your relocation expenses. How does that sound?"

Zach nearly fell out of his chair. "That sounds great," Zach accepted the job without hesitation. "How soon would you want me there?"

"Whatever works for you, but no later than the beginning of the week after next," Mr. Hollins said.

"I can make that happen. I have already listed my house for sale. My parents also live here in Tulsa. I'm sure I can get my dad to help with getting any paperwork back and forth. I am excited and look forward to joining your company, Mister Hollins."

"I'm excited as well, Zach. I believe you will be a valuable addition to the company. Call me if you have any difficulties and we can solve them together."

"You bet, Mister Hollins. See you soon," Zach said as he ended the call. He laid the cellphone on the dresser and stood there stunned. Giddy with excitement, he could not resist the desire to share the good news with his parents. He punched in their number and waited.

"Hey, Zach," his father answered. "What's up?"

"You aren't going to believe this," Zach chattered. "Sit down. You're not going to believe this. Are you sitting down? You really aren't going to believe this."

"Zach, calm down and tell me what's going on."

"The President called. I just got a job. It's in Georgia. Starts whenever I can get there. They are paying all expenses."

"Zach, slow down," Peter Templeton urged. "You're not making sense."

Zach started over and gave his dad a blow-by-blow account of all that had just happened: the call to the President, the call from the President to Mr. Hollins, the job offer, the salary increase, the telecommute requirement, everything.

"Wow!" Zach's dad exclaimed after hearing all the details of his son's good fortune. "Just yesterday you seemed so down and now, this. Your mother and I are thrilled for you, son. We will certainly miss you, but we are thrilled. Is there anything we can do to help?"

"If you could help with the sale of the house, that would be great. You know, faxing or mailing paperwork and such."

"Done. Anything else?"

"Well, since I have to be there soon, I may need someone to be here when the movers load up my stuff."

"Absolutely, next."

"That's all I can think of for the moment. My head is spinning. This all happened so fast."

"That's certainly understandable," Zach's dad agreed. "If you think of anything else, just call me and I'll see that it gets taken care of."

"If anything changes, I'll call you." Zach ended the call and slipped the cellphone in his pocket.

"Holy Cow!" Zach shouted, visions of traveling to an unfamiliar state and starting a new job at twice his old salary dancing in his mind.

Zach returned to packing up the spare bedroom, whistling and with a smile on his face.

"I should send Mister Butler a thank-you card," Zach chuckled. "None of this would have happened if he hadn't fired me."

"*Yes sir, maybe I'll just do that,*" he thought to himself as he sealed up the last box in the spare bedroom. He started whistling again as he walked out of the spare bedroom, happier than he had been in a long, long time.

Zach worked furiously the rest of the day, vacuuming, packing, cleaning, and making final preparations to make certain the house was ready for showings. The last box of personal items had been packed and stacked in the garage with all the others. All the furniture, except for the pieces that had been staged according to the suggestion made by the realtor had been moved to the garage.

Part of him was excited about the new position in Savannah and the thought of moving somewhere he had never lived before. But another part of him, the pragmatic part, was apprehensive over what difficulties might lay ahead, knowing that all major life changes come with hidden dangers and obstacles. A sense of foreboding, albeit small, began to grow inside him. Was it a premonition or just the uncertainty of moving? "*The decision has been made,*" he told himself. Convincing himself it was just sadness over leaving the house he and Angie had called home, he walked into the kitchen to make one last check of his "To Do" list.

He checked off the item that had been completed when he stacked the last box in the garage. Running his finger down the list, he smiled, realizing he had checked all the items off. The only task left was to double check drawers, cabinets, and closets to be certain nothing had been overlooked. Starting in the kitchen, he pulled out every drawer, opened every cabinet, poked his head in the pantry, and opened the refrigerator. Everything was empty and clean.

Moving to the far end of the house, he checked all the closets and the spare bedrooms. In the master bedroom, the only items left were those to be packed in his suitcase. He walked into the living room and stopped, gazing at the furniture groupings and décor items suggested by the realtor. The experts all said it was critical to remove all personal items before selling a house, but to his mind the house seemed oddly cold and uninviting. His mind drifted as he looked around the house. He could see Angie curled up on the couch sipping from her ever-present cup of raspberry tea. When they moved in, Zach had marvelled at how adept Angie had been at adding little touches that made the house feel relaxed and cozy. Every knickknack, every picture, every pillow, even the color of the walls she had carefully selected to set the mood of each room. She had fussed over even the smallest detail, not satisfied until everything was just right.

He remembered vividly the day he had arrived home from work to find Angie standing there with a huge smile, eyes sparkling, having just completed the foyer and living room.

"Was he abandoning the life he had shared with Angie," he asked himself, feeling as if her essence was slowly slipping away. Refusing to give in to the depression threatening to rear its ugly head once again, he turned and walked into the kitchen. *"He would always remember Angie,"* he vowed. She was gone and he had to move on. The decision to sell the house and begin rebuilding his life had been made and now he must follow through.

He walked through the house one last time. The papers giving his dad power of attorney for any paperwork related to the sale had been signed. His dad already had keys for all the doors. Everything necessary for the sale of the house was complete. There was nothing left to do.

He had intended to leave early the next morning, but with nothing else left to do and several hours of daylight left he decided to get an early start on the long drive to Savannah, Georgia. He threw his remaining clothes and toiletries into his suitcase and headed for the front door. A plethora of emotions roiled in Zach's mind as he pulled the front door shut and locked it. Would the move to Savannah be a fresh beginning or would depression and grief continue to shadow his every step?

He climbed into his car and started the engine. He grabbed the road atlas and flipped to the page for the state of Arkansas. Barring any traffic issues or delays, he hoped to make Little Rock before stopping for the night. He backed out of the driveway, excited to begin his trip toward a new life.

Chapter Eight

Chatham County Georgia Medical Examiner
East 67th Street, Savannah Georgia

A black panel van completed the short four block drive from Memorial University Medical Center to the Chatham County Medical Examiner's facility. The van pulled into the parking lot and backed up to the receiving entrance. George McAlpin, the morgue's on-duty diener, climbed out of the van, walked around to the back, and propped the rear doors open. He grabbed the gurney and rolled it out of the van. As the gurney slid out of the van, the wheels dropped down and locked into place. Holding the gurney with one hand, McAlpin kicked the van's doors closed with his foot and pushed the gurney toward the double doors.

He punched a large button beside the door and waited for the doors to swing open. McAlpin shook his head as he pushed the gurney down the long hallway toward the *"prep"* room. A large red tag affixed to the zipper's pull tab indicated the body had been double bagged and was to be considered a serious infection hazard. That meant it would take him at least twice as long to ready the body for the medical examiner.

McAlpin, one of three dieners employed at the Chatham County Morgue, belonged to a very small group of individuals that had the stomach for the sights and smells that came with the job at a large city morgue. As a diener, McAlpin's duties included moving and cleaning the bodies, prepping them for the medical examiner, and often assisting in the autopsy itself. Most individuals lasted less than a year, simply unable to endure the emotional anguish that came with the job. McAlpin differed from most individuals. He was a very rare bird. McAlpin, forty on his last birthday, had been at the job for nine years. Even after all those years, his empathy needle seemed to be permanently stuck on zero. Nothing bothered him. Not horrible trauma. Not long-dead bodies. Not even children. Nothing seemed to phase McAlpin.

Still early and before the day shift had arrived at the medical examiner's office, the hallway was dimly lit and deserted. As he had done hundreds of times before, McAlpin pushed the gurney down the hallways toward the *"prep"* room. Suddenly, a storage room door opened and a man stepped out, blocking McAlpin's path. McAlpin jerked involuntarily and assumed a defensive posture until he looked up and recognized the man blocking his path.

"What gives?" McAlpin snapped, outraged by the sudden and unexpected intrusion.

"Keep your voice down, you idiot," the man warned.

McAlpin bristled and took a step toward the man, "I told you the last time, I was done and I meant it."

"You are not done until I say you are done. I have enough on you to see that you spend the rest of your life in prison. Understand?"

McAlpin backed up a step, knowing the man was correct. He was in too deep and he desperately needed the money. He stood quietly and listened. The two men talked in whispers for several minutes, McAlpin occasionally shaking his head in disagreement. Exasperated, the man reached out and grabbed McAlpin's lab coat, nearly pulling him off his feet. "You will do exactly as I tell you or the next body they roll down this hallway will be yours," the man snarled. "Is that clear enough for you?"

"Yes, okay I'll do it," McAlpin sputtered, pulling away from the man's grasp.

The man turned away and hurried out the door at the end of the hallway. Visibly shaking, McAlpin grabbed the gurney and continued down the hallway into the prep room. Chastising himself for ever getting involved with the man, he angrily pushed the gurney to the center of the room. He slid the body off the gurney and onto the x-ray table, walked around behind the lead-shielded wall, and was about to start the x-ray when the wall phone began ringing.

He stripped the double gloves off his right hand and picked up the phone. "McAlpin," he spoke into the phone, his voice muffled by the face mask.

"This is Doctor Tilton. I want you to prep the body you just brought in and take it straight to the examination room."

"But there are two other decedents ahead of this one," McAlpin protested.

"Doesn't matter," Dr. Tilton countered. "This one takes precedence. Take special precautions. The attending physician wasn't able to identify the cause of death. The symptoms mimicked a hemorrhagic fever. So, we must consider the body a category three threat. Notify me as soon as the body is ready and in the examination room."

"Very well," McAlpin answered and hung up the phone.

McAlpin returned to the x-ray control room, double gloved his right hand with fresh gloves, and took several sets of images, which revealed all the intravenous catheters and other tubing still in place. Because of the suspected highly infectious threat, the body had immediately been double bagged, decontaminated, and then sealed.

In the morgue's prep and examination suite, all dead bodies were considered potentially infectious, standard precautions being implemented for every case. However, when a *Red Tag* body arrived, extremely stringent precautions were implemented to minimize the risks of transmission of known or unknown infectious pathogens. Once McAlpin had viewed and verified the x-rays, he wiped down the outside of the exterior body bag and the gurney with a solution of sodium hypochlorite for a second time. Every time he prepped a body labeled as infectious, he recalled the incident two years earlier when fellow worker Alfred Ross had been careless. A simple, yet disastrous, failure to follow protocol and an unthinking rub of his eye resulted in his contracting the H1N1 virus. Five days later, Alfred Ross died a miserable death.

McAlpin lined the gurney up beside the x-ray table, locked the wheels, and pushed the body off onto the gurney. After wiping down the x-ray table, he unlocked the gurney's wheels and pushed the gurney out into the hallway and toward the examination suite.

In the anteroom to the examination suite, McAlpin picked up the phone and punched in Dr. Tilton's number.

"Doctor Tilton."

"Doctor Tilton, this is McAlpin. The x-rays are complete and verified. I'm about to enter the examination suite."

"Very well. I'm on my way."

McAlpin, dressed in his personal protective equipment, opened the doors to the examination suite and pushed the gurney into the suite and over beside the first cadaver table. He slid the body onto the cadaver table and rolled the gurney out of the way. While waiting for Dr. Tilton to arrive, McAlpin busied himself laying out instruments, blood tubes, and various sizes of sample collection containers.

Dr. Tilton walked into the anteroom, climbed into his personal protective equipment, and donned a long, rubber apron and face shield. He pulled on double gloves and entered the examination suite. Stopping beside the cadaver table, he looked at McAlpin. "Are we ready?"

"Yes, Doctor," McAlpin answered. "Standard instrument set is on the table to your left. Sample collection containers and blood tubes are laid out and ready."

Dr. Tilton picked up a pair of scissors from the instrument table and cut the plastic tie that looped through the red warning tag and the zipper tab. He discarded the plastic tie and placed the red tag next to his clipboard to be attached to the initial findings report. Next, he unzipped the outer body bag and with McAlpin's help slipped it out from under the inner body bag. Finding nothing inside the outer body bag, McAlpin rolled it up tightly and placed it in a large "burn" bag.

While Dr. Tilton held the body up, McAlpin slid the inner bag out from under the body, careful not to disturb the intravenous tubing that had been left in place. McAlpin carefully laid the inner bag on the adjacent cadaver table. He turned back to the first cadaver table and placed the body block under the back of the body, causing the arms and neck to fall backward out of the way. Dr. Tilton stepped back out of the way while McAlpin took numerous photographs from various angles. McAlpin set the camera on a nearby worktable, picked up the fingerprint card, inked the body's fingers, and took fingerprints for positive identification.

While Dr. Tilton began filling out the autopsy record sheet, McAlpin broke open a pack of sterile Dacron swabs with plastic shafts. Using four swabs, he swabbed the top, bottom, and both sides of the interior of the inner bag. Each swab went into a separate screw-top container. He labeled each container, placed them in an evidence box, then turned back toward Dr. Tilton.

Finding nothing unusual about the clothing that had been sent over with the body, Dr. Tilton collected hair samples and fingernail scrapings and handed them to McAlpin for placements in sample containers.

Dr. Tilton began the external exam. He stepped on the audio recorder pedal and began recording, "The decedent is Victoria Jean Picket, white female, age twenty-five, red hair medium length, eyes green, height five feet eight inches, weight one hundred thirty-one pounds, no identifying scars, tattoos, or birthmarks. Gross external exam is unremarkable. There are no visible signs of physical trauma. No lacerations, no avulsions, no punctures except for two intravenous lines still in place, no abrasions, and no contusions."

Dr. Tilton slipped his foot off the recorder pedal and called out to McAlpin, "Hey, George. Help me roll the body."

The two men rolled the body up on its side. While McAlpin held the body, Dr. Tilton moved around to the other side of the table. "Hmmm, that's odd," he remarked. "There are petechiae on the back of legs and on the lower back." Petechiae are small 1–2 mm red or purplish spots on the skin or conjunctiva, resembling a rash of tiny, red dots. The appearance of petechiae on the skin is generally the result of internal bleeding, or leaking capillaries. *"That could certainly point to a hemorrhagic fever,"* Dr. Tilton thought. He scribbled a note on the autopsy record sheet and continued the external exam.

They rolled the body onto its back and Dr. Tilton began the internal exam using a standard Y incision. As Dr. Tilton continued the internal exam, he noted that significant bleeding had occurred from many of the internal organs. He specifically noted that the liver seemed unusually hard and was covered with regenerative nodules which would indicate cirrhosis of the liver. That finding seemed quite contradictory as the decedent was far too young for such a chronic condition. In addition, there was no history of heavy alcohol usage. Using a large syringe, Dr. Tilton drew blood samples from the spleen, liver, and heart and filled three vacutainers.

McAlpin was busy on the other side of the examination suite labeling sample containers. Way behind on his paperwork and in a hurry to get back to his office, Dr. Tilton dropped the vacutainers in the pocket of his lab coat. He concluded the internal exam and with McAlpin's help prepped the body for storage. Dr. Tilton zipped the outer body bag closed, sealed the zipper with red warning tape, and signed his name across the tape.

Much to the dismay of Victoria Pickett's family, viewing of the body or any preparation by a funeral home would not be allowed. A state infection control officer would likely rule that the body could be released to a funeral home, but the body would have to be buried as is.

"Hey, George. Put the body in storage until we hear from the infection control officer," Dr. Tilton called out as he pushed the examination suite door open. In a hurry to get back to his office and the mountain of paperwork waiting for him, Dr. Tilton rushed out of the examination suite, completely forgetting the vacutainers he had dropped in his pocket.

McAlpin slid the body off the cadaver table onto the gurney and wheeled it to the far side of the room. He opened an empty compartment and slid Victoria Pickett's body into a refrigerated storage drawer. After pushing the gurney back to the other side of the room, he pushed the examination suite door open and checked the anteroom. Satisfied he was alone, McAlpin lined up all the sample containers and filled another row of identical sample containers with matching sample tissues from a different decedent. He labeled the new set of containers, dumped the original set of sample containers into the "burn" bag, and headed for the incinerator.

Chapter Nine

East Kenosha Street
Tulsa, Oklahoma

In the early evening darkness, a dark blue Toyota Camry sedan sat idling in a shopping center parking lot on the southwest corner of the intersection of East Kenosha Street and North Twenty-Third Street in Broken Arrow, Oklahoma. Contract security guard Matthew Stokes, a former Tulsa police officer, sat dozing. Three months earlier, he had been fired from the Tulsa Police Department after receiving his third reprimand for using excessive force. He had turned in all but one of his uniforms, the one he currently wore, claiming it had been ripped and discarded. The fake name plate pinned above his right pocket said "Benson". A counterfeit badge, pinned above the left pocket of his uniform shirt, would fool all but another police officer.

The cellphone cradled in his lap buzzed, awakening him from his catnap. Quickly he opened the text app on the cellphone and read the brief message that had just arrived—Zachariah Templeton 315 West Elgin Street. He entered the address into the GPS app and pressed "Get Directions". The app drew a pictorial route to the address and indicated the destination was slightly over two miles away.

He slipped a 9mm pistol from the holster attached to his belt and carefully pulled the slide back to verify there was a round in the chamber. He dropped the Camry into gear, exited the parking lot onto North Twenty-Third Street, and turned left onto East Kenosha Street. Two miles later, he turned left onto North Fourth Street, drove four blocks, then turned east onto East Elgin Street.

As he turned into the driveway at his destination, he noticed there were no lights on. He climbed out of the car, walked to the front door, and knocked loudly. Twice more he knocked on the door, receiving no answer. Walking around the house, he peered into the windows. As he returned to the front of the house, he noticed the For Sale sign positioned on the front lawn. Seeing lights on in both neighboring houses, he asked them if they knew where Mr. Templeton had gone.

The neighbor on the right said they had not spoken to or seen Mr. Templeton and did not know where he might have gone. He walked to the neighbor on the left and knocked on the door.

"I'm Officer Benson," he announced as the door opened and a young woman stepped into the doorway. "I'm looking for your neighbor, a Mister Zachariah Templeton. Have you seen him recently?"

"I haven't," the young woman answered. "But my husband spoke to him briefly yesterday. As you can see, the house is for sale. My husband said he told him he was moving. I think it was somewhere in the Southeast. Atlanta, Georgia, or maybe Savannah or something like that."

"Do you know when he is moving?" Stokes asked. "I need to contact him about an important matter."

"You missed him by several hours," the woman said. "Tom, my husband, said he saw him throw a suitcase in the trunk. Before he got in the car, he shook Tom's hand and said he was leaving and wouldn't be back."

"What kind of car, ma'am?"

"A Buick Encore, I think. Light grey. I don't know what year."

"Would you happen to know the license plate number?"

"Sorry, Officer. I don't have any idea."

"Okay, ma'am. Thank you for your help," Stokes said, touching two fingers to the bill of his hat.

Stokes climbed back into his car and drove back to the shopping center parking lot. He pulled the burner cellphone from his pocket and dialed the number he had been given. After five rings, a brief voice mail announcement advised to leave a message.

"Subject is gone, several hours, moved to Atlanta or, possibly, Savannah," Stokes said. "Driving a light grey Buick Encore, unknown year, unknown license plate. Will await instructions."

Stokes shrugged his shoulders. With his job completed and nothing left to do, he put the car into gear, and headed for his one-room apartment near the mall.

Deserted Road
Southeast of Hardeeville, South Carolina

A beat up, eight-year-old Chevrolet SUV slowed suddenly as it drove down the dark, paved county road. The driver of the old Chevy spotted the small marker he had placed earlier, slowed to a stop, and shifted the vehicle into reverse. The undercarriage of the old Chevy drug on waist-high weeds as it backed down the narrow, tree-shrouded path. The driver continued backing up until the vehicle was well out of sight from the main road. The driver switched off the headlights, killed the engine, and grabbed a flashlight from the glove box.

The driver's side door opened and a man just shy of six feet tall, dressed in jeans, a dark-colored jacket, and a black ball cap climbed out and walked around to the front of the vehicle. Chevy Man leaned against the SUV's front fender and peered through the dense trees, watching for approaching vehicles.

Ten minutes passed. He watched as a dark-colored pickup sped past. Two minutes later, another vehicle flew by, blaring loud music as it passed. Five more minutes passed. Growing impatient, Chevy Man shifted back and forth on his feet. Headlights flickered through the trees as another vehicle approached. The vehicle slowed, stopped next to the marker Chevy Man had placed, and flashed a light one time. Chevy Man flashed his flashlight twice, acknowledging the signal.

The vehicle, a dark green sedan, turned into the lane, stopped in front of the SUV, and switched off its lights and engine. The driver's door opened and a sixtyish man in light brown slacks and light-blue shirt stepped out of the car. Pushing his way through the waist-high weeds, he stopped two paces short of Chevy Man. Chevy Man shined his flashlight on the man's chest. The man raised his right arm and gave the hailing sign.

The man took a step toward Chevy Man, extended his hand, and said, "I'm Kl….,"

"Shut up, you fool," Chevy Man snarled, interrupting the man. "You of all people should know we never use personal names. Not even here. I know who you are."

"You summoned me, Sir" Klaus Herrmann, the man from the green sedan, answered, taking a step backward and letting his hand drop to his side.

"The Master is deeply concerned," Chevy Man said. "Our last efforts were thwarted by incompetence. If this project does not go according to plan, the consequences will be most severe. I understand you have been given charge over the project. Be warned, if it fails for any reason, the blame will fall upon you and you alone. The Worshipful Master's fury will fall directly upon you. There will be nowhere you can hide. You know that, right?"

"Yes, I am aware," Klaus answered. "I take full responsibility. If I fail, I shall deserve, and accept, whatever judgment is befitting."

"Good," Chevy Man answered. "Have you been to the facility?"

"Yes. I visited there just yesterday."

"How is production progressing?"

"They have completed the final run," Klaus answered. "Given the potency, as it was explained to me, there would be enough pathogen to kill the entire population ten times over."

"Has the delivery vector's effectiveness been established?"

"The scientists at the facility assured me that once the trial vector was released, it immediately sought out a host. They explained that the delivery vector is genetically modified to have a life cycle of no more than twenty-four hours."

"What of the final release?"

"The senior virologistst said the contagion will spread quickly, but only near the release point because the vector's lifespan has been genetically limited using something called transcriptional activation which can be turned on and off using a specific antibiotic. The vector will live for only a day, maybe two. One of the scientists said it would take years to develop a vaccine. By the time even a prototype vaccine could be developed the population in the release area will be decimated."

"And where are the bio-containment canisters now?" Chevy Man asked.

"They are safely hidden at the agreed location."

"The delivery vector?"

"Still at the facility. I saw them. It's incredible. There are hundreds of thousands of them. It made my skin crawl."

"Return to the facility," Chevy Man ordered. "Make certain you collect an adequate quantity of the delivery vector. Split them into two groups and then hide them as well. When you have done that, collect all the work documents."

"But the scientists will object."

"Kill them," Chevy Man snapped. "They exist only to serve our needs. Besides, they are no longer useful. The facility and all its contents are to be destroyed. Be careful to make certain no records or traces of the work is left behind."

"But all that work," Klaus Herrmann exclaimed.

"It is only a small part of the Master's plan," Chevy Man answered.

"I am confused," Klaus Herrmann said, a puzzled look spreading across his face.

"The Master wishes no one man to know all aspects of the plan. The virus will be released soon, but first others must place evidence linking the current administration to the release of the contagion. That will create enormous chaos and collapse the government, which will send the country into anarchy."

"Very well, but how do I destroy the equipment so it cannot be recognized?"

"Follow me," Chevy Man replied, leading Klaus to the back hatch of the SUV. He pulled up on the lift gate and stepped back out of the way while the rear hatch swung up, revealing two four-gallon, white, plastic jars.

"Here is what you need," Chevy Man said, pointing at the white containers.

"Those two containers?" Klaus scoffed. "That is all I need?"

"To be sure, my puzzled friend," Chevy Man responded. "Do not be fooled by their small size. The substance in those white jars is the most caustic substance known to man. Let me explain. Those jars contain fluoroantimonic acid. It is, by far, the strongest of all known superacids, many thousands of times stronger than pure sulfuric acid."

"If it is so corrosive, how can it be stored?" Klaus asked, backing up a step.

"You are wise to be cautious," Chevy Man advised. "It is so corrosive, it eats right through everything, even glass."

"What are those jars made of then?"

"They are Teflon. Teflon is the only substance where the molecular bond between the molecules is strong enough to contain the fluoroantimonic acid. See the wands attached to the sides of the jars?"

"Yes, I see them."

"The acid is under pressure so you can use the wands to spray that which you wish to be destroyed. The triggers have safety catches, but still you must exercise extreme caution. It is extremely toxic and will produce massive trauma to any flesh it comes in contact with. Even a drop or two on your skin would likely prove to be fatal. It reacts violently with anything it comes in contact with, releasing highly toxic vapors."

"If it is so dangerous, how can I use it?"

"You must wear this," Chevy Man answered, handing Klaus a Teflon coated protective suit. "And use this breathing apparatus."

"What do I do with the jars when I am finished?"

"Here, use these small explosive devices. Attach one to each jar. The timers are set to thirty minutes. That should give you ample time to get far away."

Klaus and Chevy Man carefully moved the jars to the trunk of Klaus's car. Klaus climbed into the driver's seat and started the engine. Chevy Man tapped on the window and waited for Klaus to lower the window.

"I forgot to tell you, you must be quick when you dispense the acid. The cartridge in the breathing apparatus will disintegrate after only ten to twelve minutes."

"I'm glad you mentioned that," Klaus remarked. He rolled the window up, backed out onto the country road, and sped off into the darkness.

Chapter Ten

Shady Oaks Cemetery
Bluffton, South Carolina

Anna Mae Watts sat silently on a hard, metal folding chair on the end of the third row under a blue tent in Shady Oaks Cemetery, the same cemetery where her mother had been buried only days earlier. A sizable crowd had gathered for the graveside service for Victoria Jean Pickett, Anna Mae's cousin. The cemetery's gravel pathways were lined to overflowing with cars. Forced to park in the parking lot of an adjacent business, many people had walked over to join the somber crowd. At least four times as many people stood outside the tent as there were seated under the tent.

Word of Victoria Jean Pickett's passing had spread quickly through the city of Bluffton. The entire community was shocked by the death of someone only twenty-five years old. Even worse, she left behind a two-year old child and her twenty-six year old husband, Joshua Pickett. Multiple generations of the Pickett family had resided in or near Bluffton, hence the large, overflowing crowd.

Joshua Pickett, seated on the front row nearest to the casket, fought desperately against the flood of grief demanding to be released. Still in denial, his mind screamed, *"I don't believe it. She can't be gone."* For the sake of his little girl, Mazie, he refused to give in to the torrent of emotions. Mazie, just two and one-half years old, did not understand where Mommy had gone.

Tired of sitting still, Mazie squirmed in Joshua's arms. "Where Mommy," the little girl asked, looking up at her daddy.

The inquisitive look on the little girl's face and the thought of raising her alone was the proverbial "straw". Joshua's shoulders shook as the pent-up emotion poured out. Anna

Mae, seated two rows behind Joshua, had been watching, prepared to help out and entertain Mazie, if necessary. Seeing Joshua lose control, she stood up, walked up beside Joshua, and tapped him on the shoulder.

"Joshua, I'm so sorry," Anna Mae offered. "Let me help. I'll take Mazie so you don't have to worry about anything."

"Thanks," Joshua stammered, holding the little girl up toward Anna Mae.

"Am-me, Am-me," the little girl babbled, reaching out for Anna Mae.

Anna Mae took Mazie in her arms. Mazie hugged her tightly and buried her face in Anna Mae's neck. Anna Mae stepped outside the tent and walked around to the side, staying close enough that she could hear the service.

Pastor Norman Stone had also been watching Joshua as he struggled to maintain control. Upon seeing Anna Mae take charge of Joshua's little girl, he stepped up beside the casket. He surveyed the crowd, waiting for the mourners to quiet down. With all eyes on him, he began the service.

"Once again we gather here to lay to rest the body of a dear friend. A sweet soul stricken down far too early in life. It is especially difficult when one so young is taken from us. Today we lay to rest the body of Victoria Jean Picket, age twenty-five: friend, family member, wife, and mother. I share your grief dear friends, having known Victoria her entire life. It was my great joy to baptize Victoria when she was seven years old. I watched her grow into a beautiful young lady and had the privilege of performing her marriage to Joshua. I stood vigil with Joshua when she gave birth to their beautiful daughter, Mazie. I....," Pastor Stone stopped momentarily, pulled a handkerchief from his pocket, and wiped away a tear as it rolled down his cheek.

He took a deep breath, stuffed the handkerchief back in his pocket, and continued, "Not long ago I stood in this very cemetery to conduct the graveside service for Victoria's aunt. I remember the comforting words Marguerite had written on the note she had asked me to read. She asked us to not grieve for her because she was in a place where the light never fades. Take comfort knowing that Victoria is now also in that beautiful place of eternal rest."

As he had done during Marguerite Watts's service, Pastor Stone stepped beside the casket, placed his hand on it, and began his summation, "These mortal remains we now commit to the ground. Earth to earth, ashes to ashes, dust to dust. Blessed are the dead who die in the Lord. Lord, we thank you for those we have loved so dearly but can see no more in this life. We rest assured that one day we will be reunited. Receive into your loving arms your servant Victoria Jean Pickett. Amen and Amen."

Unlike the mourners that had gathered at Marguerite Watts' service, the current crowd lingered, clustered in small groups, speaking in hushed voices. Anna Mae returned to the tent and stood beside Joshua. Pastor Stone stepped under the tent, clasped Joshua's hand, and offered his condolences. Pastor Stone and Joshua talked briefly with Pastor Stone, telling Joshua to call him if he needed anything. Over the course of the next fifteen minutes, many of the mourners filed through the tent offering their condolences.

Anna Mae stood back out of the way, waiting until all those that had lined up to talk with Joshua had passed through the tent. Emotionally drained, Joshua sat down on one of the chairs. Anna Mae walked over and sat down beside Joshua. He looked tired and drawn, but he kept his emotions in check.

"I only just heard day before yesterday," Anna Mae said. "Joshua, what on earth happened. Victoria hadn't been sick."

Joshua shrugged, "Anna Mae, I just don't understand. She had a simple nosebleed, and then three days later she's dead."

"Didn't the doctors say anything?"

"One doctor, a hematologist I think, said something about not enough platelets and something he called throm-bo-cy-to something or other. My mind is a total blur. I didn't have any idea what he was talking about then and I still don't. He asked her about exposure to toxic chemicals." He turned and looked directly at Anna Mae, "Anna Mae, how on earth could Victoria have been exposed to toxic chemicals?"

"Did the doctor give you any idea why he might have suspected toxic chemicals?" Anna Mae questioned.

"I don't know," Joshua snapped. "I'm not a chemist. "I can't... I don't..." Joshua looked at Anna Mae with red-rimmed eyes, unable to hold back the tears that flowed once again, "I'm sorry. I feel numb. Half the time I just wander around like I'm in a fog."

"It's okay, Joshua," Anna Mae said, laying her free hand on Joshua's shoulder. "I understand. I know just how you feel. Really, I do."

Sitting on Anna Mae's lap, Mazie babbled something un-intelligible as she played with the stuffed animal held tightly in her grasp.

"Oh, Anna Mae, what am I going to do," Joshua sput-tered. "I'm all alone. Who will care of Mazie while I'm at work?"

"Don't worry, Joshua. We'll work something out. We really should go."

"I suppose you're right," Joshua answered, dabbing at his eyes with the soaked handkerchief clutched in his hand. "Can you give me a few minutes?"

"Certainly. I'll take Mazie and we'll go wait by the limo for you. Take as much time you need."

Anna Mae got up from the chair and with Mazie cradled over her shoulder walked toward the funeral home's limo. When she reached the limo, she turned back toward the gravesite and saw Joshua leaned over the casket. She knew ex-actly what he was going through. She wanted to rush over to the casket, put her arm around him, and weep together, but she knew he needed time alone to say his last goodbye.

Anna Mae opened the rear door of the limo and set Mazie inside. She picked up one of Mazie's stuffed animals that had been left on the seat and kept Mazie entertained while Joshua said his goodbye.

Ten minutes passed. Growing concerned, Anna Mae slipped out of the rear seat and turned toward the gravesite. She saw that several well-wishers had waylaid that Joshua. Shaking his head up and down, Joshua graciously accepted their condolences. The well-wishers turned and headed for their cars, allowing Joshua to return to the limo. Anna Mae buckled Mazie into her car seat while Joshua climbed into the front seat.

The funeral home's limo driver started the engine and drove slowly down the gravel path and out onto the street. Part way back to the funeral home, Joshua leaned over the seat and tapped Anna Mae on the knee.

"You know, I've been so busy making arrangements and attending to visiting family and friends that I haven't given a thought to what comes next. The company gave me a few days off but after that I don't know what I am going to do."

"I have a lot of vacation built up and I would love to help with Mazie," Anna Mae offered. "I have an idea. When we get back to the funeral home, why don't I take Mazie home with me and you go home and rest. Then come over to my house for supper."

"I don't want to impose," Joshua objected. "You've already been such a help."

"Don't be silly," Anna Mae countered. "I love Mazie. It won't be the least bother. We'll have a grand time."

"Well, I could use some time to unwind."

"It's settled then. When you come for supper, bring a few days' worth of clothes for Mazie. We're going to have a girl's retreat."

"Anna Mae, I can't thank you enough. I don't know what I would have done without your help."

"I'm really glad I could help. I'll call my boss tomorrow and arrange to take the next week off. That will give you plenty of time to get things figured out. If not, I'll take another week. I can do a lot of my work from home. I'm certain my boss will not have a problem with that."

"You're amazing, Anna Mae," Joshua blurted out. "That will give me some time to do some research and see if I can find out what caused Victoria's death. Something just doesn't add up."

Joshua sniffed and without thinking wiped his nose with the back of his hand. As he pulled his hand away, he noticed a small smear of blood across the back of his hand. Quickly, he hid his hand down at his side. Deep concern began to creep into his mind as the limo sped back toward the funeral home.

Smith Street
London, United Kingdom

Sha'ban Rabi Bahar, al-Ta'abin, The Snake, paced angrily back and forth across the plush carpet in his second-floor office. He stopped and stared out the second-floor window of his lavish townhouse located in the heart of Chelsea on the southwestern edge of Central London. Only four blocks north of the Thames River, he could see Battersea Park on the south bank of the Thames River. He looked downward, admiring the beautiful south-facing terrace and lush garden, the primary reason he had purchased the two-bedroom townhouse for the exorbitant price of four and one-half million British Pounds, just shy of six million in US Dollars.

Even though his buyer's agent had told him the townhouse was overpriced, he had purchased it after spending less than ten minutes viewing the property. The beautiful garden, its proximity to transportation, and being only a few blocks from his office had clinched the decision for him. Sha'ban instructed his agent to make a full-price offer in cash. Three weeks later his agent handed him the keys. The large purchase price put a dent in his available funds, albeit a small one. Through wise investments and a number of financial transactions, many of them far less than legal, he had amassed a small fortune.

Sha'ban turned away from the window and returned to his pacing back and forth across the luxurious carpet. Earlier, while working at his desk, he had received a message from his informant in America. Finally, they had located Mr. Templeton, but a check of his residence revealed he was gone again. The message from the informant said Mr. Templeton was moving somewhere in the Southeast, according to one of his neighbors. Sha'ban's face turned red as he crumpled the scrap of paper in his hand. He cursed out loud and hurled the wad of paper across the room.

Impatiently he had long waited, yearning to see the blood of the man he hated flow across the blade of his jambiya. In his business life, he was known as Bailey Gibbons, corporate financial officer of a large and highly successful financial investments firm. Only in the privacy of his townhome, did he allow the hot, Arab blood of Sha'ban Rabi Bahar that coursed through his veins to drive his emotions. His anger erupted as the vengeance he so desperately craved seemed to be slipping away. He rushed to the closet, removed his jambiya from its hiding place, and thrust it up into the air. The blood-stained blade gleamed in the bright sunlight. He uttered a solemn vow to Allah, promising that Mr. Zachariah Templeton's blood would soon mingle with the blood of the other infidels that had experienced his fury.

True to his *Al-Wala wal-Bara* (a manifestation of sincere love for Allah and a demonstration of enmity and fierce hatred toward all that displeases Allah), Sha'ban promised upon his life that his mortal enemy, the Great Satan, The United States of America, would perish at his hand.

Smiling, Sha'ban slid the jambiya back into its sheath, picked up the telephone, and punched in an international number from memory.

"Hello," a male voice answered.

"I have a task for you," Sha'ban announced.

"Yes, Worshipful Master," Timothé Alex Durand, The Grand Prince of the Royal Secret, replied, recognizing the voice of the Sovereign Grand Inquisitor.

"The Knight of Vengeance said his informant in Oklahoma located Mister Templeton, but when he went to his residence, he was not there. A neighbor told the informant Mister Templeton was moving and had already left. From what the neighbor said, it appears he is heading to the southeast US. The neighbor thought his destination was Atlanta, or maybe Savannah."

"My flight leaves Paris in less than three hours," Mr. Durand advised. "I will be on the lookout as soon as I arrive. Can you give me any details?"

"The neighbor described his car as a light grey Buick Encore. No license plate."

"That's not much to go on," Mr. Durand remarked.

"It's all we have," Sha'ban shouted. "I will send you his photograph. Use only local members you can trust. I expect you to find him."

"Yes, Worshipful Master. I will alert you the instant he is spotted."

"I have another task for you as well. Are you familiar with the delivery vector that will be used to spread the pathogen?"

"Only that I know its lifespan will be shortened to limit the range of the initial contagion," Mr. Durand answered.

"Yes, that is what the stupid Americans think," Sha'ban laughed. "The Knight has been instructed to silence everyone at the underground laboratory and then gather the vector and the substance used to limit its lifespan and take them to the secret location. I will send you the coordinates of the secret location. Watch the Knight's movements. I want you to intercept the Knight as he performs his task. When he is done, kill him, and then take the vector to the hidden location."

"But Master, that will set off a nationwide epidemic," Mr. Durand remarked.

"You catch on quickly, my friend," Sha'ban quipped. "When our tasks are done, we will release the vector and then we will catch our flights back to Europe."

"As you wish, Worshipful Master," Mr. Durand replied. The line went dead. Sha'ban returned to the window and stood staring at the river, motionless, for several minutes as he envisioned the annihilation of his hated enemy. Sha'ban turned, walked back to his desk, and pulled open the center drawer. He picked up a small black notebook and flipped through the pages. Holding his finger on one entry, he punched the number into the phone and waited.

"Leighton Air Charter. May I help you," a female voice answered.

"This is Bailey Gibbons. I need to schedule a private jet," Sha'ban declared.

"Yes, Mister Gibbons," Adele Arkwright, Leighton Air Charter's receptionist answered. "How soon will you be needing that flight?"

"As soon as possible. It's quite urgent."

"Can you hold, Mister Gibbons, while I go talk to the chief pilot?"

"Yes, I can hold. I am a frequent customer. I am quite willing to pay extra to be able to leave today," Sha'ban added.

"I'll let Mister Winfield know that," Ms. Arkwright said as she put the line on hold. A lively tune emanated from the phone receiver as Sha'ban waited. The tune completed and another one began. The second tune completed and as the third one started, Ms. Arkwright returned.

"Mister Winfield said there was a cancellation and there will be an aircraft available later today. One of our aircraft is scheduled to return to London City Airport in the early afternoon. It will require an hour or so to refuel, clean, and replenish the aircraft. So, it should be ready for departure sometime around late afternoon. Will that work for you, Mister Gibbons?"

"Yes, that will be fine. Tell the pilot to file a flight plan for Atlanta, Georgia."

"I will pass that along," Ms. Arkwright said. "And, by the way, Mister Winfield said because you are a frequent customer and the aircraft would be idle otherwise, there will be no extra charge. We'll see you this afternoon."

Sha'ban glanced at his watch and learned he would have several hours to pack and get to the airport. Knowing it would be a long flight, arriving very early in the morning hours, he made a quick sandwich. He went to the pantry, grabbed a loaf of light rye, and set it on the counter. From the refrigerator, he loaded his arms with the salt beef he had purchased yesterday at the local deli, a package of Swiss cheese, a jar of Dijon mustard, and a bottle of Russian dressing. Pushing various jars and cartons out of the way, he could not find any sauerkraut. The sandwich wouldn't be the same without sauerkraut, but he did not have time to go to the market. So, it would just have to do.

After placing his armload of sandwich fixings on the counter, he returned to the refrigerator for a bottle of his favorite soda, a locally produced soft drink made from apples. With the sandwich completed, he carried it and the bottle of soda outside to the terrace and sat down at a small, round metal table. Basking in the bright warmth of the sun, he enjoyed a leisurely lunch as he watched the boat traffic on the Thames River. Twenty minutes later, he stuffed the last bite of sandwich in his mouth and washed it down with the last swallow of soda. He picked up the dirty plate and glass and headed for the kitchen.

After rinsing the dishes and placing them in the dishwasher, he moved into the master bedroom to pack enough clothes for four days: four pairs of slacks, four shirts, socks, underwear, and toiletries. If that wasn't enough, he would buy what he needed at his destination. He quickly stuffed the pile of clothes into a small suitcase, removed a hefty stack of cash from a hidden wall safe, and hid the cash under the clothes. About to close the suitcase, he remembered one additional item he would need. Sha'ban retrieved the jambiya from its hiding place, placed it under the clothes beside the cash, closed the suitcase, and zipped it closed. Reaching in his pocket, he withdrew a wad of bills surrounded by a gold money clip. He peeled off six fifty-pound notes, folded them in half, and stuffed them in the top pocket of the suitcase, leaving a half inch of the bills exposed. Having traveled out of the London City Airport many times, he knew several of the security guards. The cash would ensure that his suitcase passed through security without being inspected.

He set the suitcase by the front door and made one last check to be certain he had turned all the lights off. He turned the thermostat down and rushed out of the townhouse. Exiting out the front door, he turned right onto Smith Street, hurried down to the corner of King's Road, and flagged down a passing taxi.

Chapter Eleven

Offices of Silverline Communications
Augusta Avenue
Savannah, Georgia

Having finished a light breakfast, Zach waited in line to check-out of the Riverview Hotel. The hotel stood at the intersection of Abercorn and East Bryan Street just five blocks from the Savannah River. Arriving after dark, Zach had not seen the commanding view from his room on the eighth floor until he pulled back the curtains after climbing out of bed.

The two hotel guests in line in front of Zach finished their checkout process and he stepped up to the desk. His room had been arranged as a pre-pay so all he had to do was hand over the plastic key card and take the receipt. He grabbed the handle of his roller bag and headed for the seating area. Zach looked at his watch and saw that the time was nine forty-five. Even if he drove slowly, the short two mile drive to the Silverline Communications office would take no more than twenty minutes and his appointment with Mr. Grant Hollins of Silverline Communications was not until eleven o'clock.. He would need to kill nearly an hour.

Zach selected a small couch at the edge of the seating area and sat down. He opened the "Homes for Sale" magazine he picked up as he exited the hotel's restaurant and began browsing. Patience not being one of Zach's strong suits, he glanced at his watch every few minutes, eager to get on to his meeting. A short, rotund man in a business suit sat down on the opposite end of the couch and asked Zach where he was from. Zach learned the man had flown in from Dallas to present a proposal for the installation of a short-hop microwave system. Having similar backgrounds, the two men struck up a conversation. Enjoying the conversation, time passed quickly. Zach looked at his watch and realized it was time to leave for his appointment. He excused himself from the conversation, informing the man he needed to leave for an appointment.

Zach grabbed the handle of his roller bag, exited the hotel, and headed for the parking garage. After exiting the parking garage onto East Bryan Street, he made a quick right onto Abercorn Street and drove east two blocks toward the river, then turned west on West Bay Street. Zach continued driving west until he spotted the sign for Jenks Street. Following Mr. Hollins' instructions, he stayed on Jenks Street for two blocks and then turned back east onto Augusta Avenue. Five blocks later he spotted the red brick building on the left side of the street Mr. Hollins had described and pulled into the parking lot. He smiled. Five minutes till eleven, right on time. He snatched his notebook from the passenger seat and headed for the front door.

Inside the building, he spotted a desk positioned under a large Silverline Communications logo. He walked up to the desk and identified himself, "I'm Zach Templeton. I have an appointment with Mister Hollins at eleven."

"Yes, Mister Templeton. We're expecting you," a blond-haired woman dressed in a dark gray business suit answered as she stood up and held her hand out. "My name is Amber Hickman. It's a pleasure to meet you, Zach."

"It's nice to meet you as well, Amber," Zach responded.

"Have a seat, Zach. I'll buzz Mister Hollins and let him know you're here."

Zach took a seat and looked around the reception area, impressed by the expensive looking, but tasteful décor. Particularly impressed by a piece of artwork on the opposite wall, he stood up and walked over in front of the piece. Very gently he tapped the corner of the artwork with the fingernail of his index finger, surprised to discover it was an original oil painting. Admiring the fine detail and blending of colors, he did not hear Mr. Hollins walk up behind him.

"Beautiful isn't it," Mr. Hollins remarked.

Somewhat startled, Zach turned around and faced Mr. Hollins. The man standing there was tall, six foot four inches at least, and elegantly dressed in a dark black suit, white shirt, and a bright, fire-red tie. "It's absolutely exquisite," Zach replied.

"Glad to have you with us. I'm Grant Hollins," he said, holding out his hand.

"Mister Hollins, it's a pleasure," Zach beamed, grabbing Mr. Hollins' hand. Zach nearly winced from Mr. Hollins' bone-cruncher grip.

"Call me Grant, Zach. Come on in to my office. I want to hear all about you."

Mr. Hollins turned and headed for his office with Zach following behind. Mr. Hollins waited for Zach to enter the office, pushed the door closed, walked around his desk, and sat down. Pointing to a chair in front of the desk, he said, "Zach, please sit down. Would you like some coffee?"

"That would be great."

Mr. Hollins picked up the phone and asked Amber to bring in two cups and a carafe of coffee. They had hardly begun chatting when Amber tapped on the door, carried in the cups and coffee, and set them on the corner of the desk. Zach picked up one of the cups and examined the logo.

"We had a bunch of cups printed with our logo as promotional items. It's yours to keep," Mr. Hollins said as he leaned forward and poured coffee into Zach's cup. He filled his own cup, sat back in his chair, took a swallow of coffee, and continued, "I have to say I was quite impressed with President Cantwell's recommendation. As I mentioned in our earlier conversation, he speaks very highly of you. The Presidential Medal of Freedom with Distinction is a *really* big deal."

"Uh...," Zach hesitated, somewhat embarrassed. "I'm not certain I deserved such a high honor. An old friend, Rear Admiral Charles Hadley, asked me to help him find a traitor. I agreed. I served my country. That's all there was to it."

"Well, from what President Cantwell shared with me, I think you deserved the award and much more. He told me about the loss you suffered and called you a hero. I must admit, I highly agree."

Not knowing what else to say, Zach simply said, "Thank you. I appreciate the kind words."

"The last time we spoke I believe we covered your work experience and background in great detail. Now, I want you to tell me about *you*. What makes you tick?" Mr. Hollins asked.

Zach and Mr. Hollins spent the next thirty minutes with Zach doing most of the talking and Mr. Hollins listening intently as Zach described pursuing the odd interference that plagued the microwave system of his former company's premier client and how it ultimately led to the failure of his company. Zach also recounted chasing an evil traitor across the country, tracking him down in Ecuador, and eventually seeing him behind bars. He left out the gruesome details of the shootout that occurred in the New Jersey high-rise apartment. The President had told Mr. Hollins abut the horrible event, but, knowing it would be a painful memory, Mr. Hollins never asked.

During the conversation, Zach learned that Mr. Hollins had also served in the Navy, but in a different specialty. Mr. Hollins had been a Cryptologic Intelligence Technician, serving in places he still could not talk about. Both men had a lifelong interest in sophisticated communication systems. In the short time span of thirty minutes, Zach and Mr. Hollins were already becoming friends. Zach smiled as he finished his second cup of coffee and sat back in his chair. He would have to call the President and thank him for recommending him to Mr. Hollins. This opportunity was exactly what he was looking for and exactly what he needed.

Mr. Hollins looked up at the clock and said, "Hey, Zach, how about lunch?"

"Absolutely. I'm starved," Zach answered.

"What sounds good? Italian, Chinese, Mexican?"

" How about Italian?"

"Italian it is," Mr. Hollins agreed. "I know just the place. Come on. Let's go."

Zach followed Mr. Hollins out of the office, down a short hallway, and out the back door into the rear parking lot. Mr. Hollins fished a key fob out of his jacket pocket and punched the Unlock button. The headlights flashed on a shiny, black BMW 735i.

"Climb in and buckle up," Mr. Hollins advised.

"Nice car!" Zach exclaimed as he slid into the passenger seat and fastened his seat belt.

"Cost a lot of money, but it's good PR for potential clients," Mr. Hollins declared. "That's also why we have the expensive décor in the office. We've been very successful and I see no reason it shouldn't show."

"Seems reasonable to me," Zach said.

"And as far as the car goes, I like it," Mr. Hollins chimed, as he looked over at Zach with a big grin on his face.

The two men spent nearly an hour and a half at the Buca di Beppo Italian restaurant. It was obvious that Mr. Hollins was a frequent and valued customer of the restaurant. The owner himself came out to greet them and made certain they had whatever they desired. Zach could hardly drag himself up out of his chair after feasting on salad, breadsticks, and his absolute favorite, Pasta Carbonara.

"Ooof. Boy, I certainly wouldn't want to do that every day," Zach chuckled, patting his stomach.

"Yeah, great food isn't it?"

"I'll say. Now I need a two-hour nap," Zach laughed.

"Come on, Zach. Let's get back to the office," Mr. Hollins said, guiding Zach toward the door.

After arriving back at the office, Mr. Hollins spent a long time showing Zach the communications server room and explaining the equipment, the company's operations, and where Zach would fit into the company structure and what would be expected of him. The two men headed back to Mr. Hollins' office and were met by Amber Hickman, the company's administrative assistant. She had several forms for Zach to sign. She laid out a W-4 and an I-9 on the desk. Ms. Hickman had already filled in all the required information. Zach signed the forms in the appropriate places. Ms. Hickman gathered up the forms and left the office, pulling the door closed on her way out.

"As I told you on the phone, normally, you will only need to come to the office two or three days a month for strategy meetings or equipment issues when they arise. You can live anywhere you want as long as it's not too far."

"Mr. Hollins, I...."

"Hold on, Zach," Mr. Hollins interrupted. "You are *not* going to do well here if you keep calling me Mister Hollins. Call me Grant. That's an order."

"Yes sir, Grant, sir," Zach laughed as he stood up, stomped his right foot, and gave Mr. Hollins a British style salute.

"Funny, very funny," Mr. Hollins snickered. "Now, the important stuff. Your salary starts as of today. I know you just got into town yesterday. Take a few days and find a place to live. The company will cover a hotel until you find something. When you get something lined up, let Amber know the address so our technician can come out and set up a computer, router, and whatever else might be needed."

"Grant, I can't tell you how much I appreciate this opportunity and all the assistance you're offering."

"You are welcome, Zach. By the way, I would suggest you look across the river in South Carolina. You might try around Hardeeville or Pritchardville. You can get more house for the money over there. Take 17A across the Talmadge Memorial Bridge to South Carolina, then follow 17A north. It'll take you right to Hardeeville. There's a Best Western hotel on the south edge of town. Any questions?"

So full of excitement he could hardly think, Zach responded "I'm certain I'll have questions later, but right now I can't think of a thing."

"Okay then, I need to finish a bid proposal before I quit for the day. Keep me informed how the house hunt goes and call my cell if you need anything. And I mean anything." Mr. Hollins slipped one of his business cards from a holder on the desk, scribbled his personal cell phone number on the back, and handed it to Zach.

"Thanks again, Grant. I'll find something as quick as I can and let you know."

Zach exited the office, amazed by the Spanish Moss hanging from the tree branches. Having spent no time in the southeast, he found the sight of the odd silver-gray strands somewhat spooky yet intriguing. With plenty of daylight left, he took a stroll down the street and explore the picturesque sights of Savannah that he had heard so much about. Two blocks down the street as he strolled along underneath a Spanish-moss-laden tree canopy along one of Savannah's cobblestone streets, an other-worldly feeling struck him as he looked further down the street.

The scene reminded him of a question posed by the writer of an article he had read in a "Local Attractions" magazine provided by the hotel. Intrigued by the article, Zach had slipped the magazine in his notebook before leaving the hotel. He continued walking for half a block, sat down on an old iron bench under a huge live oak tree, and pulled the magazine out of his notebook.

Thumbing through the pages of the magazine, he located the article. In the first paragraph, the writer asked, "*What is it about Georgia's First City that captures the souls of spirits and spurs them to stick around?*" The writer continued, "*Many news outlets include Savannah on their lists of 'America's Most Haunted Cities', claiming that Savannah, along with New Orleans and Salem, have been centers of paranormal activity for centuries.*"

Zach stopped reading and looked up and down the street at the historic, antebellum mansions, some dating back to the early eighteen hundreds. He wondered what dark secrets might be hidden inside those historic, old buildings. "*If they could only talk,*" he thought to himself.

He went back to the article and continued reading. The writer said to answer the question of how the city came to have such mysterious energy, one must dig into the city's somber history to discover the chilling reasons for Savannah's supernatural side. The article listed four categories of catastrophic conflicts that occurred throughout the centuries: bloody battles, like those resulting from the Civil War; deadly diseases, such as the ten epidemics, like the one in 1820 that decimated a tenth of the city's population; fearsome fires, such as the one that destroyed five hundred buildings in a single afternoon; and mysterious murders, like the particularly horrific murder of three sisters at 432 Abercorn Street, only a few blocks from the hotel in which Zach had stayed.

Even though he would like to have continued walking along the picturesque street, he needed to get back to his car and head for Hardeeville. He hurried back to his car, climbed in, and pulled out of the parking lot. In his mind, he was certain he remembered seeing Highway 17A on the online map he had looked at earlier. It became obvious he was mistaken. After driving around for nearly twenty minutes, he was hopelessly lost. Putting his male ego aside, he stopped at a convenience store and asked the clerk how to get to 17A.

The clerk informed Zach that 17A was also called Speedway Boulevard. Zach backtracked eight blocks and turned onto Quaker Street and then up onto the access ramp for 17A. He merged into traffic and drove across the bridge. The Talmadge Memorial Bridge was new, having been built to replace an old and outdated cantilever truss style bridge. Zach marveled as the bridge rose to one hundred eighty-five feet above the river to provide vertical navigational clearance for oceangoing vessels entering the Port of Savannah.

Twenty-five minutes later Zach completed the seventeen mile trip to Hardeeville and pulled into the parking lot of the Best Western hotel. Still early in the day, the hotel had a room available. Armed with a guest key card, he went back out to his car, grabbed his roller bag, and headed for the room. Inside the room, he dumped the bag on the bed, dug out his laptop, and turned it on. Once he had hung up his clothes, the laptop had booted up and was ready to use. He entered the WIFI password the hotel clerk had given him, opened a browser window, and began searching for realty companies.

Browsing through the long list of realty companies returned by the browser, he clicked the link for Oak Country Realty. He scanned the company's list of agents and selected a gentleman by the name of Thomas Corwin who covered the area from Hardeeville to Pritchardville. "That'll work," Zach said as he grabbed his cellphone and dialed the number listed beside Mr. Corwin's name. He introduced himself to Mr. Corwin and set an appointment for nine o'clock the next morning.

Zach had an odd feeling as he ended the call and dropped the cellphone on the bed. "*Everything is going unbelievably well*," he thought to himself. "*Maybe too well.*"

He shrugged off the uneasy feeling and headed back out to his car to go find something to eat.

Windward Court (35 Mi. SW of Washington, DC)
Dumfries, Virginia

Horns blared. Chevy Man, startled awake, jerked the steering wheel, guiding the old Chevy SUV back into the center lane of Interstate 95. Exhausted from the five hundred mile trip from South Carolina, he had briefly nodded off and veered partway into the fast lane. He blinked his eyes vigorously and shook his head to chase away the tiredness. A sigh of relief escaped his lips when he looked over at the side of the highway and noticed the sign announcing the exit for Virginia Highway 234. On the home stretch, three miles further down the highway, he flipped on the turn signal and merged into the far right lane.

After passing over the highway, he moved over onto the exit, made a two hundred seventy degree loop around the cloverleaf, and drove onto Highway 234, also called Dumfries Road. He followed Dumfries Road for two and one-half miles, then turned right onto Waterway Drive. A few blocks later, a turn onto South Lake Boulevard, a short block on Breeze Way, then he turned onto Windward Court, his street. Soon after turning onto Windward Court, Chevy Man punched the button on the garage door remote.

He turned onto the driveway that led to a grand-colonial style house overlooking the northern tip of Lake Montclair and quickly drove the old Chevy SUV into the far outside stall of the garage. Having punched the remote button when the SUV was barely half-way into the garage, the door missed the back of the SUV by a mere two inches. Chevy Man climbed out, stretched to relieve his tired and sore muscles, pulled a large grey tarp off a shelf, and threw it over the old Chevy SUV.

He pushed the door to the mudroom open, entered the house, and hurried straight through to the master bedroom. The house was still and quiet. His wife was at the Country Club for her weekly bridge club and his three children were already off to school. After a quick shave and change of clothes, he rushed back to the kitchen and grabbed a bottle of orange juice from the refrigerator and a package of chocolate-covered mini donuts from the pantry. Having gotten off to a late start, he had driven all night, stopping only once for a quick fill-up of fuel, which he paid for with cash. It was going to be a long, gruelling day with no sleep. He would definitely need the energy boost from the juice and donuts.

Hurrying back out to the garage, he climbed into a black Lincoln Navigator and backed out of the garage onto Windward Court. Reversing the route he had followed just minutes earlier, he drove the three and one-half miles back to Interstate 95. He turned onto the entrance ramp and glanced over his left shoulder, looking for an opening in traffic. Seeing a long line of semi-trucks in the far right lane, he mashed the accelerator to the floor. About to run out of merge lane, he pulled over into the lane of traffic, much to the displeasure of a big-rig truck that had to apply his brakes to avoid a collision. Chevy Man glanced in his rearview mirror and saw the big-rig's driver flashing him an obscene gesture.

The short thirty-five mile trip to Washington, D.C., would take nearly an hour. Even though it was past the morning rush hour, traffic was still moderately heavy. Once he hit the city, traffic would become much worse, exacerbated by the ever-present orange construction cones and the increased security concerns. Fifty-two minutes later, angry and frustrated with the ever-present idiots on the highways, he turned onto Seventeenth Street NW and pulled up to the White House West Gate. Chevy Man pulled out his credentials wallet and presented it to the security guard for inspection.

The security guard snapped to attention. "Good morning, Sir," he barked, motioning to the other security guard to open the gate.

Chevy Man drove through the gate, turned left onto West Executive Avenue NW, and parked in the staff parking area. He hauled his nearly six-foot frame out of the Navigator and headed for the side entrance of the West Wing. Inside the West Wing, he made his way down a long hallway and entered a dimly lit office at the northwest corner of the building.

"Greetings, Esteemed Knight," a voice called out of the darkness. A tall figure dressed in a dark grey, pinstriped suit stepped out of the shadow, his right arm extended, bent ninety degrees at the elbow, and two fingers extended upward in the grand hailing sign. "Your humble servant," Chevy Man answered, bowing at the waist. "To serve you and the Holy Order is my great joy."

"Is it done?" Mr. Suit asked.

"Soon, very soon," Chevy Man replied.

"Need I remind you of the dire consequences if we fail in our task?"

"No, Master. I am well aware of the great peril if I should fail my duty," Chevy Man answered quickly. "Everything is in place. The devices are ready. The evidence is flawless and will be planted soon."

"I hope for my sake and for yours you are correct," Mr. Suit exclaimed. "What about the *product's* potency?"

"Do not worry. It is many times what will be required. It has already been moved to the designated location."

"Good. This will be our last chance. How will it be released in multiple locations?"

"The Sovereign Grand Prince will pick up the delivery vector from the lab and then it and the *product* will be split and moved to the release locations."

"What happens after that?" Mr. Suit asked.

"Then we will go into hiding until the vector dies out and all those that have been infected have died. The planted evidence will lead straight to the President. The people will revolt and demand his head on a platter. The current administration will fall into chaos. With President Cantwell and his loyal allies out of the way, we will seize power and the Order will rule forever."

The two men shook hands, slipped out of the office unseen, and went about their daily tasks.

Chapter Twelve

Suitland Federal Center
Office of Director of Naval Intelligence
Suitland, Maryland

Soft snoring filled the room. Rear Admiral Charles Hadley sat with his hands lying in his lap and his chin resting on his chest. Exhausted from coming in several hours early to complete critical staffing reports for his superior, he had drifted off to sleep lulled by the soft whirring of the ventilation system. The intercom on his desk buzzed, startling him awake.

"Yes, Jenny," he answered, suppressing a yawn. "What is it?"

"There's a phone call for you," Jenny, his assistant, replied.

"Take a message. Tell them I'm busy and I'll call them later," Admiral Hadley said as he hung up the receiver.

A few seconds later, the intercom buzzed again. Jenny announced, "It's the Director of the CIA. He says it's urgent. He's on line two."

Admiral Hadley punched the blinking button for line two and asked his old friend, James Sandberg, "Jim, what can I do for you?"

"Is he there yet?" Director Sandberg asked.

"I would suspect so, but I haven't received confirmation of that." Admiral Hadley answered. "Jim, I have to tell you I don't think this was handled correctly. He should have been told. No sir, it's not right at all."

"I understand, but we need eyes on the ground," Director Sandberg insisted. "We're not ready to reveal what we know, as yet. This whole thing may turn out to be nothing. But if it turns out to be what we fear, we have a real problem. A real serious problem." The Director continued, "I probably shouldn't tell you this. This information is classified strictly *need to know*. I'm taking a huge risk, but I need your help. You must assure me you will not share this information with *anyone*."

"You helped me out on that last fiasco, so I'll agree. Tell me what is so urgent."

"Have you ever heard of a violent extremist called *The Snake*?"

"No. I can't say I've ever heard that name. Who is he?"

"Most people think he's just a myth," Director Sandberg said. "But just yesterday I was contacted by Thomas Calhoun, Director of the CIA's Special Activities Division. He said he has reason to believe he is very real. I can't give you specifics. Suffice it to say, I believe Director Calhoun."

"Okay, so how does that affect me?" Admiral Hadley questioned.

"If even half the stories they tell about him are true, he is the most evil, sadistic individual to ever walk the earth. He kills without warning and for the pure pleasure of it. His favorite technique is to slit the throats of his victims. Again, if the stories are true, he has over one hundred kills."

"He sounds like a real sweetheart. But again, I ask, what does this have to do with me?"

"It is said he has an elaborate network of followers. These followers are said to be extremely powerful and highly placed. To date, all efforts to penetrate the network have failed. It is well hidden and extremely secretive. We fear it may even reach to top levels in our own government. Therefore, I can use only people I am *absolutely* certain I can trust. You are one of those individuals, Admiral."

"Okay, Jim. You have my attention. Go on."

"Director Calhoun's UK informant said he came across evidence linking him to Frank Porter. Calhoun believes The Snake was the mastermind behind the entire plot."

"What!" Admiral Hadley bellowed, his nostrils flaring. "Where is he? I'll kill him myself. I'll gut him like a fish."

"Unfortunately, we don't know where he is. After putting pressure on the informant, one of the Special Activities Division agents uncovered a master forger that was to provide documents for someone called *al-Ta'abin*, which is Arabic for "The Snake". They were tracking an accomplice of the forger, but when they found him, his throat had been slit. When they went to arrest the forger, they also found him with his throat slit. In the forger's residence, they found blank passports from numerous countries, including the United States. They believe he is traveling out of the country, but they aren't certain exactly where."

"Is there any way to track him?" Admiral Hadley asked.

"They have no idea what name he might be using on the phony travel documents," Director Sandberg answered. "So, the simple answer is no."

"Do they have any guesses?"

"The evidence I mentioned earlier ties to part of the reason for arranging the recommendation for your man. Our best guess is that The Snake is heading for the United States, perhaps somewhere in the Southeast. We have alerted Customs and Immigration, but without a physical description, we don't hold out much hope of identifying him."

"Can't they squeeze the informant a little more?"

"That's not possible Admiral," Director Sandberg pointed out. "The informant and his handler have dropped off the face of the Earth. The handler was an off-the-books, deep-cover operative. He carried no ID, no cellphone, no laptop, no SAT phone, no electronics, absolutely nothing of any kind that would link him to anyone or any place. All communications were passed strictly face-to-face. The agency has literally scoured the ground. They turned over every leaf, every stick, and every twig. They looked behind every bush, every hedge, and every tree. They talked to anyone and everyone that might have had contact with him. He and the informant have simply vanished. So, as you might imagine, the trail has gone dead."

"Do they know anything?" Admiral Hadley questioned.

"The most worrisome thing is a single word the informant passed to his contact two days ago. That word
was—*Hadhramaut*. Roughly translated it means 'Death Comes'
or 'Place of Death' or something close to that. It really has the
intelligence community spooked and I mean *spooked*! They're
telling me they believe this 'Snake' character is pure evil and
given the influence he has over his adherents and the vast
reach of his network, he is a grave threat. They are still trying
to track down additional leads, but it is doubtful they will turn
up anything. Beyond that, I can't tell you anymore."

"So, what do you want from me?"

"I need to know where your man is?"

"As I said before, I don't even know if he has arrived
yet."

"This is critical, Chuck," Director Sandberg urged. "We
think he is somehow involved in this. We know there was a
link between him and Frank Porter. It is imperative he is located and warned about this monster."

"Okay, Jim," Admiral Hadley agreed. "I will call the President and get him to assign a Secret Service agent to me. I'll
send him to the area with instructions to locate him ASAP."

"Let me know when you locate him," Director Sandberg
ordered.

"When I know something, you'll know something," Admiral Hadley replied as he hung up the phone and reached for
his Daytimer. He flipped to the phone section and ran his finger down the list, stopping at the number for President Cantwell's personal cellphone. He punched in the number and
waited.

After five rings, a male voice answered, "Admiral Hadley,
I'm in a meeting. Can I call you back?"

"This is critical, Mister President. I'm afraid it can't wait."

"Well, be quick. What do you need?" the President asked,
turning away from the men seated in front of his desk.

"I just got off the phone with CIA Director Sandberg. I
can't share specifics of what he told me, but there is an urgent
need to locate our mutual friend. The one you helped get a job.

The Director told me they have uncovered a grave threat and they believe it is connected to our friend."

"How do you suggest we do that?"

"I need a Secret Service agent assigned to me for the duration. Our friend's life may depend on it."

"Stay by your phone," President Cantwell advised. "I'll call Secret Service Director Andrew Holt and have him call you."

"Thank you, Mister President," Admiral Hadley said as he hung up the phone. He sat waiting with his hand on the receiver. Two minutes later the phone rang. He lifted the receiver and said, "Admiral Hadley."

"This is Director Holt. The President said you needed an agent and that I should call you and give you whatever assistance you need."

"Thank you for calling back so quickly. I need an agent assigned to me for the duration of an issue that has come up. I need to locate someone ASAP. I'm sorry I can't tell you more, but I was advised the matter is classified strictly *need to know*."

"Very well. The President was quite clear that this is a high priority issue. I will assign Agent Anthony Kanagy to you for as long as you need him. How should he contact you?"

"Have him call this number immediately and thank you again, Director Holt."

"Consider it done," Director Holt answered as he hung up.

Admiral Hadley sat back in his chair, deep in thought as he formulated a plan to share with Agent Kanagy.

Chatham County Medical Examiner
East 67th Street, Savannah, Georgia

Dr. Luke Tilton, Chatham County Assistant Medical Examiner, sat hunched over his desk, making notes on an unfinished autopsy report spread open in front of him. He glanced up when he heard his office door open and cringed when he saw

Dr. Mark Cross, the Chief Medical Examiner, storm into the room. An irritating squeak emanated from every step as he plodded across the office in his rubber-soled shoes, stopping in front of the desk. Dr. Tilton stared at the much older man, waiting for the usual tirade he expected. Dr. Cross, nearing seventy, had a head full of snow white hair and a permanent scowl, accentuated by his sagging jowls. Dr. Cross, serving as chief medical examiner for nearly thirty years, had gained many influential allies. With those relationships came great authority and also great power. Dr. Cross refused to retire, becoming a permanent fixture at the medical examiner's office. The red splotches dotting his normally waxen appearance alerted Dr. Tilton that he was once again going to be the victim of one of Dr. Cross' tongue lashings.

"Doctor Tilton, where is the autopsy report for Victoria Pickett?" Dr. Cross roared. "It was supposed to have been completed yesterday."

"I'm still waiting for the tissue and blood results from the lab," Dr. Tilton offered in defense.

"It's your responsibility to see that all the tests are completed in a timely manner, *Doctor*," Dr. Cross bellowed. "It's also your responsibility to see that those results are entered on the final report."

"But I ca….,"

"I don't care what you think you can or cannot do," Dr. Cross interrupted. "I suggest you follow protocol and get that report finished."

"Protocol says autopsy findings are to be processed in the order decedents are received and logged into the system," Dr. Tilton advised.

Dr. Cross' face grew even more red as he bent over and looked directly at Dr. Tilton, his lips drawn tight and fire dancing in his eyes. "I'm the Chief Medical Examiner here," Dr. Cross snarled. "I say what gets done and when it gets done. The report for Misses Pickett is critical, and I want the findings completed before the end of the day. I suggest you get busy if you want to continue working here."

Dr. Tilton started to protest, but Dr. Cross had already turned away and was squeaking his way toward the door. Even though he knew it was wrong, he hoped that old buzzard would have a stroke and soon. He quickly made a few more notes on the autopsy report lying open in front of him, signed it, and laid it on the completed stack.

He sighed out of exasperation, shook his head, picked up the phone, and punched in the number for the forensics lab, in the basement two floors below his feet. Cradling the phone between his shoulder and ear, he dug through the pile of unfinished autopsy reports, looking for the preliminary findings for Victoria Jean Pickett. He located the file and flipped it open while he waited for the lab to answer.

"Forensics Lab. May I help you?" forensics technician Dennis Hudson answered, out of breath, having been busy on the other side of the lab.

"This is Doctor Tilton. I need the tissue and blood results for Victoria Jean Pickett. Doctor Cross is on the warpath, again."

"Hang on a minute, Doc," lab tech Hudson replied. Dr. Tilton drummed his fingers, waiting for the lab tech to locate the results. Getting impatient, Dr. Tilton was about to hang up when he heard Hudson's voice "Doc, I have the preliminary report right here in front of me. The tissue sample results are here, but it does not show any blood test results."

"What?" Dr. Tilton barked, knowing Dr. Cross would blow a gasket if he found out some of the results were missing. "Why aren't they there? I performed the autopsy myself. All the samples were turned in together."

"I don't know, Doc," lab tech Hudson answered. "I went over and checked all the samples that haven't been catalogued. That's what took me so long. I double checked everything. There are no blood samples for Victoria Jean Pickett in the lab."

"Well, you should know. It's your job to keep track of the samples," Dr. Tilton snapped, picturing an image in his mind of Human Resources handing him his final paycheck. "Great.

Just great! Print off what you do have and bring it up to my office immediately."

"Yes, sir," lab tech Hudson replied.

Dr. Tilton dropped the receiver back in its cradle. Developing a ferocious headache, he sat there rubbing his temples. The stress of working with dead bodies in all manner of conditions, grieving families, and a screaming, unreasonable boss once again made him question his choice to become a pathologist. Still rubbing his temples, his attention had not yet returned to the files on his desk when he heard a knock on his door.

"Come in," he called out. He looked up and saw lab tech Hudson rushing into the room. Hudson stopped in front of the desk and handed him a sheet of yellow paper.

"Sorry I yelled earlier, Dennis" Dr. Tilton apologized. "It's been a long and very trying day."

"Doc, I looked everywhere. The blood samples aren't anywhere to be found."

"Okay. I'll ask McAlpin what could have happened to them the next time I see him."

"See ya, Doc," Hudson said as he turned and rushed back to the lab to complete mounting the tissue samples he had been working on when Dr. Tilton called.

Dr. Tilton picked up the incomplete report lab tech Hudson had handed him and began scanning down the listed results. "These finding can't be right," he barked, rising out of his chair. He scanned the results a second time, a perplexed look spreading across his face. The tissue results did not indicate the slightest evidence of hemorrhagic fever. "That's not possible," Dr. Tilton exclaimed, remembering the significant bleeding he had noted during the autopsy. Dr. Cross was going to be livid because he simply could not sign off on a cause of death with such unexplained and baffling test results. Dr. Tilton was adamant he would not finalize the report until the blood samples were located or new samples were obtained.

There had to have been a mixup in either the reports or, perhaps, the samples were from a different decedent. He slipped on his lab coat, grabbed the lab report, and headed for the lab, determined to clear up the mystery.

"Hey, Dennis," Dr. Tilton called out as he pushed the lab door open. "I want to recheck the sample designators with the tag on the Pickett body."

"Doc, I'm in the middle of mounting these tissue sections on slides," Hudson protested. "Can't it wait a few minutes?"

"I guess it can. I'll send Dr. Cross down here and you can explain to him why the report he demanded by the end of day will not be complete."

Hudson jerked upright, "Well, if you're going to threaten me with having to talk to Doctor *Grouch*, I'll get right on it."

Together they walked over to the cold storage drawers and located the drawer that contained Victoria Pickett's body. Hudson pulled the latch, opened the door, and slid the body out far enough to expose the body bag label. Dr. Tilton snapped a photograph of the tag with his cellphone. He nodded his head and Hudson shoved the body back into the drawer and closed the door. Dr. Tilton compared the tag's barcode from the photo with the specimen container barcodes that had been affixed to the lab findings report.

"What?" he exclaimed when, much to his surprise, the specimen container barcodes matched the body bag barcode which matched to the decedent, Victoria Pickett. Completely baffled, he had fully expected to find a mismatch. "This just can't be!" he objected, shoving his hands in the pockets of his lab coat. The fingers of his right hand touched the vacutainers he had dropped in his lab coat pocket. He pulled the vacutainers out of his pocket and compared the barcodes to those on the finding report. The barcodes matched. "Maybe this will clear up the mystery," he said, handing the tubes to Hudson. "Dennis, I want the blood in these vacutainers tested immediately. Call me the instant you have the results. I'll be in my office."

"Will do, Doc," Hudson answered.

Dr. Tilton returned to his office and sat at his desk waiting for the results of the blood tests. Fifteen minutes later, the phone rang. "Doctor Tilton, what did you find out?"

"You aren't going to believe this," lab tech Hudson responded. "The blood type of the blood in the vacutainers does not match the blood type of the tissue samples listed on the report."

"Just as I thought," Dr. Tilton remarked. "I want the hardcopy of that report and the remainder of the blood samples up here, NOW! And do not talk to anyone on your way up. Capisce?"

"Understood. On my way," Hudson replied.

Two minutes later, lab tech Hudson pushed the door to Dr. Tilton's office open without knocking. He rushed over to the desk and handed the blood sample report to Dr. Tilton.

"Is this the only copy of the report?"

"Yes, that's the only hardcopy. The electronic results are still in the analyzer's memory."

"The blood samples please."

"Doc, what do I do with the electronic results?" Hudson asked as he handed over the vacutainers.

"Delete them as soon as you return to the lab. Do not mention this to anyone." Dr. Tilton noticed the worried look on lab tech Hudson's face. "Don't be concerned. If there is anything said about missing results, which there shouldn't be, I will tell Doctor Cross I ordered you to do it."

"What's going on, Doc?" Hudson asked. "How could the samples get mixed up?"

"The samples didn't get mixed up, Dennis," Dr. Tilton answered. "They were deliberately switched. If it had been only a mixup, the tissue samples and the blood samples would not have had the same barcode numbers."

"But why would anyone do that?"

"That is exactly what I intend to find out. Get back to the lab and delete those results before someone sees them."

"Let me know what you find out."

"Will do," Dr. Tilton assured Hudson as he held the door open for him to leave.

"Why would someone switch tissue samples," Dr. Tilton asked under his breath, repeating the lab tech's question. "What would be the reason and what would they have to gain?" he added.

Dr. Tilton became more and more suspicious with each passing minute. He stood staring out his second-floor window at the Memorial University Medical Center four blocks away. Not knowing who had switched the samples or why, he felt he could no longer trust the medical examiner's lab to test the blood samples. Independent testing of the blood and tissue samples would be necessary to verify his discovery.

Not knowing what happened to the original autopsy samples, he rushed down to the basement and located lab tech Dennis Hudson. Together they climbed into personal protective equipment and entered the examination suite. With lab tech Hudson's help, they moved Victoria Pickett's body from the storage drawer to a cadaver table. Dr. Tilton cut the evidence seal and rolled the outer body bag out of the way. He unzipped the inner body bag and folded it out of the way just enough to allow him to extract new lung tissue samples. While lab tech Hudson sealed the new samples into a specimen bag, Dr. Tilton zipped the inner bag closed. He zipped up the outer body bag, affixed a new piece of evidence tape, and signed it. Together they moved the body back to the storage drawer. In less than thirty minutes, Dr. Tilton was headed back to his office with new samples.

Feeling the samples would not be safe in his office, he decided to protect the samples by sending them offsite.

Victoria Jean Pickett's incomplete autopsy report lay open on the desk before him. It indicated no unusual findings and no cause of death, but the latest testing of the blood samples he had discovered in his lab coat pocket said otherwise. "*Where can I send the report and samples that they will be safe?*" he asked himself. After much thought, he said, "I know." He reached across his desk for his address book.

He grabbed an infectious materials, specimen bag, placed the vacutainers and lung tissue samples from areas that had shown the greatest damage in it, sealed it tight, and signed his name across the red tape seal. He scribbled a quick note and stuffed the note, copies of both lab reports, the peripheral blood films, and the infectious materials specimen bag into a padded overnight, clinical shipping pack. He addressed a mailing label to a former classmate, Dr. Michael Wilson, a senior epidemiologist at the Georgia Department of Public Health Lab, and stuck it on the shipping pack.

He swiveled his chair around and opened the email application on his computer. After typing a more detailed explanation of the tissue samples in the shipping pack, he clicked send, closed the email application, and powered down the computer.

Dr. Cross would be furious when he did not receive the report he had demanded, but Dr. Tilton did not care. Solving the puzzling mystery was far more important. He picked up the shipping pack, grabbed his briefcase, and headed for the elevator before Dr. Cross could have a chance to interfere. Getting off the elevator on the ground floor, he stepped out onto the street and dropped the shipping pack in a drop box at the corner. He headed for the parking garage, not noticing the man that exited the coffee shop across the street and followed him.

Chapter Thirteen

Best Western Hotel
Hardeeville, South Carolina

Zach Templeton sat in the Best Western Hotel's breakfast area, nursing his second cup of coffee, which had become lukewarm. Zach had awakened early, unable to get back to sleep. An early riser for his entire career, it had become a habit. Rather than sit in his empty room, he went down to the hotel's breakfast area.

After finishing a light breakfast, he had grabbed a copy of the local newspaper to kill time. Zach finished the newspaper and was disinterestedly thumbing through a magazine waiting for the realtor to arrive. Zach looked up and watched a man enter the breakfast area and begin surveying the occupants. The man's eyes settled on Zach. He waved and started toward the table where Zach was seated.

Upon reaching the table, the man held out his hand and announced, "I'm Thomas Corwin from Oak Country Realty."

Zach stood and grasped the man's hand. "I'm Zach Templeton. Glad to meet you, Mr. Corwin."

Zach sat down and pointed toward the empty chair on the opposite side of the table. "I'm really eager to find something and get settled. From our conversation yesterday, were you able to find some properties we can look at?"

"Yes, I have selected several properties I think you will like. Do you want to finish your coffee before we start out?"

"No. It's my second and it's gone cold anyway. I would just as soon get started."

"Okay, then. You said you wanted something isolated and quiet. I think we should start with a couple of houses down toward the unincorporated community of Pritchardville that fit that description. That will give me an idea of exactly what you are looking for. My car is right out front. Let's get started."

"Sounds good," Zach answered as he pushed the chair back and stood up. He dropped the half-finished cup of coffee in a trash receptacle and followed Mr. Corwin out to his car.

Zach and Mr. Corwin climbed into a light grey Dodge van. Mr. Corwin backed away from the curb, exited the hotel parking lot, and turned left onto Main Street. Mr. Corwin continued driving south on Main Street, which changed to State Route Forty-Six at the edge of town. The two men engaged in idle chatter as they headed toward Pritchardville. Still early morning, Zach noticed slight wisps of fog still clinging to the bases of the trees and bushes as the houses thinned out and they passed small farmsteads.

An hour and a half later, they had viewed three rental houses, none of which excited Zach. Standing in the lane on the third house, Mr. Corwin asked, "Well, Zach, what do you think so far?"

"The houses themselves were okay, but they seem rather close to their neighbors," Zach answered. "I was hoping for something a little more isolated and quiet. I've been living in the city and was hoping for something different."

Mr. Corwin thought for a minute, then said, "I have an idea. Let me make a quick phone call." Mr. Corwin walked to the front of his car, lifted his cellphone from its case, and punched in a number. After a short thirty second conversation, he returned to where Zach was standing.

"Someone I know had mentioned to me they were considering renting a house they own. They had a death in the family and really need the income. It's a beautiful house on Big House Plantation Road. It's really isolated. I think it might be just what you're looking for."

Zach tried to keep a mental note of the route to the house, but he lost track after the fifth turn. Zach decided ten seconds after Mr. Corwin turned down the lane, taken by the house's incredible post-card like setting. The house sat back seventy-five yards from the road on a two acre park-like lot surrounded on three sides by lush woods. Mr. Corwin drove up to the porch and stopped the car. Zach climbed out of the car and stood captivated by the beauty, but especially taken by the peacefulness. "*Wow, Angie would have loved this place*," Zach thought as he stood there listening to birds singing.

"I thought you would like it," Mr. Corwin chuckled, seeing the faraway look in Zach's eyes. "Come on. Let's have a look inside."

Mr. Corwin stepped up on the porch, pulled open the screen door, unlocked the front door, and pushed it open for Zach. "It might be a little musty. The owners intended to remodel the house, but because of the death, the house has been closed up for a while. Walk around and have a look while I open a couple of windows to let in some fresh air."

Zach wandered through the foyer and into the living room. He peeked into two bedrooms and ended up in the kitchen. Zach stood looking out of the window above the sink when Mr. Corwin walked into the kitchen.

"Marvelous view for washing dishes isn't it." Mr. Corwin said.

"Nice hardly does it justice," Zach exclaimed. "I've got to see this."

Zach unlocked the back door and walked out onto the back porch. "Does the property include the bridge?" he asked.

"Yes. The property line is about twenty feet beyond the stream that flows under the bridge."

"I'll be right back," Zach said as he stepped off the porch and headed for the bridge. Mr. Corwin leaned against the porch railing and smiled, reasonably certain his client had already made up his mind.

Zach spent a few minutes standing on the arched wooden bridge, staring down at the crystal-clear stream that passed under the bridge. He watched as the water bubbled over and around the moss-covered rocks lining the stream. With his decision made, he turned and trotted back up to the house. Zach stepped up onto the porch and the two men walked back into the house. Zach stepped back over in front of the kitchen window and took one last look at the view.

"I noticed there is furniture in the bedrooms and a couple of other pieces in some of the other rooms," Zach said. "Is that included with the house?"

"In the real estate business, everything is negotiable," Mr. Corwin answered. "Does that mean you have made a decision?"

"Yes sir," Zach replied. "It's perfect. Absolutely perfect."

"Let's head back to my office. Then I'll call the owners and see what we can work out."

Thirty-five minutes later, seated in Mr. Corwin's office, Zach asked Mr. Corwin, "Can you ask the owners of the property if it would be possible to move in right away. I'd be willing to pay an extra month's rent."

"Never hurts to ask," Mr. Corwin replied as he picked up the phone.

Zach listened as Mr. Corwin discussed Zach's offer with the owners of the property. At one point, Mr. Corwin held the phone away from his ear and informed Zach that Ms. Anna Mae Watts was getting some pushback from her father, Edwin. He said it sounded like Mr. Watts didn't really want to rent the property at all. Zach's heart sank, afraid he was going to be unable to rent the house.

Mr. Corwin put the phone back to his ear and continued listening to the conversation on the other end. After several minutes, he perked up and said, "That's great. I'll tell Mister Templeton. And thank you Miss Watts."

Mr. Corwin hung up the phone and turned toward Zach. "Miss Watts told me her father finally agreed and that your offer is quite generous. She said you can have the keys immediately and they will sign necessary paperwork later. And she said you can use as much of the furniture as you want."

"That's wonderful," Zach beamed, smiling from ear to ear. Zach slipped his checkbook out of his pocket and wrote out a check for three months rent and handed it to Mr. Corwin.

"I'll fill in a standard rental contract with all the details and you can sign it. I'll get it over to the Watts for their signatures in a day or two. Here is the key to the front door. I was told it works for the back door as well."

"I've got a couple of stops I want to make. Can I take care of those and then stop back by and sign the agreement?"

"Certainly. That would be fine."

"Is there a furniture store you would recommend?" Zach asked.

"That's easy. There's only one here in Hardeeville," Mr. Corwin replied. "Babcock Furniture. Go three blocks north, turn right, two blocks, you'll see it on the left. You can't miss it. Tell Glenn I sent you."

Zach shook Mr. Corwin's hand, thanked him profusely, and hurried out the door to his car. His first stop was Babcock's Furniture store, where he purchased a new bedroom set and a modest living room grouping. After the furniture store, he made one last stop at a supermarket to buy a few groceries, a coffee pot, a set of dishes, and some cleaning supplies.

He stopped at Oak Country Realty on his way out of town to sign the rental agreement. Zach attempted to follow the same route Mr. Corwin had taken to the house. His plan went well until he reached New River Road. From that point on, it became apparent he had made a wrong turn somewhere as he no longer recognized any of the road names. At the next intersection, he made a u-turn and pulled over to the side of the road. He called Mr. Corwin and explained his dilemma. Zach found a scrap of paper and wrote down the directions Mr. Corwin gave him. With the written directions poised on the seat beside him, Zach retraced his route until he came to the first road listed in the directions. Following the correct directions, he arrived at the house in less than ten minutes.

Zach climbed out of the car and stood there admiring the scene before him. "Remote and quiet, exactly what I need," he said. He carried in the groceries and put the cold items in the refrigerator. On his second trip out to the car, he grabbed the cleaning supplies and dumped them inside the front door. He glanced at his watch. The man at the furniture store said they would deliver the furniture between 4:00 and 5:00 o'clock. That would give him plenty of time to get some cleaning done.

First, Zach hung some bed linens on the outdoor clothes-line to air out and then spent the rest of the afternoon clean-ing. With the second floor done, he was mopping the kitchen floor when he heard the crunch of tires on the gravel driveway. Looking out the window, he and saw the furniture company's truck backing down the lane.

An hour later all the furniture had been unloaded, carried into the house, and set up. Too tired to continue cleaning, he brewed a pot of coffee, poured a large mug full, and headed out onto the back porch. He sat down in one of the two wicker chairs, put his feet up on the railing, and blew across the hot, steaming liquid. Sipping the rich, bold coffee slowly, he gazed across the backyard, wondering what his new life was going to be like.

Sudden movement to his left interrupted his reverie. A reddish-brown dog ran out of the tree line and stopped dead in its tracks when it saw Zach. Zach stood up and the dog turned and ran back into the woods. He set his coffee mug on the railing and wandered slowly toward the back edge of the prop-erty, watching the tree line where the dog had disappeared. He walked up onto the old wooden bridge that crossed the small stream skirting the back edge of the property. He took a deep breath, leaned on the rail, and gazed down at the slowly mov-ing water. *"It's so quiet and peaceful. I'm really going to love it here,"* he thought.

Zach pushed himself away from the bridge railing and headed back for the house. He had not noticed the pair of eyes that had watched him as he walked from the house down to the bridge.

The peace and quiet Zach so desperately hoped for and needed would soon vanish.

Conroy Manufacturing,
May River Road,
Bluffton, South Carolina

Anna Mae Watts, hunched over her desk, stared at the monthly production report spread out in front of her, frustrated that she could not find the error. The batch control total from production did not match the total on the hardcopy report. She leaned back and stretched to relieve the tight muscles in her neck. About to refocus on the report, she jumped when her cellphone rang. She swiveled her chair around, rummaged through her purse, and retrieved her cellphone.

"Hello," she said.

"Anna Mae, it's Joshua," Joshua Pickett, Anna Mae's cousin by marriage, screamed. "I'm scared. I can't stop the bleeding."

"Slow down, Joshua," Anna Mae urged. "Tell me what's the matter."

"My nose won't stop bleeding. Just like Victoria's," he wailed. "I've soaked two towels already. What am I going to do?"

"First, you have to calm down," Anna Mae instructed. "Wrap some ice in a towel, lie back on the couch, and press the ice against your nose. I'll hang on. Tell me when you've done that."

"Okay," Joshua stammered.

Anna Mae heard the clunk when Joshua laid the phone on the table. She heard sounds in the distance that she hoped came from Joshua getting ice out of the freezer. A drawer slammed. She heard rustling and then footsteps.

"I'm lying back on the couch," Joshua sputtered. "Anna Mae, I'm scared."

"I understand, Joshua. Stay right there. Don't move. Stay as still as you can," Anna Mae ordered as forcefully as she dared. "I'm going to hang up and call an ambulance. Then I'm coming right over. Do you understand?"

"Yes, Anna Mae. Please hurry," Joshua begged.

Anna Mae ended the call and immediately dialed 9-1-1.

"911, what is your emergency?" the emergency dispatch operator asked.

"I'm calling for my cousin, Joshua Pickett" Anna Mae barked. "He has a severe nosebleed. He has soaked two towels and can't get it to stop. His address is Forty-Five Red Knot Road. I'll be leaving immediately. I'll meet the ambulance there."

"I will send them immediately," the emergency dispatch operator answered.

Anna Mae ended the call and flew out the door of her office. She ran down the hall and poked her head in her boss's office, stopping only long enough to explain where she was headed. She threw the exit door open, sprinted across the parking lot, jumped into her car, and roared out of the parking lot.

She drove well over the speed limit the entire three and one-half miles to the Pickett house on Red Knot Road, praying she would not be stopped by a policeman. Arriving before the ambulance, she rushed into the house and found Joshua lying on the couch, deathly pale.

"Joshua, where's Mazie?" she shouted.

Joshua raised his arm, pointed at the bedroom, and managed to say, "Sleeping."

Anna Mae rushed into the bedroom and found Mazie standing up in her crib. She scooped up the little girl and held her tight.

"Am-me," the little girl cooed.

Anna Mae heard the wail of the siren as the ambulance turned into the driveway. She rushed out into the living room and with her free hand held the door open for the EMT's as they hurried in, pushing a gurney.

"He's over there on the couch," Anna Mae shouted.

"How long has he had the nosebleed?" Matt Blumenthal, the senior EMT, asked.

"I don't know," Anna Mae answered. "I just got here a few minutes before you did."

The EMT's rushed over to Joshua and performed a quick assessment. Concerned by his pallor and slurred speech, they quickly loaded Joshua onto the gurney and headed for the ambulance.

Matt Blumenthal grabbed the microphone clipped to the epaulet of his uniform shirt and depressed the transmit button, "Dispatch, Medic Two."

"Medic Two, Dispatch, go ahead."

"Dispatch, we have a male, age mid-twenties, with a severe nosebleed. Victim is very pale and incoherent. We will be transporting Code Red to Memorial University Medical Center. I repeat, Code Red!"

"Medic Two, we copy. Transporting Code Red to Memorial University Medical Center. We will inform law enforcement."

The EMT's pushed the gurney out the door and quickly loaded it into the back of the ambulance. One EMT hopped up in the back while the other EMT raced around the ambulance, climbed in the driver's seat, and roared off down the driveway.

Anna Mae rushed back into the bedroom and threw a few things into an already partially packed travel bag, grabbed Mazie's car seat, and flew out the door. She slammed the door and ran for the car. As she buckled Mazie into her car seat, the little girl cried out, "Raff-ee, Raff-ee."

Anna Mae dug a stuffed giraffe out of the bag, handed it to the little girl, and jumped into the car.

"Why are so many people sick and dying," she asked herself as she sped down the road toward the hospital.

Chapter Fourteen

Hilton Garden Inn,
Atlanta Airport

One and one-half miles southwest of Atlanta's Hartsfield International Airport, just off Southport Road, a black Lincoln Navigator turned into the hotel's parking lot and slowly drove between the rows of parked cars. The Lincoln Navigator stopped, backed up, and pulled into an empty space close to the end of the building.

Mr. John Lewin, FBI Special Agent in Charge, Southeast Division, dressed in a black business suit and wrap-around sunglasses hopped out, looked up and down the rows of parked cars, and hurried into the hotel. After briskly walking across the lobby, Lewin pressed the elevator Up button and waited. He stepped into the empty elevator car and punched the button for the ninth floor. The door slid open and Lewin poked his head out and looked both ways. Finding the hallway empty, he rushed to the end of the corridor, stopping in front of room nine twenty-three. He knocked softly three times on the door.

"Who is it?" a voice from inside called out.

"Pizza with onions and pepperoni," Mr. Lewin answered.

Bailey Gibbons, Sha'ban Rabi Bahar—The Snake, pulled the door open, holding his hand under his jacket. Sha'ban closed the door and directed Lewin toward a chair sitting beside the bed.

"Worthy Knight, have you had any success in locating Mister Templeton?" Sha'ban asked.

"Not as yet, Worshipful Master," Lewin answered. "I have all the men I can trust looking for him. If he's in the Savannah area, one of them is bound to find him, and soon."

Sha'ban removed his hand from under his jacket and walked over to the room's mini-bar. He opened the small refrigerator, grabbed a bottle of water, and asked, "Is the safe house ready?"

"Yes, Worshipful Master, it is ready," Lewin answered. "It's on Salt Creek Road about five miles west of Savannah. It is very private *and* it is very safe."

"Anything for you?" Sha'ban asked, about to close the refrigerator door.

"A water would be nice."

Sha'ban reached into the refrigerator, grabbed another bottle of water, and tossed it toward Lewin.

"What of our friend, the sheriff?" Sha'ban questioned as he moved over to the bed and sat down. "How much does he know?"

"I am not certain, Master," Lewin answered, keeping a watchful eye on the man sitting on the bed. A man he feared a great deal and with good reason. "The sheriff has been helpful, but I think his usefulness has come to an end. Also, I think he is becoming a risk."

"Contact him and determine exactly what he knows," Sha'ban ordered. "Make certain he knows what will happen if he does not remain silent."

"Yes, Master. I believe he already knows, but I will tell him again."

"Is there anything else I should know?"

"No, Master. Everything is going according to your wishes. The Sovereign Grand Prince assured me everything is nearing completion for the release of the pathogen."

"Good. Contact me the instant anyone locates Templeton."

Mr. Lewin rose from his chair and offered his hand to Sha'ban. They grasped each other's hand using the Order's secret handshake.

"Remember, Worthy Knight, we must maintain the utmost secrecy. The plan must not fail."

"Understood, Master," Lewin responded, bowing at the waist.

Mr. Lewin exited the room. Rather than walk through the lobby, Lewin went down the back stairway and exited the building at the far end of the parking area. He returned to his car and drove back to Savannah to check in on his agents' progress in locating Templeton. Then he would locate the sheriff and find out what he really knew.

Beaufort Memorial Hospital, Beaufort, South Carolina

Anna Mae had arrived at Memorial University Medical Center twenty-three minutes after the ambulance carrying Joshua Pickett had arrived, and, so far, she had been unable to learn anything about his condition. The ER admissions nurse was adamant that unless Anna Mae could prove she was family, she could not release any medical information.

Rather than argue, Anna Mae had taken a seat in the ER waiting area and was doing her best to keep Joshua's daughter, Mazie, entertained. Anna Mae looked up when she noticed someone dressed in green scrubs exit the ER treatment area and walk over to the admission desk. The man dressed in scrubs and the nurse seated at the admissions desk spoke briefly, and then Anna Mae saw the admissions nurse pointing in her direction. The man dressed in scrubs turned and headed her way.

"I'm Doctor James Volker, ER Attending Physician," the man said as he took the seat across from Anna Mae. "Nurse Carlson tells me you're related to a Mister Joshua Pickett."

"Yes, Joshua's wife was my cousin and this young lady here is his daughter."

"Okay, good," Dr. Volker said. "I'm wondering if you could fill me in on Mr. Pickett's medical history."

Anna Mae shrugged and said, "I don't really know much. Joshua and Victoria met at college and were married just three years ago. Joshua moved here from out of state. I never heard him talk about his family or any medical conditions. I'm sorry I can't be more helpful, Doctor Depue."

"Did you say his wife's name was Victoria?"

"Yes. She also had a severe nosebleed. She…"

"That's right," Dr. Volker interrupted. "I knew I'd heard that name. I remember the ER staff talking about her."

"That's correct. She died that same day."

"I'm sorry. That may have some…."

Before he could finish his sentence, a nurse dressed in the same green scrubs rushed out of the ER doors in search of Doctor Volker.

"Doctor, quick," the nurse panted. "Mister Pickett is in distress."

Dr. Volker scrambled out of the chair and without a word he and the nurse rushed back into the ER, leaving Anna Mae sitting in the middle of the waiting area.

"What is it, Mazie?" Anna Mae asked, as Mazie tugged at her arm. "Oh, I see," she said, noticing Mazie pointing toward a box of toys sitting on the far side of the waiting area.

Anna Mae picked Mazie up and moved to the far side of the waiting area. She put Mazie down beside the box of toys. Anna Mae sat down on the floor beside the toy box and dug around amongst the various toys, pulled out a bag of blocks, and dumped them on the floor. Stacking blocks was without a doubt Mazie's absolute favorite pastime. Mazie would carefully stack the blocks as high as she could and then giggle with glee when they toppled over. Anna Mae marveled that Mazie could sit for hours stacking blocks over and over again.

Anna Mae had no idea how long she and Mazie had been sitting there stacking and restacking the blocks, losing count at fifteen times. Every few minutes Anna Mae would glance over at the ER treatment area doors, wondering how Joshua was doing.

Anna Mae became very concerned when she saw Dr. Volker emerge from the ER treatment area, his scrubs soaked with sweat and a grim look on his face. He made his way over to where Anna Mae and Mazie were sitting and slumped down in an empty chair, shaking his head.

"I'm sorry," Dr. Volker groaned. "We tried everything to stop the bleeding, but nothing we tried was effective. There simply wasn't anything we could do."

Anna Mae sat there stunned.

"Are you okay?" Dr. Volker asked, reaching out and taking Anna Mae's hand.

"I don't even know his parent's names," she moaned. "What about the... the... the body?"

"I know this is difficult, but the body will have to go to the medical examiner. It's the law in all unexplained deaths."

"I understand, Doctor," Anna Mae sniffled.

"I'll have the admissions nurse come over and get your contact information to pass along to the ME's office. They will notify you of their findings and will let you know when the body will be released. I'm sorry I can't stay longer, but I have several other very sick patients that need my attention."

"Thank you doctor," Anna Mae said as he turned and headed back to the ER treatment area.

She picked Mazie up and hugged her tight as tears streamed down her cheeks. She sat down on one of the hard plastic chairs and rocked back and forth.

Her mother was dead. Victoria Pickett was dead. And now Joshua Picket was dead.

"What was happening to her beloved little town of Bluffton, South Carolina?" she wondered as she exited the waiting area and headed for her car in the parking lot.

Chapter Fifteen

Big House Plantation Road,
Bluffton, South Carolina

Zach stirred, rolled over, and opened one eye, seeing the sun streaming in the bedroom's east-facing window. At the furniture store, he had splurged, purchasing a top-of-the-line, pillow-top mattress. The luxurious mattress combined with the peacefulness of his new residence had provided him with the best night's sleep he had had in a very long time.

Knowing he had much to do, he peeled the covers back and swung his legs over the side of the bed. He stood and stretched to relieve his tired, sore muscles. "Yee-ow!" Zach wailed, grabbing his back. Straightening up slowly, he painfully realized he had overdone the cleaning yesterday. He sat on the edge of the bed to avoid bending over, snatched his trousers hanging over the bedpost, and carefully slid his feet into the legs of the trousers. After slipping his shirt on and buttoning it, he stood up and buckled his belt.

He looked at his shoes sitting beside the dresser. "Nope. Not doing that," he groaned as he turned and headed for the stairs. Grimacing with each step, he made his way to the bottom of the stairs and padded barefooted into the kitchen. Coffee. He needed coffee. After loading the coffee pot with grounds and water, he switched it on and stepped over in front of the cabinet to the right of the sink. He opened the cabinet door and grabbed a coffee mug.

As he turned and passed by the north-facing window of the kitchen, he stopped suddenly and stepped back in front of the window, certain he had seen something. Movement by the arched bridge at the north edge of the property had registered in his peripheral vision.

Pushing the curtain aside, he stared out into the backyard. The sun, risen above the horizon for less than an hour, cast eerie beams of light through the foggy mist that hugged the ground, swirling around the base of the trees. He stared for several minutes, but saw nothing. He set the coffee mug on the counter and stepped out the back door onto the porch. About to step down off the porch, he hesitated, realizing he had no shoes on. *"Oh well, they'll wash,"* he thought as he stepped off the porch and headed for the bridge.

He watched the tree line where he thought he had seen movement as he walked slowly toward the bridge. Nothing moved except for some birds skittering around in the trees. About to turn back toward the house, he noticed footprints on the wet surface of the bridge. He stopped and stood motionless, listening for movement. He heard nothing. There was no sound except for the babbling of the water flowing under the bridge.

Halfway back to the house, he stopped and bent forward slightly, testing the sore muscles in his back. Pleasantly relieved, he found that his muscles seemed to have loosened up and the pain had changed from sharp to dull. Maybe it would not be as bad a day as he had thought.

Back in the house, the coffee had finished perking. He poured his mug full and blew across the top of the hot liquid. Also splurging at the local supermarket, he had purchased the most expensive French Roast coffee on the shelf. He blew at the hot liquid again and took a careful sip of the dark and bold coffee. "Mmmmm," Zach murmured, taking another sip.

He moved to the other side of the kitchen, set the mug on the counter, and gathered items from the refrigerator and began preparing breakfast. Bacon, eggs, hashbrowns, and toast, his favorite breakfast. He turned on the flame under a skillet and dropped in three slices of bacon. On his way to the cabinet to the left of the sink to get a plate, he saw movement again as he passed by the window.

This time when he turned and looked out the window he saw a medium-sized, brownish-red hound standing in the yard looking toward the house. He turned off the flame under the skillet and armed with several slices of bread; he stepped out onto the back porch. The hound saw Zach and turned and trotted toward the trees. Zach started toward the bridge as fast as his sore back would allow.

He whistled and called out, "Hey boy, I've got some food for you." He whistled again.

The hound stopped, turned, and looked at Zach, eyeing the bread in Zach's hand.

"Come on, boy," Zach urged. "You can have it. Come on. Come and get it."

The hound took a tentative step toward Zach.

"Come on. I won't hurt you," Zach urged again, holding the bread out in front of him and waving it back and forth.

The hound took two more cautious steps, looking at the bread in Zach's hand. Another cautious step. Giving into the lure of food, the hound bounded toward Zach and eagerly gulped down the first slice of bread he offered.

"Slow down. You're going to choke yourself," Zach said as he tore the remaining slice of bread into several pieces and handed them to the hungry hound one at a time. With great effort, Zach sank to his knees and rubbed the red hound's ears. The hound reciprocated by wagging his stub of a tail and enthusiastically licking Zach's face.

"What's your name, boy," Zach asked, noticing a collar around the hound's neck.

Zach spun the collar around and turned the tag over so he could read it. "Tripp. That's an odd name for a dog," Zach said. "Would you like some more food? Come on. Follow me to the house."

Zach got up from his knees, about to turn toward the house. Suddenly, the hair bristled on the hound's back, his lips curling up as he growled.

"Huh, What's up?" Zach exclaimed.

The hound barked, turned, and disappeared into the woods.

"I wonder what that was all about?" Zach remarked. He shrugged his shoulders, turned toward the house, and stopped dead.

A slender man Zach would guess to be in his early thirties, dressed in a black suit and white shirt stood beside the porch staring at him. Instinctively, Zach reached for a weapon. His hand closed around nothing but air. If the man intended him harm, he was totally defenseless. Zach's muscles tightened as he assumed a defensive posture, a reaction ingrained in him by many years serving as a US Navy SEAL.

Noticing Zach's reaction, the man called out, "I mean you no harm. I'm Secret Service. Admiral Hadley sent me." The man closed the distance between them, stopping two paces from Zach. He held out his credentials for Zach to examine.

"Well, Agent Kanagy, explain please," Zach demanded after scrutinizing the man's credentials.

"Admiral Hadley sent me to warn you of a potential threat," Agent Anthony Kanagy responded. "I assume you remember a Mister Frank Porter."

"Yes. I most certainly do."

"The Admiral has learned that someone else was behind the plot you discovered. Someone far more dangerous than Mister Porter, if you can believe the legends."

"Legends?" Zach said, a puzzled look on his face.

"According to the legends, he is said to have over one hundred kills. Most of those kills had their throats slit. Despite that, no one has a photo of him. They call him *The Snake* because he kills without warning or remorse."

"So, what does that have to do with me?"

"It was *his* plot you discovered and spoiled, not Porter's. Porter was only an ignorant puppet. The CIA has learned through an informant that he is likely headed for the United States. CIA Director Sandberg believes and Admiral Hadley concurs you would be a likely target."

"Oh, good grief," Zach croaked, picturing his newfound peace flying out the window.

"Here is a weapon for you," Agent Kanagy said, holding out a Sig Sauer P229. "It uses .357 hollow point rounds. It will stop most threats. I have several boxes of ammunition and a holster back in my car."

"I don't know," Zach objected.

"You're going to need it. Believe me!" Agent Kanagy urged, holding the weapon out again. "From what Admiral Hadley told me, the intelligence community in Washington is really spooked. He said he's never seen the CIA Director so uneasy."

"Seems kind of dainty," Zach observed as he reached out, took the weapon, and tested its weight and balance.

"The small size makes it easily concealed and holstered in a variety of positions and locations," Agent Kanagy advised. "If you already have a favorite weapon, this would make a good back-up weapon."

"Matter of fact, I do have a favorite weapon," Zach responded. "My go-to weapon is an STI Lawman, 45 ACP. If you put a round from that anywhere on your target, he is not getting up."

"Do you have it with you?"

"Yes, but it's packed away. I haven't touched it in a long time."

"Well, I suggest you dig it out and get it cleaned and ready to use. If this guy's even half as nasty as the legends say, you need to be well prepared."

Zach stuffed the Sig Sauer behind his belt and said, "I have fresh coffee. Would you like some?"

"Thanks, but no. I'll get you that ammo and holster then I have other things to attend to. Admiral Hadley will be in touch when he has any other details. Say nothing of what I have told you, *to anyone.*"

Zach followed Agent Kanagy to his car and waited as he retrieved the ammo and holster for the Sig Sauer from the trunk of his car and handed it to him. Zach shook Agent Kanagy's hand and watched him climb into his car and drive away.

Zach walked back into the house and laid the Sig Sauer and the ammo on the kitchen table and stared at them. The peace he craved fading as visions of deadly shootouts danced in his mind. Worst of all—the vision of his beautiful wife, Angie, lying dead on the floor of Henry Tang's penthouse flashed into his mind, as raw as if it had happened yesterday.

Underground Laboratory, Unknown Location

For a second time, Klaus Herrmann climbed down the access ladder and stepped onto the floor of the hidden underground facility, making hardly a sound. Huge sums of money and effort had been expended to insulate the facility and minimize the emanation of sound or vibrations. To Klaus, it seemed liked a terrible waste of money to destroy the facility, but, then again, secrecy was paramount.

Klaus walked across the rubberized floor, the sound of his footsteps barely registering above a whisper. Out of the corner of his eye he saw a man dressed in all black coming his way. Klaus reached behind his back and pulled his weapon and shot the man slightly right of dead-center in the chest before he could react. He dragged the body where it could not be seen from the view port in the access door.

Klaus walked over to the access door and pressed a button next to the heavy door that led into the laboratory's prep area. Dr. Bristol peered at him through the small, round, glass viewing port. Klaus heard a soft clunk as the locking mechanism retracted, releasing the door. As Dr. Bristol pulled the door open, air rushed inward due to the negative pressure always maintained in the lab to prevent outward leakage of any contaminants or pathogens.

"Doctor, can you brief me on the production of the backup batch?" Klaus asked.

"Follow me to the lab's main work area," Dr. Bristol answered, pointing toward an inner door.

Dr. Bristol pushed the door open and waited for Klaus to enter. Once inside, Klaus pushed the door closed. Dr. Randall Weaver, Dr. Bristol's assistant, was seated at a long work table sipping a cup of coffee.

"Are you and Doctor Weaver the only people here?", Klaus asked.

"Yes, Sovereign Prince. He and I are all that is needed. That moron, Slater, is around somewhere. The fewer eyes the better."

"Agreed, Doctor. Sit here next to Doctor Weaver. I want you both to see this."

Klaus pulled a folded piece of paper from his pocket, unfolded it, and laid it on the table in front of them. He stepped behind the two men as they began to read and slipped his hand behind his jacket. He pulled out a Fabrique Nationale FN 509 Tactical 9mm with a long suppressor already affixed to the threaded barrel and shot both men in the back of the head. The FN 509 had long been a favorite among eastern-European assassins because of its light-weight, polymer frame, seventeen round magazine, and pre-threaded barrel.

Klaus looked down at the spent brass scattered on the floor and decided there was no need to gather it up because the entire complex would soon be destroyed. He released the access door, went back out to his car, and retrieved the two white, plastic jars containing the acid he had picked up when he had met Chevy Man. He climbed down the ladder twice, carrying one jar each time. With both jars sitting beside the access door, Klaus punched in the access code Dr. Bristol had given him, listened for the metallic clunk, and pulled the door open. He blocked the door open with a chair and moved the two white jars inside the lab.

Timothé Alex Durand (the only Illumined Elite Order member that had been informed of Sha'ban Rabi Bahar's plan), had watched Klaus from the trees. He followed Klaus after he carried the second jar down the ladder and quietly climbed down after him.

Durand peered in thru the still blocked-open door. He watched as Klaus moved the white jars over beside a worktable and turned to gather up some work papers. Durand stepped into the room, pointed his weapon at Klaus, and fired. Klaus went down, turning over an empty chair as he grabbed for something to break his fall. He tumbled onto the floor, landing flat on his back. He pointed his weapon and fired. Fired in haste, the bullet missed Durand, slamming into the wall a mere six inches to the right of Durand's head. Paint chips, bits of wallboard, and dust settled onto Durand's shoulder.

The gun fell out of Klaus's hand and clattered to the floor. He rolled to his side and struggled to his knees. He tried to stand but was unable. Growing weaker as internal bleeding from a nicked artery drained away his life, he collapsed and fell face first into a pool of blood and lay still.

Durand walked over and pushed at Klaus's motionless body with the toe of his shoe. Satisfied he was dead, he turned away. Noticing the two white jars he had watched Klaus carry in, he walked over and examined them. He turned one of the jars around and read the words *"Fluoroantimonic Acid"* in bold red letters.

"Hmmm, I wonder what that is?" he muttered out loud as he placed his hand on the lid of one of the jars and started to unscrew the lid.

Chapter Sixteen

Pickett House,
45 Red Knot Road,
Bluffton, South Carolina

Eight-year-old Jonathon Foley and his eleven-year-old brother, James, took turns tossing a football back and forth as they walked down Game Land Road, returning from playing with a group of school classmates at the local park. They turned the corner and started down Red Knot road toward their house at the end of the block.

Jonathon Foley, sporting a mop of curly, chestnut-brown hair and mischievous green eyes, poked his older brother on the arm and hollered, "James, run down the road and I'll throw you a really long one."

James, with sandy brown hair and blue eyes, took off running down Red Knot Road. "Throw it. Throw it," James shouted as he raced down the road, looking backward over his shoulder.

Jonathon drew his right arm back and heaved the football as hard as he could. Three years younger than James, Jonathon's hands were much smaller and unable to fully grasp the football. The resulting errant throw wobbled and missed its intended target by several feet. The football hit the hard road surface and bounced wildly sideways, flying into a neighbor's yard.

Jonathon raced after the wildly bounding football, chasing it up onto the porch of Joshua and Victoria Pickett's house. He bent over, reached out to grab the football, and noticed the front door was slightly ajar. He pushed the door open, stuck his head inside, and called out, "Misses Pickett?" He waited.

Receiving no answer, he called out again, "Mister Pickett?" He waited again. Still no answer.

He poked his head in the house and yelled again. Still no one answered. "Hey James, I don't think anybody's home," he yelled to his brother. "But they left the door open."

James ran over from the middle of the street and peered inside the house. "They were probably in a hurry and didn't notice the door didn't close all the way. Just pull it shut," James advised. "Come on. We need to get home."

"Okay," Jonathon answered as he pulled the door shut.

Jonathon reached down to pick up the football. He jerked back when he felt something sting his left arm. As he slapped at it with his right hand, a mosquito flew away and landed on James' shirt.

Only seconds later, James cried out, "Hey, what's that?" He hunched his shoulders and swatted at his neck. He pulled his hand away from his neck, revealing a squashed mosquito lying in his hand.

"Stupid mosquito," he exclaimed, wiping his hand on his pants leg. "Come on. Let's go. We're going to miss our show," he called out to Jonathon as he turned and trotted toward their house.

The two boys raced each other the rest of the way home. James reached the front door first and pulled at the chain around his neck. He poked the key dangling at the end of the chain into the lock and opened the door. Jonathon raced past him, dropped the football in the toy box, and turned on the television while James headed into the kitchen to get two glasses of milk and some of the chocolate-chip cookies their mother had baked earlier that morning. James returned to the living room, handed Jonathon a glass of milk and two of the cookies, and settled down in front of the television beside his brother.

"Is it on yet?" James asked, mumbling through a mouthful of cookie.

"Just starting," Jonathon replied.

Engrossed in the program playing on the television, Jonathon scratched at the angry red welt on his arm. James set his glass of milk on the floor and scratched at a similar red welt on his neck.

An hour later, as the program ended, James grabbed the empty glasses and headed for the kitchen. "Mom fixed us some sandwiches for lunch," he announced. "Come in the kitchen. Grab some chips from the pantry and sit at the table."

Jonathon pushed himself up from the floor and did as his brother had instructed. The boys ate in silence, occasionally scratching at the red welts. With lunch finished, Jonathon returned the bag of chips to the pantry and James placed the dirty dishes in the sink.

"What do we do now?" James asked. "Do you want to go out in the backyard and play catch?"

"When is Mom supposed to be home?" Jonathon asked.

"She said around 3:00 o'clock."

"I don't feel very good," Jonathon confided. "Let's just watch television."

The boys headed into the living room. Jonathon crawled up on the couch and leaned against a pillow. James turned the television on.

"You know, I don't feel very good either," James sniffled as he sat on the opposite end of the couch.

***Underground Laboratory,
Unknown Location***

Intending to find out what was in the white plastic jars, Timothé Alex Durand began to twist the lid of the jar closest to him. Gritting his teeth, he grabbed the jar with his free hand and twisted the lid as hard as he could.

"Huh, what?" he exclaimed as shrill screeching sound reverberated throughout the room. "What is that?" he grimaced as he jumped back, looking for the source of the excruciating noise. He looked toward the control panel on the opposite wall and saw a bright red sign flashing "Open Door". Completely forgetting about the plastic jars, he scurried across the room and examined the control board, looking for a way to silence the awful noise.

Rather than spending time trying to decipher and silence the alarm system, he decided to ignore the plastic jars and gather the delivery vector and move them to the delivery location. Beginning to feel nauseous due to the loud, high-pitched squeal, Durand quickly located the room where the containers of delivery vector were stored. One by one, he moved the two large containers of angry, buzzing mosquitoes into the laboratory's main room and positioned them beside the access door.

He pushed the vector containers out into the anteroom and kicked the chair out of the way, allowing the access door to close. The door swung closed and the shrill screeching of the alarm stopped.

"Good Lord!" Durand exclaimed the instant he heard the clunk of the access door closing. In a mad rush to move the vector containers into the anteroom and silence the screeching alarm, he had forgotten to set the explosives.

It would now be impossible for him to reenter the lab because he did not have the access code. The Worshipful Master would be furious.

Thinking only of the relief from silencing the alarm, Durand completely forgot about the substance he was to use to limit the lifespan of the mosquitoes. The substance sat undisturbed in the vector development area.

Inside the lab, all became quiet except for the hum of the florescent lights, the steady whirring from multiple power supply fans, and the rush of air blowing out of the ventilation system.

Timothé Alex Durand moved the delivery vector containers to his car and headed back to pick up the hidden biocontainers containing the deadly pathogen and move them and the delivery vector containers to the release locations.

151 Laurel Oak Bay Road,
Bluffton, South Carolina

Anna Mae Watts sat at the kitchen table, struggling through the heart-wrenching task of going through her mother's things. Her father, Edwin, detested business dealings and had adamantly refused, leaving the difficult task to her. The old farmhouse her parents had shared for their entire married life, the house she grew up in and still shared with her father, sat back fifty yards from the road. On the west side of Calibogue Sound, the house nestled against deep woods.

Her mother's recent death had prompted a need to examine and, likely, make changes to the property deeds for the house they lived in and the rental house on Big House Plantation Road. The tin box containing all her mother's important papers sat open on the table. Anna Mae removed everything, making piles of like items. There were no birth certificates, no property deeds, and no marriage license. Just routine papers. In the very bottom of the box, she came across what looked like a safety deposit box key. She picked it up and turned it over. Stamped into the top of the key were the numbers—1440.

Looking up from the piles of paper as her father entered the room, she asked, "Daddy, did Mother have a safety deposit box at the bank?"

"I don't know, honey," Edwin Watts answered. "I left all that business stuff to your mother."

"Did she keep any important papers anywhere other than in this old tin box?"

"I don't think so. Like I told you, I let her handle all that."

"Okay," Anna Mae sighed, knowing questioning her father any further would be a waste of time. She looked up at the clock to see if she had time to drive to the bank and see if her mother had a safety deposit box that matched the key she had found.

She dug through one of the piles of papers and pulled out a blue envelope labeled, Durable Power of Attorney. She would need that to gain access to any of her mother's accounts.

She grabbed the key and the blue envelope, pushed the chair back from the table, and stood up.

"Daddy, I'll have to go to the bank and see if Mother had a safety deposit box that matches this key," Anna Mae said to her father's back.

"Okay, honey. Drive careful," her father said, turning back to the coffeepot. He filled his cup, turned, and watched Anna Mae grab her purse and head out the door.

Thirty minutes later, she turned off the principle thoroughfare in Bluffton and pulled into the parking lot of First Fidelity Bank. Inside the bank, she located a teller, introduced herself, and asked to see the bank manager.

Anna Mae took a seat in the waiting area and watched the teller walk into the manager's office. Several minutes passed before she saw a barrel-chested man in his sixties exit the office and head her way. The man was an inch shy of five and a half feet tall with a head of snow-white hair with a matching mustache under his nose. He was dressed in light brown trousers, a tweed jacket, and striped green tie. Anna Mae had to suppress a snicker, thinking the man desperately needed the help of a fashion consultant.

"What can I do for you, Miss Watts?" Mr. Frank Keen, branch manager of First Fidelity Bank, asked.

"My name is Anna Mae Watts. I need to access my mother's account and safety deposit box, if she has one," Anna Mae answered.

"Are you a signee on the account, Miss Watts?"

"No, but I have this durable power of attorney," Anna Mae replied, holding out the blue envelope. "My mother died recently."

"You're Marguerite's daughter then," Mr. Keen remarked. "We heard about your mother. It was just terrible. May I offer my condolences?"

"Thank you, Mister Keen."

"Right this way," Mr. Keen said, pointing toward the office he had exited. "We'll have a look at that power of attorney and see what we can do."

Anna Mae walked into the man's office and sat in one of the two chairs sitting in front of a large mahogany desk. Mr. Keen followed her into the office, pulled the door closed, and dropped his overweight bulk into a black leather desk chair. He held out his hand and took the blue envelope Anna Mae held out.

"Let's have a look at this," he said as he upended the envelope and slid the contents out into his hand. He unfolded the document and read through it quickly. "Everything seems to be in order," he said, turning sideways toward the computer keyboard sitting on the side of his desk. He tapped a few keys. A few seconds later, a printer on the credenza behind him began whirring. He turned around and retrieved a sheet of paper as it rolled out into the output tray.

"If you'll sign here at the bottom," he said, pointing to a signature block at the bottom of the paper. "It's a formality. We have to have our paperwork, you know. While you sign, I'll go make a copy of the power of attorney for our records."

Mr. Keen exited the office with the papers in his hand. Anna Mae looked at the photos and various awards arranged on the shelving unit perched on top of the credenza while she waited for Mr. Keen to return.

"You said something about a safety deposit box," Mr. Keen inquired as he plopped down into his chair.

"Yes, I have it right here," Anna Mae answered as she reached in her purse and pulled out the key.

Mr. Keen reached out and took the key and looked at it, turning it over several times. "Certainly looks like one of ours," he admitted. "Let me bring up your mother's account." He turned toward the keyboard again and tapped some keys. "Yes, the record says your mother does have a safety deposit box. Box number 1440. That matches the key. I'll have someone admit you to the vault so you can check its contents." He picked up the phone and asked one of the tellers to assist Anna Mae.

"Once again, my condolences, Miss Watts," Mr. Keen offered as Anna Mae left his office and followed the teller over to the vault entrance.

Anna Mae signed the vault entry log and followed the teller into the vault. The teller inserted the bank's master key and then the key Anna Mae handed her. She turned both keys, pulled the door open, and removed the box. She escorted Anna Mae to a private cubicle, set the box down, and exited the vault.

Anna Mae lifted the box's lid and went through the contents. Lying on top, she found a manila envelope containing the property deeds for their residence and also for the rental house. She laid that envelope aside and began to sort through the other items in the box.

She found the expected items: insurance policies, birth certificates, marriage license, her great grandmother's wedding ring, and several gold coins. At the very bottom of the box was a sealed, plain, white envelope. She picked up the envelope and examined both sides, finding no markings whatsoever. As she tipped the envelope, something hard slid from end to end. She tore off one end of the envelope and dumped out its contents.

Lying on the table were two folded scraps of paper and a very odd, antique-looking key. She unfolded the first scrap of paper and instantly recognized her mother's handwriting. The scribbled note said, *"Fred Tolbert's death was not suicide."* She sat and stared at the note for a long time. *"What on Earth would a glass blower have to do with this and why would my mother know anything about his death?"* she asked herself.

The other scrap of paper looked different. It appeared to be much older and had the feel of parchment. She unfolded it. "What on Earth is that?" she asked herself out loud as she looked at three strings of odd, seemingly meaningless symbols.

She shrugged her shoulders, stuffed most of the items back into the box, and put the property deeds, the two notes, and the key in her purse. After returning the box to its slot and locking it, she removed the two keys and returned the master key to the teller. She rushed out of the bank and headed for her car. A troubling and uneasy feeling gripped her as she climbed into the car and slid the key into the ignition. Disturbing questions swirled in her mind as she backed out of the parking space and started toward home.

What had her mother been involved in?

Was her mother's death also not an accident?

Was that why the sheriff had lied to her?

What was happening to her beloved town?

The most disconcerting question she did not ask herself might prove to be the most threatening of all.

Had she just stumbled upon a dark secret she would soon wish she had never discovered?

Chapter Seventeen

Foley House,
57 Red Knot Road,
Bluffton, South Carolina

Ruth Foley, in her mid-thirties, turned off of Game Land Road onto Red Knot Road, returning from visiting her mother. Running an hour late after making a stop at the supermarket to buy groceries, she was concerned what her two boys might do, having been home alone for the afternoon. *"They're good boys, but still...,"* she thought as she pulled into the driveway and parked in front of the garage.

She climbed out of the car, walked up onto the porch, unlocked the front door, and returned to the car. She opened the trunk, grabbed several bags of groceries, and headed for the house. Upon reaching the front door, she nudged it open with her shoulder. She stepped into the house and screamed in horror, dropping the bags of groceries on the floor.

A dark red blood trail led from the kitchen into the living room. She ran into the living room and screamed again, seeing her two boys lying on the floor. Their shirts were soaked in blood. She rushed over to James, lying against the couch, a trail of blood running down his chin, staining the carpet.

"James! James!" she shrieked as she dropped to her knees beside him. "James, what happened?" She raised him up off the floor and hugged her precious child, blood staining her dress. James' eyes fluttered open and he muttered something incoherent.

"James, where's Jonathon?" She blurted out.

James managed to raise his arm and point toward the far end of the couch before his arm flopped down and his eyes fell shut. Mrs. Foley glanced in the direction James had pointed and saw two feet sticking out past the end of the couch. She propped James against the couch and rushed to the other end of the couch. "Oh, my….," the words dying in her throat when she saw Jonathon lying on the floor, a dark red stain on the carpet under his face.

She fell to her knees, grabbed her younger son, and hugged him, becoming frantic when she could not rouse him. "Phone! Phone!" she shrieked. "I've got to call 9-1-1."

She gently laid Jonathon on the floor and raced through the living room and out the front door to retrieve her purse. Dumping the purse's entire contents on the front seat of the car, she snatched her cellphone and punched in 9-1-1.

Immediately after reporting her two boys bleeding and unconscious to the emergency dispatcher, she punched in her husband's number.

"Hello," Walter Foley answered.

"Walter," Ruth hollered into the phone. "The boys, bleeding, unconscious. Walter, what do I do?"

"Ruth, slow down," Walter shouted. "What are you talking about? What's the matter with the boys?"

"Oh, Walter. It's awful," Ruth moaned.

"Ruth, I need you to tell me what's going on," Walter commanded. "What's awful?"

"I came home from visiting Mother and shopping and found the boys lying in the living room bleeding. I can't wake them up," she wailed.

"Bleeding?" Walter questioned. "Why are they bleeding?"

"I don't know, Walter. I just found them like that."

Already out of his chair and heading for the door, Walter shouted into the phone, "Call 9-1-1. I'm on my way home. I'll be there in less than ten minutes."

"I already did that," she sniffled. "They said it would be fifteen to twenty minutes. Walter, hurry!"

"I'm already out the door and in the parking lot. I'll be there as soon as I can," Walter answered as he ended the call, leaped into his car, and roared out of the parking lot.

Ruth Foley rushed back into the house to check on her two boys, relieved to find that they were still breathing. She got an old sheet from the linen closet and spread it out on James' bed. One by one, she carried the unconscious boys into James' bedroom and laid them on the bed. She paced frantically back and forth in the living room waiting for Walter to arrive.

Walter roared down the street, pulled into the driveway, and slid to a stop on top of the shrubs that lined the porch. He rushed into the house and stopped dead in his tracks upon seeing his wife standing in the middle of the living room covered in blood.

"What happened?" he barked.

"Walter, I said I don't know," she wailed. "I came home and found them like that."

Several miles away, Sheriff Lonnie Overton, on his way back to headquarters, received a call on his radio alerting him to an emergency at the Foley house. He reached down and flipped the switch for his patrol car's emergency beacon and siren. After a quick glance behind him, he stomped on the accelerator and made a U-turn as several cars dived to the side of the highway to get out of his way.

Having just turned onto Okatie Highway, Sheriff Overton was only a few miles from the Foley house. Arriving before the ambulance, Sheriff Overton parked beside Walter's car and rushed up to the door. He knocked on the still open door and walked into the house. Ruth Foley, worried and frightened, was sitting on the couch crying. Walter, doing his best to console his wife, looked up when the sheriff walked into the room.

"I received a call about two sick boys," Sheriff Overton announced.

"In here," Walter Foley said, directing the sheriff into James' bedroom.

Sheriff Overton rushed over to the bed and felt for a pulse on both boys, finding it very weak on both. He placed his hand on each boy's chest and found their breathing to be shallow and labored. Both boys were pale and their skin was cool and clammy, indicating they were going into shock.. Determining the boys were critically ill, Sheriff Overton decided to see if he could speed up the ambulance's response. He keyed the microphone clipped to the epaulet on his uniform shirt and called into dispatch, "Beaufort Dispatch, Unit four hundred."

"Unit Four Hundred, Beaufort Dispatch. Go ahead."

"I'm at the Foley house," Sheriff Overton responded. "I have assessed the two Foley boys and they are very seriously ill. Contact the responding ambulance and have them escalate their response to priority code red."

"Ten-four, Unit Four Hundred. Ambulance will escalate to priority code red."

Sheriff Overton turned the volume on his radio down, walked into the living room, and stopped in front of the boys' parents. "I've requested the ambulance to escalate their response. We'll get them here as quick as possible. Walter, do you have an old blanket I can cover them up with? At least we can keep them warm."

"Sure thing," Walter replied as he got up from the couch and headed off in search of a blanket.

Ruth Foley looked up with red-rimmed eyes and said, "Thank you, Sheriff."

"What are their names?" the Sheriff asked, looking at Walter Foley who had returned from the spare bedroom with a green comforter.

"James is the older one. The younger one is Jonathon," Walter answered.

"Do either of them have any known medical problems? Have they fallen or been injured lately?"

"No. Nothing like that. They've always been very healthy."

Sheriff Overton pulled a notepad from his rear pocket and made some notes while Walter went into the bedroom and covered the boys with the comforter.

Hearing the wail of the siren from the approaching ambulance, Sheriff Overton stepped out onto the porch and waited. He watched as the Beaufort County ambulance pulled into the driveway. The two EMT's dragged a gurney out of the rear of the ambulance and rushed up onto the porch.

"This way," Sheriff Overton barked. "In here in the back bedroom."

The EMT's rushed into the back bedroom. The senior EMT, Matt Blumenthal, dug a stethoscope and a digital thermometer out of the emergency response box and went to check the boys' vital signs. He drew the digital thermometer across each of the boy's foreheads and then listened to their chests with the stethoscope. His quick check of their vital signs revealed both boys had labored breathing and dangerously high fevers.

"I've seen these symptoms before," Matt Blumenthal called out to the other EMT. "You get their blood pressure, pulse, and respirations while I go ask the sheriff to request the air ambulance."

Blumenthal rushed out into the living room and tapped the sheriff on the arm. "Sheriff, the boys are critically ill. They need to go direct to University Medical Center in Savannah. We need the air ambulance."

Just as the sheriff keyed his microphone, the EMT in the bedroom stuck his head into the doorway and hollered, "Matt, in here now!"

Blumenthal raced into the bedroom. Walter Foley jumped up off the couch and followed the EMT into the bedroom. Walter stopped as he entered the room and stood there with a horrified look on his face as the EMT's ripped the comforter off the bed and began CPR on both boys.

"Sheriff, we need you in here," Blumenthal yelled.

The sheriff ran into the room, pushing Walter out of the way.

"Get him out of here," Blumenthal barked, jerking his head toward Walter.

"Come on, Mister Foley," Sheriff Overton urged. "Let's let them do their job."

The sheriff pushed Walter through the doorway and directed him over to the couch. Dispatch called on the radio and advised the sheriff that they had contacted the air ambulance crew and they were scrambling. Unable to just sit on the couch, Walter got up and paced back and forth across the living room, peeking into the bedroom on each pass by the doorway. Ruth Foley sat on the couch wringing her hands and occasionally dabbing at her eyes with a tissue.

Fifteen long, grueling minutes passed. Ruth and Walter looked toward the doorway as Matt Blumenthal stepped out of the room. The color drained from their faces when they saw the bleak expression on his face.

"There just wasn't anything we could do," he panted, out of breath from performing CPR. "Cancel the air ambulance."

"No!" Ruth Foley screamed as she leaped off the couch and ran toward the bedroom. Walter grabbed his wife and held her back as she broke down into inconsolable weeping.

Sheriff Overton followed Matt Blumenthal into the bedroom and surveyed the horrific scene.

"What on Earth happened?" the sheriff questioned.

"It looks to me like they bled to death," Blumenthal answered, shaking his head. "CPR was useless. That's four cases now with the similar symptoms. It doesn't make any sense."

Discouraged and frustrated, the EMT's gathered up their equipment, piled it on the unused gurney, and dragged it out to the ambulance. Sheriff Overton radioed dispatch and informed them to cancel the air ambulance and to direct the coroner to respond immediately to the Foley residence.

The sheriff wanted to scream and kick the wall, but he controlled his emotions. *"This is not right. This was not supposed to happen,"* he told himself. The nearly one and one-half hours it took for the coroner to respond, make his on-site examination, and to release the scene seemed like an eternity.

Standing on the porch, he watched as two black body bags were loaded into the back of the coroner's van. He offered his condolences to the Foleys, then climbed into his patrol car. He radioed dispatch and reported out of service and that he was headed back to headquarters. The patrol car sat idling for several minutes before Sheriff Overton slipped the car into gear and sped down the driveway, determined to extricate himself from his involvement in this insanity.

Duke Street
Beaufort, South Carolina

Sheriff Overton had driven straight to the sheriff's department headquarters. He entered the building, informed the receptionist that he was not to be disturbed, went straight to his office, and locked the door. Ten minutes later he emerged from his office, walked straight to the front door, and exited the building without a word to anyone.

He climbed back into his assigned patrol car and drove straight to his home on Westview Avenue. He parked in front of the garage, called dispatch, and reported he was out of service to take care of a personal matter. Rather than enter his house, he walked around the house, and disappeared into a workshop behind the main house.

Two steps inside the workshop his cellphone rang. "Hello," he said as he answered the call.

"We've got to stop this madness before it goes any further," a male voice ranted.

"What are you talking about?" the Sheriff countered.

"Oh, come on, Lonnie," the male voice urged. "I know about Marguerite. I know about the Pickets. I know about the lab and now the Foley boys. This is crazy. We've been lied to. We've got to stop it."

After a long pause with no response. "Lonnie, are you still there?" the voice asked.

"Yes, I'm here," the sheriff answered. "What you're suggesting is suicide. You know that, right?"

"I don't care. I'll not be a party to this evil any longer."

"You will stay quiet and you will say nothing," the sheriff warned. "If you don't, I will kill you myself. Do you hear me?"

Silence.

"Listen to me!" the sheriff bellowed. "I know you're still there. I will not warn you again."

He ended the call and shoved the cellphone in his pocket. Unable to control his pent-up emotions, he swore and kicked an empty bucket sitting on the floor. The bucket flew across the workshop and bounced up against a shelving unit on the far wall, dislodging a number of cans which fell in disarray onto the floor.

"Enough is enough," he growled as he turned and walked over to a set of shelves on the other side of the workshop. He rummaged around on the shelves, moving things aside until he uncovered a small tin box.

A short man, barely over five and one-half feet tall with a slender build, slipped into the workshop, ducking into the shadows.

As the sheriff lifted a tin box off the shelf and turned around, the short man moved out of the shadows and said, "What is that you're holding, Sheriff?"

The man raised his hand in the grand hailing sign. As Sheriff Overton looked over at him, the man announced, "I am the Knight of Vengeance. I am here under direct authority of the Worshipful Master."

Sheriff Overton, becoming very fearful when he realized who the other man was, extended his hand. The sheriff had never met the man standing before him, but he was aware that he answered directly to the Sovereign Grand Inquisitor. He had also heard the accounts of how the Knight of Vengeance dispensed unspeakably brutal vengeance to anyone who defied him. The sheriff dropped his hand as the man made no move to accept it.

"Worthy Knight, there have been too many deaths," Sheriff Overton complained. "Just today two little boys died. That is unnecessary."

"Hold your tongue, Sheriff," the Worthy Knight declared. "It is not for you to say. The Worshipful Master makes those decisions."

"But little children, surely that is unnecessary."

"Silence!" the Worthy Knight roared, taking a step closer to the sheriff. "Need I remind you of how deeply you are involved in this? The blood of those that have died is on your hands as well."

"I will not….,"

"Hold your tongue," the Worthy Knight warned. "You will do *exactly* as I or the Worshipful Master tells you to do. Remember, if you challenge us, you pay for your insolence *and* your family will pay as well. And I assure you their deaths will be exquisitely painful."

"Yes, Worthy Knight," Sheriff Overton answered.

"I suggest you hand that item over to me," the Worthy Knight instructed, as he drew his weapon from behind his back.

Sheriff Overton held out the box, pretended to stumble over a board lying on the floor, and fell against the other man.

The Knight of Vengeance fired a wild shot, but it missed its intended target.

Before the Knight of Vengeance could recover his balance, Sheriff Overton planted his meaty fist against the side of the man's head with incredible force. The sheriff still carried the muscular build he had developed during his college wrestling days. The sheriff looked down at the dazed Knight of Vengeance lying on the dirt floor. The sheriff snatched the weapon out of the man's hand and fired two quick shots into his head just to the right of his temple.

He dragged the man's limp body to the far side of the shed and hid it beneath a pile of boards, intending to return later to hide the body where it would never be found.

"The Knight of the East was right. This has gone far enough. I'm putting an end to it now!" he growled, fed up with all the killings. The decision had actually formed in his mind as he watched the two little Foley boys die.

He pulled his cellphone out of his pocket, scrolled through its contact list, selected an entry, and pressed the 'Call' icon. He listened to the phone on the other end ring four times before it switched to a voicemail recording.

"Both Foley boys just died with nosebleeds," he announced. "You are in great danger. The recent deaths were not accidents. Trust no one."

He ended the call, stuffed the cellphone back into his pocket, and retrieved the tin box which contained enough incriminating evidence to implicate a lot of very important people and see to it they spent the rest of their lives in prison. Sheriff Overton pushed the door to the shed closed and headed for his patrol car to complete another task.

Chapter Eighteen

Big House Plantation Road
Bluffton, South Carolina

Zach pushed his chair back from the kitchen table and walked over to the coffeepot to refill his cup. Passing by the kitchen window, he glanced out the window. The red hound he'd met earlier was standing in the yard looking at the house. Zach rushed over to the back door and stepped out onto the porch. As he stepped off the porch and into the yard, the hound turned and ran, disappearing into the woods.

Zach continued to the middle of the yard, then stopped and listened. After watching and listening for several minutes, he gave up and started back toward the house. Halfway back to the house, the red hound burst out of the woods and ran circles around Zach. He reached down to pet the excited hound, but the hound ran several yards toward the back of the property and stood looking at him, barking excitedly.

"Come here, Tripp," Zach coaxed, taking a step toward the dog.

The hound turned and ran toward the back of the property and stopped on the old bridge. The hound turned, looked at Zach, and started barking again.

Zach trotted down to the edge of the property. "What do you want, Tripp?" he called out.

Once again, the dog turned, continued across the bridge, and disappeared into the woods. Zach ran across the bridge and attempted to follow, stopping at the edge of the woods. The woods were far too thick for him to follow. He listened as the barking faded out in the distance. Seeing no movement and hearing no more barking, he started walking back to the house, occasionally glancing over his shoulder.

Zach nearly jumped out of his skin when there was a loud bark right behind him. Turning back toward the bridge, he saw the hound standing three feet behind him, panting.

"What's the mat....," the question died in Zach's throat as he looked up and saw a beautiful woman standing on the bridge. Their eyes met. Zach stood frozen. Even from a distance, there was something about the woman's eyes that held Zach motionless. His trance-like state was broken when she turned away and started to leave. Zach yelled as she reached the edge of the bridge. The woman hesitated, but took several more steps toward the woods.

"Please stay. Don't go," Zach hollered.

She stopped and walked back to the center of the bridge. Zach trotted down to the edge of the property, stopping short of the bridge.

"I'm a new renter here," he said. "I just moved in."

"I'm Anna Mae Watts," the woman responded hesitantly.

"The owner of this property?" Zach asked.

"Yes. Well... My father and me actually," she answered, extending her hand.

"I'm Zachariah Templeton," he responded as he stepped toward her to take her hand. "But you have to call me Zach."

As Zach started toward her, the old hound jumped in between Zach and Anna Mae, preventing Zach from getting any closer.

"He's very protective of me," Anna Mae said. "But I don't think he would bite you."

"We've already met haven't we, Tripp," Zach bubbled as he squatted down and rubbed the hound's ears. The hound jumped up and put his front paws on Zach's shoulders, nearly knocking him over. Zach squirmed and laughed as the hound proceeded to wash his face with his wet tongue.

"That's amazing," Anna Mae remarked. "He's usually quite standoffish with strangers. I've never seen him take to anyone like that, except for me or Daddy."

"We're old friends," Zach confided, looking up at Anna Mae. "I bribed him with a couple of slices of bread."

Zach stood up and reached out his hand again. "As I said before, my name's Zach." Anna Mae reached out and grasped Zach's hand. She took in a breath, feeling something she never thought she would feel. And certainly not after just meeting someone.

"Did I squeeze too hard?" Zach asked.

Embarrassed, Anna Mae found herself at a loss for words.

"My hand," Anna Mae said after a long delay, glancing down at their clasped hands.

"Oh, sorry," Zach apologized sheepishly, unable to explain the odd feeling that had suddenly come over him. Standing close to her, he could not help but see from her red, puffy eyes that she had been crying. "I don't mean to pry, but are you okay?" he inquired.

"Stupid me," she replied as she pulled a handkerchief from the pocket of her dress and dabbed at her eyes. "I tripped over a log and fell. I cut my hand trying to catch myself."

"May I?" Zach asked, holding his hand out.

She held her left hand out and turned it palm up, revealing a nasty, jagged cut running from her middle finger to her wrist. She flinched slightly when Zach took her hand and examined the cut.

"I can't believe I was so clumsy."

"I followed your dog down here to the bridge and then he took off into the woods. The woods are so thick I didn't even consider trying to follow him. How on Earth did you get here?"

"There's a hidden path just beyond the underbrush," she answered, pointing to her left. "You just have to know where to look. I grew up playing in these woods. I know where all the paths and trails are."

"Please, come up to the house and let me clean that up," Zach offered. "You can't go home bleeding like that."

"That's all right. I don't want to be a bother. I don't live far from here," she sniffled, turning to leave.

Zach reached out and touched her arm, the odd feeling returning more intensely than before. "It's no bother at all. I used to be a Navy SEAL. We're always prepared for the unexpected. Come on, let's go up to the house. Please," he insisted, pointing toward the house.

She hesitated, uncertain if she should follow this man she had just met. He was a stranger, but something about him gave off a sense of strength and safety. An unfamiliar feeling began to grow within her. She could not describe what made her feel at ease, but there was something in this man's face that convinced her she could trust him.

"Come on," Zach urged, taking her uninjured hand and gently guiding her toward the house. "That cut really needs attention. I promise I won't bite."

Zach pulled a handkerchief from his pocket and gently wrapped it around Anna Mae's injured hand. Anna Mae suppressed any remaining concern and followed Zach as he led her toward the house.

Windward Court
Dumfries, Virginia

Chevy Man paced nervously back and forth across his study, deciding if he should call his superior. Convinced it was necessary, he stopped pacing, pulled a cellphone from his pocket, hurriedly punched a number, and waited.

Thirty-five miles away in Washington, D.C., Mr. Suit, dressed in an expensive, custom-tailored, black suit walked down a corridor of the West Wing, a bright yellow, silk tie pulled up tight against the collar of his designer shirt. A matching silk handkerchief, perfectly fluffed, sprouted from his suit coat pocket. Hand crafted, Italian leather shoes clicked softly on the tile floor. He stopped suddenly and pulled a cheap burner phone from his left jacket pocket.

"You are not supposed to call me here," Mr. Suit whispered into the phone as he ducked into an unused office, pushed the door shut, and leaned against the door to be certain no one interrupted him.

"It's urgent," Chevy Man on the other end of the conversation blurted out. "I have information I am certain you will want to hear."

"Be quick. What's the problem?"

"Someone just saw a man at the Plantation Road house," Chevy Man exclaimed.

"Who?" Mr. Suit demanded. "I didn't instruct you to recruit any new members."

"I had no choice," Chevy Man offered in defense. "We couldn't watch everybody with the few eyes we had. I had to have more men."

"Okay, okay. Are you certain we can trust him?" Mr. Suit questioned.

"Yes, the Knight of Vengeance recruited him. He said he's desperate for money. When his usefulness ends, I will kill him myself."

"See that you do," Mr. Suit ordered. "So, what was the man doing at the house?"

"He said it looks like the man is living in the house. A truck delivered furniture to the house. He saw the man run out of the house and follow a dog down to the bridge. He doesn't know if the man is renting or has bought the place."

"Has this new man seen anything else," Mr. Suit asked. "Is anyone acting suspicious?"

"Not at the house, but he said two little boys got sick and died." Chevy Man stammered. "What do I do?"

"Two small boys are of no consequence," Mr. Suit snapped. "The biocontainers must be picked up now. We cannot afford to wait. The containers must be moved and prepared now before it raises any suspicions."

"But two little boys. We can't...," Chevy Man protested.

"Silence!" Mr. Suit interrupted. "In a few days, it will not matter in the least that two little boys died. Watch the house closely. There are secrets in that house that absolutely must not by revealed. Report to me if you see anything suspicious. Anything at all. We cannot risk failure. The Worshipful Master will have us skinned alive if we fail."

"Yes, sir. It shall be done," Chevy Man replied.

Mr. Suit slammed the cheap burner phone closed and swore in the darkened room. He dropped the burner phone back in his jacket pocket and rubbed his tired eyes. *"How can people be so unreliable?"* Mr. Suit asked himself.

Mr. Suit eased the door open a crack and listened for footsteps in the corridor. Hearing nothing, he pulled the door open, stepped into the corridor, and resumed his walk toward his destination. Soon. Very soon the final pieces of the plan would fall into place. A thin smile spread across his face, knowing that once the sanctimonious president was eliminated there would be no one to stand in his way.

Westview Avenue
Beaufort, South Carolina

"Lonnie, your lunch is ready," Sheriff Overton's wife, Susan called out from the kitchen.

She turned the flame down to low under the skillet, dropped a handful of ice cubes into two glasses, filled them with water, and set them on the dining table. Receiving no response from her husband, she called out again, "Lonnie, didn't you hear me? I said your lunch is ready."

Still not receiving any response, she walked into the living room to see what was keeping her husband. She saw her husband, Sheriff Lonnie Overton, staring off into space, ignoring the local news program blaring away on the television.

She tapped him on the shoulder. "Didn't you hear me?" she asked. "I called you twice. Lunch is ready."

"Huh? Oh, sorry. I guess I didn't hear you, hon," he offered in defense.

What's the matter, Lonnie," she quizzed. "You've been distracted and quiet ever since you walked in the door. Is it something at work? An accident or a murder or something terrible like that?"

"I got called over to the Foley house," he answered. "Their two little boys were horribly sick. You know, Walter and Ruth's two boys. I got there before the ambulance. As soon as the EMT's saw the boys, they were so concerned they asked me to call for Life Flight to have them transported direct to University Medical Center in Savannah"

"That's awful," Susan exclaimed. "Are they going to be all right?"

Sheriff Overton looked down at his feet and shook his head. He looked up at his wife and said, "They both had horrible nose bleeds. Worst thing I've ever seen in my life and I've seen some pretty horrible things."

"Nose bleeds," she remarked. "Isn't that what the Pickett's had? And they both died..." Dread filled her mind as the words she had just spoken sank in.

Sheriff Overton turned away from his wife overcome with emotion and kicked the couch.

"Lonnie, are you okay?" Susan questioned. She knew being sheriff was often difficult, but she had never seen her husband this upset. She walked over and laid her hand on her husband's shoulder. "But the boys will be okay once they get to University Medical Center. Won't they, Lonnie? Lonnie, tell me they'll be okay." She shook her husband. "Lonnie, answer me."

Sheriff Overton turned back toward his wife. The look on her husband's face confirmed her fear.

"The EMT's were in the bedroom for only a few minutes before they came out and said there wasn't anything they could do for either boy."

"Both boys dead," she gasped. "I can't believe it. Poor Ruth. I can't imagine what she must be going through."

"She was inconsolable," Sheriff Overton acknowledged. "Walter took her into the bedroom so she wouldn't have to watch when the coroner showed up and they wheeled the boys out in body bags."

"How are you doing, Lonnie?" Susan questioned.

"I don't know," Sheriff Overton answered as he reached out and hugged his wife. "I just don't know." He held the embrace for a long time before he relaxed his grip and stepped back.

"What about lunch?" Susan asked. "If we don't eat soon, lunch will be ruined." Susan started for the kitchen, but her husband just stood there with a troubled look on his face. "Aren't you coming?" she asked.

"No, I'm not hungry," he answered. "I have an idea. It might be a good idea if you go over and sit with Misses Foley."

"But what about you?"

"I'll be okay. I'd go with you, but I have something important I have to take care of."

"I'll go take care of putting lunch away before I go."

"Never mind. You go ahead. I'll take care of it."

"Okay. I'll call you and let you know how Ruth's doing and when I'll be home," Susan said as she leaned over and kissed her husband.

Sheriff Overton sat on the arm of the couch and watched his wife grab her purse and head out the door.

Chapter Nineteen

Big House Plantation Road
Bluffton, South Carolina

Once they had reached the house, Zach helped Anna Mae up onto the porch and directed her to sit in one of the two wicker porch chairs. Commanding her to stay put, he rushed into the house to get a first aid kit.

"Okay, let's get that hand taken care of," Zach said as he exited the back door of the house carrying a first aid kit, a stainless steel bowl, a dark brown bottle, and a pair of scissors. He knelt down beside the chair and said, "Give me your hand."

Anna Mae held out her hand and scrunched up her face as Zach unwound the handkerchief. "Looks like there's some dirt embedded in the cut," Zach announced as he peeled the last layer of handkerchief away and examined the cut more closely.

Zach ran some water into the bowl from an outdoor spigot and set it on a small table, then added some liquid from the brown bottle to the bowl.

"What's that?" Anna Mae protested when Zach moved her hand toward the bowl.

"It's just hydrogen peroxide," Zach answered. "Before I bandage it, I need to make certain it's clean. It won't hurt. I promise."

Anna Mae closed her eyes and held her breath, jerking when her hand touched the cool liquid. She relaxed as her hand became immersed in the liquid and she realized it did not hurt as promised. Zach let her hand stay in the liquid for two full minutes. He sloshed her hand in the liquid and then lifted her hand up and examined it again.

"It looks like there are still a couple of flecks of dirt in the cut," Zach confided. "They have to come out. I'll be as careful as I can."

Zach dug through the contents of the first aid kit and pulled out a narrow paper envelope. He tore off one end and slid out a cotton swab. Cradling her hand, he said, "Sorry, this may hurt a little."

Resting her hand on his knee, he eased the tip of the swab into the cut. He pulled the swab away, revealing the fleck of dirt stuck to the swab. Rotating the swab, he repeated the process and removed the remaining fleck of dirt. He returned her hand to the bowl of liquid for another full minute. A final examination of the cut revealed no more dirt.

Zach gently patted her hand dry with a kitchen towel that had been hanging around his neck. Back to the first aid kit, he grabbed a tube of antibiotic cream and applied a narrow ribbon of white cream along the cut. After placing a sterile, non-stick dressing over the cut, he wound a bandage around her hand and thumb, affixing it with a piece of tape.

"You were fortunate you didn't need stitches," Zach said. "I'm certain it will be okay, but it will probably be a bit sore. No piano concerts for a while."

"Funny," Anna Mae smiled. "I really appreciate your kind attention, Doctor Templeton. How much do I owe you?"

"I'll let you off easy," Zach answered, returning the smile. "Have a cup of coffee with me."

"Actually, I would love that."

"Great. Two cups of Zach's world famous coffee coming up. I'll be right back."

Zach gathered up the first aid supplies and went back into the house, returning with two steaming mugs of coffee. One cup went on the table in front of Anna Mae and the remaining one went on the other end of the table. He dragged the empty chair around where he could sit facing his guest.

With her injured hand resting in her lap, she picked up the mug and took a sip of the coffee. "Mmmm. That is good,"

Anna Mae observed. She leaned back in the chair and took another sip.

"So, Zach, what do you do to keep yourself busy?" she asked.

"Well, when I'm not fighting crime or saving damsels in distress, I work as a computer analyst. Business intelligence stuff mostly."

"You save a lot of damsels in distress?"

"Hundreds," Zach laughed, spilling his coffee. "Hey, that's hot."

"A bit clumsy for a superhero, aren't you?"

"Guilty as charged," Zach chuckled.

The two sat in silence for several minutes sipping their coffee, each wondering about the connection that seemed to be building between them. Zach had not felt this relaxed and open with anyone for a very long time. It felt really good to laugh.

Deep inside, Anna Mae was in turmoil over the recent mystery uncovered in her mother's safety deposit box. She desperately wanted to share her concern with someone, but could she, or should she, share it with this man she had just met? His touch was gentle and reassuring and he exuded a sense of strength that she was not used to.

She opened her mouth to speak, "Zach, I need to...."

"Don't act alarmed," Zach warned as he kneeled down and took her injured hand, pretending to check the bandage.

Out of the corner of his eye, Zach had perceived movement in the tree line at the edge of the property. Agent Kanagy's warning had rekindled Zach's sense of hyper-vigilance. Even the smallest noise or slightest movement no longer escaped his attention.

"What are you talking about?"

"I saw movement in the trees. Someone is watching us. Do not look that way."

"You're scaring me."

"Just sit still," Zach cautioned. "I'm going to pretend to go in the house. Then I'll slip out the front and have a chat with whoever is out there."

"Zach, please be careful," Anna Mae pleaded as Zach pointed at the house and stood up.

"I'll explain later," he said as he turned and entered the house. Once inside the house, Zach hurried across the living room and went out the front door, slowly easing the door closed to prevent alerting the person in the woods. Stopping at the edge of the house, he listened. Hearing nothing, he eased his head past the side of the house, checking for movement.

He sprinted across the side yard and moved quietly into the trees, being careful where he placed his feet. Search and evade techniques from the past reawakened as he crouched and made his way through the dense trees. Each step carefully considered, he moved quietly through the trees. Nearing the spot where he had seen the movement, he slowed and inched forward, looking for movement or changes in color that seemed out of place.

About to take a step forward, a twig snapped behind him. He froze for an instant, then started to turn toward the sound.

The feeling of sudden, excruciating pain flashed along the synaptic pathways in his brain. Bright flashing colors swirled and danced before his eyes, then everything went black.

Georgia Department of Public Health
1101 Church Street
Waycross, Georgia

Dr. Michael Wilson, senior epidemiologist for the Georgia Department of Public Health, walked into his office and flopped down into his chair. The day was not even half over and already he felt as if he had been at work for days. Busily working on reducing the size of the mounds of unfinished reports sitting on either side of his desk, he had been summoned to another one of the never-ending team-building workshops.

Frustrated by what he felt had been a complete waste of two hours, he stared blankly at the mountain of work. As he expected, the workshop had been like all the others he had attended; high-paid consultants spouting over-used buzzwords and offering not one single practical solution to real-world problems. Dr. Wilson was tired, overworked, and frustrated.

Dr. Wilson had excelled in medical school, driven by his lifelong dream of becoming a doctor. He had finished second in his class at the Johns Hopkins University School of Medicine, missing the top spot by only four-hundredths of a point. Graduating summa cum laude, he had had his pick of residency programs. Unfortunately, his choice of a surgical residency at Massachusetts General Hospital in Boston had been an absolute disaster. He thoroughly loved the science and the *thought* of helping patients. However, the actuality of dealing with patients face-to-face and the horror in his mind of doing something wrong and possibly killing a patient hampered his ability to function. Despite his being extremely skilled, he performed only at what seemed to be a mediocre level.

Only through sheer willpower and determination, he completed his year of residency. Not unexpectedly, the hospital board decided to not renew his contract, leaving him with a difficult choice. Another resident with whom he had become friends and had shared his difficulties, told him he knew someone that might be able to help.

His friend arranged an interview with someone at the CDC (Centers for Disease Control and Prevention). Impressed with his stellar education and skills, the CDC offered him a position as a staff researcher. After several years of exemplary job performance at the CDC, he happened across a job opening at the Georgia Department of Public Health. A single interview resulted in a very lucrative offer which he accepted the same day. Three years later he accepted a promotion to senior epidemiologist.

Despite a very successful career, an emptiness continued to grow deep inside him, fueled by his failure years earlier at Massachusetts General Hospital. Recently, that emptiness began morphing into depression. As he became more and more depressed, his attention waned, leading to the large stacks of unfinished work piled up on his desk.

"Oh, well," he muttered, dragging an unfinished report off the top of the stack to his right.

Dr. Wilson looked up from the report when a clerk from the mailroom walked in and handed him an overnight package marked "Personal". He looked at the shipping label and read the sender's name, Dr. Luke Tilton, from the return address label.

"Doctor Luke Tilton," he repeated, thinking he should know that name. Over and over he said the name in his mind, trying to remember where he knew that name from. "Luke. Luke. Luke," he repeated the first name, hoping it would jog his memory.

"Luke…, That's it," he exclaimed out loud. Luke Tilton had been his lab partner in medical school. *"That's odd,"* he thought, not expecting anything from his old medical school chum. He grabbed the "Open Here" tab and ripped the envelope open.

Tipping the padded envelope up, he dumped out two reports, a specimen bag, a set of peripheral blood films, a business card, and a handwritten note. Quickly scanning through the two autopsy reports, he unfolded the note and began reading, becoming more alarmed with each line.

Attending physician suspected an unknown viral hemorrhagic fever:
Ebola, Marburg, or Yellow Fever.
Two conflicting lab reports for same decedent enclosed.
Re-collected tissue samples from decedent do not match.
Convinced tissue samples were deliberately switched.
Decedent showed evidence of extreme thrombocytopenia.
Blood films confirm, showing many fragmented red cells.
Symptom onset and death extremely rapid (24-36 hrs.)
Independent corroboration desperately needed.
TRUST NO ONE.   *Luke Tilton, MD*

Surely his old medical school classmate was mistaken. He had not heard of any cases of hemorrhagic fever. Before examining the blood films or running tests on the blood and tissue samples, he called his old friend. Dr. Wilson picked up the business card and called the cellphone number listed on the card. An announcement indicated the cellphone was out of service or turned off. Heeding the warning on the note, he could not call Dr. Tilton's office number. Spinning around to the computer sitting on the credenza behind him, he opened a browser session and looked up the home number for a Luke Tilton in the Savannah, Georgia area. He called the number and waited.

"Hello," a shaky female voice answered.

"Doctor Luke Tilton please," Dr. Wilson requested.

"Who is this?" the female voice demanded.

"I'm Doctor Michael Wilson. I went to medical school with Luke. I'd like to speak with him about a medical matter."

"That's not possible. He's dead. He was murdered."

"I'm so sorry," Dr. Wilson said. "Are you his wife?"

"Yes. My name's Noreen."

"I received a package and a note from your husband just this morning. I hate to pry, but can you tell me the circumstances? It might be related to what your husband sent me."

"I came home from town and found him lying in the kitchen," she stammered. "The police came. They found his office ransacked. Their opinion was that it was a robbery gone wrong."

"You have my condolences. I'm sorry to have bothered you."

"Wait," Noreen sputtered. "Can you tell me what Luke sent you and why you think it's related?"

"It's a medical case," Dr. Wilson replied. "Sorry, I'm not allowed to share the details. Again, my condolences."

"Thank you," Noreen Tilton acknowledged as she hung up the phone.

Dr. Wilson stuffed the reports and the note in the top drawer of his desk, snatched the specimen bag, and headed for the department's level four biolab. He entered the biolab's anteroom and donned his personal protective equipment. After verifying all joints were sealed, the air feed line was properly seated, and positive pressure was being maintained, he pushed the door open and entered the biolab.

The first order of business was to determine if a virus was actually present in the samples Dr. Tilton had sent. Dr. Wilson split the red seal on the infectious materials bag with a scalpel and, withdrew the sample of lung tissue, and sliced off a small piece.

Rather than use the time consuming paraffin embedding technique, he opted for the cryostat sectioning technique. He flash froze the small sample using isopentane and liquid nitrogen. With the frozen sample mounted in the positioning fixture of the cryostat sectioning device, he cranked the wheel on the right side of the device to operate the microtome. As the microtome sliced up and down, he carefully advanced the sample with his left hand, slowing the movement as the sample contacted the razor-sharp blade. A thin ribbon, thinner than the thickness of a single cell, slid down the plate.

Using a fine-haired brush, he pushed a section of the ribbon onto a gelatin-coated, histological slide. The slide then went through a standard stain, wash, and dry process to prepare it for a microscopic examination under a brightfield, fluorescent microscope.

Once a virus had been introduced into a host organism, the host's cells would show distinct observable cell abnormalities, called CPEs (cytopathic effects). Presence of CPEs in the sample would prove definitely that the host had been infected with a virus. Dr. Wilson carried the slide over to the fluorescent microscope. He slipped the slide under the stage clips and adjusted the illuminator.

Seated in front of the microscope, he bent forward and stared through the binocular eyepiece. He adjusted the stage until the sample came into focus. Mumbling to himself, he spent several minutes examining the sample as he moved the sample back and forth along the X and Y axes.

"Wow," he exclaimed as he straightened up. Never in his entire career had he seen a tissue sample that exhibited every defined cell abnormality for virus infection. There were many cytoplasmic inclusion bodies, along with significant cell enlargement, swelling of cell walls, cytoplasmic stranding, nuclear inclusion bodies, and grape-like clusters.

The final step, identification of the specific type of virus, required an immunofluorescence assay. Dr. Wilson would subject the sample to commercial antibodies, each known to bind to only one specific type of virus. If the antibody linked with the virus, it would emit fluorescence or change color, thereby identifying the virus type. Becoming more and more concerned, Dr. Wilson went through every commercial antibody the lab possessed and not one produced any fluorescence or color change.

To his knowledge, the lab at the Georgia Department of Public Health had all the same commercial antibodies as the CDC had. Running his finger down the list of antibodies he exclaimed, "If the sample doesn't react to any of these antibodies, it has to be a totally new and unknown virus." A chill ran down his back as he considered the implications of the frightening statement he had just uttered.

He rushed out of the lab, climbed out of his personal protective equipment, and headed for his office. Bypassing the elevator, he ducked into the stairwell and ran up the steps three at a time.

Bursting through the door to his office, he hurried across the room and sat down at his desk. All the way up the three flights of stairs and the sprint down the hallway, he had wracked his brain trying to think of who he could call. He opened the top drawer of his desk and stared at the last line of the note—TRUST NO ONE. "What do I do? Who do I call?" he wondered.

Chapter Twenty

Big House Plantation Road
Bluffton, South Carolina

A bullet smacked into the tree beside the assailant's head, sending chunks of bark flying. The man turned and disappeared into the deep underbrush. The man that had fired the shot slipped his weapon back into its holster, turned, and disappeared in the other direction, the sun glinting off a shiny object just above the man's left shirt pocket.

Zach stirred and pushed himself up from the ground. Groggy and dazed, he leaned against a tree for support.

"Ouch," he exclaimed, gently touching the large goose egg developing on the back of his head.

Slowly, the memory of what had just happened returned. Shaking his head, he chastised himself for being careless and letting someone sneak up behind him. The blow had come suddenly and without warning. His *hunting* skills must have atrophied far more than he thought. He had not even seen his assailant. All he remembered was blurry a vision as he hit the ground: a pair of muddy boots with a distinctive red tag at the heel, and duct tape around the toe of the other boot.

Staggering on shaky legs, Zach stumbled out of the tree line, rubbing his head and heading for the house. Anna Mae, startled by the sound of a gunshot, had been watching the woods. She watched Zach exit and stumble across the yard. Zach stopped at the edge of the porch and looked up at Anna Mae.

"Zach, what happened? Are you okay?" Anna Mae questioned, "I heard a gunshot."

"Gunshot? I didn't hear a gunshot," Zach quavered. "Somebody hit me from behind. I was moving through the woods and then *wham* the lights went out. Never saw it coming. Guess I'm getting old and slow."

Picking his foot up to step up on the porch, Zach misjudged the distance, missed the edge of the porch, and went down on one knee. Anna Mae rushed over and grabbed Zach's arm to keep him from toppling over. With her help, he stepped up on the porch and rubbed his head again. He pulled his fingers away and saw his fingertips were stained with blood.

"Come over here and sit down," Anna Mae ordered, leading him by the arm. "Let me have a look at your head."

Zach eased himself down onto the chair and leaned forward. "Hey, that hurts," Zach wailed as Anna Mae parted his hair and examined the large bump.

"Looks like it's my turn to offer first aid to you, Zach," she said. "Sit still while I get the first aid kit."

Anna Mae soaked a cotton ball with hydrogen peroxide and dabbed it on the cut in the middle of the knot.

"Yeeooww," Zach cried out, hunching up his shoulders.

"Oh, come on. It can't be that bad," Anna Mae countered. "Remember. You told me it wouldn't hurt."

"Bad," Zach spit. "What did you pour on it? Alcohol?"

"It was only hydrogen peroxide. See," Anna Mae said, holding out the bottle for Zach to see.

"Well, it sure felt like alcohol," Zach complained, reaching up to rub his head.

"Don't touch it," Anna Mae scolded, batting his hand away. "If you do, you get the hydrogen peroxide again."

"Humph," Zach grumbled, dropping his hand back down on the arm of the chair.

"Sit here and keep your hand *off* that cut," Anna Mae commanded. "I'll go get some ice to put on it. Do you have plastic storage bags?"

"Yes. Third drawer below the coffee pot."

Anna Mae entered the house, located the coffeepot sitting on the counter, and retrieved a storage bag from the third drawer down. After placing two handfuls of ice cubes into the bag, she lifted a dishtowel from the dishwasher handle and wrapped it around the bag of ice.

"Here, hold this in place," she said, gently placing the bag of ice against the back of Zach's head.

Zach reached up and placed his hand on the bag of ice, moving it around until he found a spot where the pain was tolerable. Anna Mae sat in the chair opposite Zach and stared at his eyes, a worried look on her face.

"What?" Zach asked.

"I'm watching your eyes," she answered. "I want to make sure you're okay. You might have a concussion."

Zach batted his eyes open and closed a number of times.

"Well, I see you're back to your old ornery self."

"I'm sorry. I do appreciate your concern, but I'm fine. Bump on my head and I'll probably have a headache. I assure you I have suffered much worse than this."

"Did you see who hit you?" she asked, deciding to let go of her concern for the moment.

"No, all I saw was a man's legs as I went down. At least, I assume it was a man," Zach answered. "I remember muddy boots, light brown, a red tag on the heel, and duct tape wrapped around the toe of one of the boots."

A startled look flashed across Anna Mae's face as she realized she knew someone that exactly fit that description. "No. *It couldn't be. Surely he wouldn't,*" she thought.

The sudden surprise on Anna Mae's face escaped Zach's attention as he stared at the trees, trying to visualize the details from his attack in the woods. Anna Mae calmed herself internally, sat up straight, and smiled at Zach as he stood up and turned toward her.

"Come inside," he directed, pointing at the back door. "Sit in the living room. I need to make a quick phone call."

Zach held the door open and waited for Anna Mae to enter the house. Following her inside, he directed her to the couch in the living room. After refilling her cup with coffee, he walked into the bedroom, leaving the door standing open.

Cellphone in hand, he scrolled through his contact list, selected an entry, and pressed the Call icon.

"Admiral Charles Hadley's office. May I help you?" the voice on the other end answered.

"Is he in?" Zach asked. "This is Zach Templeton. It's urgent."

"Hang on, Mister Templeton. Let me check."

Zach stood in the middle of the bedroom listening to soft jazz playing softly in his ear. Not normally a nosy person, Anna Mae leaned toward the bedroom trying to pick up some of the conversation. Rubbing his forehead as a headache began to develop, Zach sat down on the edge of the bed.

"Zach, sorry for the delay," Admiral Hadley apologized. "I was just finishing up a meeting. What's up? My assistant said it was urgent."

"Admiral, we have a big problem," Zach answered. "I need to know why you sent Agent Kanagy down here. Somebody attacked me a few minutes ago. Knocked me out cold."

"Are you okay?"

"Yes, I'm okay. Got a real nasty bump on the back of my head and I'm developing a splitting headache, but other than that, I think I'll live. Anna Mae said she heard a gunshot. I didn't hear it. I must have been unconscious."

"Anna Mae? Who's Anna Mae?"

"My landlord, or one of them. It's a long story. I'll fill you in later. I need to know what's going on."

"I'm not certain I'm allowed to share that with you."

"Listen, Admiral, you send an agent down here to warn me. He hands me a weapon and then tells me I'm going to need it. And then today I get attacked in the woods. I want some answers."

Zach waited.

"Admiral, I'm waiting. I need to know what's going on," Zach insisted, the volume of his voice increasing.

"I shouldn't," Admiral Hadley admitted. "But okay. I'm climbing out on a limb here. A very skinny, very brittle limb, I might add. The CIA has some recent intel, most of which has not been shared with me. Seems they are tracking a nefarious individual they call *The Snake*. He is a legend, mostly in Europe. According to the legend, he has over one hundred kills, most of them with their throats slit. He kills without warning or provocation."

"I know that, Admiral. Agent Kanagy told me that much. So, what does that have to do with me?"

"According to a CIA informant that supposedly managed to get close to The Snake, who has since disappeared by the way, said he was the mastermind behind the bombing in Sacramento and was also directly linked to Frank Porter."

Admiral Hadley waited for Zach's response.

"Zach, did you hear me?"

"Yes, Admiral, I heard you," Zach answered through clenched teeth, the muscles along his jaw bunching into knots.

"Zach, if he was linked to Porter, it is not a big leap to believe he is fully aware that it was you that captured Porter and returned him to the United States for trial. The CIA is convinced he is on the move and likely headed here. If that's true, you would be in grave danger."

"I would love to meet him, Admiral," Zach snarled. "I have a score to settle with him. When will the CIA know if he is headed here and what his destination might be?"

"Sorry, I don't know that. I don't think the CIA knows either."

"Is there anything else, Admiral?"

"This information is *need to know* and can't be shared with anyone," Admiral Hadley answered. "Be vigilant, Zach. This guy has never even been photographed. He's like a ghost. He strikes and disappears without a trace. Oh, there's one other thing. The weapon Agent Kanagy gave you; keep it on your person at all times."

"Even in bed?" Zach quipped.

"Don't be silly, Zach," Admiral Hadley responded. "I'm serious. This is a credible threat. I'll contact you if I hear anything else. Stay safe."

"Will do. Later," Zach affirmed. He ended the call, stuffed the cellphone in his pocket, and headed for the living room.

Thinking the Admiral was probably right, Zach stopped as he walked into the living room and said, "I'll be right back. Don't leave." Continuing through the living room, he hurried up the stairs and into his bedroom. He pulled open the bottom drawer of his dresser, dug under a stack of clothes, and retrieved the weapon Agent Kanagy had handed him. Standing there staring at the 9mm Sig Sauer P229 in his hand, he thought back to the last time he had had to use a weapon.

"Haven't I endured enough? Why do I keep getting thrust into these situations?" Zach complained. He inserted a loaded clip, checked the safety, shoved the Sig Sauer into its holster, and slipped it over his belt. Passing by the closet on his way downstairs, he pulled an overshirt off a hanger and threw it on to cover the weapon.

Back in the living room, Zach plopped down in a chair beside the couch. The tail of his overshirt got snagged on the chair, revealing the menacing Sig Sauer.

"What is that?" Anna Mae gasped.

"It's a Sig Sauer nine millimeter," Zach answered. "After what happened in the woods, I think a little protection is definitely in order."

"When you were in the bedroom on the phone, I couldn't help but hear you say *Admiral* several times," Anna Mae added. "Does that have anything to do with what happened in the woods and your putting on the gun?"

"Yes it does," Zach confided. "I was talking with Admiral Charles Hadley, a former comrade from my Navy days. He's the Director of Naval Intelligence."

"Wow, Director of Naval Intelligence," Anna Mae remarked. "You go right to the top."

"I met him during my duty as a SEAL. We actually became good friends. I helped him with a couple of special ops, but I really can't say more than that."

"I understand."

"You were going to say something earlier. You know, before the guy in the woods showed up."

Anna Mae hesitated. The attack in the woods gave her ample reason to be worried, especially considering she had a suspicion she knew who had attacked Zach. She wanted to tell Zach, but she had to be certain before she said anything.

"It's nothing important," she lied. "I really need to get home. Daddy will wonder where I am."

Rising from the couch, she started toward the back door. Zach stood and blocked her way.

"Let me drive you home," Zach said. "You don't want to walk all the way home with your injured hand."

Looking down at her hand, she had to admit Zach was right. Her hand had begun to throb. Walking all the way home would not be pleasant.

"Please," Zach insisted.

"Okay," Anna Mae agreed. "You're right. My hand is starting to hurt."

"All I have to do is lock the doors," Zach said.

He switched the coffee pot off, locked the back door, and scooped up his car keys from the counter. Nudging Anna Mae toward the front door, he followed her out onto the front porch and locked the front door. Zach hurried to the passenger side of his car and opened the door for Anna Mae. Easing herself into the seat, she nestled her injured hand in her lap.

Zach started the engine and backed down the lane and out onto Big House Plantation Road. As the car started down the road toward her house, Anna Mae became more convinced than ever that something sinister was happening in the once sleepy little town of Bluffton.

__White House__
__Pennsylvania Avenue__
__Washington, D.C.__

In the middle of a meeting, Mr. Suit felt buzzing coming from inside his left jacket pocket. Abruptly concluding the meeting underway in his office, he stood and followed the puzzled attendees to the door and ushered them out.

"No calls," he yelled at his chief of staff. "I'm not to be disturbed for any reason."

Ducking back into his sumptuous office, Mr. Suit closed and locked the door behind him. Emblazoned on the entry door to the anteroom between Mr. Suit's office and the office of his chief of staff was the great seal of the Office of the Vice President of the United States.

Seated at his desk, Vice President Arthur Mead fished a cheap burner phone out of his jacket pocket.

He pressed the power button to awaken the phone and saw that he had a new text message. Opening the text app, he selected the new message and stared at the short, one-line message, "911 - KoV". The text contained the appropriate emergency code, but the message had arrived from a phone number he did not recognize.

Vice President Mead repeated the phone number out loud, closed the text app, opened the phone dialer app, and punched in the number.

A man's voice answered on the first ring and immediately blurted out, "I saw the Knight of the East watching the house on Plantation Road. He almost got caught."

"Who is this and why are you using the emergency contact code?" Mead asked.

"I was recruited by the Knight of Vengeance," Senior FBI Field Agent Alfred Grant answered. "I've called him many times and haven't been able to reach him. I thought that was important enough to contact you."

"What happened?" Mead asked. "Why did the knight almost get caught?"

"I've been watching the knight as instructed. I saw him skulking in the woods watching the man that's living in the Plantation Road house. I guess the man living there saw him. The next thing I know, the man ran into the woods and headed toward the knight. The knight hid, then hit him from behind. He bent over the man when a bullet slammed into the tree next to him. The knight took off running and disappeared."

"What?" Mead bellowed. "Who fired the shot?"

"I saw something shiny above the man's left shirt pocket. It had to be the sheriff. I ran back to my car and disappeared."

"Is anyone else suspicious?"

"I don't think so," Agent Grant answered.

"Great. Just great," Mead growled. "Silence them."

"But sir, there have already been a lot of bodies."

"Silence. It does not matter. We're almost ready. In a short time there will be nothing anyone can do. Just kill them."

"But....,"

"Did you hear me?" Mead interrupted. "Just do what I tell you to do or it's your body they will find next. Do you understand me?"

"Yes, sir," Agent Grant replied.

Shaking his head, Vice President Mead ended the call and quickly punched in another number.

In a different office on the far side of the West Wing, another cheap burner phone buzzed.

"Yes," came the answer.

"We have to move the timetable up. I have the documents ready. I want them placed by end of day. Can you arrange that?"

"But sir, that's too...,"

"We don't have any choice. There are developments down south that could jeopardize the entire plan. Somebody has moved into the Plantation Road house. We have to act before someone digs around and discovers something. The documents *must* be in place before the release if we expect to bring down the idiot."

"I'll make up an excuse and get him out of the office," Adam Conley, Deputy Assistant to the President of the United States, replied.

Vice President Mead ended the call and dropped the burner phone back in his jacket pocket. He swore out loud and slammed his fist down on the desk, worried that the plan he had spent two years putting into action could be in jeopardy. Dethroning the idiot in the Oval Office was all he had dreamed about for so long he could not remember when it had not been the driving force in his life. Nothing was beyond the limit of what he would do, not even a bargain with the Devil himself.

Vice President Mead looked like a corporate CEO or a bank president, keeping his salt-and-pepper hair clipped short and neatly combed. He wore only expensive, hand-tailored, dark suits. His suit jacket never came off unless he was alone in the privacy of his office or his home. Only the finest Italian leather shoes and vibrant silk ties rounded out his wardrobe.

Arthur Mead despised the President's infuriating "damn the torpedoes" take charge management style. He had lost count of the times he had desperately wanted to defy the idiot's policies, but President Cantwell was enormously popular and he wielded great power. Being a crafty politician, Vice President Mead knew he had to bide his time while building his own team of followers. Beside his Harvard law degree, he also possessed a master's degree in psychology. He knew people and he knew exactly how to manipulate them.

Manipulating people was so unbelievably easy he found it laughable. The only thing most Americans cared about was money and *stuff*. More and more money. More and more *stuff*. They would sell the keys to their own country to their worst enemy as long as the price was right. He never ceased to be amazed how easily the country's national security system could be bypassed. For a small number of people, the lure of money was not enough. To those he promised position and power in the empire he was building.

Despite knowing the individuals he bargained with were violent, evil men who hated the United States and everything it stood for, he aligned himself with them anyway. Like most individuals who were blinded by their own self-importance, he believed he could end the evil alliance any time he chose. He could not have been more wrong.

He was unaware that even if he were fortunate enough to be one of the three percent that survived the coming catastrophe, there would be no country left to command.

Chapter Twenty-One

East Wacona Drive
Waycross, Georgia

Dr. Michael Wilson stood in front of the desk in his home study, staring at the various items sent by Dr. Tilton. Shaken and worried by the handwritten note included with the other items, he had taken all the items home for safekeeping. Deeply worried because of the alarming results of his immunofluorescence testing of the blood sample, he knew he had to contact someone, and soon. But who?

He turned from the desk and paced back and forth in front of the window, deep in thought. Wearing a track in the plush, pile carpet, he stopped and stared out the window, racking his brain. Who could he call? There must be somebody he could trust. The CDC was out because of the warning in Dr. Tilton's note. The CDC would have been the first place Dr. Tilton would have expected him to call. So who else?

FBI? CIA? Homeland Security? There had to be somebody he could call. Someone in Washington, perhaps?

"Hmmm, a new infectious disease?" he thought as he returned to his pacing. "That's it!" he shouted, after three more passes by the window.

Six months earlier, he had attended a "Conference On Retroviruses And Opportunistic Infections" in Boston.

From one of the breakout sessions, he remembered the speaker saying, "A retrovirus is a type of RNA virus that inserts a copy of its own genome into the DNA of a host cell it is invading. Then, once infected, the virus spreads like a wildfire in dry grass."

The "*….wild fire in dry grass,*" part of the speaker's statement had painted a vivid picture in his mind. From what he had read from the autopsy report, whatever killed Victoria Pickett had spread very quick, like a wildfire. Dr. Wilson was certain he had kept the lecture notes from that conference. He walked over to a file cabinet in the corner of the room and dug through the drawer containing training materials.

"That's odd," he said to himself. "I'm certain I kept those notes."

Pushing all the files toward the back of the drawer, he started over. Halfway through the drawer, he remarked, "Aha, there it is."

He lifted the folder out of the drawer, returned to the desk, and spread the contents out across the desk. He read through the individual workshop notes until he came to the one on retroviruses. Flipping to the back page, he quickly scanned the presenter's bio. The presenter had been Major General George Whitney, MD, of the Emerging Infectious Diseases Department of the Washington, DC, VA Medical Center.

Dr. Wilson was mystified he hadn't thought of Dr. Whitney sooner as the two men had ended up sitting at the same table during the evening dinner and had had a spirited discussion about virus mutations.

"He would be perfect," Dr. Wilson declared, retrieving a rubber band-wrapped stack of business cards from the top left drawer of his desk. "I know I kept his card," he said as he slipped off the rubber band and rifled through the stack. With Dr. Whitney's business card in hand, he reached for the telephone.

He punched in the telephone number printed on the lower-left corner of the card.

"Infectious Diseases Department. May I help you?" a voice on the other end announced.

"Doctor George Whitney, please," Dr. Wilson answered. "It's urgent."

"Who may I say is calling?"

"I'm Doctor Michael Wilson, senior epidemiologist for the Georgia Department of Public Health."

"Please hold. I'll see if he's available."

"Doctor Wilson, Doctor Whitney is gathering materials for a department heads meeting. He says he can only give you a few minutes. Is that okay?"

"That's fine, but please hurry."

"He'll be with you shortly."

Dr. Wilson drummed his fingers on the desk as he waited for Dr. Whitney to come on the line. Getting impatient, he considered hanging up and calling the number again. He reached over to the phone and was about to depress the hook switch when he heard someone come on the line.

"Doctor Wilson, sorry it took me so long," Dr. Whitney apologized. "I'm due at a meeting in less than ten minutes. You'll have to make this short."

"You may change your mind when I explain why I called," Dr. Wilson began. "A colleague sent me some autopsy reports, a set of peripheral blood films, and lung tissue and blood samples. The attending physician in a suspicious death suspected an unknown hemorrhagic fever. My colleague, a local ME, concurred and sent me the samples for corroboration. I also concur, Dr. Whitney. The reason I'm calling is that the virus is a new and completely unknown virus."

"Do tell," Dr. Whitney said. "Go on."

"I sectioned the lung tissue, then mounted and stained it using standard protocols. When I performed the microscopic examination, I found that the sample exhibited every single one of the cytopathic effects. Doctor, in my entire career, I have never seen a single case where a tissue sample exhibited every listed effect."

"I can't say I have either," Dr. Whitney added. "What about the identification of virus type?"

"That is the frightening part. I subjected the sample to every commercial antibody our lab possesses. Not one produced any fluorescence or color change."

"Are you certain, Doctor Wilson?"

"Absolutely, Doctor Whitney. Otherwise, I would not have called you."

"Hang on a minute," Dr. Whitney said. He held the phone away from his head and yelled at his administrative assistant to call the chair of the meeting and tell him something urgent had come up and he could not attend.

Returning to the line, Dr. Whitney said, "Can you go over your exact procedure, from start to finish?"

Dr. Wilson repeated his earlier account, explaining each step he had performed on the tissue samples while going into much more detail. Dr. Whitney listened, interrupting twice, asking for additional explanation. Dr. Wilson concluded his explanation and waited.

"Dr. Whitney, are you still there?" he asked.

"Yes, yes, I'm still here," Dr. Whitney responded. "What you've told me is quite worrisome. If what you told me is true, and I have no reason to doubt that it is, we likely have a serious crisis. Can you overnight me copies of any reports you have and portions of the samples for testing here?"

"I certainly can. They will be on the way to you within the hour."

"I will run them through our lab here as soon as they arrive."

"There's something else I should tell you, Doctor. The last line of the note my colleague included with the samples said to trust no one. I tried to call him as soon as I received the package. I spoke with his wife and learned that he had been murdered. She said the police suspected a robbery gone wrong, but I suspect that is not what happened, especially given the warning he included."

"Don't tell anyone what you have learned or that you are sending me samples. And be careful."

'Call me when you have results from the samples," Dr. Wilson requested. He hung up the phone and grabbed an overnight envelope from his desk drawer.

151 Laurel Oak Bay Road
Bluffton, South Carolina

Anna Mae waved at Zach as he turned his car around and headed down the driveway toward the main road. Feeling apprehensive inside, she entered the house to confront her father about the items she had found in her mother's safety deposit box. Depending on how that conversation went, she would also mention the incident that had occurred at Zach's house.

She walked into the living room and dropped her purse on the coffee table. Not finding her father, she headed for the kitchen. Standing at the counter with his back to her, he turned when he heard her footsteps.

"Anna Mae, I was expecting you sooner," Edwin Watts said. "I've been waiting to start lunch."

"Daddy, we need to talk," Anna Mae declared.

"Okay. What about?"

"Not here. Let's sit in the living room."

Anna Mae turned and started toward the living room. Edwin snagged a coffee mug from the counter and followed his daughter into the living room. Anna Mae picked up her purse and sat on the couch, holding the purse in her lap. With her father settled into his favorite recliner, she drew in a breath and began.

"Daddy I went to the bank to look for the property deeds for this house and for the rental house. While searching Mother's safety deposit box, I found some odd items. Do you know anything about that?"

"You know I don't know anything about business," Edwin answered. "I never had anything to do with that stuff."

"But the items I mentioned have nothing to do with business. I found two notes and a really odd looking key."

"What do you mean a key?"

"It's old like an antique. Looks like it might fit an old padlock or something like that."

Edwin shrugged his shoulders and didn't answer.

"There were two notes," Anna Mae continued. "One was handwritten and said something about Fred Tolbert and the other one had several strings of odd characters."

She dug through her purse and pulled out the note with the odd characters. Leaning toward her father, she held out the note so he could see it. A startled look flashed across his face. He did his best to hide his shock, but Anna Mae had already noticed.

To divert Anna Mae's attention to something else, he snapped at her, "Your mother is dead. Why can't you just leave it alone? Notes. Keys. None of that matters."

Edwin leaped up out of the recliner and stomped off into his bedroom, slamming the door so hard it rattled dishes on a shelf in the living room.

Startled by her father's sudden outburst, Anna Mae stared in disbelief at the now closed bedroom door. Never had she witnessed her father react with such anger. "*It must be the grief from mother's death,*" she tried to convince herself. If not, her father's outburst would be far more troubling.

Not knowing exactly what to think, she wandered into the kitchen. Reaching up into an upper cabinet, she grabbed a coffee cup and poured it half full. With the cup in hand, she walked into the mudroom, intending to go sit on the back porch. She put her hand on the doorknob and stopped.

"My God!" she exclaimed.

She had a suspicion, but she had tried to convince herself it could not possibly be true. Sitting there beside the door was a pair of dirty work boots, a bright red tag on the heel of one boots and duct tape wrapped around the toe of the other boot. Her mind reeled. She felt light-headed.

"*No! No! No!*" a voice screamed in her mind. What possible reason could her father have for attacking Zach in the woods? Could Zach have done something to her father? The notes and the odd key? What did it all mean? The Pickett's deaths? The Sheriff's cryptic warning? What was happening? Alarming questions and frightening images swirled in her mind as she reached out to steady herself. None of it made any sense.

Unable to solve this mystery on her own, she had to tell someone. Would it be unfair to ask her new friend, Zach, to help her get to the bottom of the unexplained events. She needed help. Sudden buzzing in the pocket of her dress startled her. She leaped backward, knocking over a mop bucket which sent the mop flying across the room.

She lifted the buzzing phone from her pocket and answered, "Hello."

"Hello, Anna Mae, it's your Grammy Elsie," Elsie Bennett, Anna Mae's grandmother on her Mother's side, answered.

"Oh, hello, Grammy," Anna Mae greeted as she bent over and picked up the mop and returned it and the bucket to the corner of the mudroom. "I wasn't expecting a call from you."

"I could use your help, Anna Mae. I love little Mazie, but she is wearing me down. I'm afraid I'm not as young as I used to be."

"Grammy, I'm sorry. I completely forgot. I'll come right over and pick her up."

"Thank you, dear. I would appreciate that."

"See you in a few minutes," Anna Mae said.

Stopping by the sink, Anna Mae dumped out the coffee, rinsed the cup, and set it in the drainer. She walked into the living room, grabbed her purse, and started for the front door. Hesitating momentarily, she looked at her father's closed bedroom door, wondering if she should tell him she was leaving. Deciding against that because of his earlier outburst, she continued toward the door.

She pushed the door open and left the house without saying a word to her father. She climbed into her car and headed for her grandmother's house.

Chapter Twenty-Two

Big House Plantation Road
Bluffton, South Carolina

Anna Mae turned off Big House Plantation Road onto the driveway that led to Zach's house. She pulled up beside Zach's car and switched off the engine. She climbed out of the car, opened the rear passenger door, and lifted Mazie out of her car seat. With Mazie hugging her neck, Anna Mae headed for the house. Standing on the porch, she rapped on the front door.

"Anna Mae," Zach exclaimed as he pulled the door open. "What a pleasant surprise. I didn't expect you back so soon. And who is this pretty little lady?"

"This is Mazie," Anna Mae replied. "She's my cousin's little girl. Both her parents died recently from an unknown disease. I've been taking care of her with my grandmother's help."

Mazie eyes lit up when she saw Zach. "Me, me, me," she chattered, holding her arms out toward Zach.

"Well, okay," Zach smiled, reaching out to take the little girl, surprised she would so eagerly come to a stranger. He propped her on his hip and stepped back out of the doorway, motioning Anna Mae to come in.

"I was just about to pour me a cup of coffee. Would you like some?"

"Yes, please. I could really use some," she answered as Zach directed her toward an overstuffed chair in the living room. "Mazie really misses her daddy. Maybe that's why she is so taken with you."

"You said *both* of her parents died recently."

"Yes. It was terrible. They died only a few days apart. Joshua, that's Mazie's father, was from out of state and I'm her mother's only relative in the area except for her grandmother who's in a nursing home."

"If I'm not prying, do the doctor's have any idea what her parents died from?" Zach asked.

"The doctors seemed baffled, especially because of the similarity and suddenness of their deaths," Anna Mae divulged. "All they would say was that it was some form of blood disease."

"How are you doing suddenly being the mother of a three-year-old toddler, I'm guessing?"

"She's only two, won't be three for two months yet. I have to admit it's been quite a change, but I love her to death. The hardest part is at night when she wants her mommy."

"I can't imagine," Zach commented. "I'll go get that coffee now. Sit. I'll be right back."

Zach turned and headed toward the kitchen. As he walked into the kitchen, Mazie pointed toward the counter and babbled something that Zach assumed was, "What that?" He walked around the room describing various objects as Mazie jabbered away. Zach carried out a steaming cup of coffee and set it beside Anna Mae. He attempted to set Mazie on the couch beside Anna Mae, but she was having none of that. With Mazie clinging tightly to him, he went back to the kitchen for his cup.

Returning to the living room, he took the chair across from Anna Mae and said, "Again, I don't mean to pry, but you look upset."

"I had an argument with my dad," she answered, leaving out the discovery of the muddy boots. "I pressed him about some items I found in my mother's safety deposit box. They found her dead in her car, submerged in the May River up by Bluffton. I'm convinced her death was not an accident. As I told you, my cousin, Victoria, and her husband, Joshua, both died suddenly from what appeared to be nose bleeds."

Zach sat silently listening, holding Mazie, who had gone to sleep nestled in his lap.

"On top of all that, I received a bizarre voicemail telling me the two little Foley boys have died, both with nosebleeds. Then the man said the recent deaths were not accidents and that I was in great danger."

"Did the man say why you are in danger?" Zach asked.

"No," she answered. "Zach, I recognized the voice. It was Sheriff Overton. I'm certain of it. If he knew the deaths were not accidents, why isn't he doing something?"

"Are you certain it was the sheriff?"

"I'm positive. When they found my mother's car in the river, we had a lengthy conversation. There was no reason for my mother to have been in Bluffton. She was an excellent driver. The car had absolutely no damage. She *would not* have simply driven off into the river. I told him I didn't believe it was an accident, but he told me I was wrong. He lied to me, Zach. I could tell he was lying. It showed on his face."

"Do you have any idea why he would lie?"

"I don't have the slightest idea. He's been sheriff for a long time and is highly respected. It doesn't make any sense."

"No wonder you look stressed," Zach said as he shifted Mazie's weight to relieve his arm that was going to sleep.

"Oh, that's not all," Anna Mae added. "I found some really strange items in Mother's safety deposit box. A really odd-looking old key and two notes. One of the notes said a gentleman by the name of Fred Tolbert's death was not an accident and the other note has three lines of weird characters."

Anna Mae grabbed her purse, retrieved the note with the weird characters, and held it out for Zach to look at. Zach took the note from Anna Mae, stared at the strange symbols, and nodded his head up and down in agreement.

"They're weird all right," he agreed. "It has to be some kind of code, but I don't have a clue what it might be."

"I certainly don't have any idea why my mother would have had it," Anna Mae fretted. "She wasn't part of any secret organizations. Even if she had been, why would she have put it in her safety deposit box."

Anna Mae looked over at Zach and noticed him deep in thought as he gazed at the note, deep furrows showing on his forehead. "What are you thinking, Zach?" she asked.

"I have an idea," Zach offered. "May I make a copy of the note?"

"If you think it will help."

"I'll be right back," Zach said. "Can you hold Mazie for a while?"

Zach lifted himself from the chair and gently passed the sleeping Mazie to Anna Mae. He bounded up the stairs, rushed over to the printer, and tapped it to awaken it from its sleep mode. He lifted the top of the printer, positioned the note on the glass, and closed the top. Sitting in front of the computer, he first scanned the note, saved it, and then printed a copy. With the note and the copy in hand, he hurried down the stairs and sat on the arm of the chair Anna Mae was sitting in.

"Here's my idea," Zach panted, winded from his hurried trips up and down the stairs. "My dad worked in cryptology for the government before he retired. He was pretty good at cracking codes and ciphers. I'll call him and see if he could help us decipher this. I'll keep the copy. You put the original somewhere where it will be safe."

"I don't really have anywhere at the house that I would consider safe," she advised. "And I really don't want to drive to the bank again. Do you have anywhere here that would be safe?"

"Yes, actually. I have a fire safe in the basement. I could put it in there."

"Thanks, Zach. I'll feel better knowing it's safe," Anna Mae said, holding the note out toward Zach.

Zach plucked the original note from her hand and disappeared into the kitchen. Anna Mae heard the door to the basement open and Zach's footsteps on the stairs. Two short minutes later, she heard Zach ascending the stairs. The basement door slammed and Zach reappeared in the living room. As Zach entered the room, Mazie stirred, sat up on Anna Mae's lap, and rubbed her eyes.

"Up, up," the little girl called out, holding her arms up.

"This is getting to be a habit," Zach said as lifted the little girl up.

Repeating the game the two had played in the kitchen, Zach walked around the living room calling out the names of items as Mazie pointed at them. Perched on the top shelf of a bookcase sat an old brown teddy bear. Mazie pointed insistently at the bear. Zach snagged the bear and handed it to Mazie. She squealed in delight and hugged the bear.

"His name is Benny," Zach told Mazie. "Benny," he said again, pointing at the bear.

"Ba-ee," Mazie repeated.

"Close enough, sweetie," Zack cooed.

Mazie kept repeating her version of the bear's name as Zach turned around and walked back over to where Anna Mae was seated.

"My favorite stuffed toy when I was a little boy," he said.

"Are you sure you want Mazie to play with it?"

"Absolutely," Zach answered, hopelessly under the spell of the little girl's impish smile. "My wife and I weren't able to have children. I dreamed of having a little girl just like this."

"Weren't able to?" Anna Mae said with a questioning look on her face.

"My wife was murdered," Zach responded. "It's a long and painful story. I'll tell you sometime, but not right now, okay?"

"Sure. I didn't mean to pry."

"I moved here to get away from all the old memories and start a new life. I couldn't think of a better start than with you and this precious little girl. Oops, I hope that didn't come out wrong. I meant getting to know you. Like as friends"

"I understand," Anna Mae said. *"But would that be so bad?"* she wondered in her mind, drawing a little closer to Zach every time she was around him. Never had she met a man that radiated such strength. She determined in her mind that she was going to get to know this man better.

"Zach, Can I ask you a really big favor?"

"Sure. Go ahead, ask away."

"I need to go home and confront my father about something. Considering his last outburst, it would probably be better if Mazie was not there. Do you think you could watch her for a little while? She's really a good-natured little girl and easy to entertain.

"Well, Mazie, what do you think about that? Do you want to stay with Uncle Zach for a little while?"

Mazie nodded her head up and down vigorously.

"Will you be safe at home?" Zach asked.

"I think so," she answered. "My father's angry, but I don't believe he would hurt me. Are you really sure about watching Mazie?"

"It will be my pleasure. We'll have a great time. Is there anything special I should know?"

"I don't think so. I'll get her bag from my car. She drinks regular milk from her sippy cup. If she were to get really upset, there's a stuffed giraffe in the bag. It's her favorite. "

"We'll have an adventure. Won't we Mazie?"

Anna Mae made a quick trip out to her car and retrieved Mazie's travel bag. She thanked Zach profusely for being willing to watch Mazie. Without even thinking, she stood up on her tiptoes and kissed Zach on the cheek. Instantly embarrassed, her face turning red, she rushed out the door and jumped into her car.

Zach walked over to the door and watched as she started the car's engine, waving at her as she drove off. He reached up and touched his cheek where Anna Mae had kissed him.

Zach closed the door and turned his attention to Mazie. While she was busy playing with toys Zach had found in her travel bag, he lifted his cellphone out of his pocket, and dialed his dad's number.

"Hey, Zach, how are things going in South Carolina?" James Templeton asked.

"It's been a rather eventful couple of days," Zach answered.

"Oh, how so?"

"I'm not quite sure where to start. I met....," Zach's attention was interrupted when Mazie who handed him a toy and babbled something he did not understand. "Yes, Mazie, that's pretty," he said, handing the toy back to her.

"What's that I hear?" James asked. "Is that a small child?"

"Yes. Her name is Mazie," Zach answered. "I met a woman named Anna Mae Watts recently. She was out at the back of the property. She had cut her hand and I cleaned it up and bandaged it. Both Mazie's parents died recently. Anna Mae is taking care of her. Anna Mae was her mother's cousin. Dad, Mazie's the sweetest little thing I've ever met. Anna Mae had something important to do and asked me to watch her for a little while. I'm sorry. I know this must sound confusing."

"Details, Zach. I need details," his dad urged.

"Sorry. It would take a long time to explain. I have something really important to ask you."

"Sure, Zach. Whatever I can do to help. "

"Anna Mae's mother also died recently. She's convinced it was not an accident. When Anna Mae went through her mother's safety deposit box, she found some odd items. One was particularly odd. It's a scrap of paper with weird characters on it. I'm certain it's some kind of code. With your background in cryptology, I thought you might be able to decipher it."

"It's been a while since I've used any of those skills, but I'm willing to take a crack at it," James said. "Can you email me a copy?"

"I have a scanned image on my computer," Zach answered. "As soon as I end the call, I will send it to you."

"Anything else going on?"

"Nothing important," Zach lied, not wanting to mention the attack in the woods which would only worry his dad. "Dad, I really appreciate your help. I need to get back to Mazie. I promise I will explain everything later."

"I'm going to hold you to that promise, Zach," James responded. "I'll call you if I have any success with the code."

"Thanks, Dad," Zach said.

Zach ended the call, slipped the cellphone back in his pocket, and sat there watching Mazie, wondering what it would be like to have a daughter like her.

"Hey, Mazie, let's go upstairs for a minute." Zach picked Mazie up and two of her toys and went upstairs to his office. While Mazie played on the floor, Zach opened his email program, attached the scanned image to an email addressed to his dad, and pressed Send.

Salt Creek Road
West of Savannah, Georgia

Seated on an old thread-bare couch, Sha'ban Rabi Bahar, The Snake, nodded occasionally as he flipped through an old, tattered golf magazine. He jerked upright, hearing a floorboard on the porch squeak. Rising quietly from the couch, he picked up the Heckler & Koch P9S lying on the end table beside the couch and moved over beside the window. Carefully pushing the lower corner of the curtain aside with the suppressor screwed to the barrel of the H&K P9S, he peered at the man standing in front of the door of the old cabin.

Not recognizing the man, Sha'ban thumbed off the weapon's safety and called out through the door, "Who is it?"

"The Knight of Vengeance recruited me," FBI Agent Alfred Grant responded. "He is missing. I have important information."

"Open the door and come in very slowly."

Agent Grant twisted the doorknob and pushed the door open. He stepped slowly into the cabin, pushed the door closed, and turned to face Sha'ban.

"How do I know the Knight of Vengeance recruited you?" Sha'ban questioned, pointing the menacing weapon directly at Agent Grant's face.

"The Knight of Vengeance's name is John Lewin. I am Senior FBI Field Agent Alfred Grant. I worked under Agent Lewin. He instructed me that should I ever meet you I should say you are as fierce as Amar ibn Qahtan." Agent Grant raised his hand and gave the grand hailing sign.

Sha'ban relaxed, thumbed the safety on, returned his weapon to the table, and directed Agent Grant to sit.

"Why are you here?"

"I saw the Knight of the East skulking around the house on Plantation Road," Agent Grant explained. "There's a man I had never seen before living in the house. He saw the knight and ran into the woods. The knight hid and then hit him from behind. Before the knight could do anything else, someone fired a shot at him. It missed the knight and he turned and disappeared. The man that fired the shot had a badge on his shirt. It had to be the sheriff."

"Did you inform the Knight of Vengeance?"

"No. I have called him many times, but he did not answer, so I went looking for him," Agent Grant explained.

"Did you find him?"

"First, I went to where the sheriff lives to question him about the knight's disappearance and about the incident in the woods. The sheriff wasn't there, so I poked around in a workshop behind the house. I saw a foot sticking out beneath a pile of old boards. It was the Knight of Vengeance. He's dead. "

"Where is the sheriff now?" Sha'ban demanded.

"I do not know," Agent Grant replied, growing fearful of the man sitting across from him, having been warned of his violent and hair-trigger temper.

"Who is this man that is living at the house on Plantation Road?"

"I am not certain. It may be the man you seek. I did not get a very good look at him."

"Return to the house immediately," Sha'ban roared as he stood up and took a step toward Agent Grant. "Watch the house and determine if the man is Templeton. If it is, do not kill him. Bring him to me."

"Yes, Worshipful Master," Agent Grant stammered as he bowed, turned toward the door, and rushed out of the cabin.

Sha'ban retrieved a cellphone from his pocket and punched in a number.

"Yes," Timothé Alex Durand answered.

"The Knight of Vengeance has been found dead. One of his agents found his body in a shed belonging to the local sheriff. He is supposed to be working for us, but it appears he is having a change of heart. We must move quickly. Have you collected the delivery vector?"

"Yes, Worshipful Master," Durand answered. "The vector containers have been placed at the delivery locations. I still have to pick up biocontainers from their storage location and move them to the release locations."

"Be careful you are not discovered. When everything is in place, contact me. I will let you know when all the other matters have been completed and we are ready for the final release. You must be prepared to leave quickly."

"I shall be ready," Durand affirmed. "Soon, America shall pay for its wicked depravity and then our Holy Order shall rule the world."

"Yes, very soon, Grand Prince," Sha'ban agreed.

Sha'ban Rabi Bahar ended the call and tossed the phone on the table beside the H&K P9S. Only two tasks remained before he could unleash his plan of Hadhramaut and turn America into the "*Place Where Death Comes*".

First, he would find the sheriff and make him pay for his treachery and betrayal. Then he would hunt down his most hated enemy, Zachariah Templeton. He would slit his throat and shout praises to Allah as he watched the vile infidel's blood pour out upon the ground.

Chapter Twenty-Three

Suitland Federal Center
Office of Director of Naval Intelligence
Suitland, Maryland

Rear Admiral Charles Hadley, Director of Naval Intelligence, had just walked into his office from the daily threat assessment briefing. He dropped his briefing books on his desk and slid them out of the way. About to slip out of his uniform jacket, the buzzing of the intercom interrupted him.

He reached across his desk, poked the flashing button, and said, "Yes, Jenny. What is it?"

"Major General George Whitney from the Emerging Infectious Diseases Department of the VA Medical Center in Washington, DC, is calling for you. He says it's important. He's on line three."

"Okay, thanks, Jenny," Admiral Hadley said. After slipping out of his jacket, he tossed it onto the credenza and plopped down in his chair. He reached over and punched the flashing button for line three and said, "General Whitney, my assistant said you had something important."

"Yes, I do Admiral Hadley. Before I say anything, is this line secure?"

"Yes, for anything up to 'Q Clearance' level," Admiral Hadley answered. "If it's beyond that, I will have to change locations."

"That should be sufficient," General Whitney advised. "This information is sensitive and for your ears only."

"Hang on, General. I'm going to put you on hold while I close my office door."

Admiral Hadley walked over to his office door and poked his head out. "Jenny, no calls or interruptions." He pushed the door closed, returned to his desk, sat down, and took the General off hold. "I'm back, General. What's so important?"

"Admiral, I got your name from John Emerson, Deputy Secretary, over at the Department of Homeland Security," General Whitney said. "Deputy Emerson tells me you have an undercover resource in the Savannah area."

"Yes, that's true," Admiral Hadley answered, somewhat reluctantly. "That information was not to be shared with anyone, General."

"I understand, Admiral," the General continued. "I coerced the deputy secretary. I have learned of a possible high-level threat in the Savannah area. I told him it was absolutely imperative that I have a resource in that area that I could trust."

"I'm listening, General. Go on."

"I'll be as brief as I can be," General Whitney stated. "I'm also a doctor with the VA's Infectious Diseases Department in Washington. I received a phone call from a Doctor Michael Wilson. I met him at a conference on Opportunistic Infections some months ago. He's a senior epidemiologist for the Georgia Department of Public Health. He called me because of my work with infectious diseases. According to Doctor Wilson, a Chatham County Georgia medical examiner became suspicious when he discovered all of a decedent's tissues samples had been switched. He…"

"Sounds like a problem for the local authorities," Admiral Hadley interrupted. "I don't mean to be rude, General, but I am quite busy."

"Give me five minutes," General Whitney insisted. "I assure you, Admiral, you will want to hear this."

"Okay, General, you've got five minutes."

"Doctor Tilton, the ME, and Doctor Wilson went to medical school together. So, Doctor Tilton sent the original samples to Doctor Wilson. Doctor Tilton suspected some type of hemorrhagic fever and he wanted corroboration. In the note he included with the samples, he said to trust no one. Doctor Wilson explained to me the approach he used to identify any pathogens present in the samples. I won't take your time to explain the process as it is quite complex. What he found is both startling and frightening. What Doctor Wilson identified in the sample is a new and completely unknown virus, and if the virus is even half as virulent as he suspects, we could have a major epidemic on our hands."

Admiral Hadley continued listening for a few seconds. Realizing General Whitney had paused, he asked, "What does this Doctor Tilton think it is and does he know where it came from?"

"We can't ask him, Admiral," General Whitney replied. "He was murdered. The local police believe it was a robbery gone wrong, but that seems a little too convenient, in my opinion. Someone does not want this information to get out. If that's true, which I believe it is, it likely means the virus was engineered."

"So, you're saying bioterrorism then?"

"Yes, Admiral, that is *exactly* what I am saying!"

"Any idea how contagious this thing is?"

"Extremely. It's an unknown virus. Nobody will have any immunity to it. The infection rate would be horrendous. Doctor Wilson is beginning a statistical analysis as we speak."

"Well, that puts a whole different spin on it. What do you want from me?"

"The resource you have in the Savannah area, is he any good?"

"Let me put it this way, General. If you send a dogcatcher to catch a top-level predator, you will fail and fail badly. You need someone who not only knows how to track a predator, but knows how to think like one. Quite often, the tables get turned and the predator begins tracking the hunter. In the end, tracking a vicious predator comes down to only one cardinal rule; there are no rules."

"Is your man such an individual, Admiral?"

"Absolutely. They don't come any better, General. He has come to the aid of his country twice, and at an immense personal cost. You remember the threat of global nuclear war the

United States avoided not long ago. Well, he was the man that tracked down and brought in the mastermind behind the plot that nearly destroyed our country. The President himself awarded him the Presidential Medal of Freedom with Distinction. He's a former Navy SEAL. The most honorable and dedicated man to ever serve under me."

"Sounds like a genuine hero. I hope I get to meet him some day. For now, somebody needs to dig around quietly and see if they can turn up any information on this threat. I'll email you Doctor Wilson's contact information. He would be the starting point."

"I'll contact my resource right away, General," Admiral Hadley said as he set the receiver back on the phone. *"That can't be a coincidence,"* he thought as he considered the recent warning from the Director of the CIA regarding the legendary murderer named The Snake who was supposedly on his way to the southeastern United States.

He hated to do it, but his good friend Zachariah Templeton was about to be thrust into another chilling hunt for not only a sadistic madman but now a lethal virus.

He reached out and stabbed the intercom button, "Jenny, get me Zach Templeton's number right away."

Big House Plantation Road
Bluffton, South Carolina

After Anna Mae left, Zach sat on the couch watching Mazie playing on the floor. Zach snapped several photos with his cellphone camera that he could send to his dad. He decided he wanted to take higher quality photos for printing. Remembering his digital camera was packed away in one of the boxes stacked in the basement, he picked up Mazie and headed for the door to the basement.

Standing in front of the stacks of boxes, Zach grabbed two empty boxes and placed them on the floor for Mazie to play with. He turned back toward the stacks of boxes and studied the labels, looking for the one labeled hall closet. Hearing giggling, he turned but didn't see Mazie.

"Where's Mazie," he called out.

"Pee-boo," Mazie giggled as she popped up out of one of the boxes.

Zach jumped back, pretending to be frightened, causing Mazie to giggle with delight. Twice more Zach pretended to be frightened by Mazie's popping out of a box before returning to his task of locating his camera.

He moved and re-stacked most of the boxes before finding the one he was looking for. As he straightened up and looked across the basement, something felt off. Starting at the far end of the basement, he counted off his paces as he walked to the other side. He multiplied the number of paces by three. "That can't be," he asserted. "The length is short by over twenty feet."

Repeating the process, he came up with the exact number of paces. Assuring himself that Mazie was still occupied with the empty boxes, he moved three stacks of boxes aside and began inspecting the far wall by thumping on it. It looked like the other walls, but it sounded different. The side walls were hard concrete, but the end wall was not. When Zach rapped on the end wall with his knuckle, it sounded hollow. He inspected the edges of the wall, but stopped when he heard his cellphone ringing upstairs.

After grabbing Mazie, he rushed up the stairs, snatched the ringing cellphone from the table, and answered, "Zach Templeton."

"Hey Zach. Admiral Hadley here. How are you doing?"

"I'm doing okay, Admiral," Zach answered. "What can I do for you?"

"Something serious has come to my attention, Zach."

"Does this have anything to do with Agent Kanagy? He was pretty cryptic. Said he couldn't say much."

"He didn't know much because I didn't tell him much," Admiral Hadley replied. "Recently, I was contacted by someone that has new information that makes this situation even more ominous than I first thought."

"I don't like the sound of that, Admiral. Let's discuss….," Zach started to say, but stopped mid-sentence. "Someone's at the door. I'll have to call you back."

Zach ended the call, walked over to the front door, and pulled it open. With Mazie propped on his left hip, he looked at the beefy six foot plus man standing there, dressed in blue jeans and a dark blue plaid shirt. The way the man stood and the military-style crew cut exuded an air of authority.

"I'm Zach Templeton," Zach announced, "May I help you?"

"Sheriff Lonnie Overton," the man answered, holding out his credentials for Zach to inspect. "May I come in?"

Zach backed away from the door, ushered the man in, and pointed toward a chair in the living room. The sheriff sat on the edge of the chair and waited until Zach sat on the couch.

"I think I recognize the little girl," Sheriff Overton remarked.

"She's Anna Mae Watts's cousin's little girl, Mazie," Zach acknowledged. "Anna Mae said both her parents died recently. I'm watching her for a little while. Anna Mae had an errand to attend to."

"Yes, very tragic. Normally I would come in uniform, but I didn't want to arouse undue attention," Sheriff Overton explained. "I believe you had an encounter in the woods. Someone hit you from behind."

"How did you know about that?" Zach questioned.

"What you didn't know is that someone scared off the man that hit you. I was that someone, Mister Templeton. I put a slug in the tree right beside his."

"Huh? What?" Zach protested.

Sheriff Overton held up his hand and continued, "There have been too many deaths already. Anna Mae's mother, the Picketts, and now the two Foley boys. I didn't want you or Anna Mae added to the list. That's all I can say."

Unable to miss the obvious distressed look on the sheriff's face, Zach asked, "What are you not telling me, Sheriff?"

"This disease can't be allowed...," Sheriff Overton stopped and fidgeted with a loose thread on the leg of his trousers. "I really can't tell you...."

"Listen, Sheriff," Zach interrupted. "I still have Special Agent Presidential Detail status with the Secret Service. I already know there is some kind of plot by foreign agents. I understand that people are dying. You need to tell me what is going on."

Sheriff Overton sat staring at Zach for some time, uncertain how much he could safely reveal.

"Come on, Sheriff," Zach urged. "Out with it. If somebody is trying to kill me, I need to know."

Sheriff Overton opened his mouth, about to speak, but was interrupted by his cellphone ringing.

"Sheriff Overton," he answered. He listened for a few seconds then shouted into the phone, "You wouldn't dare! I'll..."

He ended the call, shoved the cellphone in his pocket, and bolted for the door without a word. Zach sat there dumbfounded as he watched Sheriff Overton dash out, leaving the door standing wide open. Zach rushed over and stood in the open doorway and watched the sheriff scramble into his car and roar off down the driveway like the Devil himself was chasing him.

Chapter Twenty-Four

Westview Avenue
Beaufort, South Carolina

Sheriff Overton roared down State Highway One-Seventy, sliding sideways as he turned left onto Westview Avenue. Four blocks later, he turned into the driveway toward his house and skidded past the end of the driveway, sliding to a stop mere inches from the porch. Scrambling out of the car, he slammed the door, rushed up onto the porch, and threw the door open. Lurching to a stop, a look of horror spreading across his face, he saw a man pointing a gun toward his wife's head.

"Stop right where you are!" Sha'ban Rabi Bahar, The Snake, bellowed. "Take your weapon out and toss it on the floor. NOW!"

Sheriff Overton put his hand on the grip of his service weapon and hesitated.

"Don't even think about it," Sha'ban warned, pressing his weapon against his wife's temple. "Lift it out with two fingers and drop it on the floor."

Seeing no alternative and fearing for his wife's life, Sheriff Overton lifted his service weapon out of its holster with two fingers as instructed and gently dropped it on the floor.

"Do not move, you stinking infidel," Sha'ban snarled. "It seems you cannot keep your mouth shut. You have violated your sacred vow to the Holy Order for which you will die."

Sha'ban stepped sideways away from Susan Overton and shot her dead center in the chest. With cat-like reflexes, he pointed the weapon at Sheriff Overton. "Pfffffft, Pfffffft," the suppressed weapon reported as he pulled the trigger twice. Unfortunately, the sheriff was in plain clothes and without his bullet-proof vest.

Sha'ban Rabi Bahar shot the sheriff as nonchalantly as he had the sheriff's wife. Sheriff Overton dropped to his knees, streaming blood from two holes in his chest. Looking at his wife's still form lying on the floor, he mouthed the words, "I'm so sorry." His eyelids fluttered as he fell face forward onto the blood-stained carpet.

Sha'ban shoved his weapon behind his back, stepped over beside the sheriff's motionless body, and pulled his jambiya out of its gilded sheath. Lifting the sheriff's head up by the hair, he rapidly drew the razor-sharp blade across the sheriff's throat. He moved quickly over beside the woman and slit her throat, repeating a ritual he had performed so many times he had lost count. He smiled and proclaimed, "Allahu Akbar! America shall run red with the blood of infidels," as he watched his victims' blood spreading across the floor.

Not bothering to wipe the smears of blood from the blade, he slid the jambiya back into its sheath. Sha'ban exited the house, pulled the door shut, and walked down the lane whistling indifferently as if nothing happened.

Smiling broadly, he walked the two blocks to where his car was parked. He climbed into his car, started the engine, and drove off toward the safe house to await word from the FBI agent regarding the location of the one man he hated more than any other in the entire world. After he had savored the glory of his final kill, he would release the deadly virus and escape back to Europe.

Big House Plantation Road
Bluffton, South Carolina

Still mystified by Sheriff Overton's visit and the interrupted warning, Zach scooped up his cellphone from the table beside the front door. He punched in a number and waited.

"Zach, I've been waiting for you to call back," Admiral Hadley answered. What was the interruption?"

"It was the county sheriff," Zach replied as he walked back into the living room and sat on the couch. "Earlier today I saw somebody watching the house from the woods. I circled around the front of the house and was going to confront them. Whoever it was, he got the drop on me and hit me from behind."

"Are you all right, Zach?"

"Yes. Just a nasty knot on the back of my head. The sheriff told me he took a shot at the guy to chase him off."

"Did the sheriff know him? Did he know why he was there?"

"He didn't say. He seemed really distressed. Said there had already been too many deaths and he didn't want to see me added to the list. I was about to press him to tell me more, but he got a phone call. After the phone call, he didn't say a word. Just ran out of here like his pants were on fire. You were about to tell about a serious threat earlier."

"Yes, I was. I received a call from General Whitney from the VA's Infectious Diseases Department in Washington. He informed me that a local medical examiner in Savannah discovered that all the tissue samples had been switched for a woman named Pickett that died with disturbing symptoms. Rather than report it up his chain of command, the ME sent some tissue samples to a Doctor Wilson, a senior epidemiologist, with the Georgia Department of Public Health. Doctor Wilson was so alarmed that he contacted General Whitney. The general…"

"Did you say Pickett?"

"Yes. That was the name the general used."

"The sheriff mentioned that name, but he said *Picketts*, plural, as in more than one. He also said, *'and now the two Foley boys'*. Can we check with the medical examiner to see if there is more than one person named Pickett and also two boys named Foley?"

"I'm afraid we can't do that. General Whitney said he learned that the ME had been murdered."

"Hmmm," Zach mused. "Somebody switched autopsy samples. The ME is afraid to report up his chain of command. Then the ME is murdered. Multiple people are dying with disturbing symptoms. Somebody attacked me in the woods. The local sheriff is involved in *something* that appears to be related. Seems like too many suspicious events to be just a coincidence, wouldn't you say, Admiral?"

"My thoughts exactly, Zach," Admiral Hadley remarked.

"So, what do we do, Admiral?"

"The General is extremely concerned by what Doctor Wilson reported regarding his examination of the tissue samples the ME sent. Doctor Wilson indicated there was no doubt the samples were infected with a new and completely unknown virus. The general didn't share their discussion regarding the virus's structure or the assay techniques Doctor Wilson used to identify the virus, but Doctor Wilson did say what he discovered convinced him he was looking at a deliberately engineered virus."

"Do they have any idea how contagious it is?"

"The general said extremely."

"I repeat my earlier question, Admiral. "What do we do?"

"We don't have a lot of intel yet. I discussed the virus information with CIA Director Sandberg. He and I agree that it may be related to the appearance of the individual he calls The Snake. Director Sandberg said their intel indicates he is likely headed for your area. If The Snake is linked to the virus, which we think he is, there is every reason to believe the release would be in your area. We need you to nose around. I would say the sheriff would be a good place to start."

"I'm kind of busy with Mazie at the moment. I'll see if I can locate the sheriff as soon as Anna Mae returns."

"Okay, Zach," Admiral Hadley agreed. "I'll contact you as soon as I get more information. Be careful, Zach. This guy, The Snake, is as dangerous as they come."

"Aren't I always, Admiral," Zach joked. "I'll update you after I talk with the sheriff."

Zach ended the call and laid his cellphone on the end table. Mazie looked up from playing on the floor. She grabbed one of the stuffed toys lying beside her, walked over to the couch, and climbed up in Zach's lap.

"Who is this?" Zach asked, pointing at the stuffed animal.

"Raf-ee," Mazie beamed.

She let go of the stuffed animal, rubbed her eyes, and snuggled up against Zach. *"I hope Anna Mae's talk with her father takes awhile,"* Zach thought, enjoying the contented feeling as he held the little girl tightly. He leaned back against the arm of the couch and listened to Mazie's breathing as it slowed, indicating she had fallen asleep. Putting the current threat out of his mind and savoring the simple joy of holding a child, something he had desired for a very long time, he also drifted off to sleep.

Chapter Twenty-Five

151 Laurel Oak Bay Road
Bluffton, South Carolina

When Anna Mae had arrived home, she had parked under three towering, loblolly pine trees that shaded the north side of the lane leading to the house she shared with her father. She sat for a long time going over in her mind what she intended to say to him. Ever since her mother's death, her father had been on edge, distant, and prone to outbursts of anger, often refusing to finish conversations. Determined to get some answers, she climbed out of the car and headed for the house.

With much apprehension, she walked slowly toward the old farmhouse that sat back fifty yards from the main road. The property had once been well maintained, but tall weeds now dotted the overgrown lawn, which clearly had not been cut in weeks. Flowerbeds along the front porch were unkept and choked with weeds. The white board fence bordering the property sagged at several spots where the wind had knocked it down. At the corner near the house, a crooked wooden gate swung haphazardly from broken hinges. A deep sadness filled Anna Mae's heart as she surveyed the property. Not only had the property fallen into neglect physically, the once happy soul of her family had become choked by sadness and pain.

A loose floor board squeaked as Anna Mae stepped up on the porch. She opened the front door, walked into the foyer, and looked down at the narrow, oak floorboards, scuffed and worn from many years of foot traffic. In the living room, inexpensive, wall-to-wall, tan carpeting covered the floor. A worn brown plaid sofa with heavy oak arms sat in the center of the room. On the far wall, a bookcase sat stacked with paperback books and family photos. A china cabinet sat not far away, filled with brightly colored glassware and bric-à-brac. Shocked by how tired and worn everything looked, Anna Mae stopped and thought about happier times, wishing she could turn the clock back.

Anna Mae listened. There were no sounds in the house, not even the everyday sounds one would expect to hear: no air-conditioner running, no furnace cycling on and off, no footsteps or floorboards creaking, no hum from the refrigerator; nothing but silence.

She tiptoed quietly over to her father's bedroom door, placed her ear close to the door, and listened. Concentrating on the bedroom, she nearly jumped out of her skin when she heard a floorboard squeak behind her. Whirling around quickly, she saw her father standing in the doorway to the kitchen.

"You nearly scared me to death," Anna Mae panted. "Where did you come from?"

"I was out on the back porch," Edwin Watts answered. "I thought I heard someone come in, so I came in to check."

"Daddy, come in here and sit down, please," Anna Mae urged. "We need to talk about that piece of paper with the odd characters on it."

"I have no idea what you're talking about," Edwin lied.

"That's not true," Anna Mae snapped as she pulled out the piece of paper, holding it out toward him. "Why are you lying? I saw it in your face when I asked you about it earlier. You know something that you're not telling me."

"Give me that," Edwin barked, grabbing for the piece of paper. Anna Mae jerked it back out of his reach and stuffed it back in her purse.

"You must destroy that and forget you ever saw it!" Edwin shouted.

"No, I will not," Anna Mae countered. "It has something to do with what's been happening around here. I was over at the rental house. Someone attacked Mister Templeton and hit him on the head. I know it was you, Daddy. Mister Templeton described a pair of muddy boots with a red tag on the heal and duct tape wrapped around the toe of one of them. Just like your boots sitting in there by the back door. Why did you attack him? I intend to find out what is going on."

"If you don't leave this alone and quit digging for answers you won't want to hear, you will end up like your mother," Edwin warned, getting up off the couch and starting toward the kitchen.

"I knew it!" Anna Mae screamed. "You knew all along Mother's death was not an accident. How could you lie to me? Why, Daddy, why?"

Anna Mae followed her father, waiting for his answer. "Well, are you going to just stand there and continue to lie to me? I want to know what you're involved in, now!"

Her father stood there with a grimace on his face, his lips drawn pencil-line tight. Still, he did not answer.

"Daddy, she loved you. Don't you want to know who killed her and why?" she begged.

Edwin's shoulders shook. Overcome with emotion, he broke down and blurted out, "I got involved with evil men. I had no idea what I was getting involved in. And then it was too late. I couldn't get out. I'm sorry. I never meant for your mother to get hurt. I couldn't say anything. They threatened they would hurt you."

"I don't understand, Daddy" Anna Mae blubbered. "You let them kill Mother? How could you?"

"No! No! It wasn't like that," Edwin protested. "The message on the paper…. It…. I…..”

A loud gunshot rang out. The front window exploded into thousands of tiny shards. Edwin Watts fell backward, a dark circle in the middle of his forehead streaming blood.

Anna Mae hit the floor, snagged her purse, bolted into the kitchen, and dove out the back door seconds before the front door crashed inward. Sha'ban Rabi Bahar, The Snake, rushed into the room, assured himself the Knight of the East was dead, then ran into the kitchen looking for the woman he had seen talking to the man he just killed.

Fortunately for Anna Mae, the tree line was only four short strides from the edge of the back porch. She raced into the woods and disappeared into the thick undergrowth. Having spent her entire life in the old farmhouse, no one in the county knew the woods better than she did. She started down one of the many hidden paths that meandered through the woods. Stopping suddenly when she heard the back door slam, she dived behind a wild rhododendron bush. She flattened out against the ground and breathed as quietly as she could.

Sha'ban leaped off the porch and ran into the woods, shoving his way through the dense undergrowth for several steps. He stopped and listened, hearing nothing except for a few birds his entrance into the woods had startled. After a short distance of picking his way around bushes and through the tangle of vines, he realized he had no idea which way the woman had gone. He stopped and listened again. Hearing nothing, he turned around and exited the woods, angry and frustrated. He had more important things to do than chase one woman through the woods.

Anna Mae heard the back door slam again. Slowly rising from her hiding place, she peered through the undergrowth toward the house. Satisfied the man had returned to the house, she left her hiding place. Upon locating one of the familiar paths, she ran as fast as she could toward the destination fixed firmly in her mind.

Big House Plantation Road
Bluffton, South Carolina

Sound asleep on the couch with Mazie nestled in his arms, Zach struggled to awaken from the dream playing in his mind. Machine guns were firing, Men were screaming. Mortars exploded all around him. Slowly his mind pulled back from the dream. The pounding seemed so close.

"Huh? What?" he sputtered, fully awakened by the frantic pounding on the front door. Holding Mazie tight, he struggled up off the couch, walked to the door, and yanked it open.

Anna Mae raced into the house, out of breath and panting so hard she couldn't talk.

"Anna Mae, what is it?" Zach shouted.

"Daddy…. Man…. Shot…" Anna Mae blurted out, gasping for breath between every word.

"Slow down, Anna Mae. Catch your breath first."

Anna Mae sucked in great breaths of air, finally able to string a few words together. "Somebody shot Daddy."

"When?"

"Just now," Anna Mae sputtered. "He's dead. Ran all the way here."

"Come over here and sit down while I go put Mazie in the bedroom." Zach commanded, grabbing her arm and directing her toward the couch. He went into the spare bedroom, laid Mazie on the bed, pulled a blanket up over her, and returned to the living room.

"Who's dead? What are you talking about?"

"Oh, Zach. Daddy's dead!" she wailed.

Unable to resist, she reached out and grabbed Zach in a tight embrace, desperately needing the feeling of his strong arms around her. Between gasps for breath, she sobbed uncontrollably. Zach encircled her with his arms and held her tight, knowing she needed reassurance and comfort, not questions.

Mazie, frightened by Anna Mae's sobbing, scrambled down off the bed, ran over beside Anna Mae, and hugged her leg. Jolted by Mazie's presence, Anna Mae struggled to regain her composure. She pushed back from Zach, reached down, picked Mazie up, and hugged her tightly.

"Sit down, please," Zach urged, shock still evident on her face. "Now, slow down and tell me again."

"Zach, Daddy's dead," she blubbered. "I was standing in the living room talking to Daddy when a shot came through the window. I saw a huge hole in his forehead."

"Do you know who it was? Can you describe him?"

"No. I ran out the back door and into the woods before he entered the house. He ran into the woods a short distance, but I was too far away to get a good look at him."

"Tell me everything again. Start at the beginning," Zach instructed.

"When I left here, I drove straight home and confronted my father about the piece of paper with the odd characters. He tried to take it from me and told me I should forget I ever saw it. I pushed him about my mother's death. He finally broke down and admitted he knew her death was not an accident all along. Worst of all, he was the one that attacked you in the woods. I found a pair of boots exactly like you described sitting by the back door. After the man shot Daddy, I ran. I heard him kick the door in as I ran out the back door and into the woods. He ran into the woods but couldn't find me. I ran all the way here. Oh, Zach, I'm so sorry Daddy attacked you."

"Do you have any idea why he would do such a thing?"

"It doesn't make any sense. My father had never been involved in anything unusual, except for some secret club or society."

"A secret society?" Zach questioned. "Do you know what kind of society?"

"No. He always refused to talk about it. Said he wasn't allowed to speak to anybody about it."

"Wait a minute," Zach blurted as an idea formed in his mind. "Hang on. I've got to call my dad."

Zach snatched his cellphone from the table and selected his dad's number from the contacts list. Anna Mae rocked back and forth on the couch with Mazie in her arms.

"Hey, Zach," James Templeton answered. "I have nothing for you yet. The odd characters don't match any ciphers or code systems I am familiar with."

"I have additional information that may help you decipher the characters. Anna Mae told me her father belonged to some kind of secret society. She doesn't have a name because he would never talk about it."

"That just might help," his dad answered. "It gives me an idea."

"Hey, Dad, I said I would explain later," Zach added. "Well, I got a visit from a Secret Service agent sent by Admiral

Hadley. He handed me a weapon and gave me a warning. The CIA has uncovered intelligence pointing to the mastermind behind Frank Porter. They think he is headed here from Europe. Then, I was attacked in the woods. Someone hit me from behind. The sheriff showed up here earlier. He said he fired a shot at the man to scare him off. He was going to tell me something else, but he got interrupted and ran out the door and sped off. Anna Mae's father was just murdered. I believe somehow all these events have to be related and possibly linked to that note."

"I had hoped to never hear that name again."

"Me either," Zach replied. "But, if that individual, is the monster responsible for the hundreds of thousands of deaths around Sacramento and the plot that led to Angie's death, I will chase him to the ends of the Earth."

"I understand, Zach. If it weren't for the injuries from my last run-in, I would be right there with you. You know that, right?"

"Yes, I know. You can help by deciphering those characters, and the sooner the better."

"I'm on it," Zach's dad responded. "I'll call you the instant I have something. And Zach, be careful."

"I promise," Zach said as he ended the call.

Zach laid the cellphone back on the table and sat down beside Anna Mae. He looked at her with a questioning look.

"Zach, what am I going to do?" she pleaded.

Zach reached out and cradled Anna Mae's face with both hands. "Listen to me," he said, looking directly at her. "You need to be strong for Mazie. I'm here for you."

Anna Mae smiled weakly, huge tears rolling down her cheeks.

"*We* will get through this together," Zach confided, gently wiping away the tears.

Chapter Twenty-Six

Big House Plantation Road
Bluffton, South Carolina

As the huge amount of adrenaline in Anna Mae's bloodstream dissipated, she began to shake uncontrollably from its aftereffects. Anna Mae drew in a deep breath and let it out slowly, her hands clasped tightly together in her lap. Zach had disappeared into the kitchen to get a cup of coffee to help settle Anna Mae's nerves. Returning from the kitchen, he handed her the steaming cup of coffee and sat down on the couch beside her.

Still shaking, she fought hard to hold the coffee cup level. A sudden tremor passed through her body, causing her to slosh some of the coffee out of the cup.

"Good grief," she whimpered as the coffee dribbled onto her dress. The harder she tried to control her shaking hands, the worse they shook. She looked up at Zach with pleading eyes. He took the coffee cup from her hands and set in on the table.

"Hold still. I'll get a towel," Zach said as he rushed off into the kitchen again. Returning with a hand towel, he pressed it against the stain on Anna Mae's dress. "Are you okay?" he asked.

"I can't believe it. I'm shaking like a leaf," she complained. "I'll be okay if I can just calm down." She pulled the towel out of Zach's hands and rubbed it against the stain. Picking up the coffee cup, she mopped up the spilled coffee from the table. She nearly jumped off the couch when Zach's cellphone began blaring the US Marine Corps hymn.

Zach snatched the cellphone from the table, recognizing his dad's ringtone. "Hey, Dad, I didn't expect your call so soon," he answered.

"Zach, I think I've decoded the message, but it doesn't make any sense," James Templeton advised.

"Let's have it," Zach said.

Zach listened as his dad slowly read off the results of deciphering the odd characters.

"You're right. That doesn't make sense. Say that again."

Zach furrowed his eyebrows, listening intently as his dad repeated the decoded message. "Hang on. I'm going to write that down."

Zach pulled out the drawer in the end table and grabbed a notepad and a pen. Flipping the note pad open he said, "Okay, say that again." He leaned over, placed the notepad on the table, and wrote the decoded message down verbatim as his dad repeated it for a third time. Shaking his head, he stared at the words he had just written. It still didn't make any sense.

"Thanks, Dad," Zach said. "I'll show this to Anna Mae. Maybe together we can figure out what it means."

"Zach, your mother and I are worried about you. You have been through so much already and now this."

"If we can catch this monster, maybe it will all finally end."

"I certainly hope so, son."

Zach ended the call and dropped the cellphone back on the table. Staring at the odd message, he shook his head again, still unable to make any sense of it. Scooting over beside Anna Mae, he held out the notepad and said, "Here, look at what Dad said the odd characters decoded to. Does this make any sense to you?"

> *Yaldabaoth - He who bears the Light*
> *Shamed be he who thinks evil of the garter*
> *Hidden beneath your feet*

They both stared at the puzzling message, wondering what on Earth it could possibly mean. Zach read the message out loud, hoping it might prompt some understanding.

"What on Earth does Yal-da-ba-oth mean?" Anna Mae asked, sounding out the odd word. "Is that supposed to be a person or a thing?"

"I don't know," Zach responded. "I've never heard of it either. Let me see if I can look it up."

Zach reached for his cellphone, tapped it to wake it up, and opened a browser app. He typed in the word and pressed the Search button. "I got lots of hits," he said as he scrolled down through the first few entries. "Here's one that says 'Yaldabaoth is a Gnostic god who is described as the Child of Chaos'. The next one says 'Yaldabaoth is a demented pretender god who claims to be the creator of the material world, and demands slavish obedience from his human subjects'. The rest of the entries say about the same thing."

"A false god," Anna Mae repeated. "Could that have something to do with the secret society my father was involved in?"

"A false god would make the first line make sense, but how does that relate to the next two lines ?"

"The last line says *hidden*," Anna Mae mused. "What if…. Daddy spent a lot of time over here. He said he was remodeling, but there was never any evidence of that and it never looked like he got anything done. Could he have hidden something here?"

"Did he spend a lot of time in the basement?" Zach asked. Anna Mae's question caused him to remember the odd discovery in the basement.

"Maybe. I really don't know," she answered. "Why do you ask?"

"I discovered something odd in the basement earlier," Zach said. "Let's go have a look."

He tore the page from the notepad, stuffed it in his pocket, and grabbed Anna Mae's hand. Together they headed for the basement. Zach stopped suddenly. "What about Mazie?" he asked. "I better go check on her."

He found her in the bedroom. "She must have crawled up on the bed. She's sleeping soundly." Zach announced. He slipped his hand in Anna Mae's and together they descended the stairs into the basement.

Standing at the far wall in the basement, Zach said, "Here, listen to this." He tapped the outside wall with his knuckle, then he tapped the end wall. "Doesn't the end wall sound hollow to you?"

"I agree. It does sound hollow."

"See that old gray toolbox sitting on the shelf over there. Bring it over here," Zach instructed, starting to push stacks of boxes out of the way.

With space cleared in front of the wall, Zach grabbed a prybar and a hammer from the toolbox. He hammered the short end of the prybar into the corner between the two walls. Gripping the end of the prybar, he yanked with all his strength. The wood splintered away, the prybar slipped, and Zach's hand slammed against the opposite wall. Ignoring the blood oozing from his scraped knuckles, he inserted the prybar into the hole created by his first attempt. With a much better grip against the wall, he jerked the prybar again.

The false wall pulled far enough away so he could get his fingers behind it. With a mighty heave, the wall creaked and pulled away slightly. Putting his foot against the outside wall, he pulled as hard as he could. Part of the wall splintered and fell away. With space to work, in no time Zach had the entire false wall removed.

"Anna Mae, come over here," Zach called out. "Look at this. There's a door with an old-looking padlock."

"Zach, there was an old, antique key in Mother's safety deposit box," Anna Mae exclaimed. "It's in my purse upstairs. I'll go get it."

Anna Mae ran up the stairs two at a time, snatched her purse from the couch, and rushed back down to the basement. She dug the key out of the purse and handed it to Zach.

Zach slipped the key into the padlock. "It fits," he advised as he twisted the key. The old lock fell open. Zach lifted the padlock off the hasp and tossed it aside. He pulled on the door, but it wouldn't budge. Armed with the prybar, he pried at the edge of the door. After some work, he managed to get the door open an inch. He wedged both hands into the gap and pulled with all his might. He stopped, braced his foot against the wall, took a deep breath, and pulled again.

"Arghhhh," Zach sputtered as he pulled harder. The door yielded slightly. The steel door squealed as it swung open on its rusty hinges. Anna Mae cringed as the piercing squeal increased in volume. Zach continued to pull mightily until the door stood half open.

"Hey, Anna Mae. Grab that flashlight from the ledge beside you," Zach said, peering into the darkness of the newly exposed room.

Anna Mae lifted the flashlight off the ledge and handed it to Zach. Cautiously, Zach poked his head in and pointed the beam of light into the room. The dead air escaping from the dark room smelled dank and musty. From the look of the dust and cobwebs, it appeared no one had entered the room in a very long time. Before entering, Zach directed the beam of light toward the floor. Footprints. Some of them looked recent.

"That's odd," Zach said as he swept the beam of light around the room a second time.

"What's odd," Anna Mae asked, standing behind Zach, looking over his shoulder.

"There's a thick layer of dust everywhere. It's completely undisturbed, but there are footprints on the floor. A lot of them."

From the inside, the room appeared to be much longer than Zach expected. It had to extend well beyond the foundation of the house. He ducked and stepped inside, urging Anna Mae to follow. Somewhat reluctantly, she followed.

"What does the message say?" Zach asked, handing Anna Mae the note he had stuffed in his shirt pocket.

She read the message as Zach aimed the beam of light at various objects in the room.

"Again," he requested. Anna Mae repeated the message as Zach continued aiming the beam of light at various objects. "I'm sorry. One more time, please," he said.

Zach continued sweeping the beam of light around the room as Anna Mae read the message a third time. Zach stopped when the beam of light fell upon a bizarre painting. The painting depicted a seated creature with crossed legs, having the legs, feet, and head of a goat. Folded wings sprouted from behind its shoulders. The creature's left arm pointed downward and the right arm pointed upward with the index and middle fingers raised. On a table directly below the painting, stood an eighteen-inch tall statue resembling a medieval knight. The knight was holding up his robe, revealing his left leg from the knee down. Just below the knee, a garter wrapped around the knights' leg.

Zach handed Anna Mae the flashlight and picked up the statue, examining it more closely. The statue seemed newer and not as covered by dust like the other objects. He rotated the statue in his hands several times, noticing a joint around the bottom edge of the garter. A medallion decorating the garter felt raised. Zach pressed the button-like medallion on the garter and the bottom half of the leg fell off in his hand. From inside the detached section of the leg, Zach pulled out a rolled-up piece of paper. His eyes grew large and his mouth dropped open as he read the handwritten words on the paper.

The Order of the Illumined Elite has become the most subtle and powerful of any Secret Society on Earth. I have learned the Order is pure evil and must be stopped.

Order brethren in high positions of power hold their oath to the Sacred Order far above their oath to serve the people who elected them. As such: policemen, judges, senators, and politicians, make decisions not upon truth and justice but rather based on protecting the Sacred Order and their fellow brethren above all else.

Lower level neophytes are deliberately kept in the dark and are not told what they are part of. At the upper levels, all Or-

der brethren bow down before and worship the Great Master Yaldabaoth - Lucifer, the Son of the Morning! He who bears the Sacred Light and blinds the feeble and unbelieving.

For Order members, Yaldabaoth, in Aramaic, means 'Child of Chaos' who is the originator of all evil. It is the Order's intention to spread chaos upon the entire world and then usher in a New World Order. In order to do that they are planning to destroy the United States. They intend to unleash a horrible plague of untold suffering and death, the depth of which has never been seen before.

Of those evil brethren in high places, I have uncovered the names of those men listed below:

> *John Lewin, FBI Agent - SAIC Southeast Division*
> *Bradley Jensen, Senior FBI Field Agent*
> *Adam Conley, Deputy Asst. to the President*
> *Curtis Clark, Chief of Staff to the Vice President*

You will find undeniable proof in the envelope in the hidden compartment under the table.

There are other equally powerful men, but I have not been able to find out their names. The influence of the Order reaches everywhere. Trust absolutely no one.

I only recently discovered how evil the Order of the Illumined Elite really is. I am ashamed and so deeply sorry for my part in this evil society. May God forgive me.

Signed - Edwin Watts

He handed the paper to Anna Mae and waited for her reaction.

"I just can't believe it," she choked, tears forming in her eyes. "Why would my father be part of this? What are we going to do, Zach?"

Zach had already turned away and was poking around the bottom of the table. He found a catch that released a false panel. Pushing the panel up and out of the way, he extracted a large manila envelope.

"This is incredible," he exclaimed as he scanned the photos and lists of meetings, attendees, places, and times. "I've got to call Admiral Hadley immediately and tell him about this."

He grabbed the letter from Edwin Watts and the envelope full of incriminating evidence and headed for the stairs with Anna Mae close behind. As Zach and Anna Mae reached the top of the stairs and stepped out into the living room, someone kicked in the front door, weapon in hand.

With nowhere to run, Zach and Anna Mae stopped dead in their tracks.

Atlanta Convention Center
240 Peachtree Street NW
Atlanta, Georgia

Timothé Alex Durand turned the white, Hyundai minivan he was driving off Peachtree Street into Atlanta's Convention Center and drove past the fourteen-story Grand Atrium. In the heart of Atlanta, conveniently located within walking distance of twelve thousand hotel rooms, the enormous facility could accommodate three thousand attendees in its Grand Ballroom and forty-seven meeting rooms. The enormous facility covered one-half million square feet. Durand turned into the entrance to the parking area, pulled up to the access gate, and stopped. Holding a clipboard in one hand, the security guard slid the door to the booth open, leaned out, and observed the FBI logo on the side of the van.

"ID please," the security guard requested.

Durand reached in his jacket, pulled out a leather credentials wallet, and handed it to the Convention Center security guard for inspection. The FBI credentials displayed the name Edward Fletcher. The false credentials, perfect in every detail, had been provided by John Lewin, FBI Special Agent in Charge, Southeast Division. The guard scanned down the list of pre-authorized individuals. "I don't see your name on the list Mister Fletcher," the security guard advised.

"That's right," Durand answered. "My visit wasn't planned. Someone reported a problem with our communications system."

"I'll let you in this time, but next time someone will have to call ahead and let security know you're coming." The security guard added the name Fletcher to the list on the clipboard, handed the wallet back, and pushed the button to raise the access gate.

Durand drove the minivan, disguised as a communications service vehicle, through the gate and down the center lane of the parking area. Six rows down the lane, Durand turned right and headed toward the engineering room that housed the FBI's communications equipment. Finding every parking space filled, he drove up and down rows in both directions. Unable to find a single empty space, he gave up and returned to the engineering room. He pulled to the right side of the lane as far as he could and parked, blocking in two vehicles that had parked next to the engineering room.

Every space in the Convention Center's parking area was occupied due to a very large interdisciplinary medical conference that was in progress. Several thousand interventional cardiologists, cardiac and vascular surgeons, nurse practitioners, physician assistants, and other healthcare professionals had descended on Atlanta to attend the conference.

Annoyed at not finding a parking space, Durand shrugged it off, knowing the large gathering of medical professionals was perfect for their needs. Thousands and thousands of the intensely aggressive mosquitoes would be infected with the viral pathogen and then released at the Convention Center on the last day of the conference.

Because of the extreme aggressiveness of the mosquitoes, hundreds if not thousands of the conference attendees would be infected. By releasing the infected mosquitoes on the last day, the conference attendees would board airplanes and scatter across the entire country to their homes, private practices, clinics, and hospitals. By the time any of them realized they were sick, the deadly contagion would have spread across the country. All attempts at containment would fail.

Durand climbed out of the minivan and slipped a pouch containing lock picking tools from his hip pocket. In less than a minute he had unlocked the door to the equipment room. He moved a large, empty cabinet resembling an equipment enclosure from the minivan into the equipment room, positioning it next to the existing cabinets. With the fake cabinet in place, he carried the biocontainer holding the deadly pathogen and the container holding thousands of angry mosquitoes into the small maintenance room. Looking at the container holding the angry mosquitoes, he shuddered, imagining the death and misery soon to be released. Durand placed the containers inside the cabinet, set the cover in place, and locked it.

He pulled the equipment room door closed and locked it, making certain the door was secure. Finished with his current task, he climbed back into the minivan and headed for the exit.

"That didn't take long," the security guard commented as Durand pulled up to the exit gate and stopped.

"Yeah, it was only a blown fuse," Duran lied.

The security guard recorded the exit time and opened the exit gate. "Have a nice day," he said.

Durand waved at the guard as he exited the Convention Center parking area. Everything was in place. He drove out onto Peachtree Street and headed for his hotel to gather his belongings and wait for the call from the Worshipful Master instructing him to head for the airport.

Chapter Twenty-Seven

Big House Plantation Road
Bluffton, South Carolina

"What is that you have in your hand?" Senior FBI Agent Alfred Grant yelled. "Give it to me."

Zach hesitated, looking desperately for anything he could use for cover or as a weapon.

"I said give it to me. Right now or you die!" Grant screamed.

Left with little choice, Zach started to hand the paper to the man. Frightened by Agent Grant's scream, Anna Mae leaped sideways from behind Zach, startling Agent Grant.

Instinctively, he fired the weapon in her direction. Anna Mae went down, toppling the table beside the couch, scattering the items sitting on it.

Enraged by what he saw, a scene that mirrored the day his wife was murdered right before his eyes, Zach lunged at the man with the raw ferocity of a lioness protecting her cubs. Zach tackled the man before he could react. The two men fell to the floor, knocking the weapon from Agent Grant's hand. They wrestled on the floor, each man grappling to gain control of the weapon.

Zach kicked at the weapon with his foot, causing it to skitter across the floor. Zach stood and started for the weapon. Agent Grant grabbed Zach and slammed his head against the end of the couch. Slightly dazed, Zach's reaction was a second too slow. On his knees, Agent Grant wrapped his arms around Zach's neck and began to choke the life out of him. Zach flailed and ripped at the man's arms, but he could not dislodge the man's stronger grip.

With his supply of air cut off, Zach's struggle lessened, his arms dropping to the floor. A single gunshot echoed throughout the house. Agent Grant gasped, loosened his grip, and fell backward onto the floor. Zach rolled over and pushed himself up onto his knees, coughing and gasping for air. He stared at the dead man lying on the floor, a large gaping hole where his left eye had once been.

Anna Mae had been knocked momentarily unconscious when she hit her head as she fell against the table. Fortunately, her purse had landed within arm's reach when the table fell over. Quickly regaining consciousness, she had hastily retrieved her 9mm Glock 19 GEN4 with pink hand grips and had fired one shot at the man.

"Wow! Nice shooting," Zach sputtered. "Where did you learn to...," The words died in his throat when he noticed blood running down Anna Mae's arm.

"NO! NO!" he yelled as he ran over to where she had plopped down onto the floor, the color draining from her face. "Are you all right?"

"Oh, Zach, it burns like fire," she wailed. Zach grabbed the sleeve of her blouse and split it up to her shoulder, revealing a nasty, red crease across her upper arm.

"Looks like you were really lucky," Zach said, relief flooding his mind. He pulled a handkerchief from his pocket and pressed it over the wound. "The bullet only creased your arm. It's will be very sore, but it's not serious. Hold this while I go get the first aid kit."

Zach sprinted to the kitchen and returned with the first aid kit. "Where did you learn to shoot like that?" he asked while cleaning the wound. He applied antibiotic ointment and wrapped a bandage around Anna Mae's arm.

"I grew up hunting in the woods," she answered. "Daddy taught me to shoot a rifle when I was barely eight years old and then a handgun when I was twelve."

"I'm certainly glad he did," Zach exclaimed. He closed the first aid kit and pushed it aside. He retrieved his cellphone from the scattered items on the floor. Standing over the dead man, he snapped a photo of the one-eyed man lying on the floor. Zach checked all the man's pockets, finding no ID of any kind and only a cheap, burner cellphone.

"Mazie!" Zach bellowed, already halfway to the bedroom where she was sleeping. He pushed the door open and found her standing in the middle of the room crying. He scooped her up and consoled her. Mazie hugged Zach tight and instantly settled down. A tremendous feeling of protectiveness washed over Zach as he turned and walked out into the living room.

Anna Mae had pushed herself up off the floor and met Zach in the middle of the room. Anna Mae held out her arms to take Mazie, but Mazie shook her head and clung even tighter to Zach.

"Well," Anna Mae exclaimed. "I've never seen her take to anyone like that."

"I'll walk Mazie around the room and see if that calms her down," Zach said. "Grab the tablecloth off the kitchen table and cover up whoever that is."

Anna Mae headed for the kitchen while Zach walked around the room pointing out various things to Mazie. Anna Mae came out of the kitchen dragging the tablecloth. She draped it over the dead man and waited for Zach. Zach leaned toward Anna Mae. Mazie held out her arms and allowed Anna Mae to take her.

"I've got to call Admiral Hadley and fill him in about what we found in the basement and about this guy," Zach said, jerking his head toward the dead man lying on the floor.

Zach awakened his cellphone, punched in Admiral Hadley's number, and waited. Zach filled the admiral in regarding the hidden room in the basement, the letter from Edwin Watts, the packet of incriminating evidence, and the attack by the unknown man lying on the floor.

"Zach, read me the part of Mister Watts's letter where it mentions a plague again."

"Here's what it says, '*They intend to unleash a horrible plague of untold suffering and death, the depth of which has never been seen before.*' Does that mean something to you, Admiral?"

"Remember when we spoke earlier and you said the mysterious deaths around Bluffton and you being attacked were not coincidences and then I told you General Whitney called me about a new and unknown virus in the autopsy samples?"

"Yes, I remember."

"Do you think that could be the *horrible plague* Mister Watts wrote about in his letter?" Admiral Hadley questioned, his voice tinged with fear.

"If you're right, Admiral, the dead man lying in my living room was probably involved," Zach answered. "Hang on, Admiral. I'll text you a photo of the man. He has no ID or any identifying papers."

After a brief delay while the photo arrived, Admiral Hadley exclaimed, "Holy Crow! I recognize this man, Zach. He's a senior FBI agent. He reports directly to John Lewin, Special Agent in Charge of the FBI's Southeast Division."

"All he had on him was a cheap, burner phone, Admiral" Zach added as he examined the cellphone's recent texts. "The last text he sent says, '911 - KoV'. I wonder what that means?"

"Well, the '911' obviously signifies some kind of emergency, but there's no way to know what the KoV means."

"There's only one call in the 'Recent Calls' list," Zach said. "Hang on, Admiral. I'll give it a try and see what happens."

With his free hand, Zach selected the call, clicked redial, and waited. About to end the call after seven rings, Zach perked up when a man's voice answered, "Did they find anything? Did you silence them?"

Zach held the burner phone close to his ear and just listened. "Hello. Hello. Are you there? Answer me." A look of stunned surprise filled Zach's face as the call went dead.

"Admiral, I recognized that voice," Zach blurted out. "I remember it from the award ceremony. You are *not* going to believe this. That voice belongs to Arthur Mead, the Vice President of the United States."

"You can't be serious," Admiral Hadley barked.

"I'm absolutely, beyond a doubt, certain, Admiral," Zach affirmed. "We talked for a long time that night. I'd recognize his voice anywhere."

"Zach, can you FAX me the documents in the envelope and then overnight me the originals as soon as you can?"

"Sure can, Admiral. What do I do about the body lying in my living room?"

"Do not call the local authorities. I'll send a special team to take care of it. Text me the number from the guy's burner phone. I'm going hunting Zach. We need to keep this to ourselves until we determine what exactly is going on."

"Agreed, Admiral," Zach answered. "Anything else, Admiral?"

"As a backup, email me a copy of Mister Watts' message and copies of the materials in the envelope to my private email account. I'll text it to you now." Admiral Hadley instructed. "Keep me informed if anything else develops on your end."

"Will do, Admiral. Happy hunting," Zach said as he ended the call and turned to check on Anna Mae and Mazie.

Office of the Vice President
White House
Washington, D.C.

Standing outside the Vice President's office, Admiral Hadley waited for the Capitol Police detachment to arrive. After speaking with Zach, he had quickly opened his email and kept pressing the refresh button until the materials arrived. The instant the email arrived, he detached the files, downloaded them onto a personal flash drive, verified they were complete on the flash drive, then deleted the email from Zach. After reading through Edwin Watts's letter and viewing the photos, he had printed out two sets of copies. The flash drive and one set of copies went into his office wall safe. The other set of copies he held in his hand as he stood outside the Vice President's office.

"Sergeant, stay here till I call for you," Admiral Hadley advised Sergeant Wilbur Daniels of the United States Capitol Police and the four officers standing beside him.

"What's the meaning of this?" Arthur Mead, Vice President of the United States, bellowed as he looked up from his desk, startled by Admiral Hadley's sudden entrance without knocking.

"I have a question for you Mister Vice President, but hang on just a minute," Admiral Hadley taunted as he lifted his cellphone from his jacket pocket and dialed the number of the burner phone Zach had sent him.

The Vice President jerked in surprise when buzzing suddenly erupted from his jacket pocket.

"Now for that question I mentioned, Mister Vice President," Admiral Hadley smirked. "Explain to me what the number for the burner phone in your pocket I just dialed is doing on a rogue FBI agent now lying dead in Mister Zach Templeton's living room?"

"I have no idea what you're talking about," the Vice President shouted. "I suggest you get out of my office before I have you arrested."

"You're going to have to do better than that. Much better. I have already run the phone number. We know where it was purchased. It will be only a matter of minutes before it is traced back to you."

Enraged, the Vice President leaped out of his chair and lunged toward the Admiral.

"Sergeant Daniels, in here now," Admiral Hadley called out through the open door.

Sergeant Daniels and the four officers waiting in the hall rushed into the office, surrounding the Vice President

"Sit down, you piece of garbage," Admiral Hadley snarled, pushing the Vice President toward his desk. "We really don't need the phone trace anyway. I believe these will provide ample proof of your treasonous actions, Mister Vice President." Admiral Hadley slammed down two of the photos Zach had sent. The fight drained out of the Vice President, his face going pale when he saw the photos.

"Sergeant, arrest this man," Admiral Hadley ordered. "For starters, the charge is treason. I'm sure we will come up with more charges as the investigation progresses. Get him out of here!"

Sergeant Daniels wrenched the Vice President's arms behind his back and snapped handcuffs around his wrists.

As the sergeant started walking the Vice President out the door, Admiral Hadley grabbed his arm. "Would you like to save us some time and tell us who else is involved in your scheme? It might go easier on you."

Vice President Mead's face grew red. He lunged toward the Admiral again and spit wildly at him.

"Sergeant, you may add assault to the list of charges. Perhaps the other criminals in these photos will be more talkative," Admiral Hadley declared, wiping his jacket with a handkerchief. "Oh, wait." Admiral Hadley slipped his hand in Vice President Mead's jacket and retrieved the burner phone. "You won't be needing this where you're headed. Sergeant, record that I seized this illegal burner phone from *Mister* Mead."

"And who might you be?" Admiral Hadley asked, looking at the man standing beside the Vice President's desk.

"Jensen, Sir, Executive Assistant Counterterrorism Division," Bradley Jensen answered nervously.

"What is this you two were discussing?" Admiral Hadley asked, pointing at a large map spread out across the desk. "I suggest you not lie to me, Mister Jensen."

"It's just a map. We were discussing some upcoming travel plans," Jensen lied.

Admiral Hadley stepped over beside the desk and looked directly at Jensen. "I said, do not lie to me, Mister Jensen. You are also in the photos we found. If even one person dies because of this, I will make it my life's mission to see you also get the death penalty. Do you understand me? This is your one and only chance to save yourself from the needle. What is your and *former* Vice President Mead's involvement with the Order of the Illumined Elite? Start talking."

Jensen's countenance fell as he slumped down in the former Vice President's chair, knowing he was trapped with no way out.

"Yes, we know about the Order. Start talking. NOW!" Admiral Hadley shouted as he grabbed the man's tie, nearly yanking him out of the chair.

Jensen admitted that he and the Vice President were part of the Order of the Illumined Elite, claiming the Vice President and FBI Deputy Director Curtis Clark coerced him. He claimed he was forced to assist Deputy Director Clark and the Vice President in their plan to take down the government and make Meade president. He swore that he only knew that *something* was to happen in Atlanta that would start the collapse, claiming he did not know where, only that it would happen soon.

"One last question, Mister Jensen," Admiral Hadley said. "What do you know of someone named al-Ta'abin or perhaps the nickname, The Snake?"

Jensen shook his head. "I only know that someone by that name is here. I walked in on Clark and Mead and overheard Clark mention that name and then something about a virus. They noticed me and stopped talking."

"Virus?" Admiral Hadley shouted. "What kind of virus?"

Jensen shrugged his shoulders. "That's all I know. I'm done talking. I want a lawyer."

"Well, you will certainly need one. A *very, very* good one," Admiral. Hadley responded, motioning to one of the two remaining Capitol Police officers to arrest Jenson and take him into custody.

Admiral Hadley watched as the officers handcuffed Jensen and then he followed the procession out into the hallway.

"Oh, Sergeant Daniels, go see that the President's Deputy Assistant is detained. "I'm going to go arrest the Deputy Director of the FBI."

Admiral Hadley shook his head as he rushed down the hallway, headed for FBI headquarters in Langley, Virginia, wondering just how high up the plot Zach had uncovered actually went.

"After the horrendous event in Sacramento, this may be the death knell that destroys the people's faith in their government," he thought. He lifted his cellphone out of his pocket and dialed Zach's number to fill him in on current events.

Chapter Twenty-Eight

FBI Headquarters
Langley, Virginia

Admiral Hadley and two Virginia State Troopers barged into the office of Curtis Clark, Deputy Director of the FBI, armed with a federal arrest warrant. Before Deputy Director Clark could say a word, Admiral Hadley slammed two photos down on his desk.

"Would you mind explaining those photos, Mister Deputy Director," Admiral Hadley shouted. "But, before you answer that question, you should know that at this very moment federal agents are going through your house. We found your old Chevy SUV and have already identified traces of explosives."

"You have no right to…." Clark howled.

"We have every right you miserable scumbag," Admiral Hadley snarled. "I understand federal agents have already discovered your ties to some extremely subversive individuals. It seems you do not hide things very well. Former, and I emphasize *former*, Vice President Mead and Executive Assistant Director Jensen have already been arrested and taken into custody. The charade is over. You should start talking immediately if you want to avoid a capital offense."

Deputy Director Clark glared defiantly at Admiral Hadley and laughed. "It's too late, you old fool. Many millions are going to die and then the New Order will assert itself. You are powerless to stop us."

"Don't be so sure of yourself," Admiral Hadley responded.

"You don't have the slightest idea what is going to happen. But even if you could discover it, it will be too late."

"Who else is involved in this coup attempt?"

"I will give you only one name. There is only one man that you really need to fear. They call him al-Ta'abin, The Snake. You will all die at his hand."

"We have already learned of the virus."

Deputy Director Clark's reaction was fleeting, but it did not go unnoticed by Admiral Hadley.

"I see that surprised you."

"So what. It doesn't matter," Deputy Director Clark snapped. "If you *really* have discovered it, then you would know there is no cure. Once released, the contagion will spread like an out of control wild fire."

"Not before you die with a needle in your arm," Admiral Hadley roared.

"You don't scare me, Admiral," Deputy Director Clark sneered. "I have pledged my life for the Holy Order and I will gladly give it."

In an outburst of anger, Admiral Hadley rushed around the desk, grabbed Deputy Director Clark by his jacket, and lifted him up out of his chair. "I will personally put a bullet in your head, you despicable traitor."

"Go ahead," Deputy Director Clark dared. "In front of all these witnesses it will be you that gets the needle."

Admiral Hadley released his jacket and stepped back, shaking with rage. He desperately wanted to choke the life out of the arrogant traitor sitting there laughing.

"I'm not saying another word. I believe I get my lawyer now."

No matter what threats Admiral Hadley threw at him, Deputy Director Clark adamantly refused to say another word. He just sat there stone-faced, with an infuriating grin on his face.

"Get him out of here," Admiral Hadley snarled. "Find the deepest, darkest hole you can find and toss this rotten, treasonous scum in it."

Admiral Hadley called Zach again and fill him in on everything he knew and that all those he had arrested had clammed up and stopped talking. He had nothing new to offer

Zach. The only clue was the partially open map lying on Deputy Director Clark's desk. The largest city in view being Atlanta, Georgia.

"Could that be where they planned to release the virus?" Admiral Hadley asked himself. He didn't know if Atlanta was the target and, if it was, what did they plan to do there and where did they plan to do it? Not much to go on, but it was all he could offer. Admiral Hadley dialed Zach's number and waited.

The fate of the United States would now rest on Zach Templeton.

Big House Plantation Road
Bluffton, South Carolina

Zach held his cellphone away from his ear and called out, "Anna Mae, can you go up to my office and see if you can find my road atlas. It should be somewhere in the stacks sitting on the round table."

He put the cellphone back to his ear and made some notes on a yellow pad lying in front of him.

"Somewhere in Atlanta? That's all you know, Admiral?" Zach questioned.

"Sorry," Admiral Hadley sighed. "They all clammed up and wouldn't say a word. Deputy Director Clark did mention one name we should fear. Someone he called al-Ta'abin, The Snake. That matches the name of the legendary murderer CIA Director Sandberg shared with me. I know it's not much, but that's all we have."

"Any descriptions of who we're looking for or what they might be driving?"

"No. Just the photos you sent earlier," Admiral Hadley answered. "There is only one face in the photos that we couldn't identify. Nobody knows who he might be. Everyone in the alphabet soup of intelligence agencies; FBI, CIA, DIA, NSA, and DHS, is beating the bushes and putting the squeeze on every snitch and informant they have to obtain more intel on this guy. I cropped out his image and enlarged it as much as I could. Copies have been sent to all the local law enforcement agencies in Atlanta and surrounding areas. I advised them to not approach him or any of the others in the photos if spotted. They are to call me immediately and I will relay that information on to you. I suggest you get started toward Atlanta immediately."

"Anything else I should know, Admiral?"

"Yes, Zach. Be extremely careful. Deputy Director Clark bragged that he had pledged his life to the *Holy Order* and that he would gladly give it. I am convinced these men would kill their own mother if they believed it benefitted their cause *and* they are more than happy to die for it."

"Okay, Admiral. I'll get started right away," Zach responded. "Put your head together with anybody you can think of and try to come up with a likely target in Atlanta. Atlanta is a big city and we have to narrow it down some."

Zach ended the call, walked over to a cabinet on the far side of the room, unlocked the lower section, and pulled out his personal weapon. He had the 9mm Sig Sauer P229 the Secret Service agent had given him, but he much preferred his own STI Lawman, 45 ACP because it was designed first and foremost as a duty and defensive weapon for law enforcement officers. Zach preferred it for its longer dual-spring slide assembly, allowing the magazine feed springs more time to react, producing a faster recovery time and a softer recoil. The STI Lawman's softer recoil and less muzzle movement resulted in excellent accuracy out to twenty-five yards. The trusty weapon had proved itself many times in the past. Ultimately for Zach, there was one absolutely critical feature for any weapon he carried; it must hit where he pointed it.

Zach retrieved three extra clips, two boxes of 45 ACP hollow point ammo, set the items on the table, and locked the cabinet. He ejected the empty clip and loaded it and the other clips with hollow point ammo. He shoved the loaded clip into the weapon, verified the safety was on, and laid it on the table.

Anna Mae came down the stairs from Zach's office, holding a road atlas in her left hand.

"What is that for?" Anna Mae questioned when she saw Zach lay the weapon on the table.

"Admiral Hadley just called," Zach answered. "Something's going to happen in Atlanta. He doesn't know exactly what yet, but he asked me to head that way. The men involved are evil and extremely dangerous. Whatever they're planning, it is big. One of them bragged millions were going to die."

"I'll grab a couple of bottles of water and we'll get started," Anna Mae announced, turning toward the kitchen.

"No," Zach protested. "It's too dangerous. I'm going alone."

"No, you're not," Anna Mae, protested. "Two sets of eyes are better than one. And may I remind you, if it weren't for me you would be dead. I've proven I can handle myself."

Anna Mae rushed over and stood in front of the door, blocking Zach's way. Zach really wanted to resist, but he did not have time to argue.

"Wait," Zach exclaimed, "What about Mazie? You'll have to stay here."

"We can drop here at my grandmother's house. I'll give her my friend's number from work if she needs help. I'm going with you. That's final."

No, you're not."

"Yes, I am."

'Anna Mae, I can't stand here and argue with you," Zach protested. "I've got to get started."

"You said Atlanta, right?"

"Yes. I said Atlanta. What does that have to do with you going or not?"

"Well, if you take the shortest route to hit I-95 to get you across the river into Georgia, you will pass no more than a few blocks from my grandmother's house. We can quickly drop off Mazie on the way. I can call my friend and ask her to meet us there. It won't take but a few minutes."

"I don't think so," Zach objected.

"It's either that or Mazie goes with us. Which do you want?" Anna Mae scooped up Mazie and stared at Zach. "Well, which is it?"

"Okay, okay, we'll drop Mazie at your grandmother's," Zach relented, knowing he was losing the dispute and unwilling to waste any more time. "But you have to follow my instructions to the letter. Understood?"

"Yes, Zach, I will follow your instructions *to the letter*," Anna Mae declared as she headed for the kitchen to grab some bottles of water. Returning from the kitchen with four bottles of water, she dumped them into the bag with Mazie's things and headed for the front door.

Zach stuffed the STI Lawman behind his back, raked the loaded magazines and extra ammo into a leather carry bag, grabbed the road atlas, and headed for the front door. He slammed the door and verified it was locked. While Anna Mae got Mazie buckled into her car seat, Zach dumped the carry bag on the floor behind the driver's seat and climbed into the car. He started the engine and waited for Anna Mae to climb into the passenger seat.

"Are you certain you want to do this?" he asked. "These people are extremely dangerous. I assure you they will not hesitate to kill you."

"I'm certain, Zach. Let's go," Anna Mae urged.

Zach put the car in gear and they roared off down the lane toward Anna Mae's grandmother's house. During a quick ten-minute stop to drop Mazie off, Anna Mae lied to her friend, telling her Zach had to meet a relative at the airport in Atlanta. She promised that they would return as soon as possible. Twenty minutes later they merged onto westbound Interstate Ninety-Five, headed toward Georgia.

Chapter Twenty-Nine

Interstate Highway 75
Northern outskirts of Macon, Georgia

Two and one-half hours later, with the speedometer needle indicating just below eighty, Zach's cellphone rang. He lifted it out of the case on his belt and handed it to Anna Mae.

"Hello," she answered. "This is Anna Mae Watts, Zach's friend. We are just passing through Macon on our way to Atlanta."

"Put me on speaker and turn up the volume?" Admiral Hadley requested on the other end of the conversation. "You both need to hear this."

Anna Mae tapped the Speaker icon as instructed. She leaned toward Zach, holding the cellphone between them.

"Zach, my absolute worst fear has been confirmed," Admiral Hadley shouted to be heard above the road noise. "Now, more than ever, I am convinced there is some kind of virus involved. I talked again with General George Whitney. He's the expert in infectious diseases I mentioned earlier. There isn't time to explain completely, but he is certain the Picketts and the Foley boys died from some form of engineered virus. He says he has never seen anything like it. He believes the mortality would be well above ninety percent. Assuming he and I are correct, the big event could very well be a release of that unknown virus. General Whitney did some digging and learned that there is currently a very large conference of medical personnel underway at the Atlanta Convention Center. There are over three thousand attendees and this is the last day. If a number of them are infected with this unknown virus and they leave and spread out all across the country, the result will be catastrophic and the loss of life would be enormous. General

Whitney's guess is that at least a third of the population could be dead within three to four weeks and another third of the population three to four weeks after that."

"Are you serious, Admiral?" Zach stammered.

"The General and I are dead serious," Admiral Hadley exclaimed.

"Well then, we have to catch whoever is planning this and stop them before they can release the virus," Zach asserted. "Has there been any word from any of the law enforcement agencies regarding a location of the man in the photos?"

"Nothing so far. Zach, I've arranged an escort for you. Georgia State troopers are waiting for you at the Interstate Four Seventy-Five junction, north of your current location. Drive as fast as you think is safe. They will clear a path for you all the way into Atlanta. If there are any positive sightings of the man in the photos, I will contact you immediately."

"Okay, Admiral. We'll be waiting," Zach answered. Pushing down on the accelerator, he watched the speed climb until it reached ninety. Afraid to push their speed any higher, he held it there until they picked up the state patrol escort.

Looking over at Anna Mae, he said, "Pull your seat belt tight. This could get a little dicey."

EasyGo Truck Stop
Exit 212, Interstate 75

Sixty miles further north on the interstate highway, Sha'ban Rabi Bahar, The Snake, exited the Arco truck stop, ambled over to his vehicle, and climbed in. He pulled out a cellphone, punched in a number, and waited.

"Grand Prince, where are you?" he asked the instant he heard someone answer on the other end.

"I have placed the biocontainers and the delivery vector at the agreed location," Timothé Alex Durand, the Grand Prince of the Royal Secret, answered. "I am currently parked in one of the convention center waiting areas."

"Good, my friend. Well done." Sha'ban answered. "I will be there in thirty minutes. I will feed the infected blood to the delivery vector and then I will set the timer for the release. Then we leave the vehicles in the airport parking lot and we will board our plane for home."

Timothé Alex Durand was unaware Sha'ban did not intend for him to join him on the flight home. Sha'ban intended to leave no witnesses behind, and he also refused to share rule of the coming New Order with absolutely no one. Sha'ban would give himself no more than fifteen minutes to infect the vector, set the timer, and then rid himself of Durand. As soon as he returned home, he would eliminate the two remaining Supreme Council members. The pathetic fools in the White House would either be dead or in prison and there would be no one left to challenge him. He would assume complete rule over the New World Order.

He desperately wanted to locate and kill his hated enemy, Templeton, and spill his infidel blood upon the impure ground, but there was no longer enough time. "*Perhaps, it would be better*," he thought. The coming death will be far more painful.

Smiling, he slid the key into the ignition and started the engine. He slipped the car into gear and drove out of the truck stop's parking lot. Speeding down the entrance ramp for the interstate, he merged into northbound traffic and headed for the Atlanta Convention Center.

Chapter Thirty

Interstate 75
Southern Outskirts of Atlanta, Georgia

Three Georgia State Patrol cruisers, one occupying the lane Zach and Anna Mae were driving in and the other two cruisers in the adjacent lanes, ran escort. Scattered further down the interstate, four more Georgia State Patrol cruisers began moving traffic out of the way. Anna Mae snatched up the ringing cellphone lying in her lap. She answered the call and turned on the speaker.

"Go ahead, Admiral. You're on speaker," she said, recognizing the admiral's number.

"Zach, the local PD's canvas of the Convention Center staff turned up a lead," Admiral Hadley began. "One of the Convention Center's security guards recognized the man from the photo. The parking area security guard said he admitted someone that resembled the man in the photo driving a white Hyundai minivan. The man's credentials indicated he was an FBI communications tech. The guard said he was at the Convention Center for less than an hour."

"Is he certain, Admiral?" Zach asked.

"Absolutely. Picked him out immediately. He said something about the guy seemed a little off, so he wrote down the minivan's license plate number. When Atlanta PD ran the plate number, it came back to a ten-year-old, green Honda. It has to be our guy."

"Admiral, make certain the local PD knows they are to observe only. We can't afford for the guy to get spooked. We have to grab him before he can release the virus."

"I believe they know that, but I will call them again and make certain they are aware of the risk of spooking him."

"Has anyone else spotted any of the others recently?"

"No sightings other than the one by the security guard. Atlanta PD has distributed copies of the photos to all personnel and advised them to be on high alert. I or someone else will call you the instant anyone spots anyone from the photos."

"Okay, Admiral," Zach said. "We're just passing the Interstate Two Eighty-Five junction, so we are about eight miles from the Convention Center. Let Atlanta PD know. Tell them no roadblocks. Nothing suspicious. They are to observe only."

"Will do," Admiral Hadley answered. "Zach, I know I don't have to warn you, but I will anyway. Be careful. This guy is more dangerous than a wounded lion."

"Understood, Admiral," Zach replied, nodding his head toward the cellphone.

Anna Mae ended the call, dropped Zach's cellphone in her purse, withdrew her pink-gripped, Beretta 9mm, pulled the slide back, and verified there was a round in the chamber.

Zach glanced over at Anna Mae and said, "Just what are you planning to do with that?"

"I'm going to help you," Anna Mae responded.

"No, you're not," Zach asserted. "When we get to the Convention Center, you're going to stay in the car."

"Not on your life," Anna Mae protested. "You know I can shoot. Two guns are always better than one."

"You are staying in the car," Zach barked. "It's just too dangerous. I'll tie you up if I have to."

Anna Mae stared out the windshield and muttered something under her breath that Zach could not hear.

"Don't be mad, Anna Mae," Zach begged. "This guy is a vicious murderer. I won't allow you to get hurt."

"Yeah, you already said that," Anna Mae snapped, returning her gaze to the windshield.

He shook his head and watched as one of the State Patrol cruisers dropped back until he was adjacent with Zach's car and waved as he turned off his emergency lights.

Zach slowed down to match traffic heading into downtown Atlanta. The three State Patrol cruisers lined up in the far right lane and pulled off the interstate at the next exit.

Refusing to argue any further, Zach took a deep breath and focused on the road, wondering what lay ahead at the Convention Center.

Atlanta Convention Center
240 Peachtree Street NW
Atlanta, Georgia

The Convention Center security guard looked up from the magazine he was reading and watched a white minivan pull up to the gate and stop. The driver of the minivan rolled the window down, held out a leather credentials wallet to the guard, and waited.

"Wasn't someone else from your company just here," the security guard questioned as he leaned out from the guard shack and took the wallet offered by the driver.

"Yeah, seems the equipment didn't stay fixed," the minivan's driver lied.

The security guard made a pretense of examining the wallet. He scribbled a note on the clipboard lying in front of him and handed the wallet back to the driver. The security guard had been instructed that if he saw the minivan or any of the individuals in the photos again, to let them pass and to not confront them or make them suspicious in any way.

"You can go on in," the security guard said as he punched the button to raise the security gate.

As soon as the minivan drove past the guard shack, the security guard picked up the telephone and dialed the number he had been instructed to call if he saw the minivan or the man from the photo again.

"Admiral Hadley here."

"This is Roger McClusky. I'm the security guard for the parking area at the Atlanta Convention Center."

"Have you seen the man from the photo again?" Admiral Hadley questioned.

"No. This was a different man," McClusky replied. "He was driving an identical white minivan."

"Can you describe him?"

"Can't tell you anything about his height. He looks to be average build, medium-dark complexion, jet-black hair. That's all I can tell you, Admiral."

"How do you know he's related to the other man, Mister McClusky?"

"The minivan has the exact same markings as the first one did. He pulled up to the guard shack and claimed the equipment repair the other man made didn't stay fixed. I passed him through like I was told. It looks like he went to the same place where the other man went when he was here earlier."

"If he leaves or if you see anything out of the ordinary, and I mean anything, call me back immediately."

"Yes sir, Admiral. I will do that," Roger McClusky answered.

As soon as the call ended, Admiral Hadley called Zach and warned him that someone different had just driven a white minivan into the Convention Center, but his description didn't match anyone in the photos.

Encountering the same parking problem Timothé Alex Durand had, Sha'ban Rabi Bahar pulled over to the side of the lane and double-parked the minivan. He climbed out of the minivan and entered the maintenance room.

After unlocking the false equipment cabinet, he positioned one containers filled with mosquitoes close to the ventilation exhaust duct. He carried one of the pathogen biocontainers and the other container of mosquitoes out to the minivan. Those would be released later at one of the large hotels in downtown Atlanta.

Back in the maintenance room, Sha'ban slipped on a respirator and two pairs of rubber gloves. He then retrieved one of the two bags made of synthetic skin filled with blood from the satchel he had carried in earlier. With extreme care, he opened the biocontainer and withdrew the glass, biohazard flask. He inserted the needle of a hypodermic syringe into the flask's extraction port and extracted twenty CCs of the infected fluid. After injecting the infected fluid into the blood, the biohazard flask and syringe went back into the biocontainer. He resealed the biocontainer and set it aside.

Sha'ban connected a two inch diameter hose to one end of a portable ventilator pump and the other end to a connector on the side of the mosquito container. Using another short section of hose, he connected one end to the back of the container and the other end to a "T" connector in the ventilation exhaust duct. He double taped both connections to be assured no pathogen could escape until the timer activated the system.

Sha'ban sprayed the synthetic skin bag with a pheromone that would attract the mosquitoes. He then inserted the synthetic skin bag into the container's access chamber, closed and sealed the access door, and pulled the release, dropping the bag into the container. In less than ten seconds, the bag turned black, completely covered with hungry mosquitoes.

By the time the mosquitoes were released, they would be thoroughly infected with the pathogen. Sha'ban would time the release to happen just minutes before the final session of the conference ended. Thousands upon thousands of aggressive mosquitoes would swarm around the parking lot, biting anyone and everyone within one mile.

A second time he bent over the container to make certain the sealing tape had completely sealed the hoses. Sha'ban moved over to the ventilator pump's control box and verified the timers were set for the proper time. All was now ready. He flipped the power switch on the timer and smiled, envisioning the misery and death that was about to be unleashed upon the depraved infidels.

When the timers at the Convention Center and the hotel where he would place the other container of mosquitoes tripped and pumped the mosquitoes out, he would be miles away boarding an airplane for home.

"Praise be to Allah," Sha'ban shouted. "Hadhramaut comes upon you, oh Great Satan!"

Everything had gone exactly according to plan except for two items. He could not locate Timothé Alex Durand. Durand had not been at the agreed location. Sha'ban had intended to make certain there was no one left behind to talk. He vowed that when he found him, the traitor would pay for his treachery. Durand would have been executed quickly, but now he would die a hideously painful death.

The other unfulfilled task weighed heavily on Sha'ban. Many nights he had lain awake on his bed dreaming of slitting the throat of the one man he hated most upon the entire Earth, one Zach Templeton. If it hadn't been for Templeton, the New World Order would already be in place and he would be ruler of the world. Desperately he wanted to watch as Templeton's life blood spilled out upon the ground, but there simply wasn't time. He had to be on a plane when the timers triggered the release of death. If Templeton didn't die in the coming plague, he vowed he would hunt him down if it took him the rest of his life.

Sha'ban returned the containers to the false cabinet and locked it. He picked up the satchel and headed for the minivan. Stopping with one foot out the door, he decided he would take the time to make one last check of the ventilator pump and verify the timer was set correctly.

Chapter Thirty-One

Interstate 75
Downtown Atlanta, Georgia

Quickly approaching downtown Atlanta, Anna Mae looked over at Zach and asked, "Who is this character Admiral Hadley just told you about? It sounds like you know him?"

"I know him only by reputation," Zach answered. "In Europe they say he is called The Snake. He's something of a legend. There are no photos of him and no one has seen his face or knows what he looks like. No one alive, that is."

"What does that mean?" Anna Mae asked, a horrified look on her face.

"From what Admiral Hadley told me, the legend says he has over one hundred kills. When he's operating in his guise as The Snake, he leaves no one alive that could identify him. He slits the throats of all his victims. That's how they have counted his kills."

"If he's that dangerous, how do you intend to catch him?"

"You don't catch murderous psychopaths like him. He will never allow himself to be taken alive."

Ana Mae started to say something but stopped. Picking nervously at her fingernails, she turned and watched the passing highway exit signs.

"Hey, Zach, exit Two Forty-Eight C, the one we want is next. It's just up ahead," Anna Mae called out as she compared the highway signs to the spot she had circled on the map spread out on her lap.

Zach glanced in the rear-view mirror. Seeing a break in traffic, he flipped on his turn signal and shifted over into the far right lane. One quarter mile further down the highway, he pulled off the interstate, stopped at the end of the exit ramp, and turned left onto Ellis Street NE. About to enter the intersection, a man driving a grey sedan blared his horn and made a gesture at Zach for cutting him off. Zach shrugged his shoulders and waved at the man. Zach drove four blocks east on Ellis Street then turned right onto Peachtree Street, having the Convention Center in sight, one and a half blocks to the north.

Zach turned left off of Peachtree Street and followed the signs toward the Convention Center's parking area.

"Wow," Anna Mae remarked, looking up at the impressive Grand Atrium.

Zach pulled up to the parking area guard shack and stopped, his window already down. He flopped open his credentials wallet and held it out toward the security guard.

"The man you are looking for is here," the security guard announced, reaching for the button to raise the gate. "He's in a white minivan. Six rows down, then turn right."

"Don't let anyone else in," Zach ordered as he sped past the guard shack and into the parking area.

"Anna Mae, I'm telling you again," Zach asserted. "Stay in the car."

"Not a chance," Anna Mae protested. "The two of us will have a better chance of stopping him."

Zach shook his head and followed the guard's directions, turning right at the sixth row. He saw the white minivan fifty feet ahead, parked next to an open door.

He stopped the car, looked over at Anna Mae, and pleaded, "Please, please stay here."

"No, you'll need help," Anna Mae argued.

While Zach and Anna Mae were arguing, Sha'ban stepped partway out the door and noticed a car sitting several car lengths back down the row. He ducked back inside and leaned his head out just far enough to see. The two people in the car appeared to be talking. He squatted down and squinted. A man and a woman were seated in the car. "*Are they arguing?*" he asked himself, continuing to observe them. The man in the car turned his head slightly. "Could it possibly be?" he whispered. "*Allah is indeed offering me a great blessing today,*" he thought. He recognized the man's face instantly. It was none other than his hated enemy, Zach Templeton. Sha'ban drew back into the room to wait. "Praise be to Allah," he muttered, smiling as he placed his hand on the hilt of his jambiya. "Today, you will die, infidel," he snarled as he flipped the lights off and drew back into the shadows.

"You must stay here," Zach commanded. "I have to concentrate on the guy in the room. If you come along, I'll worry about you. I won't be able to watch him and you."

"Oh, all right," Anna Mae agreed. "Don't get yourself killed."

"I'll certainly try not to," Zach replied as he quietly opened the door.

He gently pushed the door shut, reached behind his back for his weapon, pulled the slide back, and flipped the safety off. He creeped toward the open door. Reaching the open door to the maintenance room, he stepped in, his weapon pointed in front of him. The movement coming from his left was so sudden; it caught Zach unprepared. Sha'ban kicked at Zach's hands. Zach's weapon flew out of his hand and clattered on the floor. Sha'ban stomped his foot against the side of Zach's left knee. Zach crashed to the floor. Excruciating pain exploded up his leg.

A look of triumph filled Sha'ban's face as he stared at the man he hated, lying disabled only a few feet away.

"Today you will die, Mister Templeton."

Hartsfield–Jackson International Airport
Atlanta, Georgia

Bradley Anderson, Secret Service Special Agent, sat in a strategic vantage point in the departing passengers section of the international terminal, watching for anyone matching the photo that had been widely circulated to all federal and local law enforcement agencies. Special Agent Anderson, dressed in casual clothes with a magazine propped against his crossed leg, occasionally glanced at the photo stuffed into the magazine.

He tapped the message "Anything?" into his cellphone's text app and pressed Send. "Nothing" came the reply from Secret Service Special Agent Richard Forman positioned on the far north end of the international terminal. No less than a dozen Secret Service agents were stationed in both the north and south domestic travel terminals watching for anyone matching the photo.

Special Agent Anderson flopped the magazine closed, stood up, and stretched to relieve his tired muscles. Slowly he ambled over to a specialty coffee kiosk, while keeping his eyes on the flow of incoming passengers. He ordered a large café mocha latte and returned to his seat. Thinking he recognized someone in the crowd, he quickly flipped to the photo stuffed in the magazine and compared it to the face he had noticed in the crowd.

He watched as the individual hurried across the terminal and joined a line queued up waiting for the next open spot at the ticket counter. Another quick glance at the photo confirmed the man in the line did not match the photo.

Draining the last swallow of the latte, he stuffed the magazine under his arm, walked over to a trash receptacle, and dropped the empty cup in. Concerned he had been seated in the same place too long, he selected an empty seat in a different seating area.

He awakened his cellphone and sent the same message as he had fifteen minutes earlier. Ten seconds later he received the same reply as before. Another thirty minutes passed. Getting restless, Agent Anderson had been on duty for hours. He changed positions, laid the magazine in his lap, folded his arms across his chest, and yawned. Nodding off, he abruptly jerked upright, awakened by the cellphone vibrating in his pocket.

He dug out the cellphone and displayed the text message. "It's him. 5'10", thin brown hair, light brown slacks, tweed jacket, black roller bag. Walking your way."

Agent Anderson focused on the travelers streaming south from the north end of the terminal. After several minutes of scrutinizing the crowd, he picked out the man Special Agent Forman had described. From what he could see, it appeared the man already had a boarding pass in his hand. The man turned to his left and headed for the escalator that led to the security screening area and the boarding gates beyond. Agent Anderson grabbed his cellphone and tapped in a number.

"Security Supervisor," Supervisory Transportation Security Officer Ramon Alvarez announced.

"This is Special Agent Anderson. I've spotted the individual we are looking for. Five foot ten inches, thin brown hair, light brown slacks, tweed jacket, and a black roller bag. He just now started up the escalator. Make whatever excuse you need and detain him."

"Yes, sir," TSA Officer Alvarez replied. "I'll detain him and put him in interrogation room B."

"Great. I'm on my way up."

Special Agent Anderson got up from his seat and headed for the escalator. At the top of the escalator, standing off to the side of the screening area, Special Agent Anderson watched as TSA officers let the man go through the magnetometer and then pulled him aside, directing him to an interrogation room.

Special Agent Anderson showed his credentials to an airport police officer, bypassed security, and knocked on the interrogation room door. TSA Officer Alvarez handed Special Agent Anderson the man's passport and closed the door.

"Well, Mister Émile Jean-Marc," Special Agent Anderson said, looking down at the man seated on the other side of the table. "Is that your real name?"

"Of course that's my name," the man protested. "Why would it not be?"

"I think you are lying," Special Agent Anderson said, holding out his hand toward the TSA officer. TSA officer Alvarez handed him a fingerprint scanner.

"Put your index finger here," Special Agent Anderson ordered.

With the man's index finger pressed against the scanner's fingerprint window, Special Agent Anderson tethered the scanner to his cellphone then pressed Send. He disconnected the tether and tapped a speed dial number. While he was waiting for an answer, someone knocked on the interrogation room door. TSA Officer Alvarez opened the door and ushered in Special Agent Forman. Special Agent Anderson talked briefly with someone from the Department of Homeland Security biometrics lab.

"I just learned your name is not Émile Jean-Marc," Special Agent Anderson shouted, slamming the magazine down on the table. "Your real name is Timothé Alex Durand. Can you explain to me what you are doing in this country and why you have a fake passport?"

Timothé Alex Durand just sat there stone faced, glaring at the two Secret Service agents.

Special Agent Anderson placed both hands on the table and leaned close to the man's face and said, "I suggest you start talking. It will *not* go well for you if you do not."

Special Agent Anderson waited.

"We know you are somehow involved with an evil man they call The Snake."

Noticing the man's sudden change of expression, Special Agent Anderson continued, "I see you know this man. Do not lie again. I saw it in your face. We also know there is a deadly virus involved. Start talking!"

Special Agent Anderson waited again. Still, Timothé Alex Durand sat silent and stone faced.

"Still nothing to say," Special Agent Anderson shouted, shoving the table against the man's chest, nearly knocking him and the chair over.

Special Agent Anderson walked over and whispered something to TSA Officer Alvarez, who turned and left the room.

"If you won't talk here, perhaps you will if we take you somewhere where we can be more persuasive. You have made a serious mistake, Mister Durand. I assure you, you *will* answer our questions."

Special Agent Anderson stepped over beside the rear exit door. "Cuff him," he said to Agent Forman. "We'll take him out the back way."

Atlanta Convention Center
240 Peachtree Street NW
Atlanta, Georgia

Still pointing his weapon at Zach, Sha'ban noticed the bewildered look on Zach's face. "Yes, I know who you are. Does that surprise you?" Sha'ban taunted.

"How do you know me?" Zach questioned.

"Frank Porter was following my instructions. Twice I ordered him to kill you."

"You were behind the plots to destroy my country?" Zach snarled.

"Yes, but that dim-witted idiot failed. At least he killed your wife. I hope you enjoyed watching her die."

"I will kill you with my bare hands," Zach bellowed, shaking with pent up rage against the man he just learned was ultimately responsible for Angie's death.

"Shut up, you impudent pig."

Sha'ban switched his weapon to his other hand. With utter glee, he reached for his jambiya and withdrew it from its sheath.

"Today, you shall die a painful death, you infidel scum!" Sha'ban shrieked. "Your vile, infidel blood shall pour out upon the ground, Mister Templeton. Now, I, Sha'ban Rabi Bahar, The Snake, shall send you to Hell."

Sha'ban tossed his weapon aside and took a step toward Zach.

Enraged by the mere mention of Porter's name and the heartrending vision of his wife dying on the floor of Henry Tang's penthouse apartment, Zach lunged toward Sha'ban, hampered by his injured knee. The two men battled in the confined space. Driven by blind rage toward the person responsible for Angie's death coupled with the massive amount of adrenaline pouring into his bloodstream, Zach hardly felt the gashes as Sha'ban slashed at him with the gleaming jambiya.

Zach feigned sideways and grabbed Sha'ban in a bear-hug, intending to squeeze the life out of him. Sha'ban pushed backward with his legs, slamming Zach against the wall of the maintenance room. As Zach fought to regain his breath, Sha'ban summoned the strength to struggle free from Zach's grasp. Sha'ban turned, slashing the razor-sharp blade at Zach. Zach dove sideways, barely avoiding the blade as he kicked at Sha'ban's legs.

Zach backed up a step, his eyes flitting around the room trying to locate his weapon. He watched the madman's eyes intently, looking for a clue to his next move. Deep in Zach's mind memories of hand-to-hand combat were reborn, flashing into his consciousness. Looking for that one opening, he could kill the man before him with a single blow if he could land it in the right spot.

Perceiving the tiniest of movement in Sha'ban's eyes, Zach leaped sideways. Sha'ban thrust his jambiya, finding nothing but empty air. He shrieked something unintelligible, charged in Zach's direction, and thrust the dagger at Zach again.

Zach shifted his weight and threw up his forearm, pushing Sha'ban's arm sideways. With his other hand, Zach landed a powerful blow to Sha'ban's ribs. Seething with rage, Sha'ban shrieked again and lunged at Zach. Zach tucked his chin downward to protect his throat and charged toward Sha'ban, shortening the man's reach and taking the force out of the blow. Zach pumped with his legs, pushing Sha'ban backward. Both men fell to the floor.

Both men, breathing heavily, scrambled to their feet, each man looking for an opening to attack the other. Sha'ban lunged at Zach with the jambiya raised high in the air. Zach leapt backward to avoid Sha'ban's blow, lost his balance, and landed hard on the floor. Seizing the opportunity, Sha'ban kicked with all his might. Zach rolled, attempting to avoid Sha'ban's foot. Unfortunately, Zach was a half-second too slow, the heavy shoe landing just below his temple.

Out of breath and dazed from the blow to the head, Zach struggled to get up from the floor. Before Zach could get up, Sha'ban leaped on top of him, the jambiya poised at Zach's throat. Sha'ban pressed the tip of the dagger just under Zach's left ear. An enormous grin spread across Sha'ban's face as he envisioned slitting this infidel's throat from ear to ear. The vengeance he had so long yearned for was about to be his.

Chapter Thirty-Two

"The Shed"
Camp Jessup
Fulton County, Georgia

Two black Lincoln SUV's with blackened windows sat parked
in a cluster of dense pine trees behind a nondescript old shed
on Camp Jessup, a former World War I military maintenance
facility. All but a few of Camp Jessup's facilities, including living quarters, mess halls, and administrative buildings, had long
since been demolished and removed. Most of the camp had
been turned into grassy fields. Only a handful of the old buildings still remained.

From the outside, *"The Shed"* appeared to be just another
example of rampant government waste, an abandoned and
neglected government building. Unknown and hidden beneath
the building was a sophisticated, off-the-books interrogation
facility. Located a short four miles from Atlanta's International
airport, Camp Jessup sat next to the abandoned Fort McPher-
son Army base.

After refusing to talk, Timothé Alex Durand had been
dragged out the rear exit from the airport's TSA security and
had been brusquely shoved into one of the black SUV's.

Under normal circumstances, new arrivals at the facility
were brought in under cover of darkness and no vehicles were
ever left parked at the facility. However, due to the seriousness
of the current threat and an ultra-critical time constraint, Mr.
Durand had arrived in broad daylight and the vehicles were still
parked outside.

Seated on a hard metal chair, Timothé Alex Durand's left
hand was cuffed to a large metal bar bolted to the center of the
table. The four foot by six foot cinder-block room, painted a

drab, lifeless gray, was totally empty except for one chair and the table. Durand shifted his weight in the chair, staring at a two foot by three foot mirror on the opposite wall, assuming someone must be watching him from the other side. Even though he was not a US citizen, this was America and he had rights. Or so he thought.

In the viewing room, Secret Service agents Anderson and Forman stared at the man on the other side of the mirror. In other cases, they would wait until the "perp" got fidgety and nervous, but time was of the essence. They needed information and they needed it yesterday. The Secretary of the Department of Homeland Security had told Special Agent Anderson so, and in not so uncertain terms.

"What did the Secretary say?" Special Agent Forman asked after Special Agent Anderson ended his call.

Shaking his head, Special Agent Anderson answered, "The secretary said we are to get him to talk, period. No Excuses. No rules whatsoever, except for one. We aren't allowed to kill him. First time I've ever received such instructions."

"Are you serious?" Special Agent Forman questioned.

"Absolutely," Special Agent Anderson replied. "Uncertain how I feel about this, but they've ordered to find out what he knows. Let's go give our friend in there a little nudge."

The two Secret Service agents exited the viewing room and stood in front of the interrogation room door. Special Agent Anderson took hold of the doorknob, threw the door open, and angrily burst into the room.

"We're tired of playing games with you, Durand," Special Agent Anderson shouted as he kicked the chair out from under the man.

Durand tumbled out of the chair, dangling by his left hand, still cuffed to the center bar.

"Yee-ow, that hurts," Durand bleated. "You can't do that. I've got rights."

"Our friend here says we can't do that," Special Agent Anderson sneered. "Maybe we should help him up."

He reached down and helped Durand part way up and then let him go. Durand yelped in pain again.

"Oh, look. I slipped," Special Agent Anderson laughed, kicking Durand's feet out from under him. "Listen up, dirtbag," he hissed, grabbing a handful of Durand's hair and jerking his head back. "I'm running out of patience. If you don't start talking, you're going to start losing body parts."

"You can't," Durand wailed. "You aren't allowed to do that. I'll get a lawyer. I'll have you charged with assault."

"Oh, yeah. Just watch me. Hey, Rich. Set our guest up in his chair. Cuff his other hand to the center bar." Special Agent Anderson pulled a Sig Sauer P227 Tactical 9mm from under his jacket and slowly threaded a long, black sound suppressor to the barrel.

"These hollow points ought to do a real number on his knees. I sure hope this doesn't splatter on my new slacks," he said as he pulled the slide back and pressed the tip of the suppressor against Durand's knee. Special Agent Anderson flinched his hand, pretending to pull the trigger. Durand grimaced, his face filled with horror.

"Wait," Special Agent Anderson said. "Maybe if I stand behind him, I won't get any on me. Well, here goes!"

"No, don't," Durand screamed, shaking uncontrollably. "I can't take anymore. I'll tell you what you want to know."

"Rich, grab a notebook and write this down. All right, Durand start talking. And make it quick."

Special Agent Forman scribbled furiously in the notebook he had removed from his jacket pocket while Durand sang like a robin in the springtime. Giving in to overwhelming fear, he told the two Secret Service agents everything he knew. Satisfied they had what they needed, Special Agent Anderson unshackled Durand from the table and turned him over to two waiting United States marshals.

He stopped the marshals as they started out the door. "Mister Durand, if even one American soul dies because of you, it will be my great pleasure to watch them stick a needle in your arm. Get him out of here!"

Special Agent Anderson dug his cellphone out of his pocket to pass the information on to the Secretary of Homeland Security.

Conference Center
240 Peachtree Street NW
Atlanta, Georgia

The deafening roar of a gunshot echoed inside the maintenance room. Anna Mae, concerned for the life of her new friend, had disobeyed Zach's implicit instructions and had climbed out of the car and had crept up to the maintenance room. She had gasped in horror when she peered into the room, the sour taste of fear rising in the back of her throat. Reacting to what she saw and ignoring all the rules of careful aiming her father had taught he, she had rushed the shot with her Beretta 9mm. Slightly off target, the slug passed within an inch of Sha'ban's head and slammed into the wall.

Sha'ban Rabi Bahar, startled by the gunshot, let go of Zach and rolled sideways, diving for his weapon. He scrambled wildly to pick up the weapon he had tossed aside earlier.

Still shaking from a massive overload of adrenaline, Anna Mae fired and missed again. The errant slug ricocheted off the concrete floor, a fragment hitting Sha'ban's right leg, just below the knee.

"You shall pay for this with your life!" Sha'ban roared.

Zach struggled to his feet and dove on top of Sha'ban. The two men scrambled for control of the weapon, just out of reach of Sha'ban's grasp. Anna Mae pointed her weapon, but she dared not fire, afraid she would hit Zach. Zach made a desperate stab at the weapon, knocking it out of reach. Anna Mae ran over and reached for the weapon lying on the floor beside Sha'ban. Just as her fingertips touched the weapon, Sha'ban kicked her foot, sending her flying.

"Oomph," Anna Mae blurted out as she hit the floor, all the air forced out of her lungs.

The Berretta flew out of her hand, clattering across the concrete floor as it bounced out the door. Across the room, the two men continued to battle for control of Sha'ban's weapon. Zack heaved Sha'ban aside, snagged the weapon, and got to his knees. Sha'ban drew up his legs and slammed them into Zach, sending him flying across the room. Sha'ban leaped to his feet and charged full speed toward Zach.

"I'm going to kill you," Sha'ban snarled, driving his shoulder into Zach's chest, slamming him into the wall, burying punches, over and over again.

Both men crashed against one of the equipment cabinets. Zach's arm smacked into the edge of the cabinet, dislodging the weapon from his hand. It dropped to the floor. Sha'ban released his grasp on Zach and dived toward the weapon. Being closer, Sha'ban scooped up the weapon and attempted to point it toward Zach. Leaping on top of him before he could fire, Zach swiped at the weapon but missed.

Each man wrestled ferociously to gain control of the weapon, rolling back and forth, first one on top then the other. The weapon roared, but oddly muffled compared to the errant shots from Anna Mae's Berretta. The struggling stopped and both men lay still.

"Arrgghh," Sha'ban grunted as he heaved Zach's still body off and scrambled to his feet, panting and out of breath from the battle. Anna Mae had scrambled to her feet, had retrieved her Berretta, and had stepped back into the room just as Sha'ban straightened up.

With shaking arms, Anna Mae raised the Berretta, but before she could fire, Sha'ban fired his weapon. Anna Mae fell sideways, landing with a whump on the cold, concrete floor. Searing pain raced along her nerves and erupted in her brain. Intense, scorching, excruciating pain. She wanted to scream. She bit her lip, resisting the urge to cry out for Zach to save her. Cautiously, she forced one eyelid open to a tiny slit. She watched the man lay his weapon down and pick up a menacing looking dagger and start toward her. Raw, primal terror

screamed in her mind. Prickly fear gripped her. Panic threatening to overwhelm her. "*Run! Run!*" her mind screamed at her.

"*Wait. Wait,*" she commanded herself, realizing the Berretta was still in her hand. She drew in a deep slow breath and
held it, willing herself to lay perfectly still. Tightening her grip
on the Berretta, she knew she was going to get only one
chance.

With a crazed, maniacal look on his face, Sha'ban strad-
dled Anna Mae and reached down to grab her hair. Forcing
back the searing pain, Anna Mae quickly rolled to her back and
fired the Berretta.

A mixture of wild rage and shock spread across Sha'ban
Rabi Bahar's face. His face went slack, his eyes staring forward,
blank and unseeing. He teetered for a few seconds and fell
backward upon the floor, bright red blood trailing from the
dark hole in the center of his forehead.

Anna Mae dropped her Beretta 9mm on the floor and,
trailing her injured arm, raced to Zach's side and dropped to
her knees.

"Zach! Zach! Are you okay?" she yelled as she rolled him
over, using her uninjured right arm. "No," she screamed, looking down at the dark, red stain soaking across Zach's shirt.

"Zach, can you hear me?" she wailed, pressing her hand
tightly against the wound, hoping to slow the flow of blood.

"Please God, this can't be happening," she moaned. Never had she met anyone like this man. In the brief time she had
known him, deep feelings had already grown within her. She
couldn't bear the thought of losing him.

"Zach, can you hear me?" she urged again. "Zach, please!
Say something. Talk to me."

Zach raised his head slightly and his eyes fluttered open
twice as he tried to say something. He gasped and tried again
to get the words out. His head fell back. His eyes closed and he
was silent.

"Oh, Zach, I was afraid you were dead," Anna Mae sputtered, tears streaming down her cheeks as she wiped his face
with her dress.

"The equip…," Zach sputtered. He swallowed, coughed, and tried again, "Equipment…. Stop equipment…."

"Zach, I don't know what you mean," Anna Mae exclaimed.

"Must stop…." Zach gurgled. "Wires…. Wires… Rip out wires. Hurry."

Anna Mae glanced hurriedly around the room, not certain what Zach meant. Her eyes fell on an equipment cabinet against the far wall. She saw a large black wire running from the cabinet to a smaller device a few feet away.

"Zach, I don't understand," she stammered. Zach did not respond. She shook his shoulder, but received no response. Leaning down close to his face, she could not feel him breathing. Pushing the pain in her left arm out of her mind, she lifted Zach's head and cradled it in her lap.

"Oh, Zach, I already love you," she sobbed. "Please God no. This can't be." She bowed her head and pleaded with God to not take this man from her. She had only known him for a brief time, but she knew. Beyond a shadow of doubt, she believed this was the man she had been waiting for. Interrupted by a man's voice, she looked toward the door.

"Is everyone all right in here?" Roger McClusky, the security guard blurted out as he cautiously poked his head into the room "I heard a gunshot and came running. Then more gunshots. I called the FBI and an ambulance. The ambulance is pulling in now."

The ambulance screeched to a stop and two EMT's piled out.

"In here, quick," McClusky hollered. "A man's been shot."

One EMT raced into the room while the other EMT retrieved emergency equipment from the rear of the ambulance.

"Please ma'am," the EMT said. "You need to let me examine him." Anna Mae pushed herself back out of the way as the EMT gently laid Zach's head on the floor. He ripped a stethoscope from around his neck and listened intently to Zach's chest and then checked both wrists for a pulse.

"He's got a heartbeat and a faint pulse," he yelled to the second EMT. "Start an IV with normal saline. Run it wide open and hand me a compression dressing."

"Come over here and sit down, Miss and let the EMT's work," Roger McClusky urged as the EMT's worked frantically on Zach, trying to get him stable enough for the trip to the hospital.

"Hey, guys, may I?" McClusky asked, pointing at the open med kit. "I was a medic in the army. I can tend to the lady's arm."

"Sure, go ahead," one of the EMT's answered.

"My name's Roger McClusky, ma'am. I'm one of the security guards," he said as he ripped Anna Mae's sleeve open and examined the wound on her upper arm. "Looks like a through-and-through. You'll be fine, but you will need to go to the hospital to have it cleaned."

McClusky applied a sterile gauze dressing over the wound, wrapped a bandage around her arm several times, and taped it. With growing dread, Anna Mae watched as one of the EMT's started a second IV in Zach's other arm. The other EMT rechecked both of Zach's wrists and then listened to his chest again.

"We can't wait any longer," one EMT yelled at the other. They quickly loaded Zach onto a gurney and headed for the ambulance.

"Will he be okay?" Anna Mae asked one of the EMT's, fearing she did not want to know the answer.

"I won't lie to you, ma'am," the EMT answered. "It doesn't look good. Fortunately, the hospital is only a few blocks away. If we can get him there quickly, he just might have a slim chance."

"I'll see she gets to the hospital," McClusky advised as the EMT's rolled the gurney to the back of the ambulance and loaded it in. "Do you have a vehicle?" he asked, looking at Anna Mae.

"Oh, no. Zach has the keys," she exclaimed.

"That's okay," McClusky said, nudging Anna Mae toward the door. "I'll drive you over. Like the EMT said, it's not far,"

"Wait," Anna Mae exclaimed, about to step through the doorway. "Zach was insistent about some wires. Something about ripping out wires. Maybe it's that black one. There, coming out of that cabinet."

McClusky walked over and followed the black wire that ran out of a cabinet along the back wall and then over to an odd-looking device several feet away.

"Hmmm, that certainly doesn't belong here," he observed, bending down for a closer look. "Good Lord. This thing's full of mosquitoes. Thousands of them."

"That's got to be it," Anna Mae exclaimed. "Zach and Admiral Hadley talked about a deadly virus. That has to be how that monster intended to release it. Quick, we've got to disable it."

McClusky raced back over to the cabinet and pulled on the black wire, but it would not come loose. He pulled back all the slack he could and yanked at it with all his strength, throwing his weight against it. The wire slipped out from under the lugs on the terminal board, creating a blinding flash and a bright shower of sparks. The cable suddenly went slack, McClusky lost his balance, and went flying backwards, ending up on the floor on his behind.

"That should take care of it," McClusky said as he got up and dusted off the seat of his pants.

Anna Mae walked over and looked at the indicators on the timer control box. "Wow," she remarked, a shudder passing down her back as she looked at the buzzing mosquitoes and thought about what might have been.

"Mister McClusky, can you take me to the hospital now? I want to check on Zach."

Anna Mae retrieved her Berretta and headed for the door. McClusky followed Anna Mae out the door, and pulled it shut. A youngish man in a black suit came running up holding out a set of FBI credentials.

"What happened here?" the FBI agent asked.

"Secret Service, Special Agent Zach Templeton thwarted a plot to release a deadly virus," Anna Mae answered. "He was badly wounded. I'm on the way to the hospital. I've got to go."

"Not until you answer some questions," the FBI agent protested.

"Listen, sir," Anna Mae bristled. "Get out of my way. I'm going to the hospital. I'd hate to have to shoot you."

"I'd listen to the lady if I were you, son," McClusky advised.

"Follow me," Anna Mae said to the FBI agent.

Anna Mae hurried to Zach's car, dug through her purse, and pulled out Zach's cellphone. She brought up the last phone call and read off the calling phone number.

"Lock that door and post a guard," Anna Mae said to the FBI agent. "Don't let anyone in. Contact Admiral Hadley at that number and tell him the deadly virus is in there."

Anna Mae and Roger McClusky hurried to his car and sped off toward the hospital.

Chapter Thirty-Three

Atlanta Convention Center
Atlanta, Georgia

Thirty minutes after Anna Mae had departed for the hospital, a CBRN (chemical, biological, radiological, and nuclear) rapid response team from the U.S. Army Biological Warfare Center located on Fort Detrick, near Frederick, Maryland swept into the Atlanta Convention Center.

Fearing the worst, Admiral Hadley, with General Whitney's concurrence, had already alerted the Department of Homeland Security. The admiral had requested a CBRN rapid response team be scrambled and sent toward the Atlanta area.

Six U.S. Army soldiers, expressly trained in biological decontamination, climbed down out of the two response vehicles in bright yellow, Level A hazmat suits. The suits were equipped with a clear plastic full-face shield, two-way radio, steel-toed boots, chemical-resistant gloves, and a self-contained breathing system. Dressed in their large bulky suits, they looked more like an awkward cross between a sumo wrestler and a turtle than soldiers.

The CBRN response team began spraying a strong solution of bleach on every surface as they approached the maintenance room. They stopped and the lead team member motioned for the two individuals guarding the room to vacate the area. He held out his gloved hand. One of the individuals guarding the room dropped a key in the team leader's outstretched hand.

The lead team member stepped up to the door. As he inserted the key and pulled the door open, the rest of the team directed the bleach spray on him and the open doorway. Two of the team members moved into the room and sprayed down everything in sight. They switched to a solution of seventy percent ethanol mixed with one-half percent hydrogen peroxide and repeated the process. They waddled over to the container full of mosquitoes and one team member directed the spray over the container as the other member opened the access port. As the soldier directed the spray nozzle inside the container, the mosquitoes died instantly.

"Bring up the biological containment unit," the lead team member spoke into his two-way radio.

Two of the team members outside the room returned to the back of one of the response vehicles and carried a large trunk-like container to the doorway of the room. The two team members inside the room disconnected the hoses leading from the container and taped over the openings. They carried the container outside and set it in the biological containment unit, closed the lid, and ratcheted down the latches.

The two team members returned to the room and stuffed Sha'ban Rabi Bahar's lifeless body into a black body bag. They sprayed down the body bag and slipped it into a second body bag, zipped it closed, and sealed the entire zipper with red tape.

The team carried the biological containment unit and the body bag to the rear of one of the response vehicles and loaded them inside. Four of the six team members climbed into the lead vehicle and two climbed into the vehicle with the containment unit and body bag. The entire operation took less than fifteen minutes. The drivers started their engines, drove out of the parking area, and disappeared into traffic.

All exits into and out of the Convention Center had been blocked before the vehicles arrived. In all likelihood, less than ten people had any idea anything had happened.

Two hundred miles away a much larger CBRN rapid response team had descended on the hidden laboratory where the deadly virus had been engineered. The information extracted from Timothé Alex Durand proved to be accurate, allowing the response team to locate the entrance in less than five minutes. Mister Durand would be rewarded for his honesty, serving the rest of his life in a maximum security prison instead of receiving a lethal injection.

The rapid response team collected two small samples of the deadly pathogen to be sent to the CDC for research and long-term storage. All work papers were collected to be shredded and then incinerated. All laboratory glassware was crushed and the electronic equipment was beaten with sledgehammers until it was completely unrecognizable.

The incident commander toured the spaces, confirming that everything not removed had been destroyed. Team members placed two dozen targeted high explosive charges at strategic locations around the laboratory, then flooded it with ethylene oxide gas. Two bulldozers moved in and pushed three feet of dirt over the laboratory and its entrance.

The bulldozers pulled back to a safe distance. Five minutes later the incident commander verified all response team members had withdrawn to their proscribed safe locations. He picked up the detonator, flicked off the safety cover, and twisted the knob. Everyone felt the explosion more than heard it as the ground heaved upward six inches and then fell inward leaving a two foot deep depression.

Over the coming week, workers would cover the entire location with some type of sealant. Then a thick layer of topsoil would be spread and graded level. The entire area would be seeded with pasture grasses and wildflowers.

Deeply saddened, Admiral Hadley learned that Ruth and Walter Foley, Matt Blumenthal, the senior EMT, Dr. James Volker, ER Attending Physician, and two ER nurses had contracted the deadly virus. Despite being diagnosed early, herculean efforts to treat them proved to have no effect. Each one died within forty-eight hour of becoming symptomatic. Everyone remotely connected with them had been immediately isolated and no one manifested any symptoms after seven days. Two weeks passed with no further infections.

Fortunately, the general public would have absolutely no idea how close they had come to annihilation.

Atlanta Medical Center
Atlanta, Georgia

The twenty-four hours following the encounter in the Convention Center maintenance room was unbelievably grueling for Anna Mae. By the time Roger McClusky had driven Anna Mae to the hospital and she had located the emergency room, Zach had already been rushed off for emergency surgery.

About to exit the emergency room, Anna Mae felt a hand touch her shoulder. Emily Barnes, an emergency room nurse, had noticed blood seeping out of the bandage wrapped around Anna Mae's arm.

"Miss," Nurse Barnes said. "You need to have that looked at. There's blood running down your arm."

"Huh," Anna Mae responded, turning to look at Nurse Barnes then at her arm. "Blood? Oh, my!"

"Follow me," Nurse Barnes ordered, pushing Anna Mae into an empty exam room. "Sit up on the exam table."

Nurse Barnes pulled a pair of scissors from the pocket of her scrubs, cut through the bandage, and examined Anna Mae's arm.

"Is that what I think it is?" she asked.

"Yes, it's a gunshot wound. I was with my friend when he had a confrontation with a murderer."

The nurse grabbed two sterile gauze pads from a cabinet and applied one to each side of Anna Mae's arm. "Here, hold those in place while I go get a doctor."

Nurse Barnes scurried out of the exam room and located a doctor that was not busy and directed him to the exam room. Before returning to the exam room, she stopped at the admin desk and requested a police officer to respond to the exam room. After examining and cleaning the wound, the doctor told Anna Mae her arm would be fine. He dressed the wound, gave her an injection of antibiotics, and instructed her to keep the wound clean and dry.

As she exited the emergency department, she assured the security guard she was not leaving the hospital and that the police officer could find her in the surgery waiting room.

With Nurse Barnes's help, Anna Mae located the surgery waiting room and began her grueling vigil. After much pleading with the surgery waiting room coordinator, Anna Mae convinced the woman that Zach had absolutely no family in the area. The woman agreed to put her name on the list as family and promised she would keep her informed.

For two long hours, Anna Mae vacillated between flipping through months-old magazines, pacing the floor, and staring out the window. She walked over to the edge of the waiting area and looked imploringly at the woman seated at the information desk. The woman noticed her and picked up the phone. After a brief conversation, she got up from the desk and directed Anna Mae to an unoccupied section of the waiting area.

"I called and spoke with one of the nurses in the OR," the woman said. "She told me they have already given Mister Templeton six units of blood. She couldn't tell me anymore, other than it is still touch-and-go. Sorry, I wish I could give you better news."

"Thank you," Anna Mae sniffled, dabbing at her red-rimmed eyes with a soggy tissue. "I appreciate your checking for me."

"I know waiting is very difficult," the woman added. "I see it every single day. Some days I really feel like quitting. I see so much pain. But knowing I can help folks by keeping them informed, I change my mind and keep coming back."

"I don't know how you take it," Anna Mae replied, dabbing at her eyes again.

"I'll keep checking," the woman said. She patted Anna Mae on the shoulder, got up from the chair, and returned to her desk.

Anna Mae returned to her cycle of magazines, pacing, and staring out the window. Once she varied her routine, filling a styrofoam cup from the large coffee urn sitting at the far side of the waiting area. Cautiously, she took a small sip of the steaming liquid. The coffee tasted old and burnt. She added a large heaping spoonful of powdered creamer, but the burnt taste remained. After drinking half the cup, she gave up and tossed it in the trash receptacle. Back to the magazines, pacing, and staring out the window she went.

Twice more over the next three hours the woman at the information desk walked over and shared what little news she could obtain, apologizing each time because she could not offer much hope. Anna Mae was frazzled. The adrenaline expended in the maintenance room, the mad dash to the hospital, and the long hours of waiting with little hope were taking a colossal toll on Anna Mae. Nearing exhaustion, she had given up on magazines and alternated between pacing and staring out the window.

Finally, after five grueling hours, the woman walked over and said the doctor would like to speak with her. She escorted Anna Mae to a small patient conference room along the corridor that lead to the surgical suites. Anna Mae entered the room and saw a man in green scrubs seated in one of the chairs. Soaked from his shoulders down to his knees, he pointed toward an empty chair.

"I'm Doctor Daniel Singleton," the man announced, holding out his hand.

Anna Mae shook the man's hand and took a seat in one of the empty chairs, somewhat concerned by the man's solemn expression.

"I'm the chief trauma surgeon here at the hospital. I was in charge of your husband's case."

"He's not my husband, Doctor," Anna Mae corrected. "He's a really close friend. He has no family in the area. I convinced the woman at the desk to list me as family. I guess she must have put me down as his wife."

"Oh, I see. Well, okay," Dr. Singleton replied. "I'll be honest with you. The surgery was long and difficult because there was extensive internal damage. Right now your friend is listed in critical condition. The next twenty-four to forty-eight hours will determine if he survives."

"How soon can I see him?"

"He'll be in recovery for at least the next hour or two. From there he will go to ICU. If you go to the ICU waiting area and check in, someone will notify you when he arrives."

"Thank you Doctor."

The doctor got up from his chair, started out the door, and stopped. "By the way, what exactly does your friend do?" he asked.

"I'm not certain I'm allowed to tell you that," Anna Mae responded.

"Just as I was about to scrub in, I received a phone call from an Admiral Hadley," Dr. Singleton said "He was quite concerned about your friend's condition. I won't repeat what he said he would do to me if Mister Templeton didn't survive. Your friend must be very important."

"I've spoken to the Admiral, but I've never met him. I know he and Zach are good friends."

"I suspect your friend is military or law enforcement of some kind. I don't remember ever seeing someone with that many old scars."

"Something like that," Anna Mae admitted.

"I've got to go. Another case is waiting," Doctor Singleton said as he exited the room and headed for the large double doors at the end of the corridor.

Anna Mae located the ICU waiting area and checked in. Exactly two hours later the head ICU nurse came looking for Anna Mae and told her as soon as they got Zach settled and if all his vital signs were stable, she would be allowed to visit him. Another forty-five minutes passed as Anna Mae waited.

The head ICU nurse directed Anna Mae to the room where Zach had been taken. Unprepared, she gasped when she saw all the tubes, wires, and equipment attached to Zach. She staggered. Feeling woozy, she placed her hand on the sliding glass door to steady herself. The nurse led Anna Mae to a recliner beside the bed and helped her sit down.

"I'm sorry," Anna Mae squeaked.

"Don't worry about it," the nurse reassured. "Almost everyone has that same reaction the first time they walk into this place. It does look a little scary."

"How is he doing?"

"He's still critical, but his vital signs have improved slightly. Your friend there must be someone mighty special. I've been instructed to tell the ICU staff that you are allowed to stay in the room unless there is a procedure we need to do. Then we will have to ask you to leave for a time."

"He's certainly special to me," Anna Mae asserted.

Regaining her composure, Anna Mae stood up and moved over beside the bed. She reached out and laid her hand on Zach's arm, being careful to not disturb the IV lines running to both Zach's arms. She leaned down and whispered something in Zach's ear. There was no outward sign that Zach had heard her, but she didn't care. The man she loved needed encouragement. For a long time, she stood at the side of his bed, gently stroking his arm. Twice she had to move out of the way when nursing staff came in to check on his vital signs. Each time she returned to the bed and laid her hand on his arm. Tired and her back hurting terribly, she leaned down, whispered in his ear again, and retreated to the recliner.

She dozed fitfully during the night, never really sleeping for more than a few minutes at a time, instantly awakened by the slightest sound or by nurses coming into the room. Once during the night, an alarm sounded and jolted her awake. The nurses rushed her out of the room. Thirty minutes later she was allowed to return. A nurse reassured her, saying it was not unusual for someone with Zach's level of injuries to have a slight relapse.

Hours passed. Hours turned into days. Anna Mae never left Zach's room except for very short periods. She would rush down to the cafeteria, grab something quick, and hurry back to Zach's room. On the third day, one of the nurses tapped Anna Mae on the shoulder.

"Here, I thought you could use these," the nurse said, holding out a set of fresh clothes. "I think you're my size. They're nothing fancy. There's a shower just down the hall. You can put your old clothes in this bag."

Anna Mae rose from her chair and hugged the nurse, tears streaming down her face. "Thank you so much. You have all been so nice to me. I can't thank you enough. A shower and clean clothes will feel great."

Over the three days, Zach had occasionally groaned or twitched an arm or leg, but there had been no other sigh he was regaining consciousness.

Finally, as the fourth day passed into the fifth day, Zach moaned and picked up his left arm. Anna Mae flew to the bedside and grasped his hand. His left eye opened and his head turned slightly toward her. Maybe it was wishful thinking, but she believed she saw recognition on his face. For hours, she did not leave his bedside, hoping for another moment of recognition, but it never came.

On the sixth day, both Zach's eyes opened and he tried to say something. It took Anna Mae and a nurse several minutes to realize he was saying, "Mouth... dry."

Thrilled beyond words, Anna Mae believed Zach had turned the corner and had begun to improve.

One more day in the ICU and then Zach was transferred to a private room. The next day James and Martha Templeton arrived from Tulsa. Both of Zach's parents immediately fell in love with Anna Mae. She listened with keen interest as they told stories of Zach growing up while Zach cringed. In a few short hours, she felt like part of the family.

On Zach's third day out of the ICU, two men walked into Zach's room. The man in uniform introduced himself as Admiral Hadley and the man in a business suit introduced himself as CIA Director James Sandberg. They offered their sincere gratitude for what Zach had done. Admiral Hadley asked Anna Mae to follow him out into the hall.

"Miss Watts, I can't even begin to express how much this country appreciates what Zach has done and what he has sacrificed. I will see that someone is assigned to take care of him during his recuperation."

"No, Admiral, that won't be necessary."

"Huh?" Admiral Hadley questioned.

"I will take care of Zach," Anna Mae asserted.

"I guess I shouldn't be surprised," Admiral Hadley remarked. "I couldn't help but notice the way he looks at you."

"He's really something, Admiral. I've never met *anyone* quite like him."

"You have no idea," Admiral Hadley smiled. "Don't say anything to Zach. There will be an awards ceremony in Washington when he's feeling better. Call me and let know if you need something. Big or small. Whatever it is, I personally guarantee you will have it."

Anna Mae and Admiral Hadley returned to Zach's room. The Admiral and CIA Director Sandberg wished Zach a speedy recovery and said they needed to get back to Washington to prepare for the trials of the individuals that had been involved in the attempt to destroy America.

Zach steadily improved and was released from the hospital two days later. Zach's parents helped Anna Mae get Zach settled at home. They watched over Zach while Anna Mae went to pick up Mazie. Anna Mae could not imagine returning to the house she had shared with her father. So, she decided, at least temporarily, she would move some of her and Mazie's clothes to Zach's upstairs bedroom while she nursed Zach back to health. Zach would be relegated to the downstairs bedroom for convenience and necessity. Zach's knee had been seriously damaged during the confrontation, and it was uncertain how well he could ever manage stairs.

Once Zach was back on his feet, she would find a smaller house to rent and then she would put the old family house up for sale. Anna Mae called her boss and took an extended leave of absence. Concerned that neither she nor Zach were working, she called Admiral Hadley. He assured her that any financial needs they had would be taken care of.

Knowing it would be inappropriate for her to stay in the house alone with Zach, Anna Mae asked Zach's parents to stay until Zach was able to get along on his own. Within a day of Anna Mae and Mazie moving in, James and Martha had become just as smitten with Mazie as Zach had. Mazie warmed up to Zach's dad on the first day. The two of them spent hours playing together. For both Zach and his dad, Mazie was the little girl they had always dreamed about. Life slowly returned to normal for Zach. For the first two weeks, he only spent short periods of time out of bed, tiring quickly. Mazie would often disappear. Anna Mae would search and find her in Zach's bedroom, snuggled beside Zach while he read to her from one of her favorite books.

While deeply concerned over Zach's injuries, Anna Mae had never been happier in her entire life. She doted over Zach, taking care of his every need. She quickly learned Zach's favorite foods from Martha, his mother. When Anna Mae was not busy in the kitchen preparing some delectable meal, she was fussing over Zach, fluffing pillows, straightening covers, helping him from the bed to the couch, or bringing him books and magazines.

Changing the dressing on his wound was the one thing she would not do. A home-health nurse came twice a week to change the dressing and check on Zach's progress. At the end of the second week, the nurse removed the staples. From that point on, all Zach needed was a dab of anti-bacterial ointment and a simple bandage he could apply himself.

As the days passed, Zach spent more and more time out of bed. Slowly becoming accustomed to walking with a cane, his strength increased quickly.

One bright, sunny afternoon Zach's cellphone rang. Anna Mae snatched it from the end table and answered it.

"It's the Admiral," she said, handing the phone to Zach.

"Hey, Admiral. What can I do for you?"

"We need you to come to Washington to testify in the upcoming trial of Arthur Mead, *former* Vice President of the United States," Admiral Hadley informed Zach.

"How soon, Admiral?"

"How's two weeks from today?"

"I'm getting around pretty well. I'm sure I can do that."

"Good. I'll send my private jet to fly you to Washington. Why don't you bring Anna Mae and Mazie along?"

"Hang on, Admiral," Zach said, turning the cellphone away from his mouth. "Hey, Anna Mae. Would you like to go to Washington in two weeks?"

"You bet I would," Anna Mae answered, already aware of the big event Admiral Hadley had planned.

"Anna Mae says she would love to," Zach informed Admiral Hadley.

"I'll have my assistant make all arrangements. She will call you with the details. All you have to do is arrive at the airport."

"Thank you, Admiral. See you in two weeks," Zach said. He ended the call and laid the cellphone back on the end table.

Zach smiled and leaned back against the couch, thinking it would be nice to get out of the house and he was certain Anna Mae would enjoy seeing Washington.

Gulfstream G550
33,000 Feet above Northern Virginia

Kip Johnson, piloting Admiral Hadley's sleek Gulfstream G550 on a heading of zero-five-one, keyed the passenger cabin intercom, "Zach, you folks should start making preparations for landing. We are currently passing over Richmond, Virginia, one hundred eight miles southwest of Washington, D.C. Once Air Traffic Control hands us off to approach control, we will start our descent into the Washington area and we should be on the ground twenty minutes after that."

Zach looked up from the picture book he was reading to Mazie and listened to Kip's announcement. His knee throbbed from sitting for so long and a growing headache gnawed at the back of his neck.

Eight minutes later the radio in the cockpit crackled to life, "November-four-six-Mike-Lima, Washington Center, turn left, heading zero-two-seven, descend and maintain two thousand five hundred. At Casanova contact Washington Dulles Tower on one-two-zero-point-one."

Kip keyed his microphone and repeated ATC's instructions, "Washington Center, November-four-six-Mike-Lima, turn left, heading zero-two-seven, descend and maintain two thousand five hundred. At Casanova contact Washington Dulles Tower on one-two-zero-point-one, roger"

As the Gulfstream passed one mile east of the Casanova VORTAC NAVAID beacon, Kip dialed in the tower frequency and requested landing instructions. "Washington Approach, Gulfstream November-four-six-Mike-Lima."

"Gulfstream November-four-six-Mike-Lima, squawk 4377 and ident."

Kip dialed in the requested transponder code and responded, "Squawk 4377 and ident, Gulfstream November-four-six-Mike-Lima."

"Gulfstream November-four-six-Mike-Lima, radar contact fifteen miles southwest of Washington, proceed to MOSBY at two thousand five hundred, expect right traffic runway zero one right."

"Proceed to MOSBY at two thousand five hundred, expect right traffic, Gulfstream November-four-six-Mike-Lima."

Twelve miles later, Kip reported arrival at the MOSBY beacon, "Washington Tower, Gulfstream November-four-six-Mike-Lima at MOSBY."

"Gulfstream November-four-six-Mike-Lima, Washington Tower, enter right traffic for runway zero-one right. Report right downwind."

Kip began his left turn to zero-one-one and reported entering the downwind leg of his approach. "Gulfstream November-four-six-Mike-Lima, entering right downwind for zero-one right."

"Gulfstream November-four-six-Mike-Lima, cleared to land runway zero-one right. Altimeter two-niner-point-niner-five."

"Cleared to land zero-one right, Gulfstream November-four-six-Mike-Lima."

Kip steadied the aircraft on a heading of zero-one-one, lined up on the centerline of runway zero-one right. As the Gulfstream flared over the threshold of the runway, Kip eased back on the throttles to reduce the aircraft's speed. When the end of the runway and the attitude indicator's horizon line converged, Kip pulled back on the control yoke. The Gulfstream settled out of the sky and the tires touched the pavement, creating an almost imperceptible bump. Kip taxied the aircraft to the end of runway zero-one right and turned left onto taxiway kilo one.

Following the visual directions of an airport ramp worker, Kip steered the Gulfstream to the transient aircraft parking area and eased into an empty space beside a small Learjet. While the airport ramp worker placed chocks in front of the wheels, Kip set the parking brake and shut down the engines. He lifted himself up out of the pilot's seat, exited the flight deck into the passenger cabin, and opened the forward hatch.

"Great landing," Zach complimented as Kip extended the stairs.

"Thanks, I aim to please," Kip replied. "I'll have the aircraft refueled as soon as I finish the paperwork. Then, I will file a provisional flight plan. The aircraft will be ready to depart as soon as your business is done here. You have my cellphone number. Call me when you're ready to head back to Savannah."

After descending the stairs, Zach, Anna Mae, and Mazie walked into the general aviation terminal, pulling small suitcases behind them, packed with the usual items. Seeing the two adults and one small child that had been described to him, a man rushed over and introduced himself.

"Mister Templeton, I'm Martin O'Dell," the man said. "Admiral Hadley arranged for me to meet you and drive you to your hotel. The Admiral sends his regrets. He would have met you himself, but he had an important matter that required his attention."

Mister O'Dell grabbed the handles of all the bags and pointed toward a set of sliding doors and the waiting limo parked at the curb. He followed the three of them out to the limo and loaded the bags in the trunk while they climbed inside the luxurious stretch limo.

"Wow. Nice ride," Zach remarked.

"Yes. It's our best," O'Dell replied as he slid into the front passenger seat. "The Admiral requested the best we had. You will love the hotel. One of the best in town. It's only four blocks from the Capitol."

Zach and Anna Mae stared at the bright city lights as the limo wound its way through the streets of Washington. The limo turned into the entrance of the Liaison Washington Capitol Hill and stopped in front of the main entrance. Zach climbed out of the limo and held the door open for Anna Mae. He turned toward the hotel and whistled. "Nice. *Really* nice," he chimed as Anna Mae climbed out and picked Mazie up, nestling the little girl on her hip.

"You go on in and get registered," O'Dell instructed. "I'll bring the bags in."

Zach and Anna Mae entered the hotel and walked up to the registration desk. A waiting front desk clerk rushed over, ready to help them.

"Zach Templeton and Anna Mae Watts. I believe Admiral Charles Hadley made reservations for us."

"Yes, Mister Templeton. Just a minute please," the young man said, motioning to someone in the back office.

"Mister Templeton, it is an honor to have you with us," an impeccably dressed woman said. "My name is Rebecca Stevens. I'm the hotel manager. Admiral Hadley requested that I personally see to your needs while you are with us."

Zach and Anna Mae filled out their registration cards and pushed them across the counter toward Ms. Stevens. Zach slipped a credit card out of his wallet and slid it across the counter.

"Not needed," Ms. Stevens said, pushing the card back toward Zach. "Just sign your name and room number. Admiral Hadley has already taken care of everything."

"Wow. Thank you, Miss Stevens," Zach said as he stuffed the credit card back in his wallet.

"Here are your key cards," Ms. Stevens said, handing each of them a small packet containing two plastic key cards. "Your rooms are mini-suites on the VIP floor, across the hall from each other. Miss Watts, I will have a bellman bring a crib to your room for the little lady. I hope you enjoy your stay with us. If there is anything you need, let me or someone here at the front desk know."

Martin O'Dell tapped Zach on the shoulder and said, "I'll be back here in the morning to pick you up. I'll meet you here. Eight-thirty sharp."

"We'll be ready," Zach Answered.

Zach and Anna Mae located the elevator and stepped inside. Zach inserted one of his key cards into the VIP access slot and punched the button for the top floor. After a short ride to the top floor, the elevator door opened to a beautifully decorated foyer. Signage on the wall indicated their rooms were down the hallway to the right. At the far end of the hallway, they stopped in front of the door to Anna Mae's room.

"How about I knock on your door in about fifteen minutes and then we go grab something to eat.?" Zach asked.

"Sounds great," Anna Mae answered.

Whitehouse - Oval Office
Washington, D.C.

At precisely eight-thirty, Martin O'Dell had arrived at the hotel and picked up Zach, Anna Mae, and Mazie. Anna Mae got goose bumps when the limo was quickly admitted and passed through the White House gate. O'Dell parked the limo in the visitor's parking area and held the door open while his passengers piled out of the limo. Anna Mae turned and admired the meticulously manicured lawns and gardens. Mazie ran to Zach's side and held her arms up. Zach picked Mazie up and admired her brand new yellow dress with white ribbons tied in neat little bows adorning the poufy sleeves. Anna Mae had taken Mazie shopping the day before they left home. The instant Mazie had seen the pretty yellow dress hanging on the rack, she had refused to settle for anything else.

Mr. O'Dell escorted them to the lobby entrance on the north side of the West Wing. Rear Admiral Charles Hadley, waiting just inside the lobby door, rushed out to meet them.

"Great to see you, Zach," Admiral Hadley greeted, pumping Zach's hand vigorously. "And you as well, Miss Watts."

Mazie immediately stuck her hand out toward Admiral Hadley.

"And who is this beautiful little lady?" Admiral Hadley beamed as he took Mazie's hand.

"This is Miss Mazie Pickett," Zach replied. "I believe I told you, both her parents died."

"Yes, I remember," Admiral Hadley remarked. "Absolutely dreadful. Well, we need to be going. President Cantwell is waiting."

"The President?" Anna Mae exclaimed, her eyes growing wide.

"Yes. President Cantwell wants to meet you and Mazie before Zach and I meet with representatives of the Department of Justice for the preliminary deposition."

"The President? Me? He wants to meet me?"

"Don't be so shocked," Zach said. "I had a brief chat with him last night after we got back from dinner. I told him all about you and Mazie. He's a really nice guy. You'll like him."

Admiral Hadley led Anna Mae and Zach through the lobby, past the Roosevelt room, and into the President's Secretary's office. Ellen Cathcart, the President's secretary, looked up from her desk when the group of people entered the office.

Recognizing Admiral Hadley, she said, "The President is waiting for you. This way, please." She rose from her desk, walked over to the door to the Oval Office, and held it open for them.

President Paul Cantwell stood and waited as the entourage streamed into the Oval Office. As Ms. Cathcart pulled the door shut, the President walked over and grabbed Zach's hand and pumped it.

"Well, Zach, here we are again," he said. "Hardly a year ago you stood in this very spot and I offered a grateful nation's sincere gratitude for your sacrifice. How are you, Zach?"

"Mostly okay, Mister President, but the old knee isn't doing so great."

"This must be Miss Anna Mae Watts," President Cantwell said as he stepped sideways and took Anna Mae's hand. "I'm delighted to meet you. Zach has told me a lot about you."

"I'm honored Mister President," Anna Mae stuttered, a bit overwhelmed by her surroundings.

"And this must be the young lady I have been waiting to meet," President Cantwell said as he reached out and took Mazie's hand. "I understand she lost both parents because of the monster you took down, Zach."

"Yes she did, but it wasn't me that took down the monsters," Zach corrected. "It was Anna Mae. The guy had me down and would have finished me had it not been for Anna Mae. She charged into the room to protect me and took a bullet in the arm. She went down and played possum. As he stepped over her, intending to slit her throat, she shot him right in the forehead."

"Oh yes, I heard about that from Admiral Hadley," President Cantwell remarked, turning to face Anna Mae. "No wonder Zach speaks so highly of you. Miss Watts, I also offer you the sincere gratitude of a grateful nation. Your bravery and action is to be highly commended."

"Thank you, Mister President," Anna Mae beamed.

"Well, I wish you could sit and fill me in on all the details, but I understand you have a meeting to go to. Admiral Hadley, why don't you show Zach and Anna Mae the Roosevelt Room and then escort them to the Cabinet Room. I believe they are set up in there for the deposition."

Admiral Hadley opened the door and waited for Zach and Anna Mae to exit the Oval Office. He followed them out and pulled the door shut. The President waited a few seconds, poked his head into his secretary's office, and verified that his guests had entered the Roosevelt Room. He pulled the door shut, crossed the Oval Office, and exited on the Rose Garden side of the office. He hurried down the West Colonnade and entered the Cabinet Room.

Admiral Hadley spent a few minutes in the Roosevelt Room pointing out various objects of historical significance. Zach and Anna Mae would like to have spent longer gazing at the beautiful items, but Admiral Hadley ushered them out, telling them they could come back later, after the deposition.

He escorted them to the door that led to the front of the Cabinet Room. He pushed the door open and directed them into the room. Zach and Anna Mae stopped dead in their tracks as thunderous applause broke out. The large room was filled to standing-room only capacity with dignitaries, all five Joint Chiefs, and heads of the alphabet soup of government agencies. President Cantwell stood at the head of the room, waiting for the applause to die down. Finally he had to hold up his hands to quiet the crowd. He pointed toward two empty chairs at the very front of the room. Anna Mae and Zach sat and waited for the President to begin.

"Honored guests, not only did Mister Zachariah James Templeton serve his country honorably in the United States Navy as part of SEAL Team Four, three times he has answered the call of his country in times of great duress. Each time he responded with honor and high distinction far beyond what anyone could expect. Barely one year ago, it was my profound honor to present Mister Templeton with the Presidential Medal of Freedom with Distinction. Today, I stand here to award Mister Templeton with the second award of this highest honor I may bestow. The Presidential Medal of Freedom is awarded to recognize individuals who have made an especially meritorious contribution to the security or national interests of the United States. I only wish there were a higher award I could bestow on this man because he has certainly earned it. Mister Templeton, if you would, please."

Zach stood, walked over in front of the President, and stood at attention. An aide came from the side of the room and held out an open, velvet-lined box. President Cantwell lifted out the medal and draped it around Zach's neck. Zach shook the President's hand, took one step backward, and saluted. President Cantwell returned the salute, then asked Zach to move over one step.

"Miss Anna Mae Watts, please join us," President Cantwell called out.

With a startled look on her face, Anna Mae rose from her chair, passed Mazie to Zach, and stood before the President.

"Mister Speaker, would you join us," the President said, taking one step sideways.

The Speaker of the House of Representatives rose from his chair and walked to the front of the room.

"Ladies and gentlemen, I hold in my hand the Congressional Gold Medal. In the past, Congress has occasionally awarded this medal to honor recipients from the military only. This medal seeks to honor those who have performed an achievement that has an impact on American history that is likely to be recognized long after the achievement itself. It is my understanding that were it not for Miss Watts's bravery and decisive actions, Mister Templeton would not be here and our beloved country would be in the midst of a horrifying catastrophe. Therefore, breaking with past tradition, Congress has voted, unanimously I might add, to award this Congressional Gold Medal to Miss Anna Mae Watts."

The Speaker of the House of Representatives presented the medal, nestled in its presentation case, to Anna Mae. She thanked the speaker and took her place beside Zach.

"Mister Templeton and Miss Watts, long will your duty and sacrifice be remembered," the speaker said as thunderous applause once again broke out.

Unlike the heartache Zach suffered at the previous presentation ceremony, this one was a joyous occasion. He watched with delight as important dignitaries and high-ranking military officers lavished praise and congratulations on Anna Mae. But the genuine star of the event turned out to be little Mazie. Her impish smile mesmerized the attendees, captivating their attention. The room swirled with conversations and laughter for nearly two hours. Gradually the attendees filed out and returned to their duties. The Speaker of the House and two senators were the last special guests to leave, leaving only Zach, Anna Mae, Mazie, Admiral Hadley, and President Cantwell.

As Zach was about to leave the Cabinet Room and head for the airport, President Cantwell pulled him aside. He spent several minutes trying his best to convince Zach he should join his administration. Zach said he was honored, but politely refused.

The President, realizing further efforts would be fruitless, leaned toward Zach and whispered something in his ear. Zach's face turned red. The President grasped Zach's hand, hugged him, and slapped him on the back.

Anna Mae shook President Cantwell's hand and thanked him profusely for his kind words. Driven by impulse, she rushed over, gave Admiral Hadley a hug, and kissed him on the cheek.

"Admiral Hadley, thank you so much for what you have done for Zach. I understand why he speaks so highly of you."

"You're welcome," Admiral Hadley responded, slightly embarrassed. "I hope it's okay if I drop in occasionally to check in on you guys, especially little Mazie."

"We would be delighted," Anna Mae beamed.

"Well, we should get you guys to the airport. Kip is waiting to take you back to Savannah."

"What did President Cantwell say to you?" Anna Mae asked as they walked down the hallway toward the lobby.

"I'll tell you later," Zach responded, ushering her out the door.

Martin O'Dell pulled the long, black stretch limo up to the entrance of the general aviation terminal at Washington's Dulles International airport. O'Dell scrambled out of the driver's seat and opened the door for his passengers. While they climbed out, he retrieved their bags from the trunk and set them on the curb.

O'Dell stuck out his hand and said, "Mister Templeton, it was my privilege to chauffeur you and Miss Watts around Washington. If you are ever in Washington again, please call me. The next ride is on the house."

"Thank you, Mister O'Dell," Zach replied, shaking his hand. "I will do that."

Anna Mae picked up Mazie and grabbed the handle of her roller bag and headed for the entrance. Zach pulled the door open and allowed Anna Mae to enter first.

Kip Johnson, seated in the waiting area, jumped up when he saw them enter, meeting them halfway across the lobby.

"Here, let me get those," Kip said, seeing Anna Mae struggling with Mazie and her bag. He grabbed the handles of the bags and said, "Follow me."

"You guys board the aircraft and get seated," Kip said as they approached the Gulfstream. "I'll stow the bags and then we'll be on our way."

Kip quickly stowed the bags, hurried to the flight deck, and called ground control for clearance to taxi. He keyed the passenger cabin intercom, "We've received clearance to taxi. Make certain you're buckled in."

Eight minutes later, the Gulfstream was holding short of runway one-nine right. A large 767 commercial jetliner flared over the end of the runway and touched down, large clouds of blue-white smoke billowing up from its wheels. Kip taxied the Gulfstream onto the runway, lined up on the centerline, and set the brake. Once the large jetliner turned off the runway onto a taxiway, the Gulfstream received clearance to take off. Kip released the brake and pushed the throttles forward.

One minute later, the Gulfstream's nose wheel lifted into the air, two seconds later the rear wheels lost contact with the runway, and the gleaming aircraft lifted into the southern sky.

When the aircraft reached ten thousand feet and Kip advised them they were free to move about the cabin, Zach noticed saw Mazie nodding off to sleep. He lifted the center armrest, laid her down, and covered her with a blanket. He moved to the other side of the aircraft and sat beside Anna Mae.

"Now, what did President Cantwell say to you at the end of the award ceremony?" Anna Mae asked.

"It's kind of personal," Zach resisted.

"Come on, Zach. You said you would tell me later."

"Well, okay. The President said, 'Anna Mae is a wonderful woman. Don't you dare let her get away. If you do, I'll hunt you down and kick you in the behind.'"

"He did not," Anna Mae chided, her face turning red as she punched Zach in the shoulder.

"I swear. Scout's honor," Zach said, holding up three fingers on his right hand.

"When the President presented the award, he said you served in the Navy as a SEAL. What was that like,".

"Some of it was pretty rough," Zach answered? "Are you really sure you want to hear about that?"

"Yes, all of it Zach."

Anna Mae became more and more astonished by what this man had been through as she listened with rapt attention as Zach recounted some of the missions he had been part of, skipping the ones that were still classified.

Even though it was painful, he shared the hunt for and eventual capture of Frank Porter. He even shared the gruesome details of the battle in Henry Tang's penthouse apartment. As painful as it was to relive those events, it felt good to finally share it with someone.

Anna Mae leaned against him and he slipped his arm around her shoulder. Anna Mae mulled over the events Zach had shared. Astonished by what she had learned, she said, "Zach, all those horrible things. Weren't you scared?"

"Sometimes, of course," he replied. "When I was part of the SEALs, I was so focused on completing the mission and protecting other team members, there was little time to be scared. But after the heat of the battle passed, in the quiet of the night that was when the fear came."

"I can't imagine," Anna Mae responded. "But what about the times you answered the county's call and chased those sadistic criminals across the country?"

"There were times when fear rose up. Surprisingly, one of the best things that happened was when my company failed. Owning my own company had been a dream of mine for so long, part of me felt like a failure. With no company to run and no job, I had a lot of time to think. Angie was quite active in her church. She convinced me to go with her. Over the next few months, I questioned my priorities. I faced death many times, but I guess I never really gave much thought to what would happen *after* I died. One sermon, convinced me I was totally unprepared to face death. That night I accepted Jesus Christ as my Savior. Now, I no longer fear death."

"Oh, Zach, I'm so happy to hear that," Anna Mae exclaimed. Anna Mae felt as if her heart leaped in her chest. The man she was falling in love with was a Christian. She remembered vividly the night as a teenager when she had promised God she would only marry a good Christian man. "*Was this going to be the man?*" she wondered. She laid her head on Zach's shoulder, closed her eyes, and thanked God for bringing Zach into her life.

One hour and forty-eight minutes after its wheels lifted off the runway in Washington, D.C., the sleek Gulfstream settled gently onto runway one-zero in Savannah, Georgia.

Epilogue

Three days after returning from Washington, Anna Mae pulled into the driveway of the house on Big House Plantation Road and parked next to the front porch. With Zach's parents having returned to Tulsa and no longer staying at the house, it was inappropriate for her to stay there. She had made arrangements to stay with her cousin until she could sell the old family house and find a smaller house.

Zach waved from the porch, grabbed his cane, and hobbled out to the car. He kissed Anna Mae on the check and opened the rear passenger door.

"Hey, Mazie," he cooed as he lifted the little girl out of her car seat.

"How are you doing, Zach?" Anna Mae asked.

"Okay, I guess," he answered. "I don't sleep very well. The house seems so empty and quiet."

"Are you back to work?"

"Yes. Mister Hollins has been incredibly understanding. When he heard about what happened, he paid me for the time I was off work. I can only stand to sit at the computer for a couple of hours at a time. I get up and walk around for a few minutes to stretch my knee. The bad thing is; I'm making way too many trips to the coffeepot. By the way, I started a fresh pot after you called. Would you like some?"

"Sure. That sounds great."

Inside the house, Anna Mae said, "You take Mazie out on the back porch. I'll bring out the coffee."

Anna Mae filled two cups with coffee and set them on a tray. She filled Mazie's sippy cup with apple juice and added it to the tray. With the tray in her hands, she backed against the screen door and pushed it open. Immediately surprised by a cavorting red hound, she nearly dropped the tray.

"Tripp," she shouted as the happy dog washed her face with his wet tongue. "Sorry, I completely forgot about you."

"I saw him snooping around in the backyard the day we got back from Washington. He was starved. I gave him some scraps from the fridge and he moved right in. He loves lying by my feet while I work at the computer. I love having him here. Doesn't seem quite so lonely with him around."

"I'm glad," Anna Mae said, scratching behind the dog's ears. "My cousin hates dogs, so he couldn't have gone there."

Tripp wandered off to the end of the porch, sat down, and scratched at his ear. He flopped down flat, let out a big sigh, and went to sleep.

"Who's that, Mazie," Zach asked as the little girl handed him a stuffed animal.

Not waiting for an answer, Mazie took the animal back and returned to the pile of toys lying on the porch floor. Anna Mae grabbed her cup of coffee and sat down beside Zach.

"I sure miss having Mazie around," Zach said. "Angie was unable to have children. We often talked about what it would be like to have a little girl. What will happen to her with both her parents dead?"

"The court granted me temporary custody. I thought about trying to adopt her, but being single and now, not having a job…." Angie stopped talking mid-sentence.

"What happened?"

"I was the company's only accountant. My boss said they simply couldn't continue without someone to process accounts. He paid me for my vacation, unused sick time, and gave me five weeks' severance."

"I'm sorry, Anna Mae," Zach offered. "What are you going to do?"

"I don't really know," she replied. "I hired a professional cleaning company to go through the house from top to bottom. When they're done, I will list it for sale. The realtor said it should sell quickly. The proceeds from the sale should last me a while."

"I hope the realtor is correct."

"Me too," Anna Mae added.

She felt so safe and contented when she was around this remarkable man. She wondered how a man that had had such harrowing experiences and was a battle-hardened warrior could be so gentle and loving. "*An honest-to-God real live hero. And not only was he a hero, he was also a Christian,*" she thought as she leaned against Zach and sighed heavily.

Both Anna Mae's parents had been murdered, her cousin and her husband and the two Foley boys all dead from a deadly, engineered virus. Life had been cruel. Despite that, she felt more at ease than ever before. She determined she would find a way to focus on hope for the future. Maybe life in Bluffton would finally return to normal.

"Anna Mae, I really miss having you and Mazie here at the house," Zach said.

"I miss being here and I know Mazie does too," Anna Mae responded.

"Anna Mae, will you…., Ah…. Will you…."

"What is it you want to say, Zach?" Anna Mae asked, excitement building in her heart.

Zach took a deep breath and forced himself to say what he had been rehearsing in his mind for days. "Miss Anna Mae Watts, will you marry me? Then we can adopt Mazie."

"Yes. Yes. A thousand times yes," Anna Mae blurted out, tears of joy streaming down her cheeks.

Zach kissed Anna Mae and hugged her so tightly she could hardly breathe. Zach relaxed his arms and Anna Mae drew her feet up on the seat and nestled against Zach.

Zach held Anna Mae tightly and smiled.

Life was good. Really, really good.

THE END

Keith Hoar is a writer and former IBM Certified Business Intelligence Expert who consulted for numerous Fortune 100 companies. He designed executive suite business intelligence dashboards and real-time reporting systems. Keith also owned his own consulting company that designed custom software systems and sophisticated data-driven reporting systems.

Keith proudly served his country in the United States Navy for ten years. At Naval Submarine School, New London, Connecticut he assisted in training crews from both Fast Attack and Ballistic Missile submarines that patrolled the world's oceans in defense of freedom.

Keith is a PADI certified SCUBA diver with 100+ dives all over the Caribbean. Keith has published two previous novels, **Edge of Madness** and **RAGE**, edge-of-your-seat, hold-your-breath thrillers. He has also published a Christian nonfiction book, **DECEIVED: The Assault of Revisionist History**.

Thank you for taking the time to read about the author. Keith is most grateful for fans of his books, and would love to correspond with readers like you. For more information, visit https://keithhoarbooks.wixsite.com/home or you may reach him at his author email - author@zhetosoft.com

www.ingramcontent.com/pod-product-compliance
Lightning Source LLC
Chambersburg PA
CBHW031934110726
47902CB00001B/176